THE FERN KEEPERS

Damaged. Defiant. Renewed.

sara sartagne

Amazon Print edition: 9798714503788

If you'd like to keep up with Sara Sartagne's writing, why not sign up for her *no spam* newsletter and get news *first* of new releases and exclusive – free! – content.

Details can be found at the end of **The Fern Keepers**.

Acknowledgments And Historical Notes

As I continue to publish more books, it seems to me that the list of people to thank gets longer and longer. **_The Fern Keepers_** (a bit like that 'difficult second album' if you're a rock singer) is the second title in my Duality series and has been a bit of a monster to wrestle under control.

That I've done it at all is down in large part to my wonderful friends and fellow authors, who gave me feedback, offered suggestions and occasionally gave me a good talking to.

On this occasion, special thanks go to author Katherine Edgar and Jenny Smart who gently corrected my misinterpretation of historical facts; the lovely gang at Monkeys with Typewriters at Malton - Dawn, Jane and Julie; Jan Page, who urged me to up my game; and Jilly Woods who would be as good an editor as she is a writer. Thanks also to Fiona, who read my book not once, but twice and still managed to be interested.

A brief note about the history. I plundered Victorian Commons for much of my information on bills and MPs, but I have taken liberties with some of the timing of the debates mentioned in the book.

While staying as true as I could to the language, manners and dress of the time and using the ideas working their way through the period as a backdrop to Emily's story, this is a novel, not a history book, so I hope readers will forgive me the odd compromise on accuracy.

Chapter 1

At five to ten on a dismal February morning, Cat Kennedy was on the phone to her literary agent. She was describing the new ending of chapter eight of her novel when she heard a long groaning creak outside. Then there was a sound like a distant avalanche. The rumble resonated through her ribcage.

"What the hell is that noise?" she muttered. "Just a second, Creighton..."

Leaving her phone on the table, she walked to the bay window and looked out over the garden. Her eyes widened. Where once the eighteen-foot wall had been, a jagged gap split the bricks, now giving her a view to the neighbour's house. An ancient tree on her side of the wall leaned drunkenly through the bricks. The ground around its roots had heaved upwards, destroying the path through her fern garden. Even to Cat's inexperienced eye, the tree appeared in danger of toppling.

"Good grief!" she breathed.

"Catherine? What's happening?" Creighton's voice came from her phone. Whirling around, she grabbed it.

"A tree's fallen! Can I call you back?" She disconnected before he had time to answer and snatching up her padded jacket, sped through the patio doors.

She ran up the long lawn and glimpsed her neighbour's house through the tumbled bricks: a more modern, modest place than the Victorian villa she had inherited. Shoving her long dark hair off her face, she picked her way over boulders and the roots of the fallen tree. God, it must be thirty feet tall. Trying to keep her balance, she peered through the branches into the garden next door. A man was sitting on the ground by a pile of tumbled stones and forlorn-looking greenery, clutching his shoulder.

"Oh, my God! Are you hurt?" she gasped. He turned his dark head and stared at her with silver-grey eyes.

Cat's mouth dropped open. The years fell away, and she was twenty again. "*Harry?*"

Harry Moore, her lover from nine years ago, looked as shocked as she felt. "Cat Kennedy." His voice was rough. "What the hell are you doing here?"

"I live here! I moved into Cleveland House two weeks ago."

"Ah. I wondered who it was. I saw workmen sorting out the roof..." He made to stand, wincing.

"I'll come round." Cat jumped back over the tumbled stones. There were only a few houses on the road leading to the village. What were the chances that Harry would live in the one next to her? What was he doing here? How long had he been living next door?

She was breathless when she knocked at his front door, her mind still racing.

When he opened the door, his face was pale and smeared with mud. Cat remembered that he was one of the few men she could look in the eye without stooping.

"Come in," he said evenly, and led the way to a bright, airy kitchen with doors onto the garden. The otherwise perfect lawn was strewn with large stones and mortar and branches from Cat's tree.

"Are you all right?" Cat asked, her heart sinking at the mess.

"I'm fine. I got hit on the shoulder by a branch, but I don't think anything's broken. Which is more than we can say about the wall. What's the damage on your side?"

"Lots of stones, tree roots coming out of the ground, my fernery is flattened. I'm so sorry about your garden!"

He shook his head and Cat saw the pain cross his face. "You need to see a doctor about that shoulder."

"I'm fine. Don't fuss."

Okay, be a hero! Nothing much changed there, then!

Huffing, she turned to the devastation in the garden. "So, what do we do?" As she watched, a clump of earth shifted, and the tree dropped a foot lower.

Harry frowned. "We need to get a tree surgeon as soon as possible."

Cat hesitated. Tree surgeon? Like she knew any of those in Cambridge. "I can look some up on Facebook, unless you already know one?"

"I've got this." Harry fished his phone from his back pocket and scrolled, eventually punching a number with his thumb. "John? Harry Moore. A tree from next door has toppled onto the wall between my garden and the next. It's pretty big, I'd say thirty, thirty-five feet. Old age, I think. Can you have a look?" He paused. "As soon as possible, mate. Really? That's brilliant. I'll see you then."

He finished the call and glanced at her. "He'll be here tomorrow, which is a small miracle."

"God, yes! Thank you for that, I don't know anyone here yet."

Cat chewed her lip as she surveyed the mess. It looked as if it would take weeks to put right, and she didn't dare think about the cost. Harry was looking at her and she sought for something to say to break the silence. "So, this is your house?"

He nodded, his movement stiff. "Yes. I liked the village when we visited your Great Aunt May, if you remember? So when I moved forces, I looked in the area and this was for sale. I take it she's died?"

Cat nodded, tightening her jaw against the tears.

"I'm sorry for your loss," he said softly. "I liked her enormously, even though I only met her a couple of times. She was the only person to tell me off for not serving her tea in a proper cup when she visited us in the flat."

Cat blinked and swallowed hard. "Yes, I remember... Did you move in while she was still here? She never said."

"No, she'd gone into a home. I was gutted when I found out. The man who was renting her place wouldn't tell me where she was."

Cat frowned. "That's a bit unnecessary. She'd have loved to see you."

Harry pushed his fingers through his dark hair. "He might have thought he was protecting her."

"From a copper?" Cat grimaced. She had met the previous tenant, Geoff Johnson, on a couple of occasions, and always wanted to wash her hands afterwards.

"Yeah... I wasn't keen on him, if I'm honest. He loved the house but he was a bit strange. I felt sure he'd buy it."

"He made an offer, but Gam wanted me to have the place."

"Are you going to sell it?"

Cat shuffled her feet. She might have to if this book didn't do well, but the last thing she wanted was to swap life stories with Harry, particularly when hers had turned so sour of late. Let him believe she was raking it in. He might take her more seriously now than he had when she'd been a naïve twenty-year-old.

"Cat?" he prompted.

Cat gathered her wits. "I'm not sure. At the moment, it's nice to be out of London to concentrate on the next book," she said, her light words belying just *how* nice it was to be away from London.

But Harry wasn't a policeman for nothing. His eyes narrowed for a moment. "Yeah, I see your books in all the shops. You've done really well."

Hmm. He'd not read her latest reviews, obviously. "I'm surprised you moved. I thought you loved working for the Met," she said.

Harry shrugged and said nothing. Topic *definitely* off limits. "So you'll let me know when the tree man arrives?"

4

He grinned. "Yeah, I'll let you know when John the *tree surgeon* arrives."

His grin prodded her memories of the past. She studied his face. He had barely aged, though there were silver strands in the thick dark hair. He shifted under her regard then winced again.

"Should I call an ambulance?" she asked, mentally taking a bet on the response.

She won when he waved away her solicitude. "Don't be daft. I'll have a hot bath and be right as rain. Will you be in tomorrow? John will need to get into your garden."

"Oh, um—" Tension gripped her.

"Let me have your mobile, then."

Cat's shoulders stiffened as she reluctantly read out the number. But this was Harry. He was a police officer. No need to worry about it.

"We'll need to discuss the repairs when we've made the tree safe," he added firmly as he slipped the phone into the back pocket of his jeans. "It's your wall and therefore your responsibility, okay?"

Her throat and chest tightened as she thought about the cost. She nodded abruptly and returned to Cleveland House.

Cat glanced at her reflection ten minutes later. She was pale, her green-grey eyes huge in her pinched face. Her move here was supposed to be a new start, a clean break.

Sighing, she ran down the elegant, sweeping staircase, the weak February light glinting through the stained glass on the first landing and painting the walls with colour. Hypnotised, she watched motes of dust twinkle in the still air as they floated to the ground. The letterbox rattled and post dropped onto the blue, white and ochre tiles that adorned the hall floor. Her heart sank: those envelopes looked remarkably like bills. More bills, to add to the cost of rebuilding the wall.

Still, at least she was here, and away from London. Honestly, she had a lot to be grateful for. Thanks to Great Aunt May – Cat had always known her as Gam – Cleveland House was hers, all hers.

There was a lot of the house, with six bedrooms and bills to match, but it also had doors that didn't have locks on them, and elegant, high rooms she could stand up in without dipping her head like a freaky giant. She pushed away the thought of the cramped London flat she'd shared with Stephen.

"No, not going there," she muttered. Her steps echoed as she descended the last few stairs. She needed more furniture, but that would have to wait. Now, she needed to check the post and get back to Creighton.

Among the buff envelopes – electricity and gas this time – was a white envelope with handwriting she didn't recognise. Cat tore it open to find a card from Geoff Johnson, the strange little man who had been Gam's tenant while she was in the care home. She wrinkled her nose at the pink flowers and the words:

Enjoy your new home – I hope you'll be as happy as I was. To reiter-ate, please give me first refusal when/if you decide to sell. All best wishes, G. Johnson.

When she decided to sell? Cheeky bastard. Cat threw the card in the bin and went to wash her hands. She didn't know what it was about Geoff, but he made her twitch. She'd had enough of being uncom-fortable.

Pressing her lips together, she rang Creighton and was put on hold. While she waited, she looked lovingly at the heavy gold and plum curtains she'd known from childhood, the elaborate cornices and white marble fireplace that graced the drawing room. Against the plinky-plonky hold music, she said a prayer for the old lady who – she wasn't even sure it was hyperbole – had probably saved her life.

Cat smiled at the robin perching on the curved windowsill of the verandah. The bird was becoming a regular visitor, and she rewarded his visits with crumbs and bits of bacon rind. He put his head on one side, black eyes regarding her. "Yes, you're incredibly cute, but I have to get on with the book." He pecked at the windowsill and flitted away.

"Catherine? Is everything all right?" Creighton's anxious voice came down the line.

"Not exactly," Cat said, sinking wearily into her chair. "Did I tell you I had a walled garden? Well, a tree has just crashed through one of the walls, leaving me with a clear view into my neighbour's garden."

"No one hurt, though?"

"Not seriously." At least, not seriously as far as he-man Harry was concerned.

"The insurance people will sort it out, won't they?"

"No. I didn't get round to arranging insurance. I was staggered by the cost and wanted to shop around." Suddenly, her voice was clogged with tears. How was she going to pay for all the work? Gam's legacy, which she had thought would be such a lifesaver, was disappearing down the hole of repairs and expenses for Cleveland House.

Creighton was silent for a second. "Are you broke, Catherine?"

Cat hesitated. Creighton had been a tremendous support over the past six months, but he wasn't aware of *everything* about her previous relationship, and certainly not the amount of money that Stephen had siphoned out of their joint account. "A bit. Splitting from Stephen put a lot of pressure on me financially, and the last book didn't exactly fill the coffers. Money has been tight, especially with moving here."

"But you own the house?"

"Yes. I might not eat, but I have a roof over my head."

"Please eat, Catherine. You're too tall to be too thin," Creighton said, bone-dry, and she managed a weak laugh. "What are you going to do?"

Cat considered her rapidly shrinking list of options. Spend to her limit on the credit card? Get another credit card? Tucking her phone under her chin, she tapped on her hand to slow her heart rate. *Tap, tap, tap.*

"Could you borrow from your parents?" Creighton pursued.

Not a chance. "They're out of the country," she said. That, at least, was true. "I'll manage. I have savings."

"Hmm. Don't get distracted from delivering the manuscript: that's your way out of your money troubles. There's only so much I can do to hold off the publishers. They won't push back the release date again."

Cat heard the seriousness in Creighton's tone. She knew that in his tight-lipped way, he was as worried as she was about this latest book. He was acting like a combination of a sergeant-major and a cheer-leader. Or, in book terms, as a pre-development editor as well as her agent. He'd been incredibly supportive as she struggled to rebuild her confidence after Stephen, but he was running out of patience. "You'll have it on time, I promise."

Creighton ended the call. Cat gazed through the window at the jagged hole in the wall, fighting the panic that threatened to overwhelm her. Rolling her head to loosen her neck muscles, she thought tea might calm her down.

Cat cradled the mug in her hands, regarding the sparse furniture: her writing desk and three chairs, two bookshelves and Gam's sofa and huge dining table. Her chairs looked lost around it. She'd needed to escape London, but anxiety made her stomach churn. She'd left Stephen's flat with so little. Would she just rattle around in this big house?

Crucially, would she be able to write?

Her heartbeat accelerated and she began the breathing exercises the therapist had suggested after she'd left Stephen. She needed Bobbles. Strange to think that after a three-year relationship with Stephen, the only thing she missed was his ancient cat.

Recovered a little, she glanced at the bills, and calculated when the royalty cheque from her previous books was due. If there were any royalties, at least they would help her eat. The repairs would have to wait a month and she hoped Harry would be okay with that. Otherwise she'd have to dip into Gam's legacy again.

"How on earth did you manage all this, Gam?" she said to the house.

Her aunt had made some shrewd investments while working her way up the British Civil Service, but her father had never understood why she put so much money into Cleveland House. When questioned, Gam had just smiled. "I love it, and it's large enough to entertain all my friends," she'd said firmly. "It has a benign presence." Cat could still remember her mother rolling her eyes, but Cat agreed; there was a kindness about Cleveland House that soothed Cat's spirit.

Sighing, she knew Creighton was right. She needed to get on with the book, earn some money, and pay for her bloody garden wall.

Chapter 2

Emily breathed a sigh of relief as she stepped through the doors of the Mayfair house and out of the smog. Even inside the echoing hall, the murk still settled in her clothes. She nodded at the butler as she unbuttoned her walking coat, and wrinkled her nose at the smell of the gas lamps lit against the dingy morning. The butler's large hands received the grey wool coat, damp from the late winter mizzle and flecked with soot.

"Thank you, Evans. Where is Sir James?" Emily stripped off her gloves and handed them to Molly, her maid.

"In his study with Mr Castleford, my lady."

Emily bit her lip. James might be unavailable for hours, closeted with the dour-looking estate manager. She spotted a calling card on the sideboard, the writing black and stark against the thick white card. She stiffened. "Dr Schenley was here?"

"Yes, but as Sir James was engaged, he said he would call later in the week."

Her stomach tightened, but she kept her face bland.

Evans continued, his round face impassive. "Mrs Worthy asked if you would be so kind as to spare her a few minutes to plan the menus for the week."

Emily paused. She really wanted to write to Aunt Sybil and begin the book she had just purchased. But she had responsibilities. "Of course. I shall change my dress and be with her directly. Ask her to attend me in the morning room." Emily climbed the stairs slowly, trailed by Molly.

No one looking at her straight back would have guessed her feelings. She had not been accustomed to such a large staff and though she had grasped the reins in the last four years, the disdain of the imposing housekeeper who ran James' London home was like the prick of a needle to her fragile confidence.

She reached the top of the sweeping mahogany stairs, proud that she wasn't out of breath. It was progress. Molly, hovering behind her, darted forward to open the bedroom door and Emily swept into her sanctuary. The rose-pink walls seemed to welcome her. The cushions were soft and inviting, the gas light gentle.

"Shall I put out the grey silk, ma'am?"

Emily nodded. She had put aside her mourning blacks the previous week. As was the custom, they had been burned, although it had pierced Emily's heart as Molly bore them away to the fire. It seemed too soon – barely three months since she had stood, unseeing, in the dusky churchyard. It was, she thought, like shedding armour. She felt too light as she moved now, too insubstantial.

Emily sank onto the chair in front of the dressing table, slid the pin from her veiled hat, and viewed her maid in the mirror. With her nut-brown hair and brown eyes, and in her charcoal grey and white uniform, Molly reminded her of the birds flitting between the bushes in St James's Park.

Turning to her own reflection, she saw dark, almost black hair and pale skin. Thankfully, she had put on flesh over the last month. On her last visit, Aunt Sybil had exclaimed in James' presence that Emily looked like to follow her infant into the grave.

Emily had reddened as James raked brown eyes over her too-slender form. "We need to feed you up a little, Emily, my dear."

Emily shuddered. Food was unlikely to cure what ailed her.

"Milady?" Molly's quiet enquiry brought her back to her senses and she stood up to allow Molly to unfasten her walking dress.

Grey silk suited her complexion better than black, lifting her pallor and lessening the shadows beneath her blue-grey eyes. Molly nodded to herself as she patted down the folds of the full skirt, and Emily allowed herself a small smile at the maid's satisfaction in her appearance. Taking her new book, she made her way to the pretty morning room.

She disliked her interactions with the housekeeper, believing that doling out stores to create meals was demeaning to them both. But her aunt had instructed her, and Mrs Worthy expected it.

When she entered the house during that first season, Emily had suggested a change of routine.

"I'm a great one for tradition, ma'am, if you don't mind," Mrs Worthy had said. "I don't hold with provincial habits."

At the time, Emily stared at what seemed a direct insult, but gathering herself, nodded. She thought she would bring the housekeeper round to her way of thinking, but as the months wore on, it became harder to change things.

By the time Mrs Worthy tapped at the door, Emily's hands were damp. The housekeeper wished her good morning, her black dress jarring with the gentle decor of the room.

Since she had risen from her sickbed, Emily had seen an echo of pity in every one of the servants' faces except Mrs Worthy's. As the plump, sour woman inclined her head towards her, Emily wondered what made the housekeeper's heart so hard. She clutched the jet beads that hung to her waist and saw Mrs Worthy's lip twitch in what she interpreted as disdain.

Something clicked in Emily's head. She was so tired of everything – the London house, being marooned in grief, her dull, blank life and the housekeeper's barely veiled contempt. Mrs Worthy despised her? Well, the feeling was mutual.

Fired by unaccustomed anger, Emily chose a different path. "Yes?" she said curtly, placing her hands in her lap.

The housekeeper blinked, taken aback. "The menus for the week, ma'am. I wanted to discuss them with you."

"Please leave your suggestions on the table. I shall consider them and let you have my decision later."

"Of course, but..."

Emily raised an eyebrow, and Mrs Worthy seemed to gather herself. "Begging pardon, but I know Sir James is planning a dinner at the end of the week—"

"Sir James *and I* are planning a dinner at the end of the week," Emily corrected, her voice steady. "I have already discussed it with him. A clear broth, please, carp with lemon and butter sauce, and pigeon. And Sir James' preference is for service à la Russe, so please consider whether the footmen need extra support to serve each course promptly."

Mrs Worthy stared in bewilderment and Emily, who had not discussed the menu or the service with James at all, observed her expression with quiet glee. James wouldn't care as long as the food was well-cooked and each course came to the table hot. "Leave your other suggestions and I shall let you have my thoughts."

"But what about dinner today?" Mrs Worthy asked sullenly.

Emily put her head on one side and considered. "What did you have in mind?" She glanced at the cramped handwriting. "Roast ham. Splendid, that will do very well. The rest I shall consider. We can go to the storeroom later."

Mrs Worthy looked outraged before assuming an expressionless mask fell over her hard features. She nodded and made to leave.

Another thought struck Emily. "One moment. How is the new housemaid?"

"Seems well enough," Mrs Worthy said, sniffing. "They're all happy to cut corners—"

"Do you doubt your choice, Mrs Worthy?"

Mrs Worthy was silent. Emily caught an assessing glance from her, startled, no doubt, by Emily's coolness.

The housekeeper took a deep breath. "No, ma'am. She's a hard worker, sure enough, but they have to be kept up to the mark, otherwise standards slide. As you will know, ma'am."

Emily felt the barb. The servants knew Emily's background: respectable, but worlds away from James Cleveland's. And her experience did not include managing a staff of thirty-five, as Mrs Worthy was well aware. "Hmm," she said. Mrs Worthy dipped her head and scurried away.

When the door was safely closed Emily let out a breath, elated that she had, for once in nearly two and a half years, stood her ground. The menus were on the table and she would peruse them at her leisure, without the exaggerated patience from Mrs Worthy which normally accompanied them.

She sank into her favourite armchair. For a moment, the misery of the past few months receded. Such a small show of confidence! Yet it had made her feel on firmer ground, rather than unsteady, unsure. My recovery is in hand, she thought, her spirits rising.

She half-rose to find James but sat down again. She needed to be calm, not giddy. Otherwise, Dr Schenley would tell James she was hysterical. No, she should keep her counsel and bend all her effort to appearing in the pink of health, if only to frustrate the good doctor.

THE NEXT DAY, EMILY TRIED TO RECAPTURE HER BUOYANCY, BUT the spectre of a visit from Dr Schenley squashed her mood. She leafed through her leather-covered diary and read the lines written in such spirits the previous evening.

What a difference in me! Energy flooded through my body, my soul brightened, and I felt my confidence return, simply for doing what I desired rather than kowtowing to someone else! I pray this is the beginning of my recovery.

But soft night had given way to a harsher sunlit morning and her journal entry seemed like the words of a braggart. She put the book away as Molly hurried around the bedroom, laying out clothes and jewellery.

Molly began to brush Emily's hair: one hundred strokes, steady and slow. Emily regarded herself in the mirror. She had worn her ebony, wavy hair in the same way since James and she had married three years ago. He loved her hair.

"I saw Mrs Sanderson sporting a new style last week, with the hair drawn up so..." She caught a handful of hair and pulled it tighter on the top of her head. "Could you attempt such a style?" Molly nodded eagerly.

Fifteen minutes later, she stared at the image before her. Molly had looped her thick locks on top of her head, leaving her neck bare. The pearls in her ears were more visible, and in her pretty dressing gown she looked fresher, her blue-grey eyes bright.

Molly regarded her with undisguised pleasure. "I remember your wedding day, milady."

Emily laughed. "It seems many years ago!"

A soft knock on the door surprised them. James poked his dark head in and Emily's heart swelled at the sight of him. He was thinner and his face sterner after the baby. His laugh, deep and infectious, had all but disappeared. This morning, however, his dark-brown eyes swept over her and she caught the twinkle in them. "You look very fetching."

Molly bobbed a curtsy and disappeared.

Emily turned from the mirror as he approached. Her hand cupped his jaw and caressed it. She loved the soft bristles of his beard, and she spotted the recent trim. "You look very smart, James. Are you due in the House this afternoon?"

"Yes, there is an important division. If you recall, you approved of my speech." He kissed the tip of her nose and she smiled. He picked up the book on her bureau. "More novels, my love?"

They had met in Hatchards in Piccadilly, reaching for the same book. The conversation had been very polite and proper, but Emily would have been a fool not to see the interest of this tall, handsome man. And Emily was far from being a fool.

He peered at the title. *"The Mill on the Floss?* What is it about?"

Emily turned eagerly towards him. "It is about a young woman who is struggling towards a noble life," she said. "The review I read in *The Spectator* said the heroine did not have the strength of will to realise that noble life, but I am not convinced. I think she is forced to conform to society's idea of what a woman should be, intellectually and spiritually."

"It sounds as though it would frustrate you."

She nodded. "It does, somewhat, but it is splendidly written."

He smiled. "Will you come to breakfast?" he asked, and held out his arm.

She'd always liked the dining room, which was light and airy. Today, the sunlight streamed through the windows, softened by the golden stained glass. The footman George moved around in his stately way, uncovering dishes and spooning food. He approached with the teapot.

"I'd prefer cocoa this morning, George."

George picked up another pot, pouring the dark, rich liquid into her fine porcelain cup. Emily took a sip and closed her eyes in bliss; she had a sweet tooth, and this was a rare indulgence. She opened her eyes to see James smiling at her. "You'll get fat," he teased.

She smiled and nibbled her toast, rejecting the jam.

Two regular topics of conversation among her acquaintances – she hesitated to name them friends – were weight and corsets. She wriggled slightly and the steel bones of her corset pressed against her ribs and soft belly; she had submitted to Molly's efforts to make her waist an eighth of an inch smaller. While one couldn't grow fat and indolent, surely some comfort should be permitted, she had protested. She was slender enough: her grief had seen to that. But her bosom was still pert and firm, her hips flared gently from her small waist and her complexion, while pale, was fine and clear. A little energy was all she needed to show herself to advantage and prove to her husband that her health was improving...

"Are you making morning calls today?" James interrupted her reverie.

She nodded. "Yes, I am due to call on Lady Botham. I am rather tardy in thanking her for dinner last week." She paused, then forced the words from her lips. "When are you expecting Dr Schenley?"

He shot her a glance. "On Friday at the usual time, about four. Will you be here? I value his conversation because he is well connected and knowledgeable, but I know you do not always welcome his company."

Such a polite expression of the truth! She picked up her cup of cocoa again to ensure she could control her voice before replying. Could she manage Dr Schenley? He made her fearful, and of course, he had been in command at the birth...

Hold hard, Emily, she told herself fiercely. "I have no firm plans, but I expect I shall have returned from my shopping before he arrives," she said, in as serene a voice as she could conjure. James stared at her as if trying to read her thoughts, then smiled and continued his breakfast.

Emily reached for the jam and took another slice of toast. What was it James said about an army marching on its stomach? She could not manage Dr Schenley with anything less than a vigorous constitution. She needed building up!

Chapter 3

Harry's tree surgeon arrived the next day, while Cat was still in her pyjamas. Cat stumbled to the door, fastening her robe as she went.

A stocky, unsmiling man with unkempt brown hair was standing there with Harry. She glanced at her watch, appalled that it wasn't yet quarter past eight.

"Yeah, you never were good in the morning," Harry commented with a grin. "I know it's a bit early for you. This is John, come to look at the tree."

"Hi. Sorry, I wasn't expecting you until nine. Hang on..."

She left them on the doorstep as she rooted through the cupboard in the kitchen for the key to the side gate. When she returned, they were both standing in the entrance hall. Alarm curled through her. *What are they doing in my house?*

Harry gave her a sharp glance, then an apologetic smile. "I hope you don't mind us stepping inside. It's raining."

She breathed deeply and nodded. She thrust the key at John, who grunted a thank you. "I'll need the gate kept open, is that okay?"

"Yes, of course. Please make sure you return the key when you've opened the gate."

"Aye," said John and disappeared.

Silence fell and Cat caught Harry staring at her bare feet on the tiled floor. She felt her cheeks warm and pulled her robe together at the neck. "I need to get dressed."

Harry's eyes slid away and her gaze ran over his combats and thick sweater. He'd filled out since they'd split up, his shoulders broader. With his height, she imagined him knocking 'em dead when he was in uniform. Or out of it.

"Are you okay?" asked Harry. "You've gone a bit pink."

"Yes, I'm fine. Um, was there anything else?"

"Can we speak about the wall? You'll need to get some quotes."

Cat hesitated. Did she really want to have this conversation in her dressing gown? "Can you give me ten minutes to shower and dress?"

"Do you want me to wait? I could make coffee." He gestured towards the kitchen.

Cat stiffened, resenting his casual invasion of her space. "I'd prefer to speak later. Is the end of the day convenient?"

"Sure. Text me."

He left and she climbed the stairs feeling strangely disoriented.

CAT SIGHED. AT LAST THEY WERE TAKING A BREAK FROM CUTTING up the tree and the garden was quiet. She pushed the laptop away. The end of the scene where her heroine Louise faced her past demons was a good place to leave things while she grabbed a sandwich and a coffee. Damn. Make that cheese and crackers – the bread had run out yesterday. She needed to go into the village.

The sun glinted through the stained glass at the top of the drawing-room windows and she avoided looking at the hole in the wall. Thank God the rain had stopped.

She was just about to bite into some cheese when the knocker banged against the front door.

Frowning, Cat threw open the door to find a diminutive elderly lady with a jaunty yellow scarf and a big bunch of chrysanthemums assessing her front garden. She turned and smiled at Cat, delicate eyebrows arched.

"Lizzie!" Cat gasped. "What a surprise! How wonderful to see you! Come in, come in!"

"Hello, dear," Lizzie said. She stepped in and reached up to kiss Cat's cheek.

"How have you been?" Cat hugged her carefully, noting that Lizzie had lost weight and her grey eyes seemed large in her face.

Lizzie handed over the flowers and slipped off her bouclé coat. "Fine, fine. As you hadn't invited me, I thought I'd better invite myself to see how you were getting along in May's old house."

Cat blushed. Yes, she'd been busy, but too busy for Gam's oldest friend? Guilt prodded her. "I'm sorry, I should have called. I've been tied up with things: moving in and trying to get on with the next book. And now we've got a problem with the tree."

"What? Which tree?"

Cat drew her to the window and Lizzie gaped at the tumbled wall, made even more stark now most of the tree had been removed. "Goodness me! How did that happen?"

"Harry the next door neighbour thinks a couple of hundred years of rain have done it."

Lizzie shook her head, following Cat to the kitchen. "Oh dear. When are you getting it repaired?"

"I'm not sure. Money's tight, so I want to leave it until I get my finances in order."

Lizzie looked doubtful. "It's such a mess. Are you sure you'll be able to wait? This is a conservation area. I remember when May wanted to replace the windows and we had reams of paperwork to get through before we could touch anything! The council may be interested, too..."

Cat shrugged. "Well, no one's come knocking at my door yet, so fingers crossed! I was about to have lunch. Can I offer you something to eat? Or a cup of tea?"

"Lunch, at nearly three o'clock? What kind of lunch is that, Cat?" Lizzie, diverted from the wall, peered at her. "You eat, Catherine, I'll just have tea. The drawing room?"

"I'll be right in."

When Cat walked into the sitting room with a tray, Lizzie was gazing at the fireplace, a sheen of tears in her eyes. "Are you okay, Lizzie?"

Her guest said nothing for a moment, then smiled brightly. "Yes, I'm just reminiscing. I remember Burns Night with a roaring fire. May held the most wonderful parties, full of poetry and music."

"And the odd wee dram," added Cat, handing Lizzie a cup of tea. Lizzie chuckled and sat down on the old sofa, her gnarled fingers stroking the worn leather.

"Indeed." Lizzie's response was soft, and silence fell. After a moment, she blinked and looked around the room. "What happened to all the furniture?"

Cat wrinkled her nose. Her brother Anthony had picked through it like a vulture and that was *another* argument waiting to happen between Cat and her parents. "I wasn't fast enough to stop Mum and Dad clearing the place out. I claimed a wonderful chair upstairs. I think they were trying to help."

"Leaving you with next to nothing to sit on?"

Cat snorted, swallowed her tea and shrugged. The comment was unanswerable, so she didn't try.

"And how are *you*?" Lizzie asked.

"Oh, I'm fine. You know... missing Gam, trying to get on with the book. Sorting out the house."

Lizzie sipped her tea. "How does it feel to be out of London?"

Cat shot her a glance. "Is that a sneaky way of asking about Stephen?"

Lizzie put her fingertips to her collarbone and looked affronted.

"Good heavens, not at all! But since you brought it up, how are you managing without the arrogant little creep?"

Cat laughed, shaking her head. "You only met him once!" At the funeral.

Lizzie looked down her short little nose and sniffed. "It was enough. He seemed a mite controlling to me."

Oh, if only you knew, thought Cat, and picked up another cracker. "It's over and I'm fine," she responded steadily. "I'm focusing on the book."

"And how's that going?" Lizzie's question was mild, but her dark eyes were sharp. She had known Cat since she was twelve, so an outright lie was impossible.

"Slow," Cat conceded. "It's more women's fiction than romance and I'm still finding my feet. The main character, Louise, is overcoming some of her past experiences."

Lizzie nodded. "Interesting. I enjoyed your other books but they were a bit young for me. May was immensely proud of you and your writing."

"I wish I'd had better success with the last book. Gam said she wanted to see it on the bestseller lists, but I didn't manage that..." Cat's voice clogged with tears.

"Before she died? No, you didn't," Lizzie said, matter-of-fact. "But she didn't care how it sold. She wanted you to explore your talent, be completely yourself. And you're doing that. *That's* what made her proud."

Cat shook her head, lips tight. "Sadly, my editor and publisher are rather more concerned about sales."

"That's as may be. May just wanted you to follow your heart. And you can now, can't you?" Lizzie said, pouring another cup of tea. "Especially now you've jettisoned Stephen."

Cat was keen to move away from the topic of Stephen, which was making her chest tighten with unease. "Anyway, I'm glad to be here and able to write – it's absolutely what I needed. I don't know if I can afford to stay here long term, though – I was completely unprepared for the cost of running this place."

Lizzie pursed her lips. "I thought May left you some money?"

"She did, and I'm getting through it at an alarming rate. Repairs to the boiler, a new radiator, fixing loose tiles – and that was before I moved in!"

"You could always get a lodger," Lizzie suggested.

Cat paused. Did she feel brave enough for that? After Stephen, she wanted space and time. But she could use the money...

"Think about it," Lizzie said. "You need to get references and money up front, but I doubt you'd run up against many axe murderers."

Cat laughed. "You think I'm being an idiot, don't you?"

Lizzie gave her a shrewd glance. "It's good to be cautious. Stephen didn't seem a good choice."

Outside, the electric saw started up, and a knock at the door gave Cat the opportunity not to answer.

At the door was Harry, looking fed up. "I wondered if you had time now to talk about the building work?"

"Um, I have guests—"

"No, no, I must be going!" Lizzie announced, peeking around Cat at Harry.

"You don't have to go!" Cat protested.

"I must let you get on: I can see how busy you are. Walk me to my car."

As she unlocked her ancient Fiat, Lizzie threw Cat a mischievous glance. "So that's your neighbour? Is he married?"

"He's an ex. And not that I know."

"Really? How extraordinary. What are the chances of you moving next door to him? It must be fate," Lizzie slipped her arms into her coat.

"Like Stephen, that's over. Don't go there."

"So reassuring to know you once had taste." Lizzie pecked her on the cheek and ordered her to stay in touch. Cat watched the car chug out of sight, took a deep breath and returned to the house.

Harry, as she had imagined, wasn't happy about her decision to delay the repairs. "Bits of your bloody wall are all over my property! Surely it's a matter of getting the insurers in?"

"I don't have insurance."

Harry gawped at her. "You are bloody joking!"

"I was looking for a cheaper quote, and then... Things got away from me, with my deadline." Cat's head was beginning to ache.

Harry flung his hands up and Cat bristled. "Look, I'm really sorry. I'll help you clear up the mess on your lawn—"

He gave a bitter shout of laughter. "I bet you bloody won't! Because you're on a *deadline,* aren't you? Christ, some things never change!"

Cat went cold. "Yes, I am on a deadline, because writing is my *job,*" she said, steel in her voice. "I'll get it sorted as soon as I can – probably a month or so – but as it's my wall, I'll choose when to do it. At least the tree is being moved."

Harry folded his arms and stared at her. "You'll find that in a conservation area, you'll need to do it rather sooner. People take a keen interest in places like this. Don't say I didn't warn you." He turned on his heel and stalked out.

Two days later, Cat reread the letter from the local authority, requesting a meeting with her about the restoration of the wall and almost screamed in frustration. "Bloody bureaucrats!" she muttered through gritted teeth. She'd been expecting it, but not this soon. She was still seething when she heard the knock at the door.

The door stuck in the frame. Feeling the resistance, Cat tugged at it frantically. It's fine, Cat, she told herself, you're not trapped. Finally, it opened, revealing a slight man with a comb-over, hands thrust in the pockets of his duffel coat.

"Is this a good time?" Geoff Johnson, Gam's ex-tenant, smiled broadly.

"No, not really," Cat replied, still shaken from her tussle with the door.

Johnson remained where he was. "I heard about the garden wall. What a disaster!"

Cat froze. "How did you know?"

"I hear most things about Cleveland House." He smiled again, and she noticed he had something green in his teeth. "I thought you might not know about the historical importance of the house, so I informed the local authority that there had been some damage."

Cat stared at him. "You did *what*?"

"I informed the buildings officer at the council. He should have written to you by now."

"So it's you I have to thank for some officious busybody telling me how to deal with the damage?"

"You sound quite irate," he said, his thick eyebrows arching in surprise. "It's a good thing. The officer will have excellent, qualified contacts to help you restore the wall. I doubt you'd have the right sort."

"That's – very thoughtful," Cat managed to say. "I'm really busy, thanks for calling." He was still talking as she shut the door firmly.

She took a deep breath. At least it hadn't been Harry who'd reported her. It wasn't Harry's style, anyway: she knew that.

She pushed all her notes on the manuscript to one side and logged on to the savings account she'd had since she was a child. It was her repository for birthday and Christmas money, and the odd win she'd had on the lottery or the horse racing. Gam's money was in another account. The balance on the savings account was only slightly better than she remembered. Still, it was a start. She transferred the money to her bank account and trawled the internet for cheap credit deals.

The robin chirped outside her window, attracted to the garden by the upended earth and the worms exposed to its greedy gaze. "Could you lend me a few thousand quid?" Cat asked it.

The bird flew off. Cat sighed and picked up the phone to speak to the local authority officer, who was going to force her to rebuild the wall whether she wanted to or not.

Chapter 4

Emily peered at the wilting fern in the Wardian case, longing to take off the cover and rescue it. It had been over-watered, she would swear...

She turned to see Lady Botham, resplendent in emerald velvet, staring at her with one eyebrow raised. Emily forced a smile from a face that felt stiff and received a curt nod.

"It is divine!" gushed Mrs Jenson. "I perfectly comprehend why you could not have done without it!" Over her dainty cup and saucer, she indicated Lady Botham's new carpet. Emily tried to concentrate. The ladies were cooing over the densely knotted silk rug, a riot of colour which made her head ache. As Miss Chisinghurst squinted at the Turkish rug, the peacock feather in her hat brushed the floor.

"The design is very ... exotic, is it not?" Mrs Jenson twisted her head to see the carpet, covered as it was with small tables, huge vases, and chair legs. Emily heard a small crack of bone and Mrs Jenson straightened up gingerly.

Lady Botham swelled with pride. "Indeed, the monumental botanical design is typical of the region."

"But what an expense!" said Miss Chisinghurst. "Surely such

Turkish carpets cannot be worth the outlay. Particularly with the air of London, smoky and dirty as it is." She sat back on the sofa. "How on earth do you contrive to keep it clean?"

"Pah, Minnie is under-employed. Beating a carpet a few times a week is hardly onerous, and I pay her well enough."

"Oh, she is still with you?" Mrs Jenson asked innocently, and Emily pressed her lips together to stop herself smiling and took refuge behind her teacup. One of Lady Botham's continual complaints was the turnover of her servants; the conversation never turned to Lady Botham's attitude towards her servants.

"Lady Cleveland, you look a little pale. Are you well?" Miss Chisinghurst commented, bringing an immediate blush to Emily's cheeks.

"I am exceedingly well."

"Thank goodness," said Lady Botham smoothly. "We spoke about it yesterday. I'm so relieved you have put off your blacks. We were concerned at how long your recovery was taking."

Emily stiffened, torn between shame and anger. They had discussed how long she had been in mourning? She was the subject of their idle *gossip*? "How kind." Her voice could have frozen water.

Lady Botham paused in surprise. "We have only your best interests at heart," she said, leaning across to press Emily's hand.

Emily paused, conscious of the eyes of the other two women in the stuffy drawing room. She could take umbrage, or smile and pretend to be comforted by their professed concern. Emily hesitated and Lady Botham looked haughty, so she reluctantly reconsidered her position. Amelia Botham would not have offered her so much as a good morning had it not been for her marriage to James.

She smiled. "I am blessed to have such good friends," she said, crossing her fingers in the folds of her skirt.

Mrs Jenson gave a short, huffing laugh and fluffed the Valenciennes lace at her throat, her jewellery clinking. Mrs Jenson wore several strands of pearls, three brooches, and two bangles. She would be incapable of silent movement, Emily reflected.

Glancing around the room, Emily saw that her own gown, while no less fine, was less embellished than those of the other ladies. Her hair, even in the new style, sported no combs, nor the flowers in Miss Chisinghurst's blonde locks, nor the jewels which glinted in Lady Botham's dark tresses. She preferred simpler attire, but that marked her out as different, she knew.

"With no mother to guide your first steps in society, we could hardly call ourselves your friends should we not take your interests to heart!" Mrs Jenson said, with a touch of impatience.

"And with such, shall we say, *unusual* parents, I am pleased we have been able to show you how to go on!" Lady Botham added.

Emily's fingers gripped her teacup. Her parents had died in a boating accident when she was fifteen, leaving her in the loving but brisk care of Aunt Sybil. She had missed her mother and their free-ranging conversations intensely. No topic, however unfeminine, was forbidden with her mother, unlike Aunt Sybil, whose conversations were focused on the weather, society's more elevated members, and the latest fashions.

Emily recognised that her marriage to James had been a shock to society. An unknown female whose origins, while respectable, were tinged with the whiff of radical thinking should not have joined one of England's richest and oldest families. Society did not know that James had been attracted to her mind as well as her person, and had encouraged her to share her more unconventional ideas with him.

Deeply in love and keen to do James proud, Emily had been determined not to put a foot wrong in society. At first she had been grateful for the three ladies' advice, particularly after James received his knighthood. But after the baby their robust counsel was like stinging nettles to her skin, and she shrank from their company. Well, she would bear it as best she could, if only for James' sake.

"Women of the gentry have a unique position," Mrs Jenson said, to the nods of Lady Botham and Miss Chisinghurst. "Our role is to show patience and quiet fortitude, though our trials may be severe. But our menfolk require our cheerful support and unstinting enthusiasm. Moping is not conducive to their morale, nor indeed our own."

"I agree," put in Miss Chisinghurst. "Wallowing in the misery of past events cannot help matters."

Emily was rigid with fury. They thought she was *wallowing*? That the loss of her baby had not utterly shattered her heart? Oh, this was too much!

"With elections coming, many of the wives of our most eminent Members of Parliament will help them canvass," continued Mrs Jenson, oblivious to the smouldering rage that Emily was sure must be visible.

"I heard Lady Grosvenor speak on that very subject over dinner last week," Miss Chisinghurst put in, but Mrs Jenson frowned at the interruption.

"What we are saying, Lady Cleveland, is that while you may have been prostrate with grief, now is the time to put that behind you and return to your place as your husband's stalwart supporter and arbiter of his home comforts," Lady Botham finished, looking pleased that the topic, a trifle delicate for a morning call, had been covered.

"See how our conversation does you good!" marvelled Miss Chisinghurst. "You were so pale when you arrived and now your cheeks are quite pink."

Emily took a deep breath and put down her cup, folding hands that trembled a little in her lap. "I am obliged to you," she forced out.

Lady Botham inclined her head graciously, and Emily's mind raced in circles, searching for something to say. Lady Botham had five strapping children, as handsome and solid as she was; Miss Chisinghurst was unmarried and knew nothing of her pain. Mrs Jenson had borne nine children, two of whom had died in infancy. Emily had thought that of all her acquaintance, Agatha Jenson would have helped her to find some meaning in the tragedy that had befallen her. But if anything, Mrs Jenson was more unfeeling than the others. She had said brusquely on her first call after the funeral that Emily would soon recover and youth was her advantage.

The ladies were waiting for her response. She stood up, smoothing the folds of her grey silk. Her eyes found Lady Botham and her voice, although soft, was crystal clear. "I believe we are all different," she said quietly. "We are cheered and brought low by different experiences." She paused. "I find it difficult to sigh over a new carpet, however exquisite – but I shall sigh over the death of my first-born child for as long as I feel the pain. And now I must bid you good afternoon. My husband awaits my return."

There was silence. Stony-faced, Lady Botham rang the bell and the ladies murmured their farewells.

Emily left as the butler opened the door. She grasped her reticule tightly, glad to be away from that close, over-stuffed room.

SHE FIDGETED ALL THE WAY HOME IN THE LANDAU, DELIGHTED and secretly scared by what had happened at Lady Botham's house. Lord Botham was a close confidant of James, and her husband might hear of her abruptness.

Would he be angry? She hoped not. James had been all kindness through her mourning and had even shed a tear with her in private. He felt the loss of their infant son, on whom he had settled his hopes most acutely. He had paid particular attention when she set up the nursery, desiring the best of everything for their child, his heir.

She sat back against the velvet cushions as the carriage jolted towards Hyde Park and home. Thoughts tumbled around her head, forming pictures: James' face as she told him she was with child; his delight as she increased and his laughter at her ungainly movements as she navigated doors with huge skirts and a swollen belly; his anguish as he came to her bedroom after the midwife had taken their baby from that messy, bloody bed.

He had held her close while she sobbed, called her his darling, and promised he would spend his life trying to make her happy, to make her complete. But since that awful night he had forsaken her bed, choosing to spend time at Egerton's Club on St James' Street rather than return home.

To be fair, she had needed time to recover from the birth. She stared out of the window at the grey streets as they flashed by, trying to rid her mind of Dr Schenley. Throughout her labour he had prowled around the room, ignoring comments and advice from Maggie, the nurse they had engaged a month before.

When Emily, exhausted from the pain of childbirth and the sharper pain of her loss, moaned into her pillow, Maggie stroked her forehead and bade her swallow a draught of laudanum to pull her into sleep. Dr Schenley, meanwhile, had left the room to speak to James.

"Have a care this man does not come to you when you have your next," Maggie whispered. Closing her eyes, the words settled into Emily's brain as the opiates drew her into sleep. She'd been wary of Robert Schenley ever since, and took less and less of the drugs he prescribed, painfully tearing herself away from the dull oblivion of laudanum.

They slowed at a junction. Emily saw a group of young boys, ragged and dirty, tormenting a puppy at the side of the road, poking it with sticks and pelting it with pebbles. Without thinking, she hit the roof of the carriage with her parasol and called out. "Stop the carriage!"

She was opening the door of the carriage before it came to a stop, to the remonstrances of John, her coachman. "Help me past that filth, please," Emily commanded, and took his hand to climb down. She straightened her hat and advanced to the group of boys. "Whose dog is this?"

"Wassit to you?" one of the urchins replied, and the coachman clipped him around the ear for his insolence. She stared at the boy, who mumbled an apology. She bent to the dog, quivering and cowering in fear, a smear of blood on his flank where a stone had caught him. He was unprepossessing, it was true: short legs, and a wiry, matted brown coat, although that could be mud. But big, pitiful eyes stared at her as though begging to be saved.

She stood and looked at the now-wary lads. "Whose dog is this?"

There was a shuffle at the back of the group and a snotty-nosed lad was shoved forward. "'Tis mine," he muttered.

"I shall buy him from you," Emily said. John stared at her, aghast. She searched in her reticule. "Will a shilling suffice?"

The child gawped at the silver coin she held up. Then the boy who had spoken to her first stepped forward. "Two shillin' and 'ee's yourn," he said, his eyes gleaming.

Emily raised her eyebrows and moved towards him, ignoring the stench that rose from him. "You will make an admirable businessman one day, but do not presume to haggle with me. This dog will die shortly under your hands, and then what? You will have neither entertainment nor shilling." She turned back to the snotty-nosed boy. "So, which is it to be?"

"I'll take your shillin', mum," he replied, ignoring the older boy. She tossed the coin at him. He caught it and sprinted away before he could be relieved of his money by the others. Emily bent to pick up the whimpering puppy, while John whipped his muffler from around his neck and offered it to her. She smiled at him in gratitude. "Thank you! My dress would get very dirty."

She wrapped the puppy in the rough, warm folds of the muffler and it seemed to recognise it was now among friends. Emily gave him a gentle hug and laughed as he licked her face. "That will do! Goodness, we need to give you a bath. You smell frightful!"

The rest of the journey home was thoughtful. She wondered at the wisdom of picking up a stray dog, what James would say, what Mrs Worthy would say, and then impatiently pushed aside her thoughts. "Poor-spirited creature!" she scolded herself. "When a creature is in danger from a cruel master, what is there to consider?" She addressed the dog, snuggled into the muffler on her lap. "If necessary, you will live in the stables, although I would much rather keep you near me."

The dog yawned and closed his eyes.

"I can see how enthusiastic you are about that," she said gravely. "We shall see what you look like when you're clean. And give you a name. I know – we will call you Lucky, which seems apposite."

She patted the dog, who let out a sigh that shook his small body.

"Hmm. You should know, Lucky, that James' mama will not tolerate a mongrel in the drawing room, so you will need to buck up and learn some new tricks."

And so would she, she realised. Her grief still felt raw, but Lady Botham was right about one thing: James would need her help soon in the elections. As her husband, he had the right to expect it, and she should make all efforts to provide it. Many of the wives of the Members of Parliament were skilled hostesses, gathering an understanding of businessmen's interests so that MPs could properly represent them in the House. But Emily had never done such a thing and feared her awkwardness would harm James' reputation.

She would need to turn to someone for advice. But who? Perhaps Aunt Sybil would know.

Buoyed by such thoughts, she fondled Lucky's ears and he wriggled in delight. Smiling at the puppy, she looked forward to doing something. Being busy would help her grief.

A frown pinched her forehead as something struck her.

"I shall throw away the laudanum too," she informed Lucky. "It is dishonest to make it seem as though I still take it."

A gentle wag of the tail demonstrated that Lucky approved.

Chapter 5

D ave Robinson, the Historic Estates Officer from the local council, had been sympathetic to the mess, but firm.

"I'm sorry if it's financially inconvenient, but this garden wall is a fine example of Victorian architecture and part of the county's heritage, so you need to rebuild before the delay does even more damage. If you choose to ignore our advice, I'm afraid we may take you to court."

Cat took the list of suggested suppliers without a word. After she'd closed the door she logged on to the internet to investigate some of them, and her stomach sank. The suppliers sported impressive websites boasting hundreds of years in the business, and referencing their standards in maintaining historic buildings.

"At stratospheric prices, I bet," Cat muttered, closing the tabs and sighing.

Her phone buzzed. It was Lauren, her oldest chum.

—Hope the move went well and you're not TOOOO knackered? Speak tomorrow??? Don't work too hard!

Cat grinned at what seemed to be at least twenty emojis after the words. They implied that Lauren was sixteen rather than twenty-nine. A hangover from school, Cat decided. She looped a stray lock of hair behind her ear, began to text, then stopped. She couldn't put all this in a text. Instead, she sent a message to say she'd call soon for a catch-up. Then she stared into space. The computer on Gam's dining-room table called her to resume work, but her head wasn't in the right space to write.

The late February sun peeked through the drawing-room windows, mocking her inactivity. She rose and, pulling on a jacket, headed into the garden.

She meandered along the path by the lawn, noting that the daffodils were beginning to push their heads from the frozen soil. She passed the greenhouses, their windows broken and cracked. She would need to clear up all the glass soon.

Cat winced as she came to the fernery. The paths that wound through it had shifted with the roots of fallen tree and some of the ferns clung forlornly to the upturned soil.

She stepped carefully into the fernery and heaved a foot-long stone out of the path. She clucked in distress as she saw the flags cracked with the weight of the fallen wall. It would take a lot of effort to restore this. She bent to lift another boulder on to the raised bed and her eye caught a silver gleam among the mess of broken masonry, ferns and mud.

Cat dumped the boulder on the other side of the path and peered at it. Frowning, she brushed the leaves away gently and cautiously; after all, this might be an unexploded shell from the First World War.

"Or someone's lunch box!" Cat muttered, shaking her head in self-derision as she uncovered a tin box about ten inches long. It was embedded just below the top of the wall, exposed only because the top stone had been dislodged. Cat crouched on her haunches and peered at it.

"How very weird," she breathed, trying to prise it loose. She broke a fingernail before she shook her head in exasperation and dashed back to the house for a screwdriver.

35

The earth and mortar gave easily as she levered a corner of the box out. Finally, the box was in her hands. It felt strangely warm, which Cat put down to the insulating effect of the earth. There was a clasp, but any lock had long since disappeared and the lid opened with a little effort.

In the box was something oblong wrapped in oilskins. Cat closed the lid and carefully carried her find back to the kitchen, where she put it in the sink. She snapped rubber gloves on and carefully lifted the package out of the box. Holding her breath, she unwrapped it.

It was a small brown leather volume, the edge of the pages yellow and fragile with age. Cat turned the book over in her hands, and hesitantly touched the frayed ribbon that fastened the cover. She untied the ribbon – she had to tug a little – and her breath caught as a strand of the worn velvet pulled away.

"Emily Caroline Cleveland," she read on the flyleaf. "Oh my God! It's a journal…"

Cat gently opened the first page. The first entry was the first of January, 1862. Nothing to do with Gam, then.

Her mind buzzed with questions. Who was Emily Caroline Cleveland? How on earth did her journal get buried in the fernery? And *why* had it been buried there?

A faint smell of lavender drifted from the pages. The writing was elegant and slanted, but as she turned the first pages, she was aware of something strange. Weren't these someone's private thoughts? So why didn't she feel as if she was snooping?

Carefully turning the pages, she read 'Westminster', 'malady', 'mourning' and 'Mrs Worthy'. Later on, she saw the words 'Lucky' and 'Charlotte'. She read a diary entry at random:

I unearthed my watercolours and am happily engaged in reproducing a sketch of one of my favourite ferns. I feel it is not unlike and confess myself much pleased with the results so far.

A smile crept across Cat's face. Perhaps the lady who wrote this –

Emily Caroline Cleveland – had asked for the diary to be buried in the fernery to commemorate her love of ferns? It seemed a bit extreme to Cat, but then again, she wasn't a Victorian.

Some time later, the ping of a message disturbed her reading. It was from Creighton. His message was short, but to the point: How goes it?

Cat blew out her cheeks and put the diary aside guiltily. She'd barely written a word since Dave Robinson had left, wrapped up as she had been in builders and costs. And now, the diary. She picked up her phone and dialled his number.

He picked up immediately. "Catherine, how are you?"

She thought about lying to him, then changed her mind. He knew her too well.

"Snowed under with bureaucracy," she said, gloomily, and told him briefly about the council's visit and the pressure to rebuild the wall. "The suppliers all look mega-expensive. You know, been in the business for centuries, and have contracts with Historic England. I think one of them even worked on Windsor Castle..."

"Oh dear. Not good for your wallet, then?"

Cat smiled. Creighton really did understand her. "Too right! But I thought I'd ask Harry if he knew some alternative suppliers."

"And who is Harry?"

Cat hesitated. "The next-door neighbour. Astonishingly, he's an ex-boyfriend. I think we'd just broken up when you took me on. I didn't know he was next door when I moved in."

"What a coincidence. How was the reunion?" Creighton had really earned his fee keeping her motivated during the break-up with Stephen, and Cat sensed the wariness behind his mild question.

"Don't fret, Creighton: Harry and I have been over for a long time. And I'm not looking for a new partner any time soon."

"Hmm. I'm not very surprised after your last experience. I hope you'll forgive me asking about your paramour, but you *are* on a dead-line, Catherine."

"Yes, I know. But the strangest thing has happened. I found an old journal among the rubble in the fernery! It's the diary of a lady called Emily. It was in a box – it looks as if it was deliberately hidden."

"How peculiar. Do you know anything about it? I take it you've looked at it?"

Cat hesitated. Admitting that she'd just spent the last forty minutes examining the journal would not impress a man waiting for a redrafted manuscript. "Well, I've just leafed through the initial entries."

The silence at the end of the line spoke volumes. Creighton's voice was tight when he spoke again. "I'm concerned that time is getting on, Catherine."

"I know, I know! Now, about the revised chapter..." Cat sat at her computer and tapped a key to bring the screen back to life. She opened the file and took a deep breath. Louise, her female protagonist, had according to Creighton, 'taken a bit of a turn'. That, in Creighton-speak, meant that Louise was acting out of character.

"I've made some changes. You said you didn't warm to Louise, that she was too shallow and pushy when she was starting her business and would alienate those who worked with her. I've softened that and added more of her backstory, like the poor relationship she has with her mother. If you remember, her mother favours Louise's brother. I agree with what you said. It was in my head, just not on the page."

Creighton hmm-ed. "That sounds a better approach, but I'd—"

"You'd need to see the manuscript," Cat finished for him.

"Exactly. I know you need to organise the garden, but please focus. I'm beginning to get weekly calls from Raven Books and I don't enjoy the evasion."

Cat made promises she hoped she'd be able to keep.

THE NOISE IN THE BACKGROUND ALMOST DROWNED OUT everything else as Cat returned Lauren's call. "Lauren, can you hear me? Where the hell are you?"

"Hang on, let me move..." There was a muffled sound as Lauren covered the phone, then the music muted as if she'd stepped out of the room. "I'm at a launch for a new shampoo, darling! We're in some grotty nightclub off Leicester Square."

"Ah, the new job?" Cat picked up a pen and doodled. Lauren was the kind of woman who could organise a moon landing single-handedly and still find time for lunch. Foisting a new shampoo on an unsuspecting public would be a walk in the park.

"Mmm. They don't yet appreciate my talents, darling. But where have you *been*? I texted you, like, *aeons* ago!"

"I'm sorry. I've been trying to complete the rewrites and then a tree fell down in the garden."

"What? Oh my God, was anything damaged?"

"The garden wall was the main casualty. The neighbour and I can pass cups of sugar through the gap."

Cat explained about the conservation area and the demands from the local authority and Lauren made sympathetic noises. "But you have insurance, right?"

"No, sadly. I'll have to use credit." Which she needed to get sorted today. "It's a proper pain, and I've no idea what supplier to use."

"I'll say! I bet it's eating into your writing time."

Cat felt her shoulders tense; yes, it was.

"Shall I come and help?" Lauren asked. "I'm a brilliant project manager, if I say so myself, and it would leave you to concentrate on the book."

Cat blinked. "God, that would be amazing! Aren't you busy with the new job, though? I *can* manage it, but the timing's complete shite, if I'm honest."

"Don't be daft, sweetie. I'm dying to see your new place and after *this* shebang, I'm owed a few days off. Of course I'll help – anything to help the writing effort!"

The bands around Cat's chest suddenly eased. Lauren was amazingly organised and a shrewd negotiator. "Thanks, Lauren! I'm so grateful!"

"But apart from your fabulous new place crumbling around your ears, how are you? Have you heard from Stephen?"

Lauren's question caught Cat by surprise and a wave of anxiety swept over her. The break-up had been months ago but she knew Lauren still met Stephen socially. "No, why?"

Lauren heaved a sigh. "He was so gutted when you left. I wondered if he'd been, you know, trying for a reconciliation?"

"God, no! No, it's finished, Lauren." Cat forced herself to be calm. Lauren was blind where Stephen was concerned, but Cat knew just how plausible he could be, how thoroughly *nice* he seemed.

"Well..." Cat could imagine Lauren shrugging on the other end of the phone. "Seems a shame to me. I know he was a bit bossy—"

"You don't talk to him about me, do you?" asked Cat, sharply. "Because I don't want you to mention me at all."

"Hush, babe!" Lauren soothed. "Of course not: you asked me not to."

There was silence. After a moment, Cat forced herself to speak. "I'm sorry, I'm just a bit sensitive where he's concerned."

"Yeah, I get it. Listen, I'll be down as soon as I can. We finish shooting today, please God, and then I can organise with work to come and visit. Okay?"

"That would be amazing."

CAT'S FINGERS FLEW ON THE KEYBOARD AS SHE REACHED A critical point. Now she saw the right way to take the story – and her phone rang. She groaned in frustration, saw it was her mother, and swore. After a few more insistent rings, she reluctantly picked it up.

"Beanie! I thought you were going to call me when you were settled!" cried her mother. "You might have fallen down the stairs and be lying in a heap, and I'd never know!"

"Hello, Mum. I'm sitting comfortably, not with a broken neck.

Sorry, I've been busy with everything. And the book, of course." Cat ignored the childhood nickname that made fun of her height; she towered over her mother and brother.

"Oh, the book! Creighton's helping you, isn't he?"

Cat pressed her lips together and decided to change the subject. "How are you? How's the weather in Spain?"

"We're fine, but what about the house? Are you all settled?"

Cat kept the details to a minimum, aware that her mother was trying to show an interest. She looked out of the bow window at the garden and told her mother about the tree and the wall.

"Do you know how much it's all going to cost? Have you got insurance?"

"No."

Her mother sighed gustily. "Oh, Cat! Why can't you borrow some of Anthony's sense? That house is just a sink for money. I never understood why May bought it."

Cat traced patterns on the table. Her mother, not thinking to ask if Cat needed financial help, was about to go into 'Anthony is wonderful' mode; Cat would not be required to contribute.

After a few minutes of Anthony's expansion plans and his visits to China, Cat interjected. "How's Dad? And the villa?"

"Your dad's playing golf and we're having the villa redecorated. The weather's still lovely here. I was speaking to Anthony the other night and he said the weather in the UK has been dreadful – lots of rain! But you said that was what made your tree collapse, didn't you? And what of your neighbours on the other side of the wall?"

Cat hesitated. Her parents, unlike Lizzie, had thought the sun shone out of Stephen's arse, but had only met Harry a few times. Her mum probably wouldn't even remember him.

"He's a nice chap and we're sharing contractors to put it right, so I'm hoping it will be okay," she said eventually.

"I'm sure Anthony could have advised you, Beanie. You should have asked him."

Cat would rather drink battery acid than ask for Anthony's advice.

Anthony, because he ran his own company, felt he'd earned the right to run everyone else's life too. He reminded her of Stephen. "I'm sure he's too busy," Cat said.

"Not too busy for his own sister, I'm sure! Anyway, have you seen Elizabeth?"

"Yes, I saw Lizzie earlier this week."

"I felt sure you would have been in touch with her. She was so close to your Aunt May." Reproach laced her mother's words.

"I know. I've had a lot on my mind. Particularly the book, which needs to be delivered in..." She glanced at her calendar. "Six weeks."

Saying the words made her stomach flip. Six weeks!

"I'm sure it'll be fine," said her mother soothingly, and Cat ground her teeth. Her mother had always viewed her writing as an indulgence rather than a job.

"Well, it will be, as long as I get on with it. Oh, that's the doorbell," Cat fibbed.

"Really? I didn't hear it. All right, Beanie-boo, take care and speak soon."

"Bye, Mum!"

Cat disconnected with relief. Silence swept around her again, and she reorganised her thoughts, packing away her feelings of frustration and disappointment. Anthony had never put a foot wrong in front of his parents. He'd got a good degree, married a nice woman, and produced two healthy grandchildren who were neither too stupid nor too bright to cause discomfort. Not like Cat, who'd barely scraped through A levels and thrown up her dull, predictable job as a sales-person in a shoe store when she'd won a writing scholarship. Horrified, her parents had suggested she keep her job in case she became bored with writing. Cat had laughed.

Even remembering it now made her smile. Get bored with writing? She was more likely to be made a saint. She pushed herself out of her chair and went to the kitchen, cheered by the sunshine through the window. Her phone pinged again: another text. Picking it up, she frowned, not recognising the number.

—Hey Writer Girl! Still screwing people for all you can get? Think again, bitch. I know where u live and accidents DO happen. Your writing won't be the only thing to suffer. Don't think ur safe just because u ran away from London.

She stared at the screen, her heart thumping. Then her phone rang.

Chapter 6

Emily steeled herself for Dr Schenley's visit, taking up her embroidery in the corner of the drawing room, by the large window. The sun was making a valiant effort to pierce the grey London smog and its light was bright enough to sew her tiny stitches by.

She longed to open the window, but the stench from the Thames permeated everywhere. It was nothing compared to the Great Stink of three years ago, but still strong enough to make the air unpleasant. Emily recalled her distaste and wonder when she had first arrived in London. Was the whole city on fire to cause these clouds that clogged the air? And that stench! Was their fine London house built on a latrine?

As she stabbed her needle into the delicate linen Emily remembered the ladies who had hidden their smirks at her comments behind elegantly gloved hands, even though James, who had suffered from the foul air simply by going into the House, had heartily agreed. Nonetheless, Aunt Sybil had lectured her endlessly about her hastily uttered words, her curtsy, how she laughed ("Too loud and hearty for a lady, Emily!"), how she walked and carried her fan, all aimed at curing her provincialism. She winced at the memory, then smoothed out her face as a maid entered with more coal for the fire. Despite the sunshine, the early March day was chilly, so the fire was built up regularly.

Emily glanced at the maid: the new girl. She looks gaunt, thought Emily: she could do with a good dinner. Her first instinct was to speak to her, but she paused – what would Aunt Sybil say about the mistress of the house swapping pleasantries with a housemaid? The girl bobbed a curtsy and Emily watched her thin figure retreat through the door.

What Aunt Sybil would think of her conversing with a maid would pale into insignificance, though, beside what she would think of Lucky. Aunt Sybil would be horrified, much as Evans had been when she arrived clutching the bedraggled animal.

"Allow me to have your gloves cleaned, my lady," was all he'd said.

The corners of her lips curved up as she thought of the mongrel. She and Molly had wrestled Lucky into the tin bath to give him a good scrub, trying to hush his barks and growls. When he was cleaned to Emily's satisfaction, and a pale blond colour, Molly had wrapped Lucky in a towel and rubbed him dry. Once out of the water, Lucky had shaken himself hard and then discovered that he rather liked the attention of being rubbed. Molly and the dog had become, it seemed, firm friends. At this moment Lucky was in her bedroom, replete from a meal of sausages, curled up in an orange crate next to the fire. Molly was watching over him as she darned Emily's stockings.

Her pleasant reverie was interrupted by James, who cocked a dark eyebrow at her as he entered the room. "What's this about you bringing a street mutt into the house?" he asked, striding over to kiss her cheek.

"He was being beaten by some children – he's only a puppy!" she protested. "Do you dislike it so much? I should have asked you, I know, but I acted the instant I witnessed their cruelty."

He pressed her shoulder, then walked away to warm himself by the fire. "My darling, you acted like a true Christian. Although when we discussed a dog when we were first married, I thought your choice would have *some* pedigree! There are so many stray dogs in London. I trust you will not make my home into a kennel?"

"Oh, thank you!" She laughed with relief and, throwing aside her needlework, skipped across the room to fling her arms around his neck and kiss him. His big hands encircled her waist, and she shivered with delight under his touch. For a second, he didn't move a muscle. Then his mouth pressed harder and passion, dormant for what had seemed an age, flared between them. Emily's mind went blank: all she registered was James' solid, tall frame locked against hers. The taste, the spicy smell of him, filled her senses, and she gasped softly into his mouth.

A gentle knock at the door made them spring apart. Emily was panting slightly, and James' colour had risen.

"One moment!" he called. He gave a firm tug to his waistcoat, and Emily checked her face in the mirror over the fireplace. Her eyes were sparkling, her cheeks hectic with colour. Hiding a smile, she hurried back to her seat by the window and patted her skirts into place.

"Ready?" James asked with a glint in his eye and she nodded, suppressing a giggle. "Come in!"

Emily could almost believe Evans had been listening at the door: he looked so disapproving when he glided in. "Dr Schenley is here," he said, in sonorous tones.

James cleared his throat. "Show him in."

Dr Schenley always reminded Emily of a leopard she had seen at Belle Vue Zoological Gardens when she was a child. He was almost as tall as James, with fair hair and a large, well-waxed moustache. Sleek and handsome, he stalked, rather than walked into a room. He turned light-blue eyes onto her and she immediately felt hunted.

"Lady Cleveland, how are you?" He bowed, and she was obliged to hold out her hand: James held him in high esteem and it would have been uncivil to withhold a greeting. His hands were cold, and the sensation of his chilled grip stayed with her while he greeted James. "How do you do, Sir James? I hear good things about your speech last week, despite the topic."

"Thank you. Extending the franchise is a cause dear to my heart."

"You know my feelings on this," commented Dr Schenley, taking a seat on the leather sofa and crossing one long leg over the other. "One supposes that since the property qualification has been removed, the franchise is naturally extended, with no further requirement."

James smiled easily. "You are concerned about the influence of the Radicals in setting the reform agenda."

"Indeed I am! Their focus on the representation of numbers rather than interests or intelligence poses a genuine threat to the stability of our British constitution!"

Emily, listening to the discussion, wondered if the conversation might ever include her sex. Discussions of suffrage centred on *male* suffrage. Women were largely ignored, she mused, despite MPs like James wishing to expand voting rights. She sighed and regretted it as the light blue eyes of Dr Schenley swung her way. "But I forget the purpose of my call! Lady Cleveland, how are you? I hoped you would continue with your appointments."

"Thankfully, I am much recovered," Emily replied firmly.

"But my lady, your experience, while not unusual, has been traumatic! I am sure you cannot be fully recovered."

Emily bit down on her temper. While she sought for the right words to rebuff him, he began again. "You must allow me to put my expertise at your service," he said, turning to hold his hands out to James. "The fair sex is susceptible to a loss such as you have suffered, and this can have a deleterious effect on the psyche, linked as it is to the ovaries and uterus."

"Really, Dr Schenley?" James looked worried.

Emily, afraid James might promise Dr Schenley something because of his regard for her, rushed into speech. "James, you remarked only the other day that I looked well. Indeed, I have been sleeping without the aid of laudanum for some time."

"You have discontinued the laudanum I prescribed?" Dr Schenley said, with a frown.

Emily cursed under her breath, but lifted her chin. "I have found it most useful, but my mood has lifted since our last appointment—"

"Over six weeks ago—"

"My mood has lifted so *considerably* since then, that I decided a few weeks ago to gradually reduce the dose."

"You reduced the dose without medical supervision?" Dr Schenley repeated, staring at her.

"I have done this little by little. Now I sleep well, and without the heaviness that accompanied my waking." Emily endeavoured to keep her voice neutral and pleasant.

"And where is the laudanum now?" Dr Schenley asked in disapproving tones.

"I poured it away."

There was a shocked silence. "My lady, I fear you are treating your health with frivolous disregard!" Even James looked surprised.

Before she could say another word, there was a commotion outside the drawing room. Then Emily heard the barking. "Lucky!" she breathed. She stood up and threw open the door to see Evans trying to capture the mongrel, who was snarling at him from underneath a chair. Molly was spreading her skirts to block Lucky's escape route upstairs and trying not to laugh.

"Here, boy!" Emily called, and the dog shot through Evans' legs to reach her. "Yes, yes, but get down! Down, Lucky!"

Lucky crouched at her feet and she scratched his ears as she murmured what a good boy he was. Evans, red in the face, tried to recover his dignity, and she smiled kindly at him. "What a hullabaloo we have caused you, Evans. I'm sorry, thank you for keeping him safe. Molly, can you please take this little wretch back to my room and procure a collar for him?"

"Yes, my lady."

Evans, his composure only partially restored, nodded, and Emily turned back to the drawing room. Dr Schenley was speaking urgently to James. "Sir James, I have seen this before. It begins with minor acts of rebellion such as the laudanum, then progresses to nervous affliction of the brain! I beg you, allow me to recommend an asylum for an initial evaluation. As a member of the Commission, I have experience in this."

Emily stopped short, feeling the colour drain from her face.

"I am sure this is simply Lady Cleveland finding her equilibrium after her – *our* – devastating loss," James replied. Then he frowned. "There can be no need for an asylum, surely?"

"I shall send the article of which I spoke. *The Lancet*, the journal for professional doctors, holds the view that madness is a common result of disturbed ovarian function!"

Emily re-entered the room. Dr Schenley took one look at her face and turned back to James. "But I must not outstay my welcome. I bid you good afternoon." He shook James' hand.

Emily walked steadily back to her seat and picked up her embroidery hoop, which she held before her like a shield when he approached. She gave him a curt nod rather than shaking his hand, and he stiffened before nodding at her and taking his leave.

THE SILENCE THAT FELL AFTER THE DOOR CLOSED WAS ABSOLUTE. Emily could scarcely see her embroidery for tears. Would James consign her to an asylum? She drew a shaky breath and fought to find composure. She had heard her associates talk in whispers about asylums and their inhabitants: stories of women – titled society women – being shut away because they disagreed with their husbands or their fathers.

Her mind raced. She was sure James loved her: theirs had been a love match and their union had been in the teeth of opposition from his mother and his friends, who disliked her radical-thinking parents. She had pressed down her fears that she would never be truly respectable in the eyes of society. Their marriage had been characterised by open and honest conversations and he had valued her views – until the death of the baby. Since then, he had withdrawn and seemed more anxious to listen to Dr Schenley. Her eyes still smarting, she looked at him standing by the fireplace, unmoving and handsome as a statue. His expression was concerned.

"Shall I ring for tea?" he asked, after another minute of silence.

She cleared her throat, praying her voice would not betray her. "That would be lovely." She cleared her throat again. "I apologise for the interruption to Dr Schenley's visit. Lucky had escaped from my bedroom."

"He certainly kicked up a racket."

"Yes." She could think of nothing else to say on the topic and fixed her eyes on her needle, trailing bright orange silk through the linen. She needed time to think – to plot a path away from the further ministrations of Dr Schenley, or he would contrive to lock her away! And for what? Grieving for her baby? Not taking laudanum? It was absurd.

A maid arrived with the tea, setting it before the fire. James' voice made her start from her reverie. "Will you join me?"

Pouring the tea was a calming routine which cleared her mind a little. She must be firm and direct when she spoke. But before she could utter a word, James said, "Emily, my darling, was it wise to discard the sleeping draught? Dr Schenley *is* an expert and he was plainly offended."

She swallowed. "I can only repeat what I said to him: I feel much better and I sleep better than I have for months! The nightmares that plagued me are gone, and I am calm and clear-headed when I wake up."

"I engaged him because of the recommendations I have had from friends and colleagues. He has a considerable reputation as an expert on women's ailments."

"I know, and I know his bills are huge – but surely when it comes to knowing how I feel, *I* am the expert?"

James stared at her. "You feel passionately about it," he murmured.

"I feel passionately about not wanting to leave you and be placed in an asylum!"

Colour rose in his cheeks. "So you overheard our conversation," he said slowly. "I had not thought you an eavesdropper, Emily."

Her heart sinking, she reached for his hand, but he was obviously embarrassed. "I am only doing what I have always done: acting in your best interests."

She stood up, holding her head high. "Are you? Then let us have a little plain speaking, James and allow me to tell you what is in my best interests! I will not go willingly into any treatment advised by Dr Schenley, and if that includes an asylum, I will fight you tooth and nail. I am well! I feel better than I have done for months, and that is because I have not seen Dr Schenley for months."

"You are becoming hysterical! This is wild talk!"

"Hysterical? No, I am simply angry that you would even entertain such a notion. Consider how you would feel in my position."

He was silent as she walked to the door.

"Make no mistake, James. I love you with all my heart and soul, and I shall not willingly disobey you. But I will not be shut away on the whim of Dr Schenley!"

He sighed. "He is an expert in his field and we should respect that. You are unjust."

She laughed a bitter laugh. "Had you suffered at his hands as I did, James, perhaps you could understand. When I saw our baby limp and lifeless in his hands..."

She paused, gathering her ragged composure. Her speech might be clear, but it was not calm. She took a deep breath. "I am well. I have no need of an asylum. I pray you, do not listen to Dr Schenley, but listen instead to your wife."

She left him staring into the fire.

Chapter 7

Emily

Friday 14th January 1862: Dinner at Lady B's tonight at which I spoke probably twelve words. I envy her the friends she has known from childhood. Since I married J, I find myself with many acquaintances but no friends.

at jumped as the phone rang in her hand. The text on the screen in front of her seemed to be welded onto her sight. "He-hello?"

"Cat? It's Harry. I wanted to ask about the building work. And I wondered if you wanted the tree stumps for the fernery."

She sagged with relief. "Oh! I'm sorry, Harry, I have a list of suppliers but I haven't finished getting quotes."

There was a silence. "Is everything all right?" he asked. "You sound very odd."

Cat hesitated. "I've just had a really nasty text message."

"Any idea who sent it?" Harry's voice seemed to sharpen.

"No, I don't recognise the number at all." Stephen's face flashed into her head. *Although I have a good idea who sent it.*

"Come round. You sound as if you're in shock."

Five minutes later, she was on the doorstep.

"Come in, you're shaking." His warm hand grasped hers and he pulled her inside the house. "Sit down," he said, shepherding her to the sofa. "I'm going to get you a hot drink. I'll just be in the kitchen."

She nodded, clasped her hands together to stop them from trembling and began her CBT routine. By the time he returned, she was breathing deeply and her heartbeat was slowing. She recognised the leather sofa from her time with Harry, and the memories brought some heat into her cheeks.

Harry returned and thrust a cup of hot tea towards her, which she took gratefully. She took a sip and wrinkled her nose at the sweetness, but drank again, regardless. For a moment he said nothing, but simply watched her. She took a shaky breath and forced her lips into a smile. He smiled back and she realised he was in sweats. His hair was damp and tousled and there was a lemony smell about him. Just out of the shower, she thought.

"Show me the message," he said.

She found the message and passed the handset to him. He glanced at it and returned the phone, looking stern. "Nasty. Any idea who sent it?"

She sighed, holding the phone as if it might bite her. "It might be my last boyfriend – things didn't end well. I should call the police, shouldn't I?"

He nodded. "Yup. And I don't count. You'll need to accompany me to the station, madam." Cat smiled at the yokel accent and the weak joke.

"Shall I go with you?" he continued, serious again. "I can't work on your case – it would be a conflict of interest – but I can take you down. I'm too closely connected to you: it would be unprofessional."

She looked up at him and despite everything, had a feeling of falling into space. His silver-grey eyes seemed to darken. He rose from the sofa and stood with a hand on the mantelpiece.

"Of course," she said. "I don't recognise the number, but it may well be Stephen, my previous partner. I presume you can trace it, or whatever you do."

"If it came from an ordinary phone, maybe. If it came from a burner phone—"

"A what?"

"A burner phone: a phone you use and then destroy or dump. They're used by gangs to avoid detection. They're not completely anonymous; people still need to buy them and we often catch them through their credit card records. It's more difficult to trace them, but not impossible. Don't worry, we'll find the bastard who sent this."

Cat forced herself to look again at the message. "Whoever it is knows I've moved out of London."

"Did your last partner want to end it?"

"No-o-o," she said slowly, feeling herself tense up. "He refused to accept it at first, didn't take me seriously. Then he was so angry. Looking back, I reckon he didn't believe I would leave him."

Harry stiffened, but when he spoke his voice was calm. "The police will probably want his full name. Do you know where he's living?"

"I think so, and I imagine my friend Lauren will have an address if he's moved."

Harry pursed his lips and held out his hand for the phone again. As she passed it over, their fingers brushed and a jolt of electricity shivered up Cat's arm. She snatched her hand back. Harry took a deep breath, and she knew he'd felt it too.

After a second, Harry focused on the text. "The text implies that you've done them harm – 'screwing people'. I take it you've not dumped anyone else recently?"

Cat flinched and scowled at him. "No. I've been single ever since I broke up with him, and I'm not in a hurry to change that! Christ, don't make me out to be promiscuous!"

"That narrows the field," he said, placating.

Cat rubbed her forehead, her mind racing. "Something else – the text mentioned accidents. Do you think whoever sent this has *been* here? Could they have been involved in the wall collapsing?"

"Not necessarily," he said slowly. "It's not very specific. People who send texts like this want you to believe you're being watched, because it unnerves you."

"No shit!" Cat breathed.

He put the phone on the coffee table. "Okay, so it might be your ex-partner. Who else?"

She shrugged. "Honestly, I don't know. I don't have many friends, but until today, I didn't think I had many enemies, either."

He pushed his hands in the pockets of his sweats and regarded her. "No rival authors?"

Her eyebrows rose and despite the situation, she laughed. "I think you've been watching too many thrillers. This isn't *Murder, She Wrote*, you know."

"Is there anyone who might benefit from you being so unsettled that you can't finish the book?"

She huffed, but at his steely look, sat back on the sofa and thought. "I have competitors – everyone who writes does – but it's not like I have a specific rival. The publishing world is big enough for everyone. God, the field would be bloody enormous if you looked at everyone releasing a book at the same time as me!"

"At the station, they might ask you for that information, too." She stared at him and he sighed. "It might take some time to get you interviewed even if they decide you have a case, so bring whatever you need to make you comfortable while you wait."

"I might not have a case?"

He shook his head. "It's just one text. If nothing else arrives, they probably won't take it further."

"So I have to wait for *another* text?" Cat stared at him.

"You have no idea how stretched we are."

"Right," she said, rising to her feet. "I'd better go and report it."

"I'll get changed," Harry said. "It might get you seen faster if I come too."

CAT WAVED GOODBYE TO A GRIM HARRY AND CLOSED THE FRONT door. She forced herself to check the lock. She hated being locked in anywhere – it brought back memories of Stephen – but needs must...

After hanging about for over two hours at the station, she'd found the police less than helpful. Harry had warned her they would have little to go on since she didn't recognise the number, although her previous history with Stephen gave them somewhere to start. She cast another glance at the locked door and fought the urge to open it.

The officer had wearily taken her details, and a printout of a screen-shot of the message. She was now 'a file'.

She'd been shocked to her core when they suggested she call Stephen and ask him if he sent the text. "No way! I want nothing to do with him. I spent months trying to get out of that toxic relationship!"

The policeman looked weary. That would slow things down, he said. It was only one text and she wasn't in immediate danger. Despite the threatening wording, it wasn't a direct threat. So, no, they couldn't help immediately. In the meantime, would she be prepared to change her phone number so that whoever had sent the message couldn't send another? Perhaps she might consider changing her door locks?

She muttered as she peeled off her jacket and hung it in the hall. "God above, Stephen would need to bang on my door with a twelve-inch carving knife before they'd do anything!" She toed off her shoes on the tiles. Her brain acknowledged their beauty while also wondering how safe she was in Gam's lovely house. Her head ached.

Cat padded into the drawing room, slumped on the sofa and lay back against the soft, worn fabric. She felt like a rag doll whose stuffing had been ripped out. In the fading light shadows were gathering, and she dragged herself to her feet to click on some lamps. She peered into the massive marble fireplace. A fire would make the room cosy, and frankly she needed cosy right now.

Ten minutes later, she held out her hands to the warmth, lulled by the flames. Being in this house was very comforting, she reflected. Almost as if it had her back... Her breathing slowed. Had she imagined the past five hours? It seemed so surreal, like a bad dream caused by eating too much cheese.

Her watch said that it was nearly six. She would write for another couple of hours before she ate. That is, if she could concentrate. Cat threw another log on the fire. But before she focused on the book, she needed to change her phone number...

Ten minutes later, Cat was just about to send her new number to all her phone contacts when she stopped. Was Stephen still in her phone? She checked frantically. No, she'd blocked him as soon as she left. The past flickered through her brain like an old black and white movie: the memory of his handsome face, cold and angry, as he demanded to see her phone.

"Who've you been ringing behind my back?" he demanded.

"No one! Look at my phone if you don't believe me!" she'd protested and passed it to him. After a few minutes scrolling through her calls and texts, he threw it on the floor and slammed out of the room.

Half an hour later he was back, tears in his eyes, apologising. "I'm sorry. I get so jealous – you're so precious to me!"

She remembered hugging him and telling him it was all right.

Shivering, she leaned back in her chair, watching the fire dance and crackle. She started a text to send to all, then deleted it. Her mother would have a fit if Cat told her she'd received a threatening text message. Anyway, the police had asked her not to mention it to anyone in case of copycat activity. No, she'd write something about changing phone companies and forgetting to take her old number, and leave it at that.

"Not like that's never happened!" she muttered as she finished the message. It was a wonder she survived in the modern world at all, so inept with technology was she. She pressed send, hoping that it would indeed send to all her contacts.

Ten minutes later she received a text from Lauren, stuffed with the requisite emojis.

—What's up? Got a new phone & forgot 2 port the number? What are u like??XX

Cat grinned as she responded.

—Something like that. XX

Glad to have achieved something, Cat finally returned to her laptop and her main character. After two hours and several cups of tea, she had written a page she was happy with. It was like trying to walk uphill on ice: she took a step then slid back down. She tapped her fingers on the table, and after a few minutes, called Creighton.

She heard classical music playing in the background when he picked up. "Creighton? I'm sorry to call you so late. Have you got a minute?"

"Catherine, hello. I'm serving dinner in about ten minutes, so you'll need to make haste. My cheese soufflé is at a crucial stage."

"Did you get my text? About my number changing?"

"Er, let me look." Creighton promptly disconnected the call; he was even less comfortable with technology than she was. Shaking her head, Cat called again.

"Sorry about that, Catherine. Yes, I received your new number. Is that all you wanted?"

"No. I wanted to tell you why I've changed my number."

"Oh?" Creighton sounded impatient and Cat rushed to tell him everything that had happened.

Creighton was silent for a moment. "And you think it was Stephen? It certainly sounds like him. Will changing your number stop him?"

"I don't know. Hopefully. But it's really screwed up my day, what with the visit to the police too, so I'm behind a bit with the book."

"Should you be there on your own?"

"I hope to have the place crawling with workmen shortly and my friend Lauren has offered to come down and organise things, so hopefully I won't be completely alone. And I do have a policeman next door."

"Is there anything I can do?"

"If you could be your usual patient self, that would certainly help."

Creighton laughed. "I can do that. But I'm not the one you need to ask for patience," he reminded her.

"I know, I know. I'll get the manuscript to you as soon as I can."

"Take care, Catherine."

CAT'S JAW DROPPED AS HARRY TOLD HER HOW MUCH IT WOULD cost to fit Birmingham bar locks – and that was after Harry's locksmith mate had taken off twenty per cent for cash in hand. "I had no idea," she murmured and cursed not doing her own internet research.

Harry folded his arms. "Well, no one would get through the door without you letting them in. That's what you want, isn't it?"

Cat nodded, calculating how much was left in her bank account.

Harry's eyes narrowed. "I'll get him to pop round. How are you?"

His voice had softened and Cat smiled, grateful for the change from brusque to gentle. "Oh, you know, being a brave little soldier. Since I changed my number, nothing else unpleasant has arrived. So it's all good."

He looked unconvinced. "Okay, but stay in touch, won't you?"

After he'd left, Cat wandered around the house thinking about her fast-dwindling funds. She stopped at the leather chair in her bedroom. It was red and handsome and, like so much of the furniture Cat remembered, lovingly cared for. The patina of the leather spoke of parties and late-night chats; her hand caressed the chair back. She checked out an antiques website and her eyes widened at the potential value of it.

Resigned but resolved, she took a picture of it on her phone and sent it to Creighton. This was just the kind of chair he collected, if she remembered the antiques in his London house accurately.

It was only a minute before Creighton responded.

—Who does this beauty belong to?

Me, Cat texted back.

—Wanna buy it?

There was a longer pause.

—What is your price?

"As much as you can afford, Creighton," she muttered, and was about to respond when the phone rang.

"What's going on, Catherine?" Creighton demanded. "Why are you selling furniture?"

"I'm getting new furniture and I don't need it," Cat lied. "I know you like antiques, and as you're my favourite agent..."

Creighton snorted with sceptical laughter. "Very well. What do you want for it?"

Cat crossed her fingers behind her back and named the price she'd seen on the website.

"Sounds reasonable," Creighton said. "I'll transfer the cash and pick it up in the next few weeks."

Cat closed the call, and her fingers lingered on the arm of the chair.

"Needs must," she muttered. "I'll buy you back as soon as I can, I promise."

Chapter 8

Emily moaned. The monthly nurse was shaking her head and Dr Schenley was talking to her in a loud voice. "Really, ma'am, you don't need chloroform! It is not part of God's divine plan! Recall Genesis, 'In sorrow shalt thou bring forth children!'"

The feather pillow was damp and lumpy beneath her head. She tried to plead for the chloroform, but no words came.

Dr Schenley leaned his ear towards her. "What do you say, ma'am? Speak up, I cannot hear you." His eyes lit up as he looked down at her. "Aha, the little stranger comes! Let us hope this is the son and heir your husband yearns for!"

Once more Emily writhed on the bed and tried to call out, but all she heard was the high-pitched laughter of the physician. He moved forward and his face seemed to fall. She twisted her head to see a small, bloody body in his shaking hands. He thrust his face towards her and hissed at her. "You shall not blame me! It was not I!", then ran out of the room.

The nurse tutted and gathered up the pathetic little bundle. Emily caught sight of the tiny body of her newborn son and found her voice. She screamed and screamed. The noise bounced off the walls.

Firm hands gripped her shoulders, shaking her gently. "Emily! My darling, please wake up! For pity's sake, it is just a dream!" James whispered.

She threw her arms around his neck. Her heart was beating so hard that she felt sure it would come out of her breast. For a moment, all she could do was hold his broad shoulders as she sobbed. James folded her in his arms and the smooth velvet of his dressing gown cradled her cheek.

Someone entered and James spoke softly to them. "There's no laudanum in the house? Then bring some hot milk, please."

Hearing him speak of laudanum made her cry fresh tears, and he stroked her back. "Now, now, my dear. I am here. You have no cause to be afraid."

"I'm so-sorry about the laudanum!" Emily managed to say.

"Vile stuff, but it has its uses," James murmured and continued to rub her back. After many minutes, she finally regained her composure.

Molly hovered at the bedroom door with a glass of milk. James waved her in and stood up. "Stay with your mistress until she sleeps."

"Oh, James, stay with me!" Emily grabbed his sleeve and his eyes went to her face. "Please, James!"

He paused, then nodded, taking the milk from Molly, who left.

Lucky, who had been cowering in his orange box bed, jumped onto the counterpane and nuzzled Emily. James fondled his ears and put him firmly on the floor, despite a soft protest from Emily.

"Drink your milk, then he can join you." James said. "Quiet, boy!" he admonished Lucky, who had begun to whimper.

Emily leaned back against her pillows, cupping her hands around the warm milk. Molly had sweetened it with honey.

"The nightmares have returned?" James sounded grave, and Emily wondered if she should deny it. The nightmares were a sign of her weakness, an indication she was unwell. To buy time, she took another sip of milk. Glancing at his face, though, she had no course but to tell the truth. She nodded, then swallowed, unsure of his reaction.

James heaved a sigh. "You seemed to be recuperating."

She clutched his hand. "I am! This was because of the visit from Dr Schenley..."

"My darling, he is a doctor, and concerned only that you receive the best treatment. As am I. You wrong me if you think otherwise!"

"I may have spoken too forcefully earlier, James, but do not think of me as a suitable candidate for an asylum! I am sad, yes, but I am still in possession of my mind!"

"It is for rest and recuperation! Did I suggest you were insane?"

No, but Dr Schenley thinks I may be! She took a breath to steady herself and paused to choose her words with care. "My love, I seem rational to you, do I not? My malady is more connected to my grief than any corporeal part of me. You seem recovered from the death of our son and you never mention it, but it would comfort me to talk of it with you."

James shuffled his feet and stood up, fiddling with the gaslight. When it was adjusted to his satisfaction, he sat on the edge of the bed. She thought his eyes looked moist. "Perhaps you could speak to other ladies of your acquaintance. They will be better equipped than I."

She studied his handsome face, currently acutely uncomfortable. She swallowed and forced a smile. "I shall. Thank you for sitting with me, James. I am much calmer."

He hesitated. "Shall I stay until you fall asleep, like I used to? I shall need to rise early: I am due at my club before the committee."

Emily recalled the many times they had slept together like spoons, his arm casually thrown around her waist as she fitted herself to his strong thighs. After the baby, he had stayed away from her bed. At first she was so lost in grief that she barely noticed, but as the months passed she recognised the loss. She grasped his hand. "Thank you!"

"Very well. Now close your eyes."

She obeyed and felt him settle beside her, the warmth of his body a cushion around her back. His hand stroked her hair.

"It will look different in the morning, never fear," she told herself as she luxuriated in his tender touch. After a few minutes, sleep claimed her.

EMILY BLINKED AND GROANED AS LIGHT HIT THE INSIDE OF HER eyelids. James had gone: the bed cover was rumpled, but now cold.

Molly turned towards her from opening the curtains. "Good morning, milady. Morning, Lucky!"

Lucky yawned as Emily rubbed her eyes. She felt groggy, but it was a different sensation from laudanum-induced rest. Now she felt connected to the world. Perhaps being disconnected from it would be preferable.

Molly handed her a cup of tea and Emily. "I hope you rested better after I left you, ma'am?"

"Eventually, Molly. Thank you for the milk."

"I'm pleased you were able to get back off," Molly said, straightening a pillow. "Are you happy to get up?"

"What time is it? Oh my, past ten! I should have been awake hours ago!" Emily threw back the covers and Lucky began bouncing around the room, giving the odd yap and getting under everyone's feet.

With her gown finally fastened, Emily took a towel, spread it over her lap, then picked up the puppy. A mixture of rubbing his belly and tugging his silky ears kept him amused while Molly arranged her hair.

"I think we should wash your hair tomorrow, milady. I have an excellent recipe with apple cider vinegar, which should make it shine," Molly said, as she pinned the dark curls.

Emily wrinkled her nose. Her hair was so thick and long, it took hours to dry. But then she might read the periodical that James had recommended some time ago, and think about how she might support James in the upcoming elections. So she nodded and, buoyed by the thought of the quiet time to come, went to breakfast.

Evans had left her place laid and she rang the bell as she took her seat. The newspapers, unusually, were still on the table and while waiting for fresh tea and eggs, she perused them. Alongside the usual news on the miasma from the Thames was an article on the campaign for suffrage. The writer omitted any discussion of female suffrage and she tutted in disappointment.

Then a headline from a letter to the editor caught her eye: 'LUNATIC ASYLUM'. She gasped as fear pierced her, then reluctantly read on.

'Sir, I note from your newspaper last week the report of the proceedings of the London Court of Quarter Sessions, which refused to license Green Birch Asylum for the reception of lunatics. This follows a visit where women patients were discovered to have slept on mattresses that were stained, old and filthy, where many of the patients had been poorly fed, and had not left the rooms in which they slept since admittance. I applaud the court's decision. However, this long-overdue action brings into question the objectivity of the members of the Lunacy Commission, who have received several accounts of the disreputable state of this asylum. It is only with the attention of the press and the public that the lamentable condition of the patients has come to light. While the Lunacy Commission has been assiduous in its duty with other asylums, it cannot fail to astonish the public that so few of the asylums patronised by the very same doctors fall under the threat of having their licences removed. In short, sir, there are too many doctors with vested interests among the Lunacy Commission. It is not the business of these gentlemen to consider the financial implications when licences are withdrawn: their duty is to the patients."

Emily dropped the newspaper on the table and took a sip of coffee to soothe her sudden nausea. Was this the Commission that Dr Schenley was connected to? She racked her memory for the exact words he had said. Would he be rewarded if she was committed to an asylum? She glanced again at the printed words. Was this what she could expect if Dr Schenley convinced James she was not rational?

She chewed her lip. She could surely convince James of her health and soundness of mind if she supported him in his quest for re-election. But she knew so little about the procedure! For a moment she was daunted, then threw her shoulders back. "That can soon be rectified," she said aloud. "I can learn."

She rose from the table, resolved.

It was with some trepidation that she began a letter to Aunt Sybil.

I have exhausted my current companions, who have little experience in the world of politics, she wrote, after considerable thought. *They are perfectly able to tell me how to conduct myself in London, and have provided endless guidance...*

How true *that* was, she thought, wondering if Aunt Sybil would understand the barb, and hesitated, before leaving the line as it was.

... but I am determined to provide James with as much assistance as I can. Therefore I am in dire need of the advice of an experienced campaigner. Lady Grosvenor has come to my attention, but I have no entrée to her society. I turn to you, dear aunt, to ask for an introduction to someone who might support me in my first steps. I am anxious to proceed with all haste as the elections will soon be on us, so I beg you to reply today if you can.

She paused and scanned the short letter.

I am almost completely recovered, she added, ignoring the night-mares of the previous evening. She signed it, blotted it, and crossed the room to ring the bell.

As she was addressing the envelope, Evans arrived. She eyed the ormolu clock: she had missed the second morning post. "See that this catches the midday post. I expect a response."

When Emily returned from Hookhams' lending library, she instructed Molly to take Lucky for a walk and waited anxiously in her cosy sitting room for the post. She stared at her novel, reading to the bottom of a page and then starting again, unable to contain her wandering thoughts.

When Evans knocked, she almost snatched the note from the tray. She recognised her aunt's spindly, slanted script and dismissing the butler, sank into a chair to read.

I am pleased to see you are finally returned to health, wrote her aunt. Emily shook her head. Aunt Sybil was not a sympathetic creature, and had little patience with Emily's wan appearance after the funeral.

My initial thought was to provide an introduction to Lady Goring, but she is abroad at present. In any case, she knew your mother slightly and may not wish to acknowledge you.

"Well, really!" exclaimed Emily under her breath. "My mother attracts a great deal of prejudice even now, but her character was spotless!"

Therefore, my second choice is Lady Charlotte Chester and I shall write to her today. Have a care which advice you choose to take from Lady Chester, as she is extremely wealthy and has little regard for society's view of her. She may indulge in behaviour that, should you do likewise, would reflect badly on James and his family. Any unwise behaviour may also cause comparisons with your mother, which would not be helpful. However, few people know the political system as well as Lady Chester, and her advice on that matter should serve you well. Affectionately, Aunt Sybil.

"I do not know whether to be offended or pleased!" Emily murmured as she tucked the note into her pocket. Still, the thing was done. All she need do was wait for Lady Chester's card and her support to James could begin in earnest.

Chapter 9

Emily

    Tuesday, 19 February 1862: Thank God for Lucky and Molly! I feel as though I have been abandoned on a strange island, much as Mr Defoe imagined. Lost, barely surviving, and despite the many servants running the house, so, so alone.

L auren's eyes widened. "Good God, Cat, you could hold a freakin' *party* in your entrance hall! I thought you were mad moving out of London, but this is awesome!"

Cat laughed, hugged her, then took Lauren's arm and led her into the sitting room. Lauren swung around in delight. "Well, aren't you the lady of the manor? I could fit my entire flat in this room…" She strode to the bay window. "Enormous garden, too. And that's the wall, I take it? Jeez, what a mess!" She faced Cat. "But the house is amazing!"

Cat smiled. "Fancy a grand tour?" She waved a hand. "This is the drawing room, and the kitchen is through there. Not its original position: Gam told me she moved it so the food wasn't stone cold for her dinner parties. It was below stairs, but that's storage now."

"Wow. So you have a cellar now? Did this place come with a butler?"

"I wish!" said Cat, who had cleaned the place from top to bottom when she arrived. It had taken two whole days.

She took Lauren around the house, revelling in the space and the friendly feel of it. First, they walked to the sitting room on the other side of the house, the pretty paper not Victorian but a William Morris replica, complete with a teak surround to the marble fireplace. Then there was the study, with original oak panelling and a huge window that opened on to the garden.

"Didn't you want to write in here?" Lauren asked. "It seems perfect, rather than working on the dining table in the drawing room."

Cat paused. In truth, the study was about the same size as the bedroom in the flat she'd shared with Stephen. When she'd moved in and explored the rooms she had immediately felt the walls closing in on her, despite the potential escape into the garden. "Maybe later. My desk would look pathetic in here, and I'm enjoying spreading out on Gam's dining table." Lauren gave her a strange look, but nodded.

Cat was about to take her upstairs when there was a knock on the front door. She opened it to reveal Harry, looking harassed. "Hi, have you got a date for the workmen to arrive? Half the garden wall is still littering my lawn." He caught sight of Lauren. "Hi, long time no see! I live next door."

"I thought I recognised you! God, who'd have thought it?" Lauren said with a grin. She stuck her hand out and Harry shook it. "While Cat gets on with her book, I'll be dealing with the workmen."

"That's great. I don't mind who handles them as long as something happens soon," Harry said, sighing. "It's been nearly two weeks since the wall collapsed." He turned back to Cat. "Sorry to be a nag, but I was hoping to work on the garden this month."

"I'm sorry, I should have let you know. I've found one company but I'm still waiting for them to come and quote," said Cat.

Harry rolled his eyes. "Too soft by half! Please chase them: the longer this goes on, the more behind I get. Or you could let me get my contacts in to start the work?"

"It's okay, we're on it," Lauren said hastily, and Cat hid a grin. Lauren liked to keep full control of anything she was doing. "But you're right, Harry, she *is* too soft by half. If you knew how much food she should have sent back in restaurants, you'd be astonished!"

Harry laughed and Cat made a rueful face. She disliked conflict: one of the issues she'd had with Stephen. She reached for her phone. "Okay, enough teasing: I'll call them right now. I'll text you or pop round when I've got a date."

Harry thanked her and left, and Lauren stared thoughtfully at his retreating back. "Quite dynamic these days, isn't he? I'd forgotten him – he always seemed a bit pale in comparison to Stephen."

Cat ignored the comment, shuffling through the papers on the dining table to find the builder's contact details. She picked up her phone. "He was – is – a lovely man. He was brilliant when the wall came down. Hello? I'm waiting for a visit to my property. Yes, I'll hold."

Lauren wandered through the patio doors and Cat called out to her. "Be careful if you go into the greenhouses. There's a tin of arsenic on one of the shelves..."

Lauren poked her head back in, astounded. "*Arsenic?* What the hell?"

"Victorians used it as a pesticide," Cat replied. "I keep meaning to move it, but I'm not sure what to do with it..." Lauren shook her head wonderingly and disappeared.

Almost twenty minutes later, Cat at last extracted a promise that someone would be with her tomorrow afternoon. She was in the middle of a text to Harry when Lauren came back in. Her bright green sweater was misted with fine rain and she looked daunted.

"Christ, that's a lot of damage. You're lucky the tree didn't catch the greenhouse at the side of the lawn – that would have been a nightmare! It's wrecked the rockery by the wall: There's massive chunks of mortar among the plants. Are they ferns or something?"

Cat finished the text. "Yeah, it was a fernery. Really popular in Victorian times, and the greenhouses are original."

"I'm surprised they're still standing. Are you going to change the garden? I thought you could extend the patio by half, then you wouldn't have so much work to keep the garden in order. I know you like gardening, but it's huge!"

Cat paused, revolted. "Um, no, I don't plan on changing it. It's full of amazing memories of being here with Anthony and my mum and dad."

Lauren shrugged. "Well, it's your choice, but darling, do think! Just because it has history doesn't mean you should treat it like a museum! You might want to, you know, actually live here with some modern conveniences!"

"Lauren, I've got electricity, running water *and* central heating!" Cat laughed. "And before I can change anything, I need to build up my bank balance – which means finishing this damned book. Now, let me show you where you'll sleep. I'm low on furniture, but the sofa bed is remarkably comfy."

"Lead on!" Lauren slung her travel bag over her shoulder and followed Cat upstairs.

The bedroom looked threadbare. The curtains at the window were still handsome and the heavy maple wardrobes gleamed in the faint light, but the sofa bed, even covered with a fluffy duvet, seemed lonely and stark in the large room. She grinned apologetically at Lauren. "Not the Ritz, but I hope you'll be fine in here."

Lauren dropped her bag with a thump and looked about her. "Chill, Cat. It's all good. The builder's turning up tomorrow?"

"With any luck." Cat was gloomy, recalling the casual response of the receptionist.

"Okay, in case they don't, I'll look at other local builders."

"Don't forget Harry has some suggestions."

"Whoa!" Lauren held her hands up. "You don't know who they are – they could be his mates! Stay independent, Cat. Harry seems nice, but you haven't seen him for years and you don't know if he's trustworthy."

"That's the daftest thing I've heard you say, Lauren."

"Did you tell Stephen about him?"

Cat frowned. "Harry and I were over two years before I met Stephen! And it's not good form to tell your current relationship about your exes. Maybe that's where you're going wrong!"

Lauren mock-punched Cat in the shoulder. "Enough about my love life. It's just a matter of time..." She looked around and then out of the window. "Hey, this room is great. Once you get more furniture in, it'll be epic!" She skipped to the wardrobe and stroked the luscious golden wood. "This is so lovely. Was it your Gam's?" She opened one of the massive doors and poked her head inside. "God, you could rent this out as a room in some parts of London..." Her voice echoed from the depths of the wardrobe, and Cat laughed as she stepped right in.

"You can fit in it? God, I didn't realise it was that big! Are there fur coats and a back door?" she asked.

"Eh? Sorry, you've lost me," Lauren's voice came from the depths. The doorbell sounded. "Who's that?" she asked, poking her head out. Frowning, Cat clattered down the stairs to answer.

The bell rang again. "All right, all right, I'm coming!"

"No need to shout, dear," Lizzie said as Cat opened the door. She lifted a bag and gave Cat a merry smile. "I brought my lunch in case you had nothing in."

CAT HANDED THE JOURNAL TO LIZZIE, WHOSE MOUTH DROPPED open in surprise. "Where did you say you found it?" she asked, turning the pages carefully. "I need my glasses to look at the writing: it's very ornate, isn't it? Can you read it, Lauren?"

Lauren froze.

Remembering her best friend's dyslexia, Cat held out her hands for the book. "I found it in the fernery. It seemed to be buried in the rock wall, but I've no idea why!" she said. "I've read a few of the entries, but you're right. The writing is so difficult to decipher that it's slow going." She put the journal on her lap.

Lauren peered over her shoulder at it. "Was it buried because it contains loads of guilty secrets?" she asked. "A confession of a murder? Illicit goings-on in the undergrowth? That would make a fantastic story, Cat!"

"It would, but the entries I've managed to read so far are recipes and domestic stuff: hardly high drama." She opened the journal at random and the faint scent of lavender rose to her nostrils. She began to read, then gasped.

"What's the matter?" Lizzie asked.

"I can't believe I've just turned to this, but listen: *'The fernery moves on apace and my design is working well. I am delighted by the introduction of the specimens of Matteuccia struthiopteris. I have ordered Mr Newman's excellent book, which will tell me more about the history of the plants. It is a blessing to know the ferns will grow in the open air, rather than enclosed in Wardian cases to protect them from the London smog!'"* She looked at Lauren and Lizzie. "Wow, this woman built the fernery!"

"Blimey!" exclaimed Lauren. "What a coincidence, turning up that bit of the journal!"

"Coincidence? Perhaps, but this is a very special house, Cat," said Lizzie, with a smile. "Did May tell you that it has a benign spirit?"

"No!" Lauren turned to Lizzie, her face alight with interest.

Lizzie nodded. "Oh yes, it was one of the reasons why she wanted to buy it."

"Gam mentioned it, but I thought she was just winding my mother up," Cat said, turning to the back of the journal. As she did so, something fell to the floor: a folded paper so thin that it appeared to be tissue paper. Carefully, Cat unfolded it and gasped as she made out the faded lines.

"What's that?" Lauren asked.

"I think it's a plan of the fernery. Oh my God, it looks like the original!" Cat carefully spread it out on the coffee table and they all leaned over it.

"It's very faint – can you actually tell what it is?" Lauren said doubtfully.

Cat was looking back through the journal. "Yes. Whoever kept the journal – Caroline? No, Emily – plotted the planting on this paper and put more detail in the journal. See, that's a number one on the plan, and in her journal it says that number one is a – an – *Asplenium scolopendrium,* I think that's how you say it..." Cat stumbled over the unfamiliar Latin. "What a mouthful! Oh, here's another name for it: hart's tongue fern, that's much easier." She beamed at Lauren. "This is brilliant! I can use this to help me replant the fernery, so I don't have to start from scratch when the garden's cleared."

"How fascinating!" murmured Lizzie. "Do you know anything about this Emily?"

"No. I've done a bit of searching on ancestry sites, and I know she was married to James Edward Cleveland, who was a big landowner and MP, but I haven't had time to do much else. I'm supposed to be editing the book, you know."

"Well, these plans will help you pull the fernery together faster, so you can get back to the book," Lizzie commented.

"Let's go out and have a look before the builders arrive," Cat said, inspired.

The mess in the garden hadn't improved after the rain, and the mounds of soil and crushed greenery had become crumbling mud. Cat's spirits sank as they picked their way along the paths. How long would it take to fix all this, even with a plan to guide her?

They came to the fernery. To Cat's alarm, Lizzie's face crumpled at the tumbled bricks and ruined plants. Lauren also saw Lizzie's distress and her expression softened. "There, there, we'll sort it," she said, patting Lizzie awkwardly on the shoulder.

A noise floated through the huge crack in the wall and all three of them peered into Harry's garden.

Harry was near the wall, heaving at one of the blocks of stone. Beneath the ancient, dirty sweater, Harry's muscles bunched as he hauled the rubble away.

"Mmm. You said he was an *ex*-boyfriend?" asked Lizzie innocently, watching him place the stone gently on the ground. Cat waved her comment away, aware of Lauren's grin.

Harry's silver-grey gaze zeroed in on Cat and for a wild moment, she feared he had heard. He moved out of sight and she let out her breath. "He's a copper and a good man," she muttered. "It was a long time ago."

"Good job I'm here," Lauren said, nudging Lizzie's shoulder. "Keep Cat focused on the book."

Lizzie looked at the fernery and sighed. "It was so lovely: one of May's favourite bits of the garden. Will you rebuild it, Cat?"

"I hope so. Now I have the plans it will be easier, but I need to look at some old photos."

"I'll see what I can find, too," Lizzie said, surreptitiously wiping away a tear.

"With the plans, how hard can it be?" said Lauren cheerfully. "And you know what we always say..."

"Someone will have written a book on it," Cat said, in chorus with Lauren, and they both laughed.

"Perhaps Harry can give you a hand." Lizzie ran her fingers along the tiny leaves of a cotoneaster. "You'll need a strong pair of arms to help you move the stones..."

"But Harry has his own garden to sort out!" Cat gestured to the mess on Harry's side of the garden.

"Yes," admitted Lizzie. "It's a big job. Although he did seem a good sort. Perhaps he will help."

Cat was quiet, unsure of what would happen if she asked Harry for help. She sensed a hardness about Harry that hadn't been there when they'd first met. She hoped she hadn't contributed to that. Her memory still held the picture of his white, rigid face when she'd heaved her suitcases into the car.

She sighed. It had been for the best: he'd been trying to get a promotion, and she'd been doing her best to capitalise on the runaway success of her first book. They'd been stressed and impatient with each other, and it had slowly erased the tenderness between them.

Lizzie made her excuses and left, saying she'd send photos. Lauren stared intently at her phone, thumbing through websites. "You write," she said to Cat. "I'll have a look at some of the people Harry suggested."

Oh God, the book. Cat folded the delicate map and slid it between the leaves of the journal. "You're right to remind me. Let me work for another hour, then we can order a curry." As she said the words, she hoped the cash in her purse would cover it.

"I'll sort the curry, you get on with writing," said Lauren. "You don't need any more distractions, what with lover boy next door and the garden." Lauren winked at her.

"*Ex*-lover boy! God, get off my back about Harry!"

"Just keep it that way and focus, girl!"

Cat turned back to the computer and did as she was told.

Chapter 10

Emily glanced across the dinner table James' mama. Sophia Cleveland was looking down her patrician nose at the sauce Mrs Worthy had served with the lamb cutlets. James was eating heartily.

"My dear Emily, what *is* this sauce?"

"Port wine and lemon, mama. It is from Mr Walsh's excellent compendium of recipes. Lady Botham recommended it."

Mrs Cleveland sniffed and pushed the cutlet to the side of her plate. "I'm sure a good gravy works just as well."

James looked up. "If it's not to your taste, Mama, I'm sure Cook can find something that you would prefer."

"Oh, do not go to any trouble on my behalf! You know I am the least particular of eaters, and not at all fussy. I am sure pudding will sustain me if I am hungry at the end of the meal."

Emily pressed her lips together and James winked at her. She relaxed as well as she could. The family dinner with his mother was proving much more of a trial than the dinner for twenty she had hosted the previous night with James' fellow parliamentarians and their wives. Knowing few of the ladies present had made her a careful, quiet observer, as they talked of parliamentarians she did not know and debates in the House of which she had only a vague notion. She confessed as much.

"You must come to hear them speak," said one of the ladies, smiling.

"But how?" Emily felt sure that women were not allowed in the House.

"Come to the Ladies Gallery," said another. "We gather in the space above the ceiling of the Commons Chamber. We cannot see very much, and it is cramped and not very comfortable, but it is worth the exertion."

Emily nodded eagerly.

The meal had been a great success, and she basked in the warmth of James' compliments on her management. She had hoped to speak to him about her intention to support him in the election, but his gentlemen friends had stayed far longer than she expected. She resolved to talk to him at breakfast, but her plan was thwarted by an emergency committee sitting which lasted most of the day. She was eager to speak to James before she heard from Lady Chester.

Mrs Cleveland sighed gustily and the candles, put on the table to create an intimate glow, flickered. Emily kept her eyes on her plate and put the last piece of lamb in her mouth, chewing thoroughly. Dabbing her mouth with a napkin, she decided a visit to Mrs Worthy was in order to pass on her compliments, regardless of her mother-in-law's opinion.

"Delicious, Emily," said James from the end of the table and she smiled at him as the footman cleared the plates. She nodded at George to top up her glass.

"Emily!" said Mrs Cleveland urgently, in a low voice. George paused mid-pour, his rubbery face frozen.

Emily looked quizzically at her mother-in-law. "Yes, Mama?"

"Excessive consumption of alcohol is unfeminine!" Mrs Cleveland sat bolt upright, her mouth a thin line.

Emily hesitated, then lifted her chin. "I shall have a little more, thank you, George." Carefully, slowly, he added an inch of red wine to her glass. She took a sip and held the glass up against the light, staring into its ruby heart.

James put his head on one side and frowned. "Mama is being solicitous."

No, she is being dull. Emily drained the glass. "She is too kind. There, I have finished. Are you coming through for tea, James, or shall we leave you here?"

He was silent for a moment, then pushed his chair back. George sprang to pull the chair back for Mrs Cleveland.

"We will all go through." His voice was quiet as he offered his arm to his mother and with a smirk, she accepted. They left the room.

Emily threw her napkin on the table, torn between amusement, irritation and disquiet. It seemed unlikely that she would speak with her husband that evening.

THE NEXT DAY EMILY FOUND JAMES IN HIS STUDY, FROWNING AT A thick report. "May I speak with you?" she said, hovering at the door.

He looked at her, eyebrows raised, and her heart sank. "I can come back..."

"No." He sighed, putting the report down and rising to wave her into the chair opposite. She sat down and arranged her skirts carefully, as if at an employment interview. Which it was, in a way.

"You are standing for re-election," she began. "I would like to help by hosting some of your dinners and speeches. I have asked Aunt Sybil to write to Lady Chester—"

"Lady Chester? Lady *Charlotte* Chester?"

Emily paused. Aunt Sybil had advised her; surely he could not object? "I asked Aunt Sybil who could guide me. Lady Chester was her suggestion."

"Charlotte Chester is an eccentric. I grant you that she supported Lord Chester through all his campaigns, but since his death she has said some ... odd things. I'm not sure I approve. My mother certainly would not approve."

Emily stared at him, unsure what to say. His mother would object? What on earth had this wretched Lady Chester said to cause her displeasure? "I – I am sorry. I relied on Aunt Sybil to advise me. Did she do wrong?"

James stroked his beard reflectively. "She is not as well-connected as Mama. I wonder why you did not solicit *her* advice: Mama is considerably better informed. Your Aunt Sybil is hardly in society since our marriage, is she? She barely leaves Gloucester."

Emily bowed her head and cursed her impetuous note to Aunt Sybil. But to who else could she turn? Aunt Sybil was her last remaining relative, and she was hardly close to James' mother. The idea of asking for Sophia's advice made her queasy.

"In any case, I am reluctant to accept your offer of help," continued James, and she raised her gaze to his face. "You cannot support my campaigns: you are not well enough," He rose and stared out of the window at the street.

Emily sat up straight in her chair. "Not well enough?"

"No: the return of your nightmares makes me concerned for you."

"But that was only one night!"

"Your behaviour in front of Mama last night bordered on insolence!"

At this, Emily's mouth dropped open. She stood up and gripped the edge of James' large mahogany desk. "Partaking of wine is *insolent?*"

"Don't be obtuse. Mama is quite correct: excessive drinking *is* unfeminine. I saw how dismissive of her sentiments you were. That is not what is due to a lady of her years!"

"I may have been a little impatient, but I would not call a glass and a half of wine excessive. Why, you will drink five or six times that and think nothing of it!"

"I am a man! Women do not have the constitution to take much wine. Imagine your role as a hostess in the elections, where men of commerce make a point of emptying as much of as a cellar as they can. It is too much of a risk!"

Emily's head whirled with the injustice of it. "Was I intoxicated? Did I slur my words as we drank tea?"

"No, but my concern was your demeanour towards my mother, where her consequence must exert some influence over your behaviour, surely - but no. You continued to ignore her counsel and humiliated her in front of George!"

Emily opened her mouth to say something, but recalling her careless words to her mother-in-law, thought again. "I am sorry if I was disrespectful," she said finally, forcing the words through gritted teeth.

"You were," James said curtly. "I see this as a symptom of the wider constitutional affliction of which Dr Schenley spoke. I tell you, Emily, I am concerned for your wellbeing. A retreat, indeed, may be the most beneficial course of action. Supporting my election activity –unthinkable!"

His words rushed through Emily's head and she deciphered their meaning syllable by syllable. He would send her away! She would be thrown into an asylum and never see the light of day again, sleeping on filthy sheets and manacled to the bedposts! She stepped back, clasped her hands together, and drew a deep, steadying breath.

"Might I make a suggestion?" She was proud that her voice was calm, and that the tremor in her hands had not transferred to her words.

James nodded, and pride straightened her backbone. "I cannot convince you that I am well. I may not accompany you on your election travels, and I do not wish to remain in London during the summer: the air becomes unbearable."

"So, you will return to your aunt?"

Emily shook her head. She would commit murder within the week if she went to stay in Gloucester with Aunt Sybil. "I would prefer to go to Cleveland House, if that is acceptable. I have not visited since we were first married, but I enjoyed the countryside and there will be plenty of opportunity for quiet reflection." Cleveland House held wonderful memories of James and the joyous first months of their marriage. It would also take her away from Dr Schenley's ministrations and the threat of incarceration. Perhaps quiet and solitude would allow her to build her strength, and God willing, she could bear James another son.

If he ever came near her again.

James looked out of the window. At long last he turned to her, and his dark eyes were sad. "That seems sensible. I shall visit you after the election."

They stared at one another and Emily felt disembodied as she drank in the sight of him. But she must be firm. "I shall take Molly and leave on Thursday." She swept out of the room.

Chapter 11

Emily

Saturday 17th February 1862: I have been a poor-spirited crea-ture! I realise that if you are prepared to battle and endure a little discomfort, there is always a path to a better situation.

Cat frowned as she looked at the screen. Her words were proving difficult to wrangle. The house was blissfully quiet, though, and she was able to focus until a message pinged on her phone. It was Lauren.

—Tx for the flowers, u shouldn't have! let me know if u need me again! XX

Cat smiled, truly grateful for her help. The contractors Cat had chosen had sucked their teeth and offered a price only a little less than extortion. Lauren had smiled sweetly, sent them packing, then badgered Harry for his contacts.

Her old school friend had ripped into the job. She'd been charming to Harry's builders, briefed the contractors, stopped one of them cutting through a power cable, and pressed Cat on the logic of her deci-sions about what to tackle first in the garden. And throughout she'd chivvied Cat to just *get on* with the book. In short, Lauren had been a star, which was why Cat had sent flowers.

Cat had also been glad of Lauren's company at night for the four days she had stayed. She'd had no more vile messages, but the police hadn't progressed with the investigation. Perhaps it was as Harry said: after that one text, there would be no more.

A shaft of sunlight glanced off her laptop screen, making it unreadable. She rose to pull the curtains. Finally, the weather had changed for the better. The workmen would turn up again on Wednesday and she'd need to pay attention to what was happening outside, but for now she could focus on working a bit of energy into her writing, which seemed to be on life support.

If only she could stop worrying about her lack of money! She had kicked that can down the road a bit, though. While Creighton was vague about when he would collect her chair, he had paid for it and the money was in the bank – until she handed it to the locksmith. She was now the proud possessor of a brand-new credit card with a dizzying credit limit, but she knew there would be a reckoning eventually.

"So let's hope this book does well!" she muttered. She deleted a paragraph, then another, and tried again.

THE FOLLOWING DAY, DAVE THE LOCKSMITH STOOD BACK AND admired his handiwork. "There you go. You'd need a police battering ram to get through that."

"Shh, don't tell my neighbour!" Cat joked, glancing at Harry, who was watching from the bottom stair. Harry grinned as Dave packed up and Cat counted the money into the locksmith's hand.

"I shaved a bit off the side of the door," said Dave. "It was sticking. You'll need to paint it." Cat nodded. Soon, he roared off in his van.

She closed the door, which felt a little clumsy with the new levers, then reopened it. It opened smoothly and she was relieved. She could get out easily.

"All good?" Harry asked, and she smiled. Silence fell between them and thickened as they stood looking at one another.

They both began to speak.

"Do you—"

"The workmen—"

Harry grinned. "Sorry, you first."

"The workmen will come again on Wednesday."

"That's good. I know Lauren's gone back to London. I was going to ask if you were okay on your own."

As she considered the night in front of her, Cat knew she didn't want to be alone. "I've got a motion-sensitive light and one of those doorbells with a camera, but after I've fitted them, would you like to come round for a glass of wine? You said it would be good to catch up."

She saw a flicker in his eyes which might have been surprise, then was gone. "Do you need help fitting the light?"

"Nah, I'm a dab hand with DIY." Cat grinned.

"Sounds great. How about we order in?"

"Sure! The local Chinese is brilliant." Cat thankfully dismissed the haphazard contents of her kitchen cupboards.

As they discussed the food, she recognised that Harry was engineering the discussion so that he would call the takeaway and pay. She was touched, but mentally counted the cash in her purse, in case she'd misread his intentions. He left, promising to return in a couple of hours.

Cat dug out her screwdriver and managed to mount the light to her satisfaction, then spent some minutes darting about in front of her door to position the arc of the sensor. She glanced at her watch and tutted; she'd run out of time to get the doorbell fitted if she was going to change.

The bedroom will look even larger without the chair, she thought as she shrugged herself out of her tee-shirt. Still, cash was cash. She'd replace the furniture when she started earning again.

She pulled a pair of jeans and a clean sweater, dragged a comb through her hair and grabbed a lip gloss. She caught sight of herself in the mirror. Her eyes sparkled, more green than hazel; she put it down to the additional exercise.

WHEN HARRY ARRIVED CLUTCHING AN ENORMOUS BAG OF Chinese food ten minutes later, she was building a fire against the cold late-February night. "Not lost your appetite, I see!" She laughed, eyeing the containers of food.

He grinned. "I didn't like everything on the set menu, so I ordered a couple more dishes. It will always freeze."

He closed the front door and double-locked it. As casually as she could, Cat leaned past him and unlocked it. "Not expecting an invasion, are we?" she said lightly. "Come on through."

As they drank the wine, the slight restraint that had threaded through the conversation gradually evaporated. Cat fetched another bottle.

"The workmen are getting on well," commented Harry, spooning food onto his plate.

"Have some rice, too. Yes, I'm seeing less of your front lawn!"

"Mmm. I'll be able to focus on sorting out my garden soon, rather than organising Charlie and his crew."

She asked what he had planned for his garden, and listened, impressed, as he told her about his plans for a deep border and a greenhouse. "Alongside the day job, of course."

"How did you end up in Cambridge?" Cat asked, as she nibbled on a prawn cracker.

He shrugged. "I was going nowhere in London," he said, after a pause. "I dipped a promotion. My superintendent sat me down and told me that my face didn't fit." His eyes avoided hers.

"I thought you were really happy at the Met," she commented, watching him closely, and he flinched. She kept quiet, hoping he would say more, but he shook his head.

"How did you get involved with Stephen?" he asked, turning the tables on her.

She sighed and picked up the bottle of wine, offering it to Harry. He shook his head and she emptied the last inch into her glass. "I met him during the promotion of my third book: he was a guest at some party organised by the publisher. He was in public relations and we hit it off. He was funny, caring ... or I thought so at first. My friends loved him, Mum and Dad were on the brink of buying the wedding stationery – it was like the planets had aligned or something. I imagined I was in love."

"But it changed?"

She said nothing and he leaned forward. "Cat, you suspect him of sending abusive text messages. *Something* happened!"

"It was so gradual. He did so much for me when I moved in with him. I ate what he cooked, I went where he wanted, I dressed in the stuff he bought me." She stopped, feeling herself grow tense, and surreptitiously tapped on her thigh.

Harry waited.

"I found some old pictures on my phone from before we met. I didn't recognise myself. My hair was different; I wore completely different clothes. That was when I realised I didn't see my friends any more, only his. I also realised that he criticised – gently – everything about me. Then I stopped writing. That's when Creighton stepped in."

"What happened?"

"When Creighton phoned me, Stephen cut off my calls. He said Creighton was stifling my talent, bollocks like that. When Creighton called in person, Stephen shut the door in his face and locked me in. He said all kinds of crap: no one loved me like he did, I was such a failure and he was only protecting me... It was awful."

"How did you get out?"

"Stephen was in the loo and I happened to look out of the bedroom window. Creighton was hanging around in the street. I opened the window, and he said he'd help me when Stephen left for work. He came with a locksmith who broke into the flat. I grabbed what I could carry and left."

Harry whistled. "Stephen locked you up?"

"Yeah. He was the reason I left London. It seems so obvious, looking back, but I didn't see it at all when I was in it. Not until it was too late."

"You told the police all this?"

She nodded, close to tears, and he covered her hand with his. It was warm and comforting, a little rough from the work he'd been doing in the garden, and his touch reawakened memories of their time together. He froze, as if he could see her thoughts, and pulled his hand away.

Cat smiled at him to try and dispel the uneasiness. "Shall we sit by the fire? Do you still take your coffee black?"

He nodded, and she gathered the dirty plates and headed to the kitchen. When she returned with the drinks, he'd packed away the uneaten food, stacked the containers neatly on the table, and stuffed the rest of the rubbish in the bag.

They sat on opposite ends of the sofa.

Harry spoke softly, haltingly. "At the Met, there was an incident. Everyone said that someone had died because of me. It wasn't true, but I couldn't bear the whispering, the looks, the comments behind my back. I had to leave."

Cat stared at his face, suddenly aged by the words he had spoken. Harry gazed into the fire.

She swallowed. "How did it happen?"

"We were staking out a drugs gang. My radio had a fault – it made too much noise – so I turned it off while we waited for the gang to do a drop. John was watching on the other side of the street and he saw me run into an alley that I'd forgotten was a dead end. When I didn't respond to his radio call, he came to get me. They saw us and started shooting. We were both hit, but mine was only a flesh wound. John died later that night." He paused, remembering. "They suspended me for not following procedure."

"I'm so sorry," Cat murmured, unsure what else to say. His face was a mask. Cat longed to say something to bring him back, to make him Harry again. She reached out and touched his knee.

He turned to her, his gaze darker in the flickering light of the fire, and his mouth twisted into a cynical grimace. "I was lucky to get the post here. News travels, obviously." Cat couldn't think of a response. "Anyway, that was a long time ago and I'm happy enough here. Have you heard anything from the station since you reported the text?"

Cat knew when she was being moved along. "Not yet. But as you said, it's one text."

"Have they spoken to your ex? He sounds sufficiently unhinged."

Cat shifted in her seat. "I haven't heard. But I thought you couldn't work on the case."

He grinned ruefully, and to her relief, became the Harry she remembered. He shook his head and picked up his coffee. "You're right, I can't get involved. Unprofessional conduct and all that. My chief would go mad if he found out I was discussing the case with you."

"Shame. I could do with talking to someone, since your colleagues don't seem bothered."

He laughed. "I can only sympathise from a distance. I ought to keep my nose out."

When Harry stood up to go, Cat hesitated as he turned to her. A kiss was out of the question. Shaking hands would be ridiculous. So she hugged him, feeling ridiculously safe with his arms wrapped round her.

"Lock up and sleep well," he said, his voice husky. Then he was gone.

Chapter 12

Lucky bounced around at her feet.

"Down, Lucky! Will you give me no peace?"

Lucky looked so woeful at her sharp tone that Emily couldn't help smiling. That ruined her attempts to control the puppy, who placed his paws firmly on her lap, his tail wagging so hard that his small body twisted from side to side. In some ways Lucky had been a blessing, distracting her from the pain of leaving James. However, in other ways...

"Naughty!" tutted Molly. She scooped up the dog and bore him away. "So please ma'am, I'll take him to the garden and see if I can't tire him out," she added.

Emily nodded, and moved to sit at the huge walnut desk that dominated one side of the morning room. It was handsome, inlaid with delicate leaf and flower designs, but too large for the room. If she remained here longer, she might move it to the study or her sitting room. She counted it another blessing that this house was beautiful: comfort seemed to ooze from its walls. She opened her journal, her hands smoothing the leather cover.

The breeze moved the curtains at the window and she sighed,

gazing at the sunshine that glittered through the leaded windows. Their train journey had only taken an hour and a half, yet how far she seemed from London! But she must not repine. She squared her shoulders and dipped her pen in the inkwell.

> *How I miss James! But I intend to recuperate as best I can alone, and set myself the task of being the wife James expects. My invitations to the neighbours for my at-home have been dispatched. Perhaps there will be someone with whom I can form an acquaintance. The cook here, Mrs O'Donnell – with whom I am resolved to leave the key to the store cupboard – has a fine hand with pastries. That should tempt them to come, even if my company does not.*

Resolved, she blotted the diary and slipped it into the drawer by her bed.

EMILY'S HAND WAS STEADY AS SHE SIPPED HER TEA. POLITENESS required that morning callers stayed no longer than half an hour. She resisted the temptation to glance at the clock.

Her guests, Colonel and Mrs Phillips, perched on the edge of the sofa and nodded at Mrs and Miss Sherwood-Taylor. The wife and daughter of the Reverend Sherwood-Taylor, who had sent his apologies, commented on the fine weather. The late sun outside was in stark contrast to the arctic atmosphere in the bright drawing room. Emily kept her face passive as Mrs Phillips stared down her bony nose at the room. Her small eyes darted about as if calculating the value of the ornaments. Emily wasn't sure whether to be amused or indignant.

So far, the conversation had probed her family (insufficiently impressive and tinged with radicalism) and her familiarity with the local area (found wanting by the Colonel). Emily felt the Phillipses' disapproval spread through the room. Hence the safe topic of the weather, now exhaustively explored by the Sherwood-Taylors.

"Lady Cleveland, it has been a while since you condescended to visit the area," said the Colonel through a thick moustache. "If I might be so bold, does the smog of London bring you to the greener country-side of Cambridgeshire? I understand that Sir James will be campaigning for his seat, but it had struck me that you might be by his side, particularly given your upbringing."

The heat ran over Emily's throat and face. She put her cup and saucer down and forced a smile. "My husband is perfectly in control. I should be in the way."

"And your place is to create a relaxing home for him to return to. Do you not agree, ma'am?" said Mrs Sherwood-Taylor comfortably to Emily, taking another of the delicious fancies that Mrs O'Donnell had baked that morning.

"Indeed, to what role should her ladyship be more suited?" added Mrs Phillips, and Emily's chin rose at the implication that this was all she was good for. She drew a deep breath and arranged her skirts around her.

"Quite so, quite so." Colonel Phillips grunted, and Emily saw his wife dig him in the ribs. Cream clung to his whiskers and he dabbed at his mouth with his napkin.

A howl split the air, followed by scrabbling at the door.

"Mercy me!" cried Mrs Phillips, jumping up. "What is that noise?"

Emily's heart sank. She knew that noise. She could just hear Molly scolding Lucky behind the drawing-room doors.

"Excuse me," she said, walked steadily across the room and threw open the double doors. Lucky erupted into joyful barking. Molly wrung her hands and began to apologise, but Emily shook her head. "No matter. Do you have his lead? Excellent. Put it on him and give the end to me."

Emily led Lucky into the drawing room, his tail wagging like a metronome. Colonel Phillips looked aghast and the ladies shrank back.

"What – what breed is your dog?" asked Mrs Phillips in a thin voice.

Emily looked at Lucky and put her head on one side, recalling the German she had learnt from one of Aunt Sybil's acquaintances. "He is a new European breed called a Mischling," she said, using what she hoped was the German word for mongrel.

The Colonel nodded sagely. "Yes, yes. I believe I saw one in London at the Great Exhibition in fifty-one."

"Undoubtedly," Emily said gravely, patting Lucky on the head. The dog sighed in contentment and laid his head on the hem of her dress.

"I am nervous of dogs," declared Mrs Phillips, looking hard at Emily.

"Are you?" Emily raised an eyebrow. "How very unfortunate." She glanced at the grandfather clock, and Mrs Phillips sprang to her feet.

Emily rose and held out two fingers. "Thank you for coming," she said, hoping she sounded more sincere than she felt, and Mrs Phillips pressed her lips together.

The other callers also took their leave and Emily was left alone with Lucky. "You are such a horror," she told him as she took a delicate custard tart from the plate. "As if my situation was not sufficiently insecure, you do not add to my cachet!"

Lucky wagged his tail.

Well, that had been little short of a disaster. The Phillipses had done their best to strip away her fragile confidence. They had been quietly dismissive while they chomped through the pastries, disapproving while she poured the tea, and astounded that she could demean herself to pass a plate around.

The soft chime of the doorbell interrupted her dismal thoughts. Who is that? she thought, frowning. She was not expecting further callers.

The door opened and Watson, a man as round as he was tall, announced in sonorous tones, "Lady Chester, ma'am. Are you at home?"

Emily gaped, and said she was indeed at home, and stood to greet her unknown guest.

Emily stared as a beautiful lady, not in her first youth, but with twinkling black eyes and glorious titian hair, swept into the room swinging her parasol. Lucky jumped up and obviously saw a kindred spirit, as his tail wagged so hard that it caught the spindly leg of a side table and the vase on it wobbled dangerously.

Emily steadied the vase and Lady Chester laughed, a low, musical sound. "Well held! I trust Lady Sybil mentioned that she wrote to tell me of your change of direction?"

Emily stepped forward and put out her hand. Lady Chester's hand-shake was firm and warm. "No, it probably slipped her mind. I do beg your pardon, won't you please sit down? Watson, could we have fresh tea?"

Emily felt the presence of the older woman settle in the room like sunshine. She was cheered, though somewhat horrified when Lucky promptly rolled over for a belly scratch from her visitor. But Lady Chester laughed again and obliged until Lucky's pink tongue hung out in bliss.

Lady Chester waited until Watson had left and leaned forward. "I saw your other visitors leave," she said. "They looked astoundingly dull. Were they?"

Emily's mouth dropped open and then she laughed, the sound floating to the ceiling. "I cannot pass comment on my guests – that would be the most appalling manners," she said, with a smile. "But Lady Chester, I am afraid you have followed me to Cambridge for no reason."

"You must not think I am put out; I live but twenty minutes' drive from here."

"That puts my mind at rest – at least for the inconvenience of your journey. I had intended to ask your advice in supporting my husband's re-election campaign." She took a deep breath, "However, he considers me too early in my recuperation to support him."

Black eyes fixed on her and Lady Chester arched an eyebrow. "You have been unwell?"

Emily racked her brain for how to explain the loss of her baby without becoming maudlin. While she was thinking, Watson returned with tea and set about clearing the dirty plates, which afforded her another few minutes. When she had finally handed Lady Chester her tea, she managed to say, "I had a difficult birth."

Lady Chester sat very still. "I take it your baby died?" Her voice was so gentle that tears started in Emily's eyes. Unable to speak, she nodded.

"My poor dear," Lady Chester responded quietly. "I daresay lots of people said that you're young and you have plenty of time. They are fools. While it may hurt less as time passes, I believe the memory never completely fades. You have my sincere condolences."

Emily could barely breathe. With the exception of James, who had comforted her through his own grief, these were the kindest words anyone had ever said to her about her child. In a mere five minutes, this stranger had reached in and warmed her heart.

She smiled at Lady Chester through her tears. "I am *so* pleased to meet you."

THE FOLLOWING WEEK, LADY CHESTER CLAPPED HER HANDS AS she surveyed the garden. Emily smiled at her guest's enthusiasm.

On her first visit, Lady Chester had stayed much longer than the prescribed thirty minutes, but rarely had Emily enjoyed an hour more, speaking of women's suffrage and Emily's mother – topics she never discussed in a morning call. The door had barely closed on her unconventional visitor when Emily reached for pen and paper to write a brief note inviting her to return for dinner.

The invitation was accepted with alacrity, and Lady Chester suggested that she might arrive early to see the garden before the daylight faded.

Emily was delighted, though hesitant to form a close attachment so quickly. Yet Lady Chester was unlike any other woman of her acquaintance. She remembered her aunt's warning that Charlotte Chester cared little for the niceties of polite society, but Emily found her guest's frankness refreshing.

"This is just too perfect! Your roses will be glorious in the summer with so many buds," Lady Chester said.

Emily laughed. "None of this is my doing, I'm afraid."

"Really? But you do not visit here often, do you? Do you not keep a garden in London?"

Emily told her about the London house and the long, narrow garden established by James' parents before his father died. Lady Chester's bright black eyes rested on Emily's face as though reading between the words she spoke. Emily's tentative efforts to add to the planting had been firmly rebuffed. It was as if the garden was a painting; pretty, but unchanging. Something to look at, but not be involved in.

"So I am afraid that after a while, I let the gardener do what James' mother said," Emily recalled. "At times I almost felt I was being patted on the head and told to run away and play!"

Lady Chester laughed and Emily flushed at her own indiscretion. What on earth she was thinking of, telling tales of James' family to a stranger?

Lady Chester darted a glance at her and patted Emily on the arm, her expression now sober. "I take it we can be private between ourselves?" she asked. "Apart from the servants, of course, who have ears everywhere."

Emily nodded and gathered her composure. They walked along the path until they reached a shady part of the garden.

Lady Chester put her head on one side. "Ah, you have a problem here. This gets so little sunlight that it would be difficult to grow anything."

"But this is ideal for a fernery," Emily said slowly. "I have long wanted to grow my own ferns outside of a Wardian case."

"You like ferns?"

"They captivate me. Their very existence is a miracle. Fern plants can drop millions of spores on the ground, but only the few that find ideal conditions will grow. And their shape and form are so numerous. They range from the glossy leaves of the *Asplenium scolopendrium* to the delicate, almost transparent leaves of the maidenhair fern."

She paused, suddenly embarrassed at her enthusiasm, but Lady Chester looked on approvingly. "A fernery would give an impressive point of interest, Lady Cleveland. You could design one!"

"I?" Emily's eyes widened. "I know a little about ferns, but I know nothing about designing gardens."

"You know more than many of my acquaintance. And as to design, your imagination and perusing a few journals will suffice." Lady Chester waved away her protests. "I know a little, and the rest I imagine we can get from Mr Moore's excellent book. Shall we discuss it over dinner?"

EMILY LAY PROPPED UP ON THE SCENTED PILLOWS AND BREATHED a sigh of contentment. Molly, brushing Emily's gown to remove Lucky's hairs, glanced at her. "Are you tired, milady?"

"A little," Emily admitted. "But very content with dinner tonight. It was a lively evening. I have not had such fun for a while."

Molly held the gown up and squinted at it, pursing her lips as she saw yet another dog hair. "I caught sight of Lady Chester as she arrived. Her gown was exceedingly fine. I wondered if you would consider such a style, milady?"

Emily reflected. One could almost judge Lady Chester's gown as plain until you looked at the cut and quality of the silk. Not for Lady Chester the frills and adornments that Emily had seen in London. Her taste was simpler: even, one might say, more elegant.

"Charles Worth," Lady Chester had said airily when Emily had remarked on it. "Empress Eugénie's official dressmaker."

Emily had nodded, her eyes sliding over the gown covetously.

"Perhaps I could search in *Domestic Magazine* for some patterns, milady?" Molly prompted.

"Well," murmured Emily, weighing up the cost of a gown from the Empress Eugénie's wardrobe and the possibility of seeing a pattern for it in the *Domestic Magazine,* and considering it unlikely. "You can certainly look."

"I will do that." She put the gown in the wardrobe and turned to Emily. "Do you have everything you need, milady?"

"Yes, thank you. Please wake me at eight o'clock. There is much to do tomorrow."

Molly bobbed a curtsy and slipped away. Emily waited until she heard Molly's footsteps echo down the hall, then reached towards the locked drawer by her bed. She slid out from beneath the covers, her feet hunting for her slippers. Lucky raised his head, and when he realised a walk was not in the offing, settled down again.

Emily took the journal to her escritoire and pulled out the chair. She thought for a moment, then began to write.

I have a new scheme afoot; one that will challenge me and delight James. I am embarking on the design of a fernery in the garden. Lady C. has convinced me to study ferns more closely and I wrote tonight for a copy of Mr Thomas Moore's History of British Ferns. I believe I can create something beautiful, and perhaps the endeavour will ease my loneliness and my grieving.

She scribbled a few lines about the need to speak to Seth, the gardener. He would need to arrange additional labour so the work could begin promptly. Tomorrow she would sketch more detail. She would make the fernery a luxurious bower of beautiful greenery and gentle shade.

She closed the journal, well pleased with her day's work.

Chapter 13

Emily

Friday 17th March, 1862: I cannot lead him to see my progress, my fresh energy. It is as if he sees an ancient daguerreotype of me taken years ago, rather than me as I am now.

C at stood up in disgust and raked her hands through her hair. The building noise outside was screwing into her temples, but that didn't excuse the twaddle she had just typed.

As she sat down again to what she had started to call 'the damned manuscript', her phone buzzed. "Didn't I switch you off?" she muttered, tensing as she picked up the phone. She sagged a little with relief. It was Lauren.

—How's the work? Shall I come up & kick ass for you?

Cat's finger hovered over the reply button. She wasn't sure she wanted company at the moment, given the state of her manuscript.

—Hi babe, she responded. I'm getting on fine. Can I give you a call in a week or so?

A minute passed and then there was a sharp buzz.

—No probs. Off to South Africa, filming at a vineyard, so signal may not be good for text. Email if u want me.

The usual suite of emojis followed and Cat grinned.

"Cat? Ms Kennedy?"

The shout from the front door made her jump. It was Charlie, the small, rotund gaffer in charge of building the wall. He poked his head around the door to the drawing room, as usual, in mid-sentence.

"... so what me and the lads have done is leave some gaps, a bit like air holes. If you don't like 'em we can block 'em up, but speaking personally, I think they look authentic."

"Hi, Charlie." Cat smiled at his cherub-like face, which radiated innocence – highly implausible, given the cash-in-hand deals that characterised the repair work. "Sorry, I was concentrating on something else. What were you saying?"

He tutted, complaining that she never listened to him, and repeated what he'd said. Apparently, some stones had shattered when the wall tumbled down. Rather than add to her bill with more materials, they'd made a pattern of the gaps.

He led her into the garden. They'd almost completed the pale greyish-gold stone wall, but between thigh and shoulder height the builders had left holes in the rows, forming a diamond pattern. Charlie was right: it did look authentic.

"I love it, but does Harry? After all, it's his wall too."

Charlie waved her concern away with a wink. "He's cool with anything you want," he said, grinning knowingly at her. He swaggered off, his short form in his black donkey jacket reminding Cat of a small dinghy on a choppy sea.

She blushed and retreated indoors, but the conversation had broken her concentration and after twenty minutes she closed her laptop. Having made the inevitable cup of tea, she settled on the sofa and took up the journal.

"Emily Caroline Cleveland, thank you for the fernery plans. What else do you have to say for yourself?"

She stroked the worn leather and carefully opened the pages. Cat pushed aside the faint feeling of intruding on this unknown woman and read on, concentrating to decipher the florid writing. She dipped into the journal at random, catching phrases. One almost made her cheer:

I felt my confidence return, simply for doing what I desired rather than kowtowing to someone else! I pray this is the beginning of my recovery.

Recovery? Cat frowned. Recovery from what?

"What happened to you, Emily Caroline?" she murmured as she delved further into the journal. Her eyes widened as she saw an entry from late May 1862:

Our relationship, which had seemed so full of fire, is now flickering to embers through lack of fuel. And although it is gross and unfeminine to admit such thoughts, I feel desire gnawing constantly at me, as though I could not be whole without his embrace. At night I pace the floor yearning for the relief that congress with him brings. My passion churns through me and unreleased, I am sickened.

"Wow!" Cat muttered, fanning her face. "There's more to you than a crinoline, Emily!"

She came across a page near the front of the journal that appeared as if someone had dripped water on it. The ink was smudged, and compared to the previous entries of elegant, looping letters, the hand-writing was jagged and disconnected. Most of the words were unreadable, although she could work out the words Dr Schenley – whoever that was – and 'my darling'.

Then she read: *My infant – oh! The pain is unbearable.*

Cat gasped, taken by surprise at the stark anguish. Whatever had caused Emily to write this? Then she recalled she had spotted the word 'mourning' and carefully turned the pages to find it. Yes, there it was.

As she read that entry and others, she realised that Emily had been mourning the loss of her baby. "Oh God, what a shame!" she whispered as she read, her throat tight and painful with tears for this woman whose grief seemed written in blood.

With a start, Cat saw it was past six o'clock and the daylight was fading fast. She closed the journal reluctantly. Despite the pain in its pages, this journal was like a new friend, and she wanted to know more.

But she returned to her laptop.

THE LETTER THAT ARRIVED A WEEK LATER LOOKED LIKE ANY other circular, Cat almost didn't open it, but the envelope looked official. She wondered nervously whether it might be from her publisher. Who was still waiting for her manuscript.

So she opened it. As she looked at the crude cut-out letters, her first thought was that really, she should have known better.

PATHETIC. THINK I DON'T KNOW ABOUT THE NEW NUMBER? I'M STILL COMING FOR YOU.

She put the letter down on the kitchen counter and, trying to control the panic bubbling in her throat, forced herself to finish making her coffee. The low-slanting spring sunshine glinted off the brass handles on the kitchen cupboards and she silently blessed Gam for the gift of Cleveland House. It calmed her a little.

When she had her coffee in hand, she turned back to the counter. The letter lay on the polished marble, black letters stark on the white paper, making ugly words.

Her hands shaking, she took a photo and sent it to Harry. He phoned her back less than a minute later. "Are you okay?" he demanded.

"Yes, at the moment," she responded. "A bit shaky."

"Put gloves on, put it in the envelope and go to the station on London Road. I'll meet you there. Who was your contact?"

She fumbled in her bag for the contact details. "A Constable Davis."

"Right, see you there."

CAT DIDN'T REMEMBER THE JOURNEY. SHE DROVE CAREFULLY TO the station with the envelope in her bag, as though she was carrying an unexploded bomb.

Harry was waiting outside and looked closely at her as she walked towards him. What he saw appeared to satisfy him. "Good stuff. Ready?"

She composed herself. "Yup. Does this letter change things?"

"Let's talk to Constable Davis and see."

While Constable Davis was sympathetic, that was all he was. They didn't have the resources to do much, he explained.

"No forensics?" Harry asked.

"No, sir. Unless the victim is in danger of physical attack."

"You need to wait until someone comes at me with a gun?" Cat burst out.

"Who do you know in London? That's the postmark. Do you recognise anything else about this message?" Constable Davis asked calmly.

Cat slumped in her chair and gestured helplessly. "I know *hundreds* of people in London! And no, I recognise nothing about it, otherwise I'd tell you."

"Who did you tell that you'd changed your number?"

"Only the three hundred people in my phone book!"

"Including your ex?" put in Harry.

Constable Davis looked at him impatiently. "Sir..."

Harry raised his hands. "Sorry, sorry," he said. "Not my investigation, I know."

"With respect, there doesn't seem to be much investigation going on anyway!" Cat said hotly. Two pairs of eyes swung towards her. "I live alone, I've had two threatening communications, and you're doing nothing about it!"

"Cat—" Harry began, but a gesture from the constable quietened him.

"As DI Moore has raised a good point, we may as well have your answer." Constable Davis leafed through his notes. "*Was* your ex – Stephen Fergusson – included in any communication about the new number? You said you'd broken up with him because he was very controlling..."

"Yes, and I blocked him on my phone when I left," Cat said tightly.

"And he locked you in your shared flat and a friend had to break you out?"

She nodded. "But he doesn't know where I'm living now. So if it is Stephen, I'm not sure how he got my address."

"You have shared friends?"

Cat stared at him, her head beginning to ache. Constable Davis looked steadily at her, and she bit her lip. "Yes, I suppose we still have some shared friends, so one of them might have passed my new number and my address to him. God knows why, though. Everyone knows we've split up."

"But how well known were the circumstances of your break-up?"

"Not well known," Cat muttered. "I felt so incredibly stupid that I hadn't seen it coming. Only Creighton, my agent, knew anything about the details."

"I see," said Constable Davis, closing his notebook. "We may contact Mr Fergusson and ask some general questions, and maybe your agent. Is there anyone else?"

"What about Geoff Johnson?" Harry said suddenly. "He has a motive: he wants you out of the house."

Cat raised her eyebrows. "You think so?"

"Who's this?" asked Constable Davis. Cat briefly ran through her history with Geoff Johnson. It seemed far-fetched to her, and she said so.

"You can't be too careful. It's possibly worth bringing him in." The constable stood up and took the letter. "I'll add this to the file. Call us if you get any further messages. We'll contact you when we have further information."

Cat walked to her car in silence, Harry alongside her. "So they'll interview Stephen and Geoff Johnson?" Cat asked as she opened the driver's door.

"For Fergusson, it depends how busy they are in Camden, which is where I guess they'll deal with it," Harry replied. "They might have a conversation with him, and if Geoff's easy to trace, they may phone him for a chat. But don't think the note will go to forensics and they'll look for DNA, or anything you see on TV. Doesn't happen like that."

"Silly me. Fancy thinking that the police were here to solve crime."

Cat got into her car, slammed the door, started the engine and slid down the window. "Thanks for the moral support."

He shrugged. "No problem. Catch you later?"

"Maybe." Cat drove off in a temper which lasted until she reached her house.

There was a postcard on the mat. Carefully, bearing in mind the last letter she'd received, she turned it over.

It was from Lizzie. *How is the writing? Love, Lizzie*

She dug out her phone immediately. "How sweet of you!" she said when Lizzie answered.

"Don't be idiotic," Lizzie said crisply. "So, how are you?"

"I – I'm fine," Cat replied, after a slight pause. "The writing is going okay. Could be better, but I'm doing rewrites after Creighton's feedback."

"*Are* you fine?" Lizzie asked. "You don't sound too sure."

Cat shook her head, cursing Lizzie's antennae.

"Cat?"

Cat sighed. "I've had a bit of bother." Then she remembered that the police had asked her not to mention the investigation and winced.

"What kind of bother?" Lizzie asked.

"Oh, money. You know, the usual thing. I got turned down for a credit card and that's pissed me off."

"Hmm," Lizzie said. "Well, there's a nursery which specialises in ferns near me and I wondered if you would like to visit it. I presume the wall will be complete at some stage?"

"Yeah, they're getting on really well. I'll call you when I'm ready to start, shall I?" And when I've worked out what money I have left.

Cat ended the call and a warm glow spread through her. She would ring-fence some of her funds to make a start on the fernery. It had been important to Gam, and Gam had been, hands down, Cat's favourite relative. While Lizzie could never replace her, she was making it her business to ensure Cat didn't feel the loss so keenly.

Out of nowhere, she thought about Lauren. Cat hadn't heard from her, but perhaps she hadn't returned from South Africa yet. She'd been so excited about the trip and Cat had been thrilled for her. But Lauren, who would send photos whenever she was on a jaunt, had been strangely silent. Cat shrugged. Perhaps the mobile signal really had been bad.

A buzz came from her phone. Slowly, Cat picked it up.

—I can still get to you, can't I? God, you're crap. Run, Kitty Cat, run. I'm coming to get you…

Chapter 14

Emily smiled broadly as Seth Lovell's scratchy voice detailed their progress. It was a splendid day. She was wearing a new dress, sewn by a local dressmaker under strict instructions from Molly. Its charcoal-grey silk was relieved by delicate white lace at the throat and sleeves. Although it did not achieve the elegance of Mr Worth, it was a fine imitation and it became her. She had received a telegraph from James' agent to say that she would read of Sir James' re-election in the *Times*, should she care to look. Emily had spent the morning buried in the tiny script of the newspaper, relieved that James had retained his seat.

Seth's grizzled head nodded at the walls they had built from earth, stone and the rocks that the team of labourers had dragged into the garden. This was the final part of the work on the ground. Emily had noticed how poor the soil was, and that would not do. Seth and his team had added manure and dug in a dozen large bags of grit which would help aerate the soil.

Among the mud, of which there was an abundance, she glimpsed where ferns and greenery were taking root. Lucky sniffed and trotted around, and she reflected ruefully that the dog would need to be wrapped in a towel and scrubbed before he could be allowed into the house again.

"Oh, the wall will appear just as I envisaged when it is planted!" she cried, pointing to the waist-high wall along the path, meandering through the trees so that the traveller was unseen.

Seth paused in his monotone commentary and touched his battered hat. "Yes, ma'am, but beggin' your pardon, we ain't so sure when the ferns will be 'ere."

"Are there delays? I was not aware."

Another labourer, younger than Seth and slightly less rumpled, stepped forward. "Ma'am, the salesman came Tuesday, all apologetic-like, but he says there's delays on the ferns comin' from Devon."

"How long? Did he say?"

"'Bout two weeks."

Emily frowned, then hid her irritation with an effort; the delay to the ferns wasn't the fault of the men in front of her. "Very well, I shall write to the suppliers. But what you have accomplished is splendid. Please continue with the stone around the fountain."

She returned to the house, depositing Lucky in the kitchen where he could be made respectable for company again.

Settled at the writing desk, she paused. She had never written a letter of complaint in her life, but she was angry that her custom had been taken so casually. She penned a note to John Dadd's North Devon Fernery and Rosary in Ilfracombe, expressing her indignation that while the salesperson had spoken to her workmen, he had omitted to call on her personally. She would be obliged if the ferns that she had paid for could be delivered next Thursday at the latest, otherwise she would be put to considerable inconvenience.

She read her letter through and nodded, satisfied that she had conveyed what she felt. She had just pulled the bell to summon Watson when he arrived, enquiring whether she was at home to Lady Chester and the Reverend Sherwood-Taylor. She was.

"Lady Chester, how lovely to see you!" She shook hands warmly with her friend and turned to the neat, precise man beside her, his moustache and goatee carefully trimmed. "Reverend, it was an excellent service last Sunday. Please sit down." She looked away from Lady Chester, whose eyes were dancing at her white lie.

The reverend flushed pink and harrumphed as he took his seat. Watson returned with a maid and some refreshments.

"Are you well, Lady Cleveland?" asked the reverend.

"I am. And how are your delightful wife and daughter?" Emily handed him a cup of tea.

"Well enough, well enough," he said, nodding hard. "Felt I ought to visit to show my respects. Parish work, you know, parish work." He slurped his tea, and the noise made Emily blink in surprise. She avoided Lady Chester's delighted smile.

Reverend Sherwood-Taylor put down his tea and stroked his chin. "I have heard of your efforts to redesign the garden," he said, sounding hesitant.

Emily twinkled at him, but his next words wiped the smile from her face. "Sir James' father was very particular about the layout, very particular, but I am sure you have spoken to Sir James about any changes, and that this current upheaval has his blessing." He nodded towards the garden. "Did you work on the design together?"

The question was mild, but Emily breathed in sharply. She was just about to speak when Lady Chester laughed softly. "I hope you won't be responsible for ruining Lady Cleveland's surprise, Reverend. This work is to celebrate Sir James' victory in the recent elections."

"Indeed!" The reverend's eyebrows rose up his pale, thin forehead.

"I am certain Sir James will allow his wife some latitude in the garden as a welcome-home gift," Lady Chester said firmly.

Reverend Sherwood-Taylor picked up his cup again. "I only hope that you have steered clear of the cult for ferns," he said. Emily stilled, her eyes widening. "Improvident fern-hunting maniacs are ravaging the countryside! I believe Devonshire has been almost *completely* denuded of some of its native ferns, which now languish in unsuitable soils all over the country."

Emily could feel the colour rising in her face. Lady Chester, with a quick glance at Emily's face, clasped her hands firmly around her parasol. "I am sure Lady Cleveland only buys from reputable nurseries. Isn't the weather glorious for this early in the spring?"

Finally, the reverend took his leave. Emily bit her lip and shifted uncomfortably. Lady Chester leaned forward and patted her hand. "My dear, do not be concerned. You have purchased from Dadd's, have you not? A most respectable nursery."

"Yes, but I did not know of the impact I might have! What if James has views about this? Oh, I'm such a fool! I only wanted to show him..."

Lady Chester shot her a shrewd glance. "How competent you were? That you were recovering?" she asked lightly.

Emily hung her head. "Am I so transparent?"

"Only to those who know how to use their eyes," Lady Chester said gently. "Come, show me the progress in the gardens. You can do nothing about the ferns now. They will arrive in due course, and you will astound Sir James with your ingenuity!"

Emily twisted her hands and nodded, reining in her misgivings.

Lady Chester was quiet as she surveyed the fernery taking shape under the careful hands of Seth and his crew. As she waited for a word from her guest, Emily's stomach churned. "Do – do you like it? Is it adequate?"

Lady Chester turned to her, black eyes shining, and clasped her hands together. "Adequate? It's magnificent! It will be like a faery bower! Oh, ma'am, what talent you have!"

For a moment, Emily couldn't speak. Words of praise were strange to her ears. She nodded jerkily, willing the tears not to fall. Seeing her emotion, Lady Chester turned away, walking slowly along the path.

Emily gathered her scattered thoughts. One part of her shrank from the thought that James would be displeased by her alterations, and worse, that she had succumbed to the craze for ferns. But the other revelled in the praise of her new friend: a balm to her spirit, which had been battered by so much misfortune. With new eyes, she saw her vision for the fernery and it looked splendid. More than splendid.

She caught up with Lady Chester. "I wish you would call me Emily."

Lady Chester looked at her and, after a moment, put out her hand, "Charlotte."

Emily shook Charlotte's gloved hand and together they walked through the garden.

EMILY WAS SQUINTING AT THE WATERCOLOUR WHEN WATSON announced Lady Chester. *Charlotte*, she reminded herself as her guest breezed through the door. She rose, smiling at the energy that the redhead brought with her whenever she entered a room.

"How are you?" she said, wiping her hands on the rag she kept near her paints and brushes.

"Delighted to see you at your easel again!" Charlotte beamed at her and it struck Emily afresh how different Charlotte was from the pale, uninteresting people in London. Even Charlotte's clothes seemed brighter: the colours rich, even bold. Today she was wearing a beautifully cut cream silk Zouave jacket over a dress trimmed with mint-green braid. The skirt was full, but Charlotte navigated through the side tables and pedestals with ease and settled gracefully on the sofa. She twinkled at Emily.

"Another Worth creation?" Emily gestured at the dress.

Charlotte shook her head, smoothing the silk. "My dear Emily, not all my dresses are by the master! This is from Mme Vignon, after the American fashion. Now, what are you working on? How is the fernery developing?"

"I am making good progress but my ferns are delayed, so I have picked up my paintbrush instead."

Charlotte made her way across the room and peered at Emily's work. The painting was only about eight inches square, but what it lacked in size it made up for in delicate precision. A shocked expression crossed Charlotte's face and her lips parted. "This is *adiantum capillus veneris,* is it not?" she said in awed tones.

Emily laughed. "Yes, it's maidenhair fern. I confess, I am rather pleased with it. I know some people consider them dull, as they are for the most part green – but oh, what variety in that colour and leaf shape! Look how the sunshine filters through the leaves! I declare they fascinate me endlessly."

Charlotte turned to her. "Emily, will you forever hide your light under a bushel? This is wonderful! I could almost imagine the plant in front of me!"

Emily was touched by her friend's enthusiasm and felt a blush creep up her throat. "Indeed, I am gratified that you like it so much," she murmured. "Thank you, Watson," she said as the butler bustled in with tea and freshly baked biscuits.

They took their seats, but Emily saw a slight frown between Charlotte's brows. Handing her a steaming cup, she waited for Charlotte to speak.

After stirring her tea thoughtfully, Charlotte raised her eyes. "I think you should write some notes on your illustration and send it to a publisher," she said quietly.

Emily chuckled. "I believe you are letting your partiality interfere with your judgement, my dear. My illustration cannot possibly be good enough for public viewing."

Charlotte tutted and grabbed her reticule, extracting a crumpled journal. She leaned forward and placed it on the tea table. *Phytologist: a popular botanical miscellany.*

Emily picked it up and turned the pages. "This is about new plant discoveries," she said, drawn to the content. "Does it appear monthly?"

"It does. I am acquainted with Alexander Irvine, the editor," Charlotte said, watching Emily. "He has been searching for content on ferns for some time. I'd be happy to make an introduction, and he would be delighted to receive your illustration."

"Oh, I could not!"

"But why not? Your illustration is fine indeed, and if you are concerned about the propriety – why, botany is one of the few sciences in which women may be active!"

"But..." Emily went to look at her watercolour, examining it with her head on one side. "Surely there must be better illustrators than I."

"Compare, my dear," Charlotte said drily, opening the page to a lacklustre illustration of a peony. It wasn't even accurate.

Emily pursed her lips. "What would James say?"

Charlotte waved a hand. "Pah! If you are so bashful, submit it with an instruction that you remain anonymous."

All Emily could hear in the quiet drawing room was her breathing. She could never do this. James would be surprised. Her mother-in-law would be horrified. Aunt Sybil might well disown her. But her work was good. In her heart of hearts, Emily knew it. Was her illustration good enough to be published, though?

"What harm could it do if you are anonymous?" asked Charlotte mildly, observing her from beneath long lashes. "Shall I introduce you? Would you like me to offer your illustration and negotiate payment?" Charlotte popped a biscuit in her mouth.

"Payment?" exclaimed Emily.

"Oh yes," Charlotte nodded. "It will be paltry, but you can use it to purchase more ferns, perhaps?" Emily hesitated, and Charlotte leaned forward. "You are talented, Emily. You design brilliantly and you breathe life into your illustrations. Please let the world see you as you are, not as just another socialite who married well."

Emily hesitated, tempted. She would like to be seen. Before she had built the fernery she had felt she was gradually disappearing, buried in layers of grief and social pleasantries. If her submission was unnamed, surely that would protect her reputation? James and his family would never know who the artist was, even if they saw a copy of the journal. Surely the risk was minuscule?

After a moment, she nodded. "Very well, then please write to your Mr Irvine. He may use the illustration as long as I remain anonymous."

"I shall take it to him myself."

Chapter 15

Emily

Wednesday 22th March 1862: I have completed my watercolour and I own that I am pleased with it. But it is the act of creation that gives me such pleasure. The outcome may only be for my satisfaction, but the process is a joy, regardless of the result.

The following morning was busy. First, and most urgent, Cat had to change her number. Just before she changed her number, she received a text from Lauren.

—Hiya! Passing yr place later – r u in?

"When did you get back?" wondered Cat as she responded.

—Yes, but need to shop. When u coming? How was the trip?

—Client cancelled. About 12?

—Cool. U OK?

—Bit rushed c u later.

Cat frowned. No emojis – Lauren *must* be rushed! It was such a shame about the trip: Lauren had been really excited about visiting South Africa.

She phoned her mobile company again, to the bemusement of the customer services representative, then sent another 'message to all' with her new number but no explanation as to why. Doubtless those who knew her well would put this down to her normal ditziness with technology. On this occasion, she was happy to let them think what they liked.

Afterwards, she put crumbs on the windowsill for the robin, now named Batman, and pushing the last twenty-four hours out of her head as best she could, took another look at her cupboards. With the remainder of Creighton's chair money still in her account, she went to a supermarket.

Cat was dragging the groceries out of the car boot at ten to twelve when Lauren pulled up in her brand-new Mini with the Union Jack on the roof.

"Hiya stranger!" Lauren called as she parked with her normal accuracy.

Cat smiled. It would be good not to think about the lunatic sending her threatening messages. Even though she needed to write, she needed a break to do something normal...

"Be more enthusiastic! I'm offering to buy you lunch!" Lauren laughed as she slid elegantly out of the car. She was wearing a bright pink miniskirt with spike-heeled knee-high boots, and a huge plaid scarf over a tight black top. Cat glanced down at her usual jeans and T-shirt and shrugged away a twinge of envy.

Lauren slung her handbag over her shoulder and grabbed two bags of shopping. "Any booze in here? Writers need to keep up their alcohol levels. Never did Hemingway any harm."

"Hemingway never drank while he was writing," Cat said, following her to the front door. "And it's an urban legend that his favourite drink was the mojito. It was the daiquiri." She fished out her house keys.

Lauren looked on as Cat wrestled with the new locks. "God, are you hiding the Crown Jewels in there?"

Cat blushed as she realised that Lauren had no idea why she had changed the locks, and she couldn't tell her, a friend she'd known since school. "I had a problem with the previous lock," she said.

Lauren lugged the bags into the kitchen and Cat gave her an enthusiastic hug. "Well, this is a lovely surprise!"

"Just passing, darling. I'm on a recce this afternoon for a new product launch – I can't tell you what or I'd have to kill you – but I thought I'd pop over and see if you had time for lunch. I've found a fab Italian with mouth-watering pasta."

Cat opened her mouth to plead that she needed to write, but the light in Lauren's eyes made her change the sentence. Lauren looked almost as if the world depended on Cat's answer.

She grinned. "Love to, but how long have you got before your meeting?"

"It's at three thirty and it will take me about half an hour to get there, so we've plenty of time." She paused and her blue eyes looked Cat up and down. "Do you want to freshen up before we go?"

Cat could take a hint. "Should I get changed?" she asked.

Lauren grinned and nodded. "Shall I put this lot away in the meantime?"

"You're a pal." Cat blew a kiss at her elegant friend and ran to her bedroom.

Her wardrobe, after some riffling, produced an emerald sweater and a navy corduroy skirt. Cat thrust her feet into her flat boots, pulled a brush through her dark hair, and was ready.

Almost ready, she decided, heading back to the dressing table. The sweater brought out the green in her eyes and made her hair shine. She riffled in a drawer for a lip gloss and slicked some on her mouth. The raspberry gloss added a lushness to her lips, and she nodded at her reflection, satisfied.

Lauren was just closing the key cupboard, juggling three tins of tuna, as Cat arrived. Cat mock-tutted. "Not there – here," she said, opening the cupboard where the tins were stored. "You can't get the staff these days."

"What did your last slave die of?" Lauren turned to look at Cat.

"Ah, that's the Cat Kennedy I remember," she said, winking at her. "I was afraid I'd have to get those jeans surgically removed."

"I'm working!" Cat protested. "I don't need to dress up to sit and type all day."

"Chill, girl. Now, are you ready? Got all the keys to lock up Fort Knox?"

"Cheeky cow," Cat said, without heat, and grabbed her bag.

THREE HOURS LATER, CAT WAVED AT THE DEPARTING MINI. ONCE it had gone, a frown wrinkled her forehead. Lauren had seemed on edge, her laughter brittle. Cat wondered if the job was getting to her, or the disappointment of that cancelled business trip. Although Lauren had brushed it off, Cat thought that beneath her expertly applied make-up, she had looked tired and stressed.

She walked up the path to the house, tall and grand, the leaded lights of the entrance hall twinkling in the sunlight. On the pillars, the gargoyles, smoothed out by the wind and rain of many years, looked more cuddly than frightening.

The sight of the house gladdened her heart and once again she sent a tiny prayer of thanks to Gam. This house would keep her safe; she knew it in her gut. As she stepped through the door, the house seemed to embrace her. She leaned on the door and looked into the hall, the watery spring sunshine casting a warm, buttery glow on the tiles.

Cat shrugged off her jacket and headed for the drawing room. She needed to start work again, but paused at the bay window and looked out at the garden. The tulips were unwrapping their flowers, showing flashes of scarlet and yellow. She let out a sigh of pleasure. Admittedly, she could have done without a three-hour break in her day, but it had been nice to see her best mate. She saw a missed call from Creighton and guiltily rang him.

"This latest section where Louise meets her half-sister – very good, very good," he boomed.

Cat's eyes widened. The compliment was so unexpected that she sprang into defensive mode. "What do you want to change?"

Creighton chortled. "I don't want you to change anything; I wanted to encourage you to write more like that! It has great emotion: I was really rooting for Louise." Cat waited for the *but*. "Are you still there?" he asked.

"Yes, I'm here. Thanks. I— I'm pleased you like it."

"Capital! Continue in this vein and everything will be fine!" Creighton rang off, leaving Cat stunned.

She opened her laptop and found the section she'd sent him. She'd written it after she put the journal down, and it had been effortless, fluid.

A movement outside the window made her glance up. The robin was perched on the sundial. It put its head on one side as if asking where she'd been all afternoon.

Cat smiled, then her eyes caught the light shifting by the fernery. She looked, then looked harder. "I could have sworn..." she said to herself as her brain tried to make sense of shadows that swirled almost like a skirt. Then the shadows were gone and the sunlight seemed clear and steady.

She shook her head and sat down at the dining table to write.

SOMEONE BANGED ON THE DOOR AND SHE JUMPED. SHE WASN'T expecting anyone. Cautiously, she looked through the spyhole in the door. It was Harry, looking as if he'd come from the office, and she breathed a sigh of relief.

"You seriously need to chill, Cat," she muttered as she started to unlock the door. "You're imagining axe murderers around every corner, you idiot."

"Hello!" she said to Harry as she threw open the door.

He scowled at her. "I've been trying to ring you for twenty minutes! Haven't you got your phone on?"

She raised her eyebrows and he looked a little shamefaced. "Okay, so you haven't got your phone on. Sorry. I was worried."

"No, I was working. Apologies. Coming in?"

"I just wanted to check on you," he said, stepping inside as she waved him towards the drawing room. "Ah..."

Cat followed his gaze to the dining table and wrinkled her nose. Once she got into the swing of writing it would take a brass band to disturb her. The table was piled with books, a thesaurus, printouts with scrawled notes, a cereal bowl and several half-drunk cups of tea. She moved forward, piling up papers to create some order.

He laughed. "Don't tidy up for me! Now I know you're okay, I'll leave you in peace. Charlie tells me they'll finish on my side of the wall tomorrow morning, so is there anything else they can do in your garden?"

"Is there any chance they can replace the edging on the path? You know, before the path splits in front of the fernery." She strode to the window and he followed. "There. See how the edge has come away?"

"Where?" He leaned closer. She could smell him and feel the warmth of his body. Her mind went blank. "Oh yeah, I see where you mean."

He moved away and she swallowed. "Right. Yes. So, um, if you could ask them to do that I'd be grateful." She stared into his eyes and for a moment it seemed all the air had been sucked out of the atmosphere.

He moved away, then murmured something and walked to the door.

Following him, Cat glanced at her phone and frowned. "You didn't ring me fifteen times, did you?"

"No, I rang twice." The hairs rose on Cat's arms. "Let me see," he said, suddenly professional. She handed the phone to him. "Well, someone definitely wanted to speak to you: you have fifteen missed calls. Do you recognise this number?"

He held the phone out and Cat went rigid. "Stephen," she whispered.

Harry took her hand. "He left a message. Shall we listen to it together?"

Cat nodded, barely able to breathe.

'You have three new messages.'

Stephen swore down the line and put the phone down. The second message was the same. Then, 'Third new message, received today at three thirty-four pm.'

"Catherine, long time no speak." Stephen's cold voice rang out in the quiet room. "I'd ask how you are but frankly, I don't care. Thanks to you, I've spent the last three hours in a shithole of a police station being questioned by a snotty-nosed copper about a crisis which is probably all inside your tiny little mind. I suggest you leave me out of it before I get my lawyer involved."

'End of messages.'

By the time the answerphone clicked off, Cat was shaking. Harry, about to speak, looked at her face, then pushed her towards the sofa. "Sit down before you fall down."

A couple of minutes later, he thrust a cup into her hand. "Drink this, it'll help." She took a sip and almost gagged at the amount of sugar in it. Another sip, and the blood began to pump through her veins again.

She raised the cup in a shaky salute. "We have to stop doing this. Thanks."

"I take it that was the ex?" She nodded. "He sounds a right charmer. They pulled him in for questioning, then. At least they're taking you seriously."

Cat nodded again, not sure she could manage complete sentences. Hearing Stephen's voice again was like reliving a nightmare.

"Cat, this bastard didn't hurt you, did he? He didn't beat you up?" His voice was gentle, and it helped her pull herself together.

"No. Although he might have done if I'd stayed." A thought struck her. "How did he get my number again?"

"Someone shared it with him – but who?"

Lauren.

Cat stared into her cup of tea, realisation dawning. God above, Lauren had shared the number with him! She placed her mug carefully on the coffee table and held out her hand for her phone.

Harry gave her a quizzical look. "Shall I go?"

She shook her head as she dialled the number. "No. I might need something stronger than tea after this. Lauren? Hi, this is only a quick call. Did you give Stephen my new number?"

She heard a deep breath. Lauren's voice sounded strained, her laugh artificial. "Darling, I'm trying to pave the way for a reconciliation! I didn't think it would do any harm."

"Lauren, I'm not sure how much clearer I can be. I never want to speak to Stephen again. He's a controlling, unpleasant man. I wouldn't willingly go back to him if he was the last man on earth!"

"I'm sorry," Lauren said quickly. "I only meant good, Cat, I swear! We were talking over a drink, and you know how forceful and persuasive he can be. I thought—"

"You thought wrong! When I next see you, I'll play you his bloody message!"

"Cat, I'm sorry. We're still mates, aren't we?"

Cat could hear the panic in Lauren's voice, but she wasn't ready to forgive her, still feeling suffocated after hearing Stephen's voice. "Don't give him any more information about where I am or what I'm doing. I'll speak to you soon." She ended the call and let out a breath. Then she glanced at Harry, approaching with a glass of wine.

"Yes, tea is definitely inadequate on this occasion," he said, sitting beside her on the sofa. "So it was Lauren?"

Cat took the glass and swallowed a mouthful of wine. Her hands had stopped shaking, at least. "It was. She's got an incredibly warped idea of Stephen and how he was with me. Mind you, he was always charming in front of other people. No wonder she thought I was an idiot for breaking up with him."

Harry raised his eyebrows. "Didn't you tell her what he did?"

"Not at first, no: I wasn't sure if I was imagining it. I tried to tell her when things became unbearable. To be honest, though, I wondered if she understood what I was saying. She kept making excuses for him. You know – a bit old-fashioned in his ideas of what women should wear, a touch overprotective. *Overprotective?* He freakin' locked me up!"

Harry stood up. "I'll see what the investigating officer at Camden had to say about your ex. It sounds as though they released him without charge."

"What does that mean?"

"Exactly what you'd think. They'll have brought him in, asked to see his phone and phone records, and asked him about his relationship with you. If they found nothing on his phone and got nothing from what he said, they'd have no other option than to release him. Although I bet he was nicer to my mates in Camden than he was to you."

"Yeah, that's pretty typical. Two-faced bastard."

"I'll let you know what I find. Stay cool."

Chapter 16

Emily ripped open the envelope with unsteady hands. She had written to James, and telegraphed him after receiving the news of his success in the election. Until today, she had received only brief communications in return. Part of her thrilled to see her name in his bold script.

She was in her sitting room, the fire burning merrily to warm the room against a sullen grey sky outside. The thick embossed stationery was stiff as she unfolded it.

My dearest Emily – Thank you for your congratulations. I am pleased the election business is over, even if the result was not in doubt. The House has finally announced its Easter recess and by the time this reaches you, I should be on the train to Cleveland House.

Emily leapt to her feet and rang the bell violently, bringing Watson at a run. "Quick, fetch Mrs O'Donnell! Sir James will join us later today!"

Mrs O'Donnell, plump and pink-faced from haste, arrived a few minutes later, Lucky bouncing around her. Emily remembered too late that as mistress of the house she should be a monument of calm, even while others were rushing about. She took a deep breath, then instructed Mrs O'Donnell in what his lordship might like for dinner – and luncheon, should he arrive hungry.

Mrs O'Donnell pressed her lips together and nodded, her face showing a servant's neutrality. Emily was in sympathy with her. It would have hurt so little for James to write sooner, so that this frantic activity might be avoided.

"Oh, how like you, James!" she murmured as Mrs O'Donnell left the room, her stiff, straight back leaving Emily in no doubt of her annoyance. Lucky put his head on one side, his pink tongue hanging from the side of his mouth, and Emily grinned at him. "Would a little notice be too much to ask, Lucky?"

Having set the staff in an uproar, Emily sat down to read the rest of the letter.

I trust you are in good health and recovering your strength. In truth, I am eager to come to you. It seems an age since I last beheld your sweet face, and I yearn to hold you and make sure you are hale and hearty. I have missed your precious presence, which until recently I had not realised was so essential to my comfort. Your loving husband, James.

Emily felt her body heat up. James never expressed himself in florid language. This, tame as it might seem to others, was passionate for James. She folded it carefully, then unbuttoned her bodice and slipped it next to her skin, a tingle of excitement rising in her at her husband's imminent arrival.

EMILY TRIED NOT TO LOOK AT JAMES' FROWN AS HE MURMURED TO Seth. Her palms were damp, and she hid them in her skirts. Lucky, sensing her unease, stood quietly at her feet.

For her, their reunion had been little short of miraculous. James had ignored Watson, pulled Emily into his arms and kissed her, hard. His hand caressed her hair, then her face, before he saw Mrs O'Donnell waiting to curtsy and drew back.

Emily led him into the drawing room while the servants collected his bags. Once the door closed, James again took her in his arms and kissed her, whispering how much he had missed her. Only the arrival of the tea things had brought a very satisfactory reacquaintance to a close.

But that now seemed a long time ago. James stood silent in the fernery. So far, apart from his start of surprise when she had led him into the garden, he had given her no clue to his feelings.

He turned, thumbs hooked into his waistcoat, and she forced herself to speak. "Do – do you like it? I have had to enrich the soil, hence it looks disturbed..."

He smiled slightly and the scone she had eaten with her tea turned into gravel in her stomach. "You have obviously worked very hard," he said. "Shall we return to the house?"

They walked without speaking along the path, her heart beating as if she had been running. She took a seat in the drawing room and clasped her hands firmly in her lap. She recalled Charlotte's words, that she, Emily, was talented. Charlotte would not have been untruthful ... would she?

James sat down across the room from her and crossed his legs. Emily resented how relaxed he was, when she was so tense. Abruptly, she unclasped her hands and leaned back, then raised her chin and rolled her shoulders to loosen them. The movement drew the fabric taut against her breasts. James' hot gaze fell on her for a split second, then moved away.

He picked a piece of fern from his trouser leg. "I'm glad Seth has been here to help you," he said finally. "I would have been displeased if you had toiled alone to dismantle the garden."

Emily's brows drew together in a frown. "Seth and the others have done much of the heavy labouring. But dismantling? The work has been meticulously thought through! You cannot think that I would alter the garden carelessly."

James uncrossed his legs and leaned forward. "I hoped you would rest, as Dr Schenley directed. Your health is of the utmost importance, and it will not benefit from poking around in the dark and damp."

At the sound of Dr Schenley's name, Emily shivered involuntarily.

"See? You are chilled even from ten minutes outside!" James rose to poke the fire, then added a log and came to sit beside her. "My darling, I know you – we – have suffered in recent months, but I hope we can soon try again for a son."

"Or a daughter."

"Or, indeed, a daughter, though that might simply serve to delight Cousin Freddie." James' laugh grated on Emily's ears. "I found out yesterday that his wife Cecily is with child."

Emily knew what that meant. Her hands, already cold from thinking of Dr Schenley, turned to ice. Should Cecily give birth to a male heir and Emily not produce a son, the estate would revert to Freddie's side of the family. This was why James was here, and so attentive. It had nothing to do with her as a person, and more the fact that she was of child-bearing age. She swallowed. "I have been so well since I came here! The fernery has given me a reason to get out of the house. I feel so much stronger for the fresh air and the exertion of directing the men! And *I* think the result a success."

He patted her hand. "My love, I do not want you to do anything to risk your recuperation. Being well enough to bear our son is more important than a fernery, is it not?"

Emily rose jerkily to her feet. "I shall do nothing to put our chances of a family at risk," she began, and he relaxed. "But I cannot see how planting a few ferns is detrimental to that aim. If you wish to improve my health, for pity's sake let me be useful! I have had great joy so far from the project. I hope you do not plan to prevent me completing it?"

He looked as if she had slapped him.

"Will you allow me to finish it?" she demanded.

He stared at her. "If it means so much to you, then yes, of course," he murmured, spreading his hands.

"Thank you. I shall see that your rooms are ready," she said, and swept out.

EMILY SIGHED. SHE NEEDED TO SPEAK WITH CHARLOTTE, WHOSE indefatigable good spirits would chase away her megrims. Her reflection in the mirror was pale and sad. She sat up straighter on the bed. She needed to take herself in hand, rather than be so easily swayed by the attitudes of others!

She closed the journal just as James opened the door. Lucky raised his head from his bed in the corner. Calmly, she placed the journal in the drawer and closed it softly. She turned the key and placed it in her jewellery box.

"I see your mutt is still with you," James said, hovering by the bed.

"Where else would he be? He is almost my constant companion. I believe he knows, to use a vulgar phrase, on which side his bread is buttered." Emily looked fondly at Lucky, who wagged his tail.

"Surely he does not accompany you to dinner?"

"No, Molly takes him for a walk while I eat. It is a routine we have established."

"I shall see you in the dining room," he said, after a pause. She nodded, then moved to the dressing table so that Molly could finish her hair.

After he left, neither of them spoke for a minute. Then Molly said lightly, "Would ma'am like me to lay out the cream peignoir?" The maid's face was innocent in the mirror.

The cream nightdress was a confection of lace and silk which, although it buttoned to the throat, felt sinfully soft and slippery against the skin. It had formed part of Emily's wedding trousseau. While she loved it, Emily had not worn it for a long time, feeling it an incongruous garment to wear for illness and nightmares. Recalling James' cold comments about the fernery, she shook her head.

Molly made a moue with her mouth, sliding the last ebony comb into Emily's thick locks, then bobbed a curtsy.

The atmosphere at the long table was congenial, but formal and careful. "I expected you would leave London earlier," she said.

"The House was in chaos," James replied, heaving a sigh. "They couldn't agree when we would break for recess, and then Russell was trying to introduce a new Reform Act. When Mr Disraeli pointed out that this would enfranchise more than two hundred thousand new voters, Russell found himself almost alone, poor chap. Many Liberals are opposed to it, believing we would hand the running of the country to half-educated men."

"Half of the labourers building my fernery can neither read nor write, but they reason clearly and intelligently. Would it be such a bad thing?"

"Palmerston is also against the measure," said James. "He believes the proposal excites the working class and is in danger of tipping the balance of power to the unions, who are agitating enough without further incitement."

"Where do you stand on the issue?"

James paused, running his fingers along the stem of his glass. "I am torn," he admitted. "Part of me is terrified of conferring such power on what would be a new class of citizen, unused to our institutions. My father would have been appalled at the idea. The world as he knew it would change irrevocably."

"But surely your father supported progress?" Emily asked gently.

James chuckled. "Only if that progress paid homage to our lineage. Family was the most important thing to him. In his view that required stability, not change."

Emily's heart sank. What would James' father have thought of *her*? And their marriage? Given the disparity between their stations, Henry Cleveland would have disinherited his eldest son; her charming mother-in-law had more or less said that to her before the wedding.

"And what of the other part of you?" she asked.

"That believes all men should have the vote, particularly since I toured the cotton mills in Manchester. Such men I met there, with such excellent qualities! Hardworking, God-fearing, many more honest than gentlemen of my acquaintance."

"But if the Prime Minister opposes it, there is little chance of success, I presume?" Emily's voice was sad.

"It is a slim chance – very slim."

Emily clasped her hands together, chilled. Watson, who was waiting on them, crossed to the fireplace to place another log on the fire. She smiled gratefully at him.

"Tell me," James said, after a long draught of wine, "how have you occupied yourself in my absence?"

"I have made a friend of Lady Chester." Emily heard the defiance in her tone. "And I have begun to paint again. I am documenting the plants I place in the garden."

"She responded to your aunt's letter, did she? A rare handful, that woman. Be careful she does not drag you into schemes that might rebound on the Cleveland name."

"Do credit me with some sense!"

Conversation paused as the plates were cleared.

"Show me your work tomorrow," James said, with a smile, but for once his charm failed. He joined her for tea rather than remaining in the dining room with his solitary port, but no sooner had she poured the tea than Emily stood up.

"I am tired and I am going to retire early. Goodnight."

James looked startled. "But—" His face took on a pleading look. "I'll come and say goodnight in a little while, shall I?" He got to his feet and stroked her cheek. His dark-brown eyes flickered in the firelight and she pressed down the traitorous yearning building in her body.

"Are you not tired after your journey, James? Would it not be best to see you tomorrow?"

He sighed. "You may be right. We shall dine together again tomorrow night?"

They had not shared a bed since the baby. Remembering his silky skin made her weaken, until she remembered that his primary concern was to produce another heir. She stood taller. Was being a brood mare all she was good for? No. She had, as Charlotte said, other talents.

She summoned a smile. "Of course." She gave him a peck on the cheek and went to her cold and suddenly very lonely bed.

Chapter 17

Emily

24 March 1862: Mr Lovell tells me he is tackling the flower borders, but to my mind they still contain too many weeds! I am ungrateful; he and his motley crew help a great deal and I know I should count my blessings.

The following day, Cat's anger had subsided; perhaps she had been too hard on Lauren for giving her number to Stephen. After all, while she'd hinted about the hell she had suffered in the latter part of her relationship, she hadn't gone into detail. Lauren, who was a positive soul, would have put on her rose-coloured glasses and decided that Cat was exaggerating or going through a bad patch. And they had been friends for years, since school.

"Ha!" Cat snorted, blocking Stephen's number again. She dithered over calling Lauren and eventually put the phone down, unsure how to begin the conversation.

The April day was blowy but dry and she walked slowly around the garden, admiring the waving daffodils and vibrant tulips, and delighted at the swathes of colour filling the borders. Until her health failed, Gam had been an avid gardener, forever pottering and planting.

Cat paused by what had been the fernery. The collapse of the garden wall had dislodged the stones that shaped the path through it, hiding it from the rest of the garden.

"Almost like a grotto," she mused, trying to imagine it. Her confidence to follow through on Emily's plans was not high, but with her finances so precarious, she couldn't afford a gardener. She'd have to do it herself. Perhaps she could involve Harry. After all, he'd asked if he could help. In the depths of her subconscious her brain labelled that course of action 'complicated', but she was sorely tempted.

Or she could sort out all her garden problems and follow Lauren's suggestion to pave it and make one big patio. She shook her head. The suggestion was typical of Lauren, a city girl through and through. As far as Cat knew, Lauren didn't even have a houseplant in her sleek London apartment.

Lauren had come a long way from their school days, transforming herself into a voluptuous young woman, and she had, when finally diagnosed, overcome her dyslexia. Cat watched in admiration as Lauren found shortcuts to get round her word blindness. One reason Lauren was so wedded to her phone was that she ran her entire life through it; she used apps to read content aloud to her, she set alarms so that she never missed appointments and even managed business correspondence on her phone. No one speaking to Lauren would ever suspect that she had any difficulties.

But fifteen years ago the teachers had not diagnosed her, and everyone believed Lauren was just slow and stupid. *Lauren* believed she was slow and stupid. To her everlasting shame, Cat had shared this universal view, although she refrained from teasing Lauren, not wishing to be cruel.

But when she walked into the loo one break time and found Lauren in tears, Cat stopped dead. As the sobbing girl tried to hide her face, she passed Lauren a piece of toilet paper to blow her nose, patted her awkwardly on the shoulder and sat with her until the bell for the next lesson. From that day, she set out to deflect and challenge the insults that came Lauren's way. Even today, her mouth tasted sour at the cause of Lauren's misery: a few cruel girls.

Mind you, defending Lauren from taunts had given Cat one of the few lessons from school that she'd never forgotten: being an outsider. It was lonely and thoroughly unpleasant, and it forced them to rely on each other.

Their friendship remained firm even after leaving school. Cat remembered a whirlwind of concerts and festivals where Lauren sized up the security, catering and lighting crews running the events. At the end of one concert, Lauren sidled up to a ticket checker for a chat. The next thing Cat knew, Lauren was a steward for the next huge gig. Now she headed up a division in a multinational events firm.

Cat shook her head. Lauren was a strange mixture – so canny in some ways, so naive in others. She could spot false merchandise and forged tickets from ten paces, but she was still dazzled by Stephen's charming smile.

But who hadn't been dazzled? She shook her head at her own blindness, and when Stephen's gentle cruelty and undermining comments had become impossible to miss, her continued belief that he could change.

"You're weak, Cat," he'd said, as she had asked, almost in tears, to go for a drink with her friends. "You'll get sucked back into your old life with your no-hoper mates and their insignificant ambitions. You deserve more, and I intend to make sure you fulfil your potential. I think it's better you stay in tonight, don't you?"

Lauren had been the only one of her old set of friends to make it into their flat. Cat barely recognised her determined, go-getter friend in the simpering, smiling woman that Lauren became in Stephen's company. Stephen had isolated Cat from her old friends, and she was stranded when she discovered how much money Stephen was spending from their joint account; she could only be grateful that Creighton had suggested she invest some of the royalties from her first book. Stephen didn't know about that money, so she at least had something when she walked out. Her royalties from her early books had decorated Stephen's flat, or bought him expensive designer clothes.

Cat kicked a loose stone in the path. "Never again," she muttered. She never wanted to be in anyone's power like that again. If that meant being single, well, so be it.

Cat refocused on the garden, which seemed to beckon her to stay and walk a while longer in the breeze and forget the past. Cat pulled her cardigan around her more tightly and traced the path again. The peace of the place seemed to soak into her bones, and by the time she'd reached the patio door to the drawing room, she had made some decisions.

She would tackle the fernery, with guidance from Lizzie. She would ask Harry for help. She needed the muscle, and he'd pressed home the point that the police investigation of her stalker made it impossible for him to become involved with her. And that was fine. He needed to be absolutely professional and she— Well, that was fine.

And she'd leave things with Lauren for the moment. She'd send a postcard saying something silly which would make her laugh. Then, most likely, Lauren would pick up the phone and their relationship would be back to normal.

WHEN GEOFF JOHNSON RANG THE DOORBELL HE WAS RED IN THE face. Cat knew this because she was viewing him on her phone from her new doorbell camera. She sighed. She knew what this was about, and when she opened the door, she left the chain on.

"Good afternoon," Geoff said stiffly, straightening the collar on his grubby raincoat and putting his face close to the gap. "I imagine you know why I'm here?"

"Have the police paid you a visit?"

"They have. I'm not at all pleased at the impact that two policemen and a panda car have made on my neighbours!"

"I'm sorry. They wanted to know everyone that I might have a problem with. As you wanted this house, and indeed, insisted that Gam sell it to you, I had to mention you."

"Really? I'll have you know that I have a spotless reputation in this area – or at least I did until your thugs turned up at the door! I'm astonished there aren't other characters from your past who would fall under suspicion, since I'm sure that in your line of work you've met some shady individuals! I see no reason why I, a perfect tenant who never so much as fell behind with the rent, should come to the attention of the police." Geoff was thin-lipped as he wound himself up and clenched his fists. "You have no real feeling for this house, nor will you give it the attention and money it deserves. But *I* would!"

Cat looked at his white knuckles and suppressed a shiver, taking a step back from the door. His pale blue eyes looked wild. She needed to get away...

No! She was in her own house and the police were asking legitimate questions. Shaking, Cat forced herself to remain where she was and took a deep breath.

"First of all, they're not *my* policemen, and if it was PC Davis, he doesn't look in the least thuggish. Secondly, I suspect that after the police had finished talking to you, they told you to stay away from me." His skin mottled even further and Cat put her chin up. "Please do so. I intend to live in this house, and I won't be scared out of my inheritance! And if I do sell Cleveland House, it's extremely unlikely that it will be to you."

"We'll see about that!" he spluttered and hurried away, his brown shoes crunching on the gravel.

CAT DIDN'T NORMALLY TYPE 'THE END' WHEN SHE FINISHED A manuscript. She'd found from the experience of writing all her other books – even the successful one – that when you reached the end of the story the work *really* started.

So usually she didn't celebrate finishing a story. However, this one, finally, was worth reading. She sat back in her chair and breath whooshed out of her lungs as she punched the air.

Cat stood up and stretched. She needed another read through before it went first to Creighton, then the editor at the publishing house. But for now, she closed the laptop with a satisfying click. She would read it next week.

She considered texting Lauren, picked up her phone, and hesitated. The silence from North London had been deafening since she posted the card to Lauren nearly a week ago. Cat wrinkled her nose and put the phone down. Lauren might be globetrotting again. Tension gnawed at her stomach.

A text buzzed and she grabbed her phone, thinking that it might be her best friend hearing her thoughts across the miles. It was Lizzie, asking if she would like to visit the fern nursery. She had attached a scan of some ancient photographs of the fernery before the wall collapsed.

Cat peered at the photos, their colours faded. One was of Lizzie and Gam in front of the fernery, clutching garden hoes. They were both dressed in miniskirts, their arms around each other's waists, and smiling at the camera. Their dazzling happiness from nearly fifty years ago touched her, making her heart ache again with the loss of Gam. She blinked away the tears.

On impulse, Cat punched in Lizzie's number.

"You must be psychic!" Cat smiled. "I've finished for the moment, so I have time to talk ferns! The photos are great, and with the original plans from the journal, I'm sure we can make a start."

"You've finished?"

"Until the editor rips it to bits, anyway. I need another read-through before I send the manuscript over to Creighton for his thoughts, but at the moment my time is my own! When can you come?"

They arranged to meet and, the call over, Cat looked out of the window. The dappled light through the leaves made her smile and contentment spread through her veins. It was ridiculous, but she felt the garden seemed pleased that she had come to the end of the manuscript.

Cat walked through the patio doors. The slowly emerging leaves were soft and fragile, freshly green, cheerful.

"Almost as if it was smiling," Cat murmured. Then she tutted to herself and turned back to the house.

Chapter 18

Breakfast the following day was akin to walking on wet stones: one misstep, and you could be in for a dunking. She peeked at James over her cup as Watson moved around like a large, rotund ghost. Despite retiring early, shadows showed under James' eyes. He shook the paper to remove a crease just as a footman came in and whispered in Watson's ear.

Watson cleared his throat and addressed Emily. "There is a delivery for you, Lady Cleveland. From Ilfracombe."

Emily grabbed a napkin, patted her lips and set down her cup. "That will be my ferns! Thank you, Watson." She threw down the napkin and pushed back her chair.

James looked up, perplexed. "The ferns will wait while you finish your breakfast, Emily."

"Ah, but I won't!"

Emily hurried into the garden, Lucky barking excitedly at her side, thrilled that he was having a run in the garden with his mistress before noon.

Seth handed her a note from Mr Dadd. He was very sorry that he could not complete her order just yet, he wrote, but hoped the interim delivery would give her pleasure. The rest, for reasons completely outside his control, would follow, and she would receive a communication in due course. He was her devoted servant, &c.

"Grovelling little man!" Emily muttered as she crammed the note into her pocket.

The ferns that had arrived were luscious and glossy. Emily stroked their leaves and exclaimed over their beauty. She turned to Seth, who was standing wordless, watching. "Bring the trays over to the fernery, please. Treat them gently: they have had a long journey! And bring the water-sprayer, so that we can revive them. Oh, James! I didn't see you there."

"No, you were too busy being in transports over your ferns," he replied, holding her arms while she regained her balance. He looked her up and down, and she smoothed her thick apron with her gloved hands. "I suppose you're going to plant them?"

"Don't be silly, James. Of course I'm going to plant them! That is the fun part!"

He was silent then. She ignored him and walked down the path. He followed her and, watching his face, she explained what she was hoping to achieve.

"I thought this part of the garden sufficiently sheltered to create a fairy grotto. The walls are high enough to create something like a ravine which one can walk through, making one feel quite enclosed and secret. Anyone standing here" – she pulled him gently to stand beside her – "is invisible to anyone at the house."

"Really?"

Emily all but rolled her eyes. Did he know how like a sulky child he sounded?

"Beggin' your pardon, ma'am, I've put the ferns by the arch," said Seth.

James took a step away. "I'll leave you and your mongrel to your pottering," he said, and strode off.

"*Pottering*, is it?" Emily clenched her fists as she watched his straight, tall figure disappear down the path.

Lucky whined, and she bent to fondle his ears. "No, not you, Lucky! Just another top dog with his nose out of joint."

The planting should have taken about an hour, but the activity was so soothing that Emily lingered in the garden, much to Lucky's delight. The labourers had found an old ball and between planting, Emily played fetch with the mongrel. Thus, it was nearing lunchtime when she finally pulled off her leather gauntlets and put her hands on her hips to survey her work.

Seth touched his hat. "I reckon it looks grand, ma'am."

She beamed at him. "Indeed, although there is more to do! But thank you, Seth."

Her back twinged as she plodded to the house but her spirits were light. Lucky seemed to sense this and trotted happily beside her, his tongue hanging out. She shooed Lucky in before her and laughed as he flopped onto the nearest cushion. "You have no stamina!" she teased.

"You look exhausted," James commented from the armchair, over the top of his *Times*.

She swung round, clutching her throat. "James, you startled me! How long have you been there?"

"Hours. Since I left you knee-deep in mud after breakfast," he replied, folding the newspaper. He looked her up and down; she shifted from foot to foot under his gaze. "Are you too busy to join me for lunch?"

Her eyebrows rose at his tone. But while his voice was cool, his eyes seemed to plead. "I shall change first. Please don't feel obliged to wait."

When she returned to the dining room half an hour later, he was cradling a glass of wine.

"I thought you would have eaten without me," she said, nodding at Watson, who pulled out her chair.

"I've been looking at your painting."

"Oh! You've been in my sitting room?"

"You told me that you had spent some time painting, and I have to say that your industry has been rewarded. It is a splendid likeness."

Emily was alert for mockery in his voice, but there was none. She beamed at him and picked up her soup spoon. After a few moments, she said, "Your admiration of my sketch is gratifying. There is a demand for such illustrations..."

"Really? A demand from where?"

"From journals. For enthusiasts, and scientists." Emily swallowed. "I had thought to send my illustrations – my illustration," she amended swiftly, "to the publisher of this..." She rose, retrieved the journal Charlotte had given her, and handed it to him. She held her breath as he flicked through the pages.

He paused, then smiled kindly at her. "Is your illustration of a standard to be published?" he asked gently. He picked up his cutlery. "I applaud your ambition, but you do not need to do this, Emily. Certainly I would be unhappy if you were selling your efforts. That would not be becoming to the family."

Words tumbled over themselves in her brain. She looked at his firm jaw and for a moment had a vision of her honeymoon, waking up in a Paris hotel and trailing her fingertip down his face. Her cheeks flamed as she recalled her first experience of being loved and loving back. He had been tender, gentle, reassuring.

As quickly as the heat came, ice followed. So much had changed since those heady days of love and discovery, when he had seemed to value her mind and her ambitions as well as her body. A return to them seemed impossible. One of the illustrations was already in London, although the journal could easily reject it – and would, if James was correct. But if the journal did wish to use it, she would remain anonymous. James need never know.

She put down her spoon, her appetite forgotten and her back ramrod-straight. "Very well," she said.

Emily drained her wine glass and rose to her feet. The clock struck and she shook her head, hardly believing that it was only eight o'clock. Had they been sitting at the table for only an hour?

The throbbing at her temples made her feel dizzy. Tea would help.

"I shall be in the drawing room," she said to James, who nodded with a puzzled expression.

The silence had lain between them like a blanket, suffocating her spirit and making her watchful. He had ventured several safe topics at dinner and she had barely responded. She yearned to return to their previous ease, but neither of them seemed capable of reaching the other.

In the drawing room, she settled in her favourite chair by the fire and gazed into the flames. Her husband, a grown man of five-and-thirty, was indulging in a fit of the sulks. Since the conversation about submitting to the journal, he had seemed distant. Twisting her hands in her lap, she wondered if she should write to Charlotte and withdraw her illustration.

The door closed with a click and she jumped. "You startled me!"

"I beg your pardon. I do live here too, you know." He leaned his arm on the mantelpiece, his long fingers toying with a tassel on the mat that ran along the marble.

Emily pulled the bell for tea. The only sound in the room was the crackling of the fire.

"You seem different," he said.

Her eyes darted to his face. "I? No, I am just the same. Rather dull and dreary."

"You are neither of those things. And you are different. You speak your opinions so freely."

Her chin lifted. "I recall you saying in the early days of our marriage how pleased you were that I had an opinion."

One side of his mouth lifted in a smile. "Yes, indeed. It was what drew us together, was it not?"

"But it no longer appeals?" The words came out of stiff lips.

He looked at her, surprised. "What? God, Emily, how your imagination runs away with you!"

A knock at the door heralded Watson, which ended further conversation. Emily took a few sips of the tea she no longer wanted and placed the cup in the saucer.

As soon as he closed the door, James looked at her impatiently. "I love you. I like many things about you. You are my wife." His tone brooked no argument, and the strength left Emily's limbs. She suddenly longed for her bed.

She heaved herself from the sofa. "I am glad I have redeeming qualities, as well as being an invalid."

He threw her an impatient glance. "You are retiring?" She nodded. "I shall call in on you when I finish my tea." Emily's hand trembled a little as she opened the drawing-room door.

She was staring in the dressing-table mirror when he knocked softly and stepped inside her bedroom. He came to stand behind her and placed his big hands on her slender shoulders, squeezing slightly. "You seem very tense."

"I'm tired."

He kissed the side of her neck and her eyes fluttered closed. Breath sighed from her as his fingers trailed along the straps of her evening gown, making her skin rise in goosebumps. He cupped her small breasts through the silk of her gown and drew her to her feet. His dark eyes glowed like embers and the blood thumped in her temples. "Come to bed," he said softly, and she swallowed.

He nipped the side of her mouth before teasing her with small kisses and gathering her close to him. His body pressed against her and the thoughts fell out of her brain like jelly: slippery, hard to grasp. She had an objection, didn't she? Something about being more than a brood mare?

There was a knock at the door. Molly tumbled into the room with Lucky at her heels and stopped short.

"Not now," said James, pleasantly, lifting his head.

Lucky growled and Molly grabbed his collar.

"No! James, I'm sorry, but I'm very tired," Emily protested, wriggling free. Molly hovered uncertainly in the doorway. "Wait outside, please, Molly. I won't be a moment."

The maid left, pulling a reluctant Lucky with her.

James stepped away, his eyes stormy. "You're tired?"

"I— Of course: I planted nearly thirty ferns today!"

James drew in a great breath. He tugged down his waistcoat and his lips tightened. "That is another reason for leaving things to the experts, Emily. Save your strength for offering comfort to your husband."

He strode out of the room and she sank onto a chair as though she were a marionette whose strings had been cut.

EMILY OPENED THE DOOR TO THE STUDY, CLUTCHING THE NOTE from Charlotte. She stopped short as she saw James at the desk, writing a letter of his own. He started and pushed the paper out of sight. "What is it? I am rather busy."

She flinched at the brusqueness of his voice. "I apologise. I shall be in my sitting room." She backed away, then paused. "Are you writing to your mama?"

Their gazes locked. "Yes, I am writing to her about the memorial to Charles and my father."

She nodded. James' brother Charlie had died in the Crimea. Charlie's death was rarely spoken of, but Emily had heard whispers among her female acquaintance that Henry, James' father, had never recovered from the news. James had sworn to take his seat in Parliament and make Charlie proud. His mother spoke of this often, but Emily believed that James' efforts were directed towards the memory of his father, despite their many disagreements.

Now, though, looking at her husband's dark eyes, Emily knew James was lying. Whatever the letter was about, it was not about the memorial.

"Please let me know if there's anything I can do," she responded lightly. Once in her sitting room, she sat in the window seat and opened Charlotte's letter, her stomach fluttering with nerves.

Alexander loves it and will pay you twenty pounds. Happy and eager to offer you further commissions. Please reply by return. I shall call on Thursday if convenient. Affectionately yours, C.

Emily sat back against the window frame with a whoosh of air from her lungs. The painting was sold! And the journal wanted more of her work!

James would be so angry, though. She was expressly disobeying his wishes. Her excitement dissipated like smoke. She should ask Charlotte to withdraw the illustration and forget these ridiculous notions.

The door banged, and through the window she saw James stride onto the gravelled drive. He was carrying a letter.

A shiver ran through her. He had a secret.

Emily went to her writing desk and scribbled a reply to Charlotte.

Delighted. I look forward to continuing our conversation on Thursday.
E.

She glanced at Charlotte's note and tossed it into the fire. She watched it burn until it was blackened and illegible.

Now she had a secret, too.

Chapter 19

Emily

Wednesday 29th March 1862: Lucky is learning new tricks. He can now sit on his haunches and look appealing – or as appealing as a mongrel can. I believe J has taken to Lucky, for all his insults over his lack of breeding and the wiry coat that will shed no matter how much Molly brushes him.

Cat looked rather doubtfully at the pile of earth and broken stones that had been the fernery, and then at the specimens she'd bought with Lizzie. Some were glossy and emerald, while others were delicate and frothy, like pale-green lace. Although the ferns hadn't cost her a fortune – there was a sale on, Lizzie had told her – they were so beautiful that she wanted to ensure they had the best chance of survival. Once again, she looked at the space in the garden and worried that the ferns would not fill it.

Earlier, they'd made a careful list of all the ferns in Emily's original design.

"That's maidenhair fern," Lizzie commented, pointing at the

writing as she scribbled *Adiantum capillus-veneris*. "You're turning into a pteridologist."

"A what?"

"A fern addict. Fern hunting was a craze in Victorian times and Emily was a fan, if this list is anything to go by. I don't recognise all of these, so some of them might be rare," Lizzie mused. "This one, for example, the Forked Spleenwort—"

"It sounds like some dreadful disease!"

"It does rather, doesn't it? I think this is one of the rarest ferns in the country." Lizzie glanced at her. "It might cost a lot of money to buy one, and that's if we can find it."

"Oh."

"Don't fret, dear. We'll find something that looks like it instead."

And they'd headed off to the specialist nursery, Cat buoyed by the conversation and enthused about a new hobby that didn't involve a screen and a keyboard.

Cat rubbed her nose and tried to recapture those feelings of optimism. She estimated Lizzie to be less than one hundred pounds wet through. She wouldn't want to be shovelling earth or heaving stones around.

"Right, where's your tools?" Lizzie asked, proving her wrong.

They worked carefully and slowly for the next hour, clearing rubble and branches from the tree that had crashed through the wall which Charlie and his team had missed.

"I thought your friend Lauren would be here to help," Lizzie said, after a while.

"Lauren works internationally and she's been out of touch for a bit, so I imagine she's away," Cat replied.

"Ah. Shame, we could use an extra pair of hands."

"Lauren's great, but I doubt gardening is one of her talents." Cat grinned. "Harry said he'd help, but he needs a bit of notice. I might ask him to help me build the little bank that's in the plans. See?"

Cat pointed at the plans and Lizzie stepped over a pile of earth to get a closer view. "Oh yes! That will look splendid! Is that where we need to put the two maidenhair ferns?"

"Um... Yes, and then the *osmunda regalis* at the back."

They toiled on until three thirty, when Cat called a halt. "I need tea before my tongue glues itself to the roof of my mouth," she declared. "Same?"

Lizzie nodded and walked back to the house with her. The weather was warm for early April and Cat dragged a couple of kitchen chairs and a folding table out to the patio. "Sit down, you look exhausted," she said to Lizzie, who smiled, but sank gratefully onto the chair.

Cat quickly made tea, cut a couple of slices of fruit cake and headed out with the tray to find Lizzie gazing at the garden, shading her eyes from the sun slanting through the trees. She glimpsed traces of tears on Lizzie's cheeks and fiddled with the mugs and teapot, giving her time to recover. As Gam's closest friend, Lizzie would miss her too.

Without a word, she placed the tea in front of Lizzie and sat down. Eventually, Lizzie sighed and picked up her tea. The air was still and Cat felt peace sink into her weary bones. "I reckon we should clear a little more of the path and then call it a day," she said.

Lizzie reached across and patted her hand. "May would have been so happy at the work you're doing," she said, her voice sounding rusty. "She loved this garden, and the fernery in particular."

Not able to trust her voice, Cat nodded and grabbed a slice of cake. After forcing down a bite, Cat managed, "I hope so."

"Definitely, my dear." Lizzie's voice grew a little stronger, and Cat nodded again.

"Shall we finish off?" she croaked. Lizzie gave her a smile of such sweetness that Cat's throat tightened again, and she leapt to her feet to clear the mugs.

It only took ten minutes to plant two more ferns and move the rest to the shelter of the garden wall. Cat, finally in control of herself, turned to Lizzie. "Thanks so much for your help. I'll talk to Harry and call you to see if you're available to help again, but don't feel obliged."

"I'll be available," Lizzie said, stripping off her gloves. "I do enjoy spending and planting other people's money!"

Cat laughed and waved her goodbye.

Later that night, Cat groaned as she crept into her bed, muscles complaining at the unaccustomed exercise. Lizzie could give her forty years – how did she feel? She made a note to call her in the morning, then yawned widely.

She didn't recall turning off the light.

A WOMAN CAT DIDN'T RECOGNISE, WITH LUSTROUS DARK HAIR pinned on top of her head, walked towards her. Her eyes were dull. She came out of the sunlight, and the rays seemed to dance around her. She wore a white pin-tucked blouse with a frill at the high neck. She was carrying a book, and Cat recognised it as the journal that lay on her dining table. As Cat watched, the woman drew out a heavy chair to sit at a wooden writing table that shone with polish. The chair ruckled the ornate rug which glowed in blues, greens, and gold.

The woman sat down, opened the journal, dipped a pen in the ink bottle and paused, staring blindly at the wall. Her knuckles were white as she gripped the pen and she gave a shuddering gasp as she wrote. Then the tears came. They flowed down her cheeks and dripped from her nose to the paper, blotting it and obscuring the words she had written. Impatiently, she searched for a handkerchief and wiped her eyes, but still the tears came, her breath tearing at her throat. Eventually the woman threw the pen aside, put her head on her arm and sobbed as though her heart would break.

It was a dream, Cat knew, created from her imagination and the contents of the journal. The woman was Emily. Cat longed to comfort her but feared the grief Emily bore might never heal.

Emily disappeared as though covered by water, sinking deeper and deeper into the distance, and Cat was now standing in the garden at

Cleveland House. As Cat looked around, she saw a white metal structure like a pagoda, with a love seat in the centre. Emily was seated with a bearded, handsome man. He laughed, and the rich, full noise seemed to come straight from his belly. Shyly, Emily put her hand into his. Their heads moved closer and they kissed. Was this James? Contentment washed through Cat and she relaxed, feeling her own tears drying on her cheeks.

Emily turned and seemed to look straight at Cat. Nervously, Cat smiled and Emily smiled gravely back at her. "Be brave. *You* are all you need to succeed," she said in a low, musical voice. Cat nodded, and the scene disappeared.

CAT OPENED HER EYES JUST BEFORE THE ALARM, A WARM SENSE of contentment in her bones. She remembered her dream and lay still, trying to recall the details. She felt very well rested and refreshed in a way that didn't happen often. With a smile, she stretched.

"Ouch!" Pain shot through her arms as her muscles reminded her of the four hours she had worked in the garden the previous day. Mentally, she might be on top form, but physically she was a wreck. There might be a solution to that, though. She got up gingerly and slipped on her robe, then headed to her bathroom and the wonderfully deep, luxurious roll-top bath.

She perched on the edge and turned on the taps. Soon, steam clouded the mirror and the windows. Water swirled into the white porcelain and on impulse Cat added a generous dash of bubble bath.

Jeez, if this is how I feel, I wonder how Lizzie is? She walked back to the bedroom and texted Lizzie.

Moments later, a response flashed onto her screen.

—Are you stiff? Sorry to hear that. I've just come back from my morning swim. Check the ferns to make sure they don't dry out. I recommend aspirin for the muscles.

Cat rolled her eyes and returned to the bathroom, calculating the difference in their ages. "What a wuss you are, Cat Kennedy! Ohhhh..." Her muscles unclenched as she sank into the tub. She shut her eyes and relaxed, luxuriating in the bubbles in a way not possible in a shower. Her brain sorted through everything that had happened over the past month.

When she raised her eyes to the bright light that bounced off the chunky taps and tiles, she was resolute. The letter and the texts were scary, but they were meant to frighten her. She was made of sterner stuff than that.

What had Emily said to her in the dream? *You are all you need to succeed.*

Cat stood up and reached for a towel. She wrapped it firmly under her arms, welcoming its rough touch. She stared at her face in the mirror, her dark hair mussed and damp at the ends, but her eyes clear and bright.

The book was finished, and it was good. Actually, more than good; it might be the best thing she'd ever written. She'd started work on the fernery. She'd put locks on her front door that would defend a castle. And if she needed a friend in a hurry, she had Harry.

Harry in a hurry. A giggle escaped her as she recalled the wedding of one of Harry's cousins. In that interminable time that photographers take between the ceremony and the wedding break-fast, he'd grabbed her hand. She'd been wearing a wrap-around dress...

She turned from watching the photographer, who was trying to get the toddlers to look at him. "Is everything okay?"

"Not really. Come with me," Harry had said, and pulled her into an empty room.

She'd stared at him. "What's up?"

"I haven't kissed you in over an hour," Harry said solemnly. "And this dress is driving me wild."

Cat knew that tone. Her throat went dry. Her heart missed a beat, and she felt a persistent throb between her legs.

"So if you wouldn't mind stepping into this closet," Harry continued, opening a door and steering her in.

She laughed softly. "So, a kiss, you said?" She peered through the gloom at shelves covered with odd bits of crockery and table covers.

"That will do for starters."

His lips found hers and, pulling her towards him, his hardness pressed against her stomach.

"What happens to an off-duty police officer who's found *in flagrante?*" Cat enquired, as she brushed her hand over his trousers. His breath caught in a satisfying way and she calculated how long it would take for them to have sex and tidy themselves up before guests started filing in.

"No idea. And right now, I don't care. Oh my God, you're wearing stockings!" His hand ran up her leg, paused at the touch of bare flesh, then his fingers brushed her damp knickers. It was her turn to gasp.

The phone rang and Cat jumped, hot and bothered. She swore softly as she searched for the phone. "H-hello?"

"Cat? It's Harry."

"Um, hi."

"Are you okay? You sound weird." Cat could hear the frown in his voice, and felt the flush rise over her chest and neck.

She pulled the towel tighter and gathered her scattered thoughts. "Yes, I'm fine."

"You texted about the fernery?"

"Um, yes, were you serious about helping?" Cat tried to block out the past ten minutes. "We've started, but there's loads more to do."

Harry didn't reply at once. Cat imagined the bigger stones she wanted to rearrange to make a pathway through the ferns and build up walls. She couldn't ask Lizzie to help with that.

"Sure. Let me know when."

She sagged with relief. "That would be brilliant. I'll check with Lizzie, too."

She'd just have to keep her reminiscing to a minimum.

Chapter 20

Charlotte was examining the newly planted ferns from Dadd's. She leaned in to view the delicate lines of the feathery leaf in the dappled sunshine. "It's such a beautiful specimen," she murmured, and Emily smiled at her lover-like tone. The specimen in question was an *osmunda regalis,* the latest addition to the garden, its huge bright-green fronds uncurling and quivering in the spring breeze.

"It will turn bronze in the autumn, you know," Charlotte added, straightening up.

"Yes. The water will reflect the leaves as it grows." Emily indicated the nearby pond. "It will appear to such advantage!"

"Sublime."

James poked his head out of the window, clearly searching for them, and cursed as Lucky rushed past him.

"I fear our peace is at an end," said Emily. "Here's Lucky – and possibly my husband."

"What? Oh dear, he looks rather grim. Was he always so?"

"Oh, no! We have had many happy times, but..." She paused. "He was so disappointed about the baby ... and of course he is busy at the House."

"He was not the only one to suffer!" Charlotte sounded indignant. "Have you told him the news about the journal?"

"Please do not mention the illustration! I am in his bad books and speaking of the journal will make things worse. Please, Charlotte, promise me!" Emily said under her breath.

Charlotte's eyebrows shot up, but she nodded, and a social smile lifted her lips as James approached.

Lucky trotted up, his tongue hanging out, and Emily made a fuss of him. After James had scanned the borders, he inclined his head to Charlotte.

"Sir James, your wife has done a sterling job on the fernery, do you not think?" asked Charlotte. "It looks splendid, and it is still in its infancy!"

James looked unconvinced and stooped to pat Lucky before he replied. "Sadly, I do not share the nation's enthusiasm for ferns. The garden looks nice enough, although I am no judge."

Emily felt the heat rise up her neck and face at his assessment and bowed her head while she took refuge in patting Lucky. She blinked hard to clear the water from her eyes.

"Indeed, so few people *are* excellent judges, I find," Charlotte replied. When Emily straightened up, Charlotte's eyes were narrowed and glittering.

James' chin rose and Emily hastily intervened. "Come, Charlotte, I must go indoors, otherwise I shall be one big freckle!"

"You spend too much time out here," said James.

"This air is much more beneficial for Lady Emily's constitution than the smog and filth of London, though," Charlotte declared. "She is in looks since she arrived, and her stamina is much improved." Emily tugged at Charlotte's arm, but she did not move.

James stared at her. "As my wife expends all her energy in the garden, leaving none for her husband, you will understand my lack of enthusiasm."

"I confess that I am a little tired. I would dearly love a cup of tea!" pleaded Emily, and Charlotte finally turned with her towards the house.

As they walked, Lucky disappeared into the glasshouse which leaned against the south-facing wall of the garden. Emily called him, but he did not appear. With a sigh, she approached the glasshouse.

Seth, who was digging over one of the beds, raised his head at her calls, then dropped his spade and leapt over the path. "Beggin' your pardon, ma'am," he wheezed as he strode into the glasshouse with more speed than she'd witnessed from him before.

Lucky was sniffing at some apples strewn across the soil. Seth reached out a large hand and grabbed Lucky by the scruff of his neck, and he whimpered.

Emily gasped. "Mr Lovell! What is the meaning of this?"

"Poison." Pulling a rag from his pocket, Seth wiped a fine dusting of powder from Lucky's muzzle.

"Poison?" Shocked, Emily gazed at the apples on the ground.

"Aye, arsenic. For the rats." He gestured to a red tin on the shelf at the end of the glasshouse.

Emily's mouth moved, but no words came. Had Lucky licked anything? Would he die? Oh, she should have kept him closer!

"What's going on?" James' shadow fell across the door of the glasshouse. "Good God, Emily, what's the matter?" he said as he saw her face.

"I— Lucky has been poisoned!" she cried.

In one step, James took Lucky in his arms and examined him closely.

"I wiped off what I could," Seth said, twisting his hands.

"Well done, Mr Lovell, I can see you have cleaned off most of the powder." Lucky raised uncertain eyes to James' face and his lips turned up at the corners. "Yes, yes, I know. It's all very frightening, isn't it? A bath is in order for you, my boy."

"A bath! What is the purpose of that?" Emily tried to keep her voice calm. Charlotte appeared by her elbow.

"To clean off any powder on his fur so that he won't lick it," James replied.

"And if he has already eaten some?" Emily's voice wobbled.

"We will need to force salt water down him to make him sick," Charlotte said, and James and Seth nodded agreement. With James' hand holding Lucky's muzzle shut so that he could not lick anything, they hurried into the house.

THE AFTERNOON DRAGGED ON. LUCKY WHIMPERED AND SHOOK, and the stench of his vomit was almost unbearable.

James kept a firm hold on the puppy, whose frantic efforts to get free grew weaker with every chime of the clock while Charlotte held open his jaws and Emily poured salt water into his mouth. Charlotte closed his jaws and rubbed his throat, murmuring to him that he was a good boy and this would be over soon.

When Charlotte suggested that Lucky was vomiting nothing more than water and they could do no more, Emily stroked Lucky's ears. "I'm so sorry, sweetheart. We need to give you a bath, and then we will let you sleep." She beckoned to Molly, who was standing, distressed, in the corner of the room. "Molly, he doesn't understand why people who love him are doing such dreadful things to him. I hope he will let you bath him."

James' head shot up at her words.

"James?" Emily said, uncertainly. "A bath will remove the rest of the poison, will it not?"

He seemed to rouse himself and nodded.

Emily turned back to Molly, "Take care you do not get the arsenic on your skin."

Molly, still crying, wrapped the limp puppy in her apron and left the room.

"We should clean ourselves," Charlotte said after the door closed.

In agreement, they moved to the scullery to scrub their hands and faces, throwing the kitchen into disarray as pots and pans were cleared to allow them access to the sink. Then silence fell; they were exhausted.

Charlotte, exclaiming at Emily's pallor, led her to the drawing room and made her sit down. James seated himself beside Emily and took her hands. "Lord, Emily, your hands are like ice! Lady Chester, would you oblige me by ringing for tea?" He squeezed Emily's fingers gently. "Emily, Lucky is well-named. I would bet a large sum of money that he will be perfectly well."

The lines of his face had become less severe, and she raised a hand to his cheek. He turned his lips to her palm, and she shivered as a response shot through her. He smiled and kissed her forehead. "Tea will warm you up. Try not to worry, Emily. I shall look in on Lucky this evening."

She nodded, conscious of Charlotte's sharp gaze. With a shrewd glance at Emily, Charlotte excused herself.

As soon as the door closed, James drew Emily into an embrace. "My darling, you've had a nasty shock. Shall I ask Lady Chester to leave?" he murmured into her hair.

She snuggled into his shoulder. "No, thank you. Charlotte is a true friend: none of my London acquaintance would have stayed all afternoon to help save a puppy. Tea will revive me, I am sure."

James smiled wryly. "Indeed. Unlike me, you have not been mistaken in Lady Chester's character. Neither she nor you flinched from the unpleasantness, and I am proud of you."

Exhausted though she was, Emily glowed at his praise and kissed his cheek. He gazed at her and pressed her closer to him. Her lips parted and for the first time that afternoon, she relaxed as his kiss, warm and gentle, filled her whole world. When it ended at last, his eyes searched her face. "Now you have more colour in your cheeks," he teased, and she laughed softly. "Tea would restore you even more, though. Where is it, I wonder?"

On cue, there was a knock at the door and Watson entered with a tea trolley, decanter and glasses. "Lady Chester said that my lady had suffered a shock, so I took the liberty of bringing the brandy."

"Oh, thank you! How thoughtful!" Emily smiled at the butler.

Charlotte re-entered the room. James greeted her more warmly than he had earlier, and the conversation flowed easily. Charlotte and James talked about the debate currently raging in Parliament on the extension of suffrage, and Emily looked on in surprise. Unlike the carefully negotiated discussions along well-charted topics which Emily had observed in her London calls, their talk was honest yet respectful. It was as if someone had ripped away a curtain and they had all remembered what was important, she mused as she sipped her tea.

"Lady Emily, what do you think of the suffrage debate?" Charlotte asked suddenly.

Emily frowned as she formulated her response. "We educate many more ordinary people than used to be the case. They are men and women of steady habits and character, who serve our leaders, which enables them to lead us."

She glanced at James, who was staring at her intently. "I know there is trepidation, but I am convinced that the measure will promote the happiness and prosperity of those who should have a voice in things that concern them. So, yes, I think suffrage should be extended."

"To women, too?" James' dark eyes were fixed on her.

She put her head on one side. "I had strong views on this when we met, and they haven't changed," she replied. "The debate currently only addresses half our population. Men guide the nation, it's true, but they do not do so alone. They are supported by an army of others: not only their secretaries and colleagues, but wives and mothers who are significant figures in their lives. As the fairer sex, we may not make big decisions in our current position, but we are rational creatures when you include us in debates – as you do now – and we could contribute enormously."

"Bravo!" Charlotte beamed at her, but Emily focused on her husband's face, which was grave and thoughtful.

He smiled. "Yes. Your argument is well made."

Emily smiled back, feeling as though she had returned to the time when she was first married, and the discussion moved on.

Eventually Charlotte took her leave, pressing her hand as she did so. Afterwards, James and Emily checked Lucky and then sat by the fire. He read the *Times*, and she returned to her novel, speaking occasionally. As long as Lucky suffered no ill-effects, Emily thought cautiously that she might count herself happy. Then worry about Lucky and the business of the illustration returned to her, and she chewed her lip.

James raised an eyebrow and reached for her hand. "I checked not half an hour ago, and Lucky was still sleeping soundly. He has had no convulsions. As I said, I think he will live up to his name. Are you sure he is not a cat with nine lives?"

She smiled, but her stomach churned as she remembered her deception. Still, as an anonymous contributor, she could keep her misdeeds from James. After she had delivered the next illustration, she would paint no more. Her mind was made up.

LUCKY AWOKE LATER THAT EVENING AND TO THE RELIEF OF ALL, appeared to have cheated death. Mrs O'Donnell fed him tidbits of poached chicken and salmon and Molly found a soft blanket for his bed. His tail wagged weakly.

Emily felt her heart swell with joy as she chucked him under the chin, but she refrained from too much fussing. Lucky was still unsteady on his legs and additional rest would be more conducive to his recovery. James had warned her that the ill-effects of the poison might show themselves at a later date: they would just have to hope and be patient.

Emily's throat was tight as she walked downstairs. As they reached the drawing room, James held the door open for her and examined her closely. "You have a little more colour, but please oblige me by reducing your activity over the next two days. You are still delicate."

"I am much stronger than I was!" she protested. An awkward silence fell as she remembered his previous coldness towards her. "James, do you object so strongly to my work in the fernery?"

He sat on the sofa, flicking his coat-tails out as he did so. "Well... I suppose not. I am still concerned that you are over-exerting yourself, but you are obviously happy."

"Oh, it gives me such joy!"

He regarded her quizzically. "That much is clear. I never thought to see you so animated over a plant."

Something in his voice made her glance at him. Heavens, was he jealous of the garden? She reordered her thoughts as she sat down next to him. "I know I must not overstretch myself," she said, pressing his arm. "Your advice is sensible. Perhaps we could go for a drive together tomorrow? We are always saying that we should make more use of the barouche."

James kissed her. "Capital idea! I shall speak to Watson before dinner."

Chapter 21

Emily

   3rd April 1862: I crave connection with others who share my hopes and interests and for something to make me feel of use! The fernery gives me purpose as well as conversation and seems to make the world a less lonely place.

C at cleared her supper dishes from the table. The gloom was settling outside and Cat, who loved the sun, yearned for long summer days. She took the dishes to the kitchen and stood with her hands in the hot soapy water, staring out at the darkened garden. Frustration nagged at her; she knew she should get on with the garden so that the plants had time to bed in, but her funds were so low.

She shivered as she saw her reflection in the window. The dusk seemed threatening, and she stacked the dishes as quickly as she could.

She sank onto the sofa in the drawing room and reached for Emily's journal. She turned the delicate pages and read a few entries, making sense of the initials and the curling pen strokes.

Getting a picture of Emily from the journal was like doing a jigsaw without a photo on the box. As Cat read, she smiled at some of the phrases. There was a reverend who was 'as neat as a pin' and a colonel with 'a moustache like a broom head'.

As Cat counted the people Emily wrote about, she concluded that the previous mistress of Cleveland House hadn't had many friends. The name Charlotte appeared several times in the later pages of the diary. "Not sure where *you* came from," muttered Cat. Charlotte seemed to be a regular visitor and eventually she connected the letter 'C' in the journal with her. 'J', Cat thought, was Emily's husband.

Then she came across an entry that read:

I feel as though I have been abandoned on a strange island, much as Mr Defoe imagined. Lost, barely surviving, and despite the many servants running the house, so, so alone.

Cat's eyebrows rose. Life was not all roses for Emily. She read on.

I intend to recuperate as best I can alone, and set myself the task of being the wife James expects.

After a moment she closed the journal and shifted uncomfortably on the sofa. Here was a suffering woman, lonely in a mass of people. A mother who had lost her baby, yet was determined to conquer her situation. She, Cat, had this splendid roof over her head and friends who cared about her. What did she have to whine about? Okay, she had a psycho pestering her and no money, but *really?*

Perhaps she should borrow some of Emily's resolution.

"Time to pull on the big girl pants," she said to the house.

CAT WRINKLED HER NOSE AT THE POTS OF FERNS STANDING patiently by the shed. With Lizzie she'd sorted through the soil, taking out the smaller rubble. Now it was time to tackle the larger pieces:

those stones and boulders that were still whole. She'd been in the garden since just before eight – a minor miracle for her – and had managed to break most of her fingernails in the hour that followed. She was filthy, and her shoulders ached. But to her astonishment, she was having a wonderful time.

She reached for the photocopied plan of the fernery and peered at Emily's copperplate handwriting. Her gaze darted to the garden, then back to the plan. Hang on, the path went *that* way... She rotated the paper again. The plan and the ground in front of her clicked together and she saw the design. "Ohhh! Now I get it!"

The plan showed a boulder and then a raised wall, which was currently missing. Cat took the biro from her ponytail and scribbled a note, then tapped the pen against her teeth as she considered the pile of enormous stones delivered by the garden centre the previous day. It was astonishing how much rocks cost and she'd hesitated, given her finances, but she was due a royalty cheque soon which would improve her cash flow. She looked again at the massive boulders, pushing the pen back into her hair. "That one would go there..." she mused.

Her phone rang. "Anyone home?" Lizzie asked.

"Coming!" Cat sprinted through the house to find Lizzie and Harry standing at the front door. "Oh my God, you're on time!" she cried.

"Not everyone is habitually late, you know," Harry said mildly, and she grinned at him.

In the garden, Cat spread out the plan on a chair and they clustered round it. "I'm trying to rebuild this path," she explained. "Then we can put ferns on the top and in the cracks between the rocks. That leaves these enormous things to be pulled into place," she added, waving a hand at the boulders.

Harry's eyes narrowed and he pursed his lips. "We'll need a plan to shift these, unless you want a hernia."

"What, you can't move them alone? I don't know what the police force is coming to," Cat teased.

Harry ignored her and disappeared, returning ten minutes later with a pickaxe and half a dozen round posts, each about four feet long.

Lizzie frowned for a moment, then her brow cleared. "Ah, of course! You've been to the pyramids, haven't you?"

He winked at her while Cat looked on, mystified. "We'll use the pickaxe to lift one end of the rock and slide the posts underneath," he explained. "Then we can roll the rock using the posts as wheels, instead of lifting it. We've got more chance of lifting the smaller ones."

"Brilliant!" Cat smiled.

"Shall we see if it works?"

It was back-breaking work, even with the posts. At the end of an hour, Cat remembered how she'd felt when she'd once run a marathon. Harry stripped off his jacket and sweatshirt and the T-shirt he was wearing grew damp with perspiration. His scent tickled Cat's nose as they heaved the smaller rocks into place. She was close enough to feel the heat of him on her arms as they gripped the stones together.

Finally, they were done. "The cement should set in a couple of hours, but don't put any ferns in until at least tomorrow," Harry said, wiping the back of his neck and his forehead with a huge handkerchief.

"No fear!" said Cat, collapsing on the lawn. "I'm done for today. It's possible I'm done for the entire month!"

"Then have a drink and relax," said Lizzie, walking up with a tray.

"Lifesaver," sighed Harry, grabbing a mug of tea.

They drank in silence, and Cat, looking at her new wall, did a little jiggle of joy. "I know it isn't finished, but I can't thank you enough."

"You need more compost," Lizzie observed.

Cat nodded. "I'll get some next week. But can I offer you pizza tomorrow as a thank you for all your work today?" No one spoke. "It's not much, I know, but..."

"That would be lovely," said Lizzie firmly. Harry nodded, a strange smile on his face.

HARRY SHOOK HIS HEAD AS SHE OFFERED THE PLATE TO HIM. "I won't be able to move if I have another slice."

Lizzie leaned over and snaffled the last piece of pizza. "I, on the other hand, can quite happily manage that."

Cat laughed as petite Lizzie made short work of the pizza. She topped up Lizzie's glass and waved the bottle at Harry. He shook his head. "Shall I help you clear up?"

"No, make yourself comfortable. I'll brew some coffee."

As she stacked the dishwasher and broke up the pizza boxes, Cat hummed. It had been a good night.

"I'm no faint heart, but I'm not sure I could do what you do," Lizzie was saying as Cat returned with a laden tray.

Harry laughed. "We're well trained. Most of us just want to make a difference."

Something in the way he said the words intrigued Cat. "And are you?" she asked, passing him a mug. "Making a difference, I mean?"

His lips tightened and he shrugged. "I'm doing what I can, although I could do more in a higher rank. You get more influence the more senior you are."

"So are you going for Detective Chief Inspector? That's the next rank up, isn't it?" Cat marshalled her scant knowledge of policing.

"Yeah, well remembered," he said, and sipped his coffee.

"You're trying for a promotion?" Lizzie asked, looking at them over the rim of her mug.

"In a week or so. Although if I get through, I'm not sure of the next step. There aren't any vacant Chief Inspector positions at the moment in Cambridgeshire."

"So they'll keep you hanging around until there's a job?" Cat frowned. "You're not the most patient person, Harry."

He grinned. "Not ideal, I grant you, but it often happens. I'll be waiting until someone retires or moves on. Or I'll have to."

"What, move on?" Lizzie asked.

He nodded. "I'd rather not move forces, though. I moved here because I like the area and I want to put down some proper roots."

Cat was silent. While he didn't seem miserable, Harry wasn't properly happy. He was missing ... what was it? She gazed at the handsome man in front of her.

Sparkle. He seemed as though someone had turned him into a black-and-white version of himself. He glanced at her and she hurriedly looked away.

"But I'm getting ahead of myself. I have to pass the Board first," he said easily.

"I'm sure you'll do well," Lizzie said. "Let us know what happens, won't you?"

He grinned at her. "Are you looking for friends in high places?"

She laughed, and began to tell a story of a trip to Italy where Gam had begun a conversation with a man on the plane. "He seemed a very ordinary little man," she said, her eyes gleaming in the lamplight. "But he seemed quite taken with May and me. We said goodbye while we were picking up our luggage and thought that was that. But when we were driving out of Naples, a lorry clipped our back fender."

She shook her head, remembering. "It was a complete disaster. The driver stopped his lorry in the middle of the road and began to harangue us. I speak Italian, but he gabbled so fast that I couldn't keep up. The traffic was building up and everyone sounded their horns – oh my, the *noise!* May was beginning to lose her temper..."

"Oh jeez..."

"Well, yes." Lizzie threw Cat a rueful glance. "Things were coming to a head. The lorry driver was steaming with rage and May was about to blow a fuse when a policeman arrived. He strode up to the lorry driver and let out a stream of Italian abuse. My dear, they were practically nose to nose! Then the lorry driver went pink and turned to us with an apology! I never did work out what the policeman said – I thought I heard the word 'royalty', but I could have been wrong. We were so relieved to get it all sorted out, and move the car. It was only when I climbed behind the wheel that I realised how familiar the policeman looked. He was the man we'd chatted to on the plane! He winked at me and I invited him for a drink that evening. It's amazing what uniform can do for a man!"

Harry chuckled. "Did he join you?"

"No, he told us he was on duty." Lizzie sighed. "That was a wonderful holiday."

"You and Gam were always going somewhere," Cat said.

Lizzie smiled. "We enjoyed each other's company."

"You were never tempted to marry?" Harry asked curiously.

"No. I never found a man I liked enough."

"Well, it's good he didn't chat you up on duty – that would have been *very* unprofessional!" Cat joked. "Not like Harry here."

Harry shot her a glance and put his head on one side. As he'd talked about the promotion she had seen his hesitation. She wanted to encourage him – but felt awkward. He'd made it perfectly clear that he couldn't get involved with her because of the case, and probably wouldn't welcome it.

Perhaps it was time to wrap the evening up. She stretched to put her mug on the tray and winced. "God, I feel like I've been run over by a truck!"

"Yes, I'm feeling weary," Lizzie admitted, getting carefully to her feet. "I'll talk to you later in the week."

Harry saw Lizzie to the door, then turned to Cat and gave her a hug. "Nice evening," he said, and left, leaving her with her mouth open and her heart skipping.

Chapter 22

The room was quiet. A recovering Lucky was curled up by her feet, and Emily was so engrossed in her book that she didn't notice James enter her sitting room. She jumped as he sat down, smiling. "I beg your pardon!" she said, hastily closing the pages of Mr Thomas Moore's *History of British Ferns*.

James chuckled, holding out his hand for the book. "Am I being cuckolded by a fern?"

"That," said Emily, passing him the book, "is the silliest thing I have heard you say."

James flicked through the pages and put his head on one side. "The illustrations are not very good, are they?"

Emily froze. Stay calm, she told herself.

"The book contains some very useful information," she said, studying her fingernails. "I use it to gather advice on my growing mediums and where in the garden to place the ferns."

"Your sketch bears comparison with some of these. Where is it? I thought I saw another picture, but it is not on your easel now." He waved a hand at her empty easel.

"Charlotte was so taken with it that I gave it to her. Shall we have tea?" She jumped up to pull the bell.

He shook his head. "Watson is laying up for lunch. Actually, I wanted to talk to you about something."

"Oh?"

"No need to worry. You look as if I'm about to accuse you of something!" James scratched a still-dozing Lucky on the head. "The fernery is almost complete, is it not?"

She nodded, feeling her heart thump against her ribs.

"I thought Mama might enjoy looking at it. I plan to ask her to come and stay for a few days, if you have no objection?"

Her breath came out in a rush. "Oh! Yes, of course!" He kissed her cheek lightly and offered his arm to take her to the dining room.

Her sense of relief that her illustration was still a secret was so strong that the objections she had to Sophia Cleveland visiting them did not surface until she sat down to lunch. They nagged at her, intruding into an otherwise lively conversation with her husband.

She was proud of her work in the fernery, an achievement built quietly, piece by piece. She did not need her mother-in-law coming in like a battering ram to flatten it.

But perhaps she had misjudged Mrs Cleveland? Perhaps James' mother would admire the alterations she had made to the gardens and be pleased with her new interest, which was helping her spirits and her physical recovery?

As Evans removed her plate, she asked James, "Do you really think your mama will like the fernery?"

James' eyebrows rose. "Of course! You have, as Lady Chester said, created an excellent fernery. I admit that until we spoke further of it, I had little notion of the cunning design you have built."

"In that case, I'll be happy to explain it to her."

"I shall write this afternoon."

"Will you receive visitors today?"

He shook his head, sighing. "Regretfully, no. I have a speech to write."

169

Emily laughed. "You look as though you were going to have a tooth drawn! Is it so awful?"

He threw down his napkin, pushing his chair back. "It is. I am treading a perilous path on a delicate subject."

She looked at him quizzically. "Too delicate for my ears?"

"I fear it may be."

"Sir, I count myself a robust creature in matters of the intellect, even if my body is less strong. I am all ears."

"Let us go into the drawing room."

Emily took a seat in the drawing room, full of curiosity. James paced the room. "Well?" Emily said.

James stopped and faced her, rocking on the balls of his feet. "This is not for the ears of a lady."

"Oh, for goodness' sake! Have we not talked of everything?"

"Very well." He paused for a good minute and she steeled herself to remain still. "As you know, we maintain a great body of men who protect the Empire." He paused, and she nodded. "My committee has received information that out of almost ninety-eight thousand soldiers, nearly fourteen thousand have been admitted to hospital with venereal disease."

Emily's eyes widened in shock – at the baldness of the comment, the topic and the numbers. Looking past her, James continued. "As you can imagine, there is great concern in the military that so many men are contracting this disease. To increase the efficiency of the armed forces, we need to decrease the cost of treating it."

"The men catch the disease from common women ... prostitutes?" Emily rolled the word around in her mouth before speaking.

James stared at her, then inclined his head, a flush on his cheeks. "Men are subject to strong urges," he said. "The committee is considering a recommendation that alongside the usual edicts against prostitutes, there should be additional measures to contain the disease, particularly in garrison towns."

"What are the proposed measures?"

James sighed. "That policemen can arrest prostitutes within a certain radius of the town and bring them in for compulsory checks."

Emily narrowed her eyes. "Compulsory? And the men?"

"The men are subject to no such regulation."

For a moment Emily was quiet as she thought this through. She lifted her eyes, puzzled. "But might not the men also spread the disease?"

The glance James gave her was complex: it mingled relief, surprise, and respect. He sat beside her in one swift movement. "Exactly! I know we are dealing with women of the worst sort, but the soldiers they consort with may also carry the disease that beleaguers our army and endangers the safety and stability of the country!"

"Tell me what you must do with your speech, James," Emily said carefully. She was trying not to think of the potential implications for those women whom the newspapers decried and the clergy despised. She wondered what a compulsory examination might entail and shrank from the images that came into her mind.

"I need to show that while the situation demands bold action, introducing such legislation implies that prostitution is a necessary evil. Thus the women become merely instrumental."

"Ah... and the counter-argument is that *because* they are prostitutes, and already fallen, these women need less protection than soldiers." Her voice was quiet.

James laughed. "How quickly you grasp my problem!"

Emily shook her head, remembering the women she had glimpsed on her return from the opera or the ballet in London: sharp-faced, desperate girls, thin from lack of nourishment, at the mercy of the bitter weather and the constable. How had they fallen so low? They were women, as she was. "How do women fall like that?" she asked.

"It is easily done, if the chaplain at the House is to be believed." James leaned back and gazed into the distance. "Many consider them vicious, born from birth to the trade, but there are many pathways to such debasement. A disagreement at home, a brutal husband, so many mouths to feed that honest work is inadequate... There are many reasons. I want to suggest other solutions – educating the men in harmless and improving recreations, thus creating a greater sense of self-control. Even providing women guaranteed free of disease would be better than a law that takes a shared enterprise and blames one half."

"It warms me to know you care so much for laws that apply equally to males and females," Emily said softly.

"Are you surprised? My father held himself to be a model of fairness, and I hold myself to his standards." James drew himself up.

In the discussions which Emily had had during her engagement, nothing Mrs Cleveland had said about James' father had made her consider him an advocate of women. She patted his arm. "Of course. I see what a bind you are in, trying to protect the women compelled to bear the brunt of the enforcement. Perhaps you could consider it a constitutional matter?"

He looked at her and stroked his beard. "By Jove, Emily, you may have something there."

To her delight, he kissed the tip of her nose and left her.

EMILY'S STOMACH FLUTTERED AT THE SOFT KNOCK ON THE DOOR. Molly paused, hairbrush in the air.

"Come in!" Emily called. "You may go," she murmured to Molly.

Molly bobbed a curtsy and disappeared. In the mirror, Emily saw the maid's eyes twinkling.

James stood aside to let Molly pass and hesitated by the open door. Emily hesitated, too. The thought of the illustrations nagged at her, even though she wanted him. She should tell him. She *would* tell him.

He ran a finger around his collar, and she realised that he was nervous. She smiled at him and he shut the door. "I... I thought I'd see how you were," he said.

"I am as well as when you saw me at dinner, not a half hour ago."

He grinned at her, transforming into the carefree man who had teased her, wooed her and finally, in the teeth of opposition from his friends and family, married her. His gaze skimmed over the cream peignoir sliding and rustling against her skin. Hesitatingly, he raised a hand and stroked the side of her neck. "You smell delicious."

"My scent reaches that far? I thought you would need to be closer."

"Do you know, I think you're right."

James pulled her towards him and buried his face in her dark, thick hair. Emily sighed and closed her eyes. When his mouth found hers, she whimpered in need, her breasts taut and sensation pooling between her legs. He backed her gently towards the bed and leaned over her as she fell backwards, her hair spread over the white sheet like dark wine. He pulled the tie on the neck of her peignoir and kissed her down to the hollow between her breasts. She raked her nails through his hair and he growled, breathing hard.

"While I have much admired your waistcoat, it is superfluous to the occasion," said Emily, tugging at the buttons on the elaborately patterned silk.

"I'm pleased you noticed it," he said, standing to shrug off his jacket.

"I notice everything about you," Emily said, raising herself on her elbows to observe him hungrily as he stripped. When finally he turned back to her, naked and aroused, she was wriggling with impatience.

He knelt on the bed and ran his fingers across her collarbone, then flicked the lace at her neck. "Delightful as this is, I consider that like my waistcoat, it is superfluous."

She giggled, and held her arms aloft, shuffling her body until the silk slid away. He tossed her nightgown onto a chair and gazed at her. Heat rose through her at the fire in his eyes.

Emily linked her arms around his neck and pulled him towards her, her lips seeking his mouth, his shoulder, anywhere she could reach. His eyelids lowered and a deep sigh escaped him. She raised her knees to cradle his long, lithe body, revelling in the silkiness of his skin, the rough hair around his erection. "I have missed you," she murmured between gasps as he sucked her nipples and trailed his fingers across

173

her stomach. When his middle finger dipped inside her, she sucked in a breath.

"And I have missed you."

Their sighs and gasps floated through the room, tangled with murmured words of love, until Emily grasped James' hips and pushed herself towards him. "Please, James." Her whisper was loud in the quiet room.

He thrust into her smoothly. She cried out, a soft moan of desire and welcome which he captured in his kiss. Emily tossed her head from side to side, then tensed as the waves of pleasure began to rise. It was only a few seconds later when she clutched his shoulders and uttered a wordless cry of completion.

He groaned, gave one last rock of his hips and then, breathing heavily, rested his forehead on hers. A moment later, he eased his weight away and lay beside her. She snuggled in and he kissed her forehead.

Just as she was falling into sleep, she heard him whisper, "I love you, Emily."

CHARLOTTE WATCHED AS EMILY HANDED JAMES A CUP. HE SIPPED and smiled warmly at Emily, then glanced at the clock on the mantelpiece. "I have another appointment with Castleford, so I must leave you," he said, sounding genuinely disappointed. He put his cup on the table and ruffled Lucky's ears before nodding to Charlotte and leaving. Emily smiled.

"You are glowing, my dear," Charlotte commented as Emily offered her a plate of still-warm biscuits. "Has James reconciled himself to your development of the fernery?"

"He is glad that it makes me happy."

"Ah. So you haven't yet told him about the illustrations?"

Emily looked up sharply. "Ssh! I am waiting for the right time!"

Charlotte leaned back in her chair. "Loath as I am to interfere, the longer you stay silent, the more awkward it will be when you do tell him."

Emily wriggled in her seat and looked away. "I hope he need never know, as I am submitting under the cover of anonymity. Our marriage is so cordial at the moment. I ... I don't want to change it."

Charlotte regarded her steadily. After a moment, Emily sighed. "It seems such a little thing to you, but James and I have always been open and honest with one another. To admit doing something against his express wishes would damage our relationship, I am certain."

"He has no secrets from you?" Charlotte asked, her head on one side.

Emily's mind recalled the image of James striding out of the house with a letter in his hand. The letter which, she was sure, was not addressed to his mother about the memorial to his father and brother. She fiddled with the lid of the teapot and said nothing.

Charlotte hunted in her reticule and brought out a piece of paper. "This is from the journal. Alexander is pestering me for additional illustrations. What shall I say to him?"

"Oh!" Deep down, Emily was thrilled that her work was in demand. But she could not continue if this sick churning guilt was how she felt after submitting just two illustrations. "Could you tell him that I am busy developing my fernery? At least put him off until I have spoken with James..."

Charlotte looked her in the eye. "I can do that. But my dear, please find the courage to tell James of your brilliance!"

Emily nodded and offered Charlotte another biscuit.

Chapter 23

Emily

Monday 27th April 1862: How far a little praise can lift one's spirits! While I know the world and I are not less troubled, for a moment, things are easier and our burdens lighter to carry.

Listening to Lauren talk at a hundred miles an hour, Cat couldn't help grinning. "I've been crazy busy at work, but I loved your postcard – real old school!"

"I just wanted to say hi," Cat said, remembering their last conversation and unsure how – or if – to mention it. She waited to see what Lauren would say.

"It's lovely to speak, darling. How's the garden?"

"It's great! You ought to come and see."

"I might do that... How's the book?"

"With Creighton." Pride edged Cat's voice.

"Omigod, you *finished* it?"

"The final draft," Cat put in hastily. "I imagine Creighton will have his comments and until I hear from him, it won't go to the publisher. Then *they'll* have edits. But yes, the first draft is done."

"We must celebrate!"

Cat laughed. "When it's finalised. Hopefully, that won't be too long. Oh, hang on, Creighton's calling. Can I call you back?"

"Make sure you do – we need to plan the celebration!"

"And commiserate over South Africa. You must be gutted!" Cat disconnected the call to Lauren and switched to Creighton. "Hi, Creighton."

"Hello, Catherine. I'm sending my suggestions to you. Can you please give them your urgent attention?"

"Of course, but—" Cat paused, uncertainty making her stumble. "Is – is it okay? Do you like it?"

There was a pause and her nerves jangled.

"It's the best thing I've read from you." Creighton sounded serious.

"Oh! Oh, great! I think..." Cat struggled to collect her scrambled thoughts.

"You've reached a new place in your work," he continued, thoughtfully. "I believe the move to Cambridgeshire has enabled you to reach into your emotions in a way that makes the other novels seem ... lightweight."

"Oh."

"That's a good thing, Catherine, and we will speak about future books when this is put to bed. But now you need to focus on the draft for Raven Books. You don't have much time."

"Yes, yes of course! I'll get on it straight away."

She was still for a moment after the call ended. For a second, she gazed at the computer as though she couldn't remember how to turn it on. The call had left her bemused when she had hoped to feel uncomplicated happiness. Good grief, what on earth had he suggested in the edits if he liked it that much?

Finally galvanised into movement, she opened Creighton's email.

Two hours later she sat back, realising that she hadn't moved, drunk or eaten anything, or even visited the bathroom since Creighton's call. She blew out her cheeks and looked through the window. At least it was still light.

"Tea," she muttered, and got up, her joints creaking. She wouldn't finish the edits tonight, but she would make her deadline at the end of the week.

She was stirring her tea when the doorbell rang. It was Lauren, carrying a bottle of tequila.

CAT RUBBED HER EYES. GOD, SHE WAS KNACKERED, AND IT WASN'T even midday. But at least she was alone and the house was quiet. She took another gulp of water. It was so unfair that alcohol didn't seem to touch Lauren. She'd left at just gone nine this morning, looking disgustingly bright eyed, while Cat nursed a banging headache and the impression that she'd been put through a spin dryer. The night had been frantic, and Lauren so high-spirited that she'd verged on hysterical.

Now the black letters on her screen nagged her. Change me if you dare, they taunted. If you *can*. She rested her forehead on her hand. Frankly, she doubted that she'd ever learned to read and write.

A sharp rap at the door made her wince.

Harry's gaze ran over her. "Good morning," he said. "Or is it?"

"Hmm..." She led him into the drawing room. "Lauren came yesterday to help me celebrate the end of the book. Or rather, the completed first draft."

"I saw her car." Harry took in the papers, the laptop and the big glass of water and raised an eyebrow. "Are you working on something else already?"

"No. Same book but taking Creighton's comments into consideration. Lauren was a bit premature."

"Ah. And now you're trying to catch up?"

"Trying being the operative word."

"Why didn't you tell her you were still working?"

"Our last conversation wasn't a happy one, if you remember. When she turned up on my doorstep to celebrate, it was an olive branch. I could hardly turn her away, could I?"

Harry scratched his ear. "Right... Anyway, I've brought you a couple of bags of compost for the planting. I can do it, if you're writing. I'll need to bring the wheelbarrow through the side gate, though."

Cat was taken aback by his thoughtfulness. "Oh, thank you!"

He shrugged. "No probs. Have you had any more nuisance calls?"

It was a very casual question, but he looked watchful. "No. Perhaps they got scared off by police questioning."

"Stephen Fergusson sounds like a controlling, narcissistic bastard. If it is him, he may not stop."

Cat was so depressed at the thought that she didn't answer. Instead, she pulled open the cupboard door to look for the gate key. She couldn't see it, and tutted, cursing her hangover. "Where did I put it...? There should be two...Oh, here it is. Just use this, it's the duplicate. There's another one somewhere, but this should open the side gate." She opened the patio door.

Harry went through, grinning at her. "You never did have a head for booze."

"There's no need to look so smug!" She snapped.

He saluted as he walked up the path and she returned to her disapproving manuscript.

After a couple of coffees, Cat's head finally cleared and the editing picked up pace. Her growling stomach told her it was way past lunchtime. Before she could make sandwiches, Harry popped his head through the door. "Come on, you need to do this!" he said, smiling.

"What?"

"Plant the last fern," he announced, holding it up.

She smiled, the heaviness in her temples finally dissipating, and pushed back her chair.

Outside, he handed her the fern and a trowel. "There you go."

"I feel like the Queen. Shouldn't there be a ribbon? Or a fanfare?"

"I can record the moment on my phone to send to Lizzie, but I don't run to brass bands."

She smiled at him gratefully. "You're a star! Make sure you get my good side!"

"Do you have a bad side?"

She flushed and concentrated on planting the final specimen, a wonderful painted Japanese fern, its leaves tinged with pale grey which glistened silver in the shade of the trees.

"Ta-dah!" she said after she patted it in, and grinned at Harry, who was filming her. "Thank you both *so* much! Without your help, I'd still be dithering. You've been marvellous!"

She blew a kiss at the phone, and Harry froze, then lowered the phone. "I'll just clear up, then leave you to the rest of your day."

Cat stared at him. "Can't you stay for a cuppa and a sandwich? It's the least I can do."

His headshake was a definite refusal. "No, I must get on. I'm glad it's finished."

She was silent as they walked to the front door. He said goodbye and she watched his tall figure stride away.

CAT WAS UPSTAIRS COLLECTING LAUNDRY WHEN SHE HEARD THE letterbox clatter. She looked at the time. Half past two in the afternoon: late for the post.

She walked carefully downstairs, her arms full of sheets. As she reached the hall, her phone buzzed in her back pocket. Juggling the washing and her phone, she answered it without looking at the screen. "Hello?"

"Have you called the police yet?" a metallic voice asked, and she almost dropped the phone.

"Who is this?"

The metallic voice laughed. "Wouldn't you like to know? Have fun!"

The line went dead.

"But – hello? Hello! Damn you..." Cat froze, her pulse hammering in her throat. On the mat was a large white padded envelope. Willing herself forward, she picked it up.

Oh my God, what if it's a bomb? She pulled herself together. "For goodness' sake, this isn't an episode of CSI," she muttered. She grabbed the envelope and took it to the drawing room. She was sliding a knife into the flap when the doorbell rang, and she jumped.

It was PC Davis, with a female colleague. Cat's mouth fell open. "What are you doing here? How did you know?" she gasped. PC Davis frowned at her and she gestured for them to come in.

"I was in the neighbourhood and thought I'd call round to update you, rather than ring," he replied. His frown deepened. "How did we know *what*?"

"I've just had a phone call asking if I'd called the police yet, and a moment before that, *this* arrived," Cat explained, pointing at the envelope.

PC Davis picked it up and looked carefully at it. "Hmm," he said. "Hand-delivered. Are you expecting anything?"

"No."

"Let's have a look, then."

He prised open the envelope seal and gently drew out half a dozen photographs printed on A4 paper. They looked grainy, and had obviously been printed on a normal office printer. All of them showed Cat in the house: at the patio windows, peering out of the kitchen window, at the front door taking out rubbish, and one of her taken at night, drawing her bedroom curtains.

"Shit," Cat whispered in shock. When had these been taken? She focused on the sweater she was wearing in the kitchen shot. She had worn that on Monday, after Lauren had left her with a hangover.

"I wore that sweater two days ago," she said. Her mouth felt numb.

"Are all these rooms at the back of the house?" the female officer asked, and Cat nodded.

PC Davis peered out at the garden. "Let's take a look. Come with me, PC Southwell."

While they were in the garden, Cat sat staring at the photos. She wrapped her arms around herself. How dare this arse creep around taking photos? Forcing herself to pick one up, an uneasy doubt crept into her mind. While the garden wrapped around the manor, sturdy fences with gates blocked the access on either side. Whoever had sneaked into her back garden would either have gone through Harry's garden and scaled the huge wall at the back, or got through the locked side gates. She jumped up and ran outside.

When she reached the gate on the left-hand side of the house, the hasp was hanging loose. She called PC Southwell, who tutted in frustration at the lack of prints.

"Did you forget to lock it?" asked PC Davis, coming over.

"I never *un*locked it!" Cat said, wringing her hands.

"Where's the key?"

"In the key cupboard in the kitchen. I could swear I had two copies of every key in the place, but I've lost one. Gam was always losing them."

"Could someone have broken in and stolen one?"

The hairs on the back of Cat's neck stood up. Someone was in my house? "I – I can't think," she said. The implications made her shiver. Who had been in her house? There was Charlie, and the lock guy – but she'd been there all the time, and Dave the locksmith had never left the front door. Geoff, who might be trying to drive her out of the house, had never got through the front door after Cat had moved in. Lauren had been in, but they'd been together all last night. Stephen didn't know where she lived, she hoped. And she had given Harry a key to the side gate, but he'd handed it back. Had he left the door open?

She thought back to the call, and that strange metallic voice. "There was a phone call earlier," she said, and told PC Davis as much as she could remember. He was scribbling when the doorbell sounded. For the second time, Cat froze.

"I'll get it," PC Southwell said, walking to the front door. It was Harry.

"Harry! What are you doing here?" Cat asked, jumping to her feet.

"I saw the police car and feared the worst," he said, with a grin, and PC Davis smiled politely.

Cat told him briefly what had happened. "Did you lock the gate after you were here the other day?"

"I did. So if forensics come, they'll probably find my fingerprints on the padlock."

"Can I ask why you were using the gate, sir?" PC Davis asked evenly.

Harry looked slightly embarrassed. "I was planting some ferns, if you must know. Cat asked me to give her a hand in her garden."

Cat nodded. "That's right. But the key was missing before you came round," she said thoughtfully. "I couldn't find the actual key, remember? I had to dig out the duplicate. So it was taken before you came round." Harry nodded.

"Who has visited the house?" PC Davis asked, while the other constable scribbled furiously.

Cat listed everyone. "So, apart from Harry and Lauren, no one else has been in my house."

"What about Lauren?" Harry asked.

Cat stared at him, then laughed. "Don't be daft! We've been friends since we were at school! And quite apart from being my closest mate, Lauren was incapable of stringing together a sentence the last time she was in the house with me, let alone stealing a key! And that's even if she knew the right one to take!"

"Were the keys labelled?" asked PC Southwell.

"Well, yes... but, honestly, that would mean anyone could nick them!"

Harry shrugged and looked at the photographs. "Something to add to the file," he said, and PC Davis nodded. "Are there any prints?"

"None that we can see, and we'll never get forensics out to check," said PC Davis. "They might come tomorrow, but the locks look clean to me." PC Davis said.

Silence fell, then Cat spoke. "You said you came to update me?"

"Yes. My colleagues in Camden interviewed Stephen Fergusson

and I called on Geoff Johnson. Although they weren't required to talk to us, both did. They both denied any involvement. The law says that we must have good cause to extract data from their phones, and it must be pursuant to a reasonable line of inquiry—"

"So Stephen's previous threatening and controlling behaviour doesn't equal 'good cause'?" asked Cat, breathing hard.

"We were unable to identify any evidence that either person had been calling you," said PC Davis, his face expressionless. "We will of course continue with the case, but currently we have no reasonable suspects."

Cat fumed, but there was nothing else she could say. The police officers left, advising her to double check that all the gates were secure. She closed the front door, blowing her cheeks out, and returned to Harry, who was hovering by the sofa. Now that the fury had drained out of her, her legs felt like lead.

"Coffee?" she said, and he nodded. As she clattered mugs and spoons, tension crept into her shoulders and neck. What could she do? When would this stop?

Harry focused on her as she placed his mug on the table. "You okay?"

She stared at him.

"Fair enough, that was a stupid question. What are you going to do?"

"I'll be fine. That prick might be lurking outside, but he can't get through the front door without a battering ram if I lock myself in. I'll be fine," she said again, mostly to convince herself.

Cat sipped her drink. To her surprise, Harry prised the mug from her fingers, put it down and took her hand. She drew an unsteady breath and he squeezed her fingers. "Cat, I know you said you'll be fine, and that door would keep out the average tank, but let me know if there's anything I can do."

She leaned away to look at him, eyes wide, and forced a smile. "I'm a big girl. I'll be okay."

He shrugged. "Call if you need me."

Chapter 24

James' mama opened her parasol with a snap, swung it over her shoulder and stared haughtily at the garden. "I suppose it looks pretty. Your contribution to the gardener's work seems quite successful," she said, after she had scanned the garden with eyes which had none of James' warmth.

Seth opened his mouth to correct Mrs Cleveland but Emily shook her head at him.

James, who had followed them into the garden, came bearing an envelope. "For you," he said to Emily. He turned to his mother and held out his arm. "Mama, let me show you the whole. It is quite magical in the far corner: truly an enchanted grotto, especially with the sun shining through the trees."

Mrs Cleveland smiled sweetly and took his arm. As they walked away, Emily could hear the icy tinkle of her mother-in-law's laughter. "James, your partiality for your wife should not lead you into over-stating her contribution."

Beside Emily, Seth heaved a sigh. She smiled at him, some of her indignation soothed by his frustration over Mrs Cleveland's refusal to acknowledge Emily's design. He tipped his hat and lurched off.

Emily looked at the envelope James had handed her. The postmark was Cambridge but the handwriting was unknown to her. She tore it open, unfolding the stiff cream stationery.

Madam,

May I introduce myself: I am Lord Thomas Bainbridge, chairman of the Cambridge Pteridological Society. Lady Chester has spoken most warmly of the fernery you are creating at Cleveland House. Our select and informed society meets every other week. From what Lady Chester tells me, we would benefit from seeing how you have arranged your fernery and integrated it into the wider garden. Forgive the impertinence, but might I solicit an invitation on behalf of our humble group? You would not find us uneducated in the study of ferns.

I remain your obedient servant, Thomas Bainbridge

Emily's first response was pleased – how kind of Charlotte to recommend her so highly! But as she heard the conversation at the end of the garden, she chewed her lip. James might not like people tramping all over the garden; his mother certainly would not. She would have to broach the subject away from Sophia's ears. Perhaps Charlotte could assist her, as she had mentioned the fernery to Lord Thomas.

"Emily?" James' voice roused her from her musings. He was standing with his mother, who was squinting at the clear blue sky as though she expected rain. Doubtless Sophia was searching out an opportunity to be unhappy.

Emily smiled at James. "I beg your pardon! I was wool-gathering. Shall we go inside?"

"Is all well?" James asked, gesturing at the letter.

Emily tucked it into her pocket. "Merely a social matter."

She penned a note to Charlotte, begging her to come to dinner and save her. Then, she reasoned, her mother-in-law would have someone other than herself to scold and belittle. An equally brief note came from

Charlotte in the four o'clock post, saying that she would be delighted to act as a second target and offering to wear her most daring gown.

It was late afternoon when Mrs Cleveland retired to rest before dinner, leaving Emily alone with James, who was reading. Emily put aside her embroidery and crossed the room to sit on a stool by his chair.

He shot her a knowing glance. "I see something is afoot. What would you have me do?"

Emily twinkled at him, drew the letter from her pocket and passed it to him.

"Thomas Bainbridge, eh? I did not know he was enamoured of ferns."

"I do not know the gentleman. Before responding, I wanted to ask if you would object to the group visiting the fernery. I would like to hear the thoughts and views of knowledgeable strangers, if only to be certain that my friendship with Lady Chester is not clouding her judgement about the success of my fernery."

He laughed. "My love, Lady Chester is not the type to mince words. If she has praised you – and she obviously has to this gentleman – you should have confidence in her sentiments."

She smiled and rose. "I shall write back to Lord Thomas. Thank you, James."

He captured her hand and kissed it. "Your gardening brings you great pleasure; I am happy to do all I can to promote that."

Emily smiled. At least she had moved on from 'pottering'.

EMILY DABBED HER MOUTH WITH A NAPKIN TO HIDE A SMILE. MRS Cleveland's stunned expression at Charlotte's glorious gown was a memory she would treasure.

When Charlotte had thrown off her cloak in the hall, Sophia's jaw dropped, then her lips thinned. While not a vain woman, Sophia Cleveland prided herself on her youthful appearance, and Lady Charlotte Chester had seriously discomfited her. Charlotte's damson-coloured dress, the hue so rich that you could almost taste the fruit, had only a sprinkling of jet beads on the bodice as embellishment. Her white shoulders rose from the very low-cut décolletage and pearls gleamed softly around her neck. She looked like a queen.

James had been startled, but was too well-bred to do anything other than compliment Charlotte on her looks. Emily, dressed in pale-grey silk, was momentarily jealous of Charlotte's appearance, and then she recalled the cause of her sober attire, the death of her baby.

She blinked several times and lifted her head to find James' tender dark-brown gaze on her. He caught her hand and lifted it to his lips, and Emily's heart clenched. She smiled and some of the shadows around her thoughts lifted.

The conversation was general: the latest Royal Academy exhibition and the scientific lectures at Westminster Hall, where Charlotte was a regular attendee.

"That reminds me, Mama – we are expecting a group of enthusiasts from the Cambridge Pteridological Society later this week," James said, helping himself to the mushroom fricassee.

"You are?"

Charlotte beamed at Emily. "Thomas has written to you?"

"He has. They will visit on Thursday."

"But what is this society?" asked Mrs Cleveland, sounding querulous.

Emily explained and Mrs Cleveland all but rolled her eyes. "Not more ferns? Truly, I don't see the attraction!"

"Lord Thomas has a veritable passion for them," Charlotte said, with a smile. "Has the craze sweeping through fashionable circles passed you by, Mrs Cleveland?"

Mrs Cleveland bristled at the implication and leaned across the table to James. "I hope you won't allow Emily to become obsessed, James. Heaving plants around is very menial work for a woman in your wife's position, and who can appear feminine when covered in dirt? Indeed, she grows more like her mother every day."

"Mama, I am right here," Emily said, through gritted teeth.

Sophia Cleveland continued speaking to James. "Your father planned these gardens. I am not at all sure that he would approve of Lady Emily becoming so involved in their ... redevelopment."

"Mama, there is no harm in Emily doing what she has done. She has developed great skill and working in the garden has helped to build her strength. Indeed, I am pleased at the bloom in her cheeks."

"And what do *you* think, ma'am?" Charlotte said, turning to Emily. "It is your constitution under discussion. What is your view?"

Emily was torn between laughter and annoyance. She saw James' eyebrows rise and while she cared little for her mother-in-law's opinion, she did not want to embarrass her husband. She leaned across the table, ignoring Mrs Cleveland's disapproval, and clasped James' hand. "My husband has it exactly right. The fresh air helps me sleep more soundly and I have much more energy than I did in London."

"And wouldn't you agree that everything needs renewal, Mrs Cleveland? Lady Emily has breathed new life into the garden," Charlotte said sweetly.

"You knew it as my husband left it?" Mrs Cleveland's voice was acidic.

Charlotte's eyes glittered when she smiled. "Oh, I am *much* too young to have visited when your husband was alive, but Lady Emily indulged my curiosity when I first paid my respects, before she embarked on her design."

Hectic colour rose to Mrs Cleveland's cheeks at Charlotte's gentle dig, and Emily saw James frown at their unrepentant guest.

She rushed into speech. "I am sure the society would be fascinated to hear how Mr Henry Cleveland originally planned the garden, Mama. If you are available on Thursday, I am certain the enthusiasts would be eager to know the original design."

Mrs Cleveland pressed her lips together and James moved the conversation on.

Thursday was fine with bright sunshine. As she looked at the garden, Emily's chin lifted and she smiled with satisfaction. The shadows over the fernery were gentle and flickering and though there were still some gaps – John Dadd had written yet again to apologise for the delay – she thought the fernery appeared to advantage.

"Lady Emily!" Lord Thomas called from the depths of the fernery, and Emily hurried down the path. "I must ask about your splendid *Hymenophyllum tunbridgense*. I have found mine does poorly in its current position, yet yours is thriving." He gestured to the tiny fern, tucked between two stones in the dripping waterfall that Seth had constructed.

Emily laughed. "I feared it would not hold its place when I planted it, given the precarious situation of the boulders. But clearly, the damp air serves it well. Is yours planted near water rather than having direct contact, my lord?"

"Ah, I see my error. I have my gardener spray it daily, but water dripping over it would be beneficial and, in addition, save his labour. Thank you, ma'am. Even unfinished, your fernery is a triumph!"

James, who had been watching from a distance, strolled over and Lord Thomas drifted back to examine the waterfall.

"Your fernery – and you – are a hit, my dear!" James murmured. "I have been accepting plaudits all afternoon."

"Everyone has been most kind."

"Her ladyship is much too modest, Sir James," Charlotte commented as she joined them. "Her ingenious design and the perfect placement of the specimens make the fernery successful. Oh... I see you have more guests."

Charlotte's voice implied that they were less than welcome, and when Emily turned to see Reverend Sherwood-Taylor bowing over Mrs Cleveland's hand, she swallowed her sigh of dismay.

"Ah, another of the neighbourhood's worthy but slightly dull citizens," James said. Smothering a giggle, Emily went over to shake hands and welcome the new arrival.

"Just so, just so... Ah, the lady gardener herself! How d'you do, ma'am?"

"Reverend, welcome. I did not know you were interested in the fernery."

"The power of the Deity is not proclaimed in Creation in more impressive language than by the very humble weeds that we tread beneath our feet!" Reverend Sherwood-Taylor proclaimed, surprising Emily with his poetic turn of phrase. "We must learn to understand the language in which He addresses us, be it ever so mysterious. Yes, ever so mysterious."

Mrs Cleveland nodded regally.

Somewhat bewildered, Emily offered the reverend refreshments. He continued, "Indeed, I must keep up with the pastimes of the ladies to remain current, so that I may do the work of the Church more readily."

"Ladies' pastimes?" Emily said carefully, aware of the sharp gaze of her mother-in-law. In the corner of her eye, she saw Charlotte and James approaching. While the reverend shook James' hand, Charlotte received the barest nod.

"You implied that botany is not a serious topic, sir," Emily pressed.

The reverend noisily sipped his tea and nodded. "Oh, indeed! While I am heartily in favour of ladies' involvement in the sciences, it is hardly the realm to which they are suited. Botany, insofar as ladies are involved, is a splendid compromise. Amusement, you know, for the fairer sex."

Emily heard Charlotte take a deep breath, as if about to go into battle. She was about to intervene when James spoke, his tone deceptively mild. "Are you belittling my wife's endeavours, Reverend? This garden has been significantly remodelled."

Emily registered the surprise on the faces of the group, in all likelihood for completely different reasons.

The reverend put his head on one side, reminding Emily of a sparrow. "Ah, but is it for the better? We are in the age of change, I am told, but not all change is welcome."

"And in any case, Emily hardly shifted the soil!" Mrs Cleveland put in, twirling her parasol. "Her gardener took the lead, did he not?"

"I must protest, ma'am. Lady Emily has been at the head of the fernery's development from inception to completion – not a bystander watching from a distance!" Charlotte said firmly. "Indeed, she planted the ferns with her own hands. Is that not correct, ma'am?" Charlotte turned to Emily, her eyebrows raised.

"You planted the ferns?" Mrs Cleveland interjected. "Oh, but that is such menial work!"

Emily, who had been preparing to calm the choppy waters of the conversation, changed her mind. "I did indeed. I love handling the plants, and as you yourself said, Reverend, there is something of the divine in that. I am afraid, though, that I do not agree with your assessment that botany is only amusement for the gentler sex. Gentlemen are also involved in botany, and we have intrepid fern-hunter groups who number several ladies in their company."

The reverend turned stiffly to James. "I do not decry Lady Emily's fernery, Sir James. The fern enthusiasts present will provide testament to her efforts, I am sure." He bowed to James and held out his arm to Mrs Cleveland, and they bustled away.

Emily watched them go, divided between laughter and exasperation. Charlotte was much less conflicted. "Did he actually say that botany was only 'amusement for the fairer sex'? Odious little man!"

Emily pressed her arm, aware of James' intent gaze. "Hush, Charlotte! Could you offer Lord Thomas and the group some refreshments?" she murmured.

Charlotte nodded and walked away.

At a polite cough, she turned to see Watson. "Oh, Watson, did you want me?"

"Two telegraphs have come for Sir James." Watson offered a silver tray.

"Two? How extraordinary." James frowned and took them.

Emily watched him open them. A shadow fell across his face at the first, and darkened at the second. "Is all well?" she asked, anxiety rising in her.

He shook his head. "I must go to London."

"Why? What has happened?"

"There are problems with the committee, and—" He paused as if searching for words.

Emily placed her hand on his arm. "What is it, James?"

James cast her a grim look. "Freddie's wife has given birth to a son."

Chapter 25

Emily

Friday 5th May 1862: I am very weary. No wonder, given my sleepless state. No sooner does my head touch the pillow than my mind races with possible choices, and I toss and turn until the maid comes with my morning tea. I refuse to take laudanum: weary as I am, I detest the sensation of being behind a glass screen during my waking hours.

Cat pushed her chair back from the desk and raised her arms above her head. "Yesss!" She punched the air, then pressed send on her email. The book was on its way to her publishers. God, she hoped they liked it.

It was only ten thirty. Time for a cuppa, and then perhaps she'd go for a walk. Or she could read some more of the journal, or do some titivating in the garden. Her time, on this bright Saturday, was her own.

An hour later, she opened the front door and found a milk bottle on her doorstep. She tutted. "They've delivered to the wrong house."

She hovered, not knowing what to do. Should she take in the bottle, or leave it out so that the milkman could re-deliver it once he found out his mistake? Perhaps they'd delivered to her instead of Harry. She tucked the bottle under her arm and walked to Harry's house.

Rock music accompanied hammering as she walked up the path. She smiled as she recognised the band. She and Harry shared a love of live music; they'd been to many concerts together.

She leaned on the bell. After a few seconds, the music became quieter and a dusty Harry opened the door. She held out the bottle. "Morning! I recognise that tune. Just wondered if you were missing a pint of milk?"

Harry grinned. "The latest album is brilliant." He glanced at the milk bottle. "Not me. Must be along the road, but that's a fair step."

"Oh well, I suppose I'd better give it a home. I hate waste—"

"Wait. Give it to me." Harry's smile had disappeared and his eyes were intent on the bottle.

"What?"

"Give me the bottle and come inside."

She handed him the bottle and followed him indoors to the sink. "What's wrong? Why are you taking the top off?"

He slid a knife into the foil top and she saw a dark shadow in the neck of the bottle. "Wh-what's that?"

"I'm not sure, but I suspect it's a mouse." Harry's voice was grim as he probed the bottle with the knife.

Cat shrank back in horror as a dark sodden shape fell into the sink and the milk glugged down the plughole. "Oh my God!"

Harry looked at her sharply. "Here." He thrust a battered washing-up basin at her and she threw up. She turned away, tears running down her face, mortified and shaking.

Harry calmly took the basin and disappeared into the downstairs toilet. When he returned, Cat was tapping a routine on her hands, trying to stop trembling.

"We need to report it," he said gently, and she nodded. "I'll get changed and come with you."

It was late afternoon when they returned. This time, the police had asked more pointed questions about Cat's move to Cambridge and her relationship with Stephen, and more about Geoff. After all, they said, he was local. The experience had been brutal, almost implying that she deserved what was happening. The police would talk to Stephen again, and she prayed to the universe that her ex-lover didn't have her new phone number or her address.

She flung her bag on the sofa and sank down beside it. She leaned her head back and closed her eyes. She wouldn't cry. She absolutely wouldn't cry. Damn, where was her handkerchief?

A warm hand squeezed her shoulder. "Can I get you anything?"

"Unless you can give me superpowers to search out and destroy everyone who wants to do me harm... Nope, I don't think so."

He chuckled, and she felt the squashy sofa dip beside her. Silently, tears trickled down the sides of her face. Neither of them spoke.

After a few moments, Cat scrubbed at her eyes and sat up. "Okay, yes, there is something you can do."

Harry turned his head to look at her. "Name it."

"Can you teach me some self-defence skills?"

He stared at her, then looked thoughtful. "That's not a bad idea. Okay, I'll change into sweats. You should, too."

Ten minutes later, they had pushed the furniture to the sides of the room and Cat was facing him.

"First, never stand and fight when you can run," Harry warned her. "The object is to stay alive, not exchange punches with some guy who's attacking you." Cat nodded. "Okay, so if someone comes up behind you and does this—" He wrapped his arms around her, pinning her arms to her sides. For a second, they both stilled. She felt his heartbeat against her back and his thighs tense against the back of her legs. Her nipples leapt to attention. She heard him clear his throat.

"What next?" she blurted out.

196

Harry lifted her off her feet. Cat struggled, but couldn't break his grip. "Okay, caveman, how do I get out of this?"

"Reach behind you and find the front of my thigh. Yes, just there: that's the sciatic nerve. Dig your fingers in and squeeze... Ow! Okay, okay, you've got it! Bloody hell, Cat, stop!"

"Oh, I'm sorry! Are you all right?" Cat peered down at him as he clutched his leg.

He groaned. "Yeah ... you've got that one." He took a deep breath and straightened up.

A few more manoeuvres and Cat was enjoying herself. Harry looked a little the worse for wear, only just escaping the kick she aimed at his groin. "Whoa! That was close... That's good. Remember, when you kick someone in the groin, don't use your foot – use your shin. Less chance of damaging yourself."

Cat nodded.

"So, eyes, nose, groin and knees are the vulnerable areas," Harry said. "Dig your thumbs in the eyes, twist the nose, kick the groin and use the heel of your foot on the knee. And if someone comes at you with their hand like I'm doing now, grab it with both of yours, twist underneath and shove their arm up their back. Ready? You try."

Cat followed through on the move and, to her delight, succeeded. Harry winced and she let his arm drop immediately. "God, sorry, did I really hurt you?"

He bent over with his hands on his knees, breathing rather faster than normal. "Jeez, Cat, I wouldn't want to meet you in a dark alley!"

She smirked. "You should be so lucky!"

His eyes met hers and she went hot all over.

A flush crept over Harry's face and he bit his lip. "I think you know all you need now. I'm going to get a shower. Let me know if that creep calls again, or if anything turns up on your doorstep that you're not expecting."

Cat trailed after Harry to the front door and put her hand on his arm as he opened it. "I seem to thank you every five minutes lately," she said. "But thank you."

He raised a hand, then disappeared down the path.

FIVE DAYS LATER, CAT SAT IN THE SLEEK LONDON OFFICE AND stared at the portly man in front of her. "You don't like it *at all?*" she whispered.

Her publisher, David Sanderson, leaned back in his black leather chair and looked at her over the top of his glasses. "It's not our usual fare," he said, spreading his hands. "We might take it with some changes, but it would require a considerable rewrite. It wasn't what we were expecting; your synopsis implied something quite different."

Cat frowned, trying to make sense of his words. Didn't the synopsis reflect the story? She found it hard to remember.

Creighton sat beside her, tense and straight-backed. David pushed several sheets of paper towards her and Creighton. When she turned them over, she found detailed notes about the required changes. Her mouth dropped open and Creighton's eyebrows drew together sharply.

"You want me to change Louise's name?"

"Our market research shows it's too old-fashioned a name to attract the younger demographic."

"And her child is now a girl?" Cat stared at him, aghast.

David shrugged. "Our market research team is very thorough. Sorry, we need – we *want* this book to be a success, so we're giving it every chance. And we want to cut out a couple of characters to make it read better."

Cat's hands shook with fury. If she made all these changes, it would not only rip out the heart of the book, but it wouldn't be her book any more.

"Oh, one more thing..." David said mildly, and she waited. "We'd like to change the title."

Cat's temper subsided completely, and she was calm. She looked at

Creighton, silent beside her. "Can Creighton and I have a chat?" she said.

"Yes, that's a good idea." David heaved himself to his feet. "I'll give you some privacy."

Cat bit her lip as the publisher closed the door and forced herself to reread the suggested amendments to her novel. After a moment, she turned to Creighton. "This is a demand for changes, not a request. They won't publish me if I don't do it." She frowned. "It wasn't *that* dreadful a book, was it?"

"Do you want to do them?" asked Creighton, looking at her intently.

Cat hesitated, then shook her head. "I know this is whistling six months' work and my contract down the wind, but no. I don't want to make these changes. It wouldn't be my book, just something the bloody marketing people wrote."

"It might make you a lot of money," Creighton reminded her.

She knew. But her gut churned at the idea of this book not being published as she'd written it. Her past experiences with Stephen were knitted into the pages: not the events, but the emotions. It was part of her catharsis.

She sighed. "I know. And I could use the money right now. What do you think about the book? I thought you liked it."

"I do. I like it a lot, but David's right. It's not – what did he say? Not their usual fare." He leaned forward and patted her hand. "It's streets ahead of anything he normally prints!" A strangled laugh escaped her.

Creighton twinkled at her. "If you can hold out a little longer for cash, Catherine, I can look for another publisher. But that depends on you holding your nerve."

Cat reflected. She was having to hold her nerve a lot at the moment. Would this make it worse? Maybe, but not *much* worse. She could always live on baked beans for a few months. "Do you believe in the book?" she asked, searching Creighton's face.

He smiled. "I do. Do you believe I can find you a decent publisher who appreciates your talent?"

"I do."

"Then I believe we're married," he said wryly. "Let's give David the news that he can stick his deal. You've delivered the book, he's paid you no advance, and he's decided not to publish it."

Isn't" there a termination clause?" Cat chewed a nail.

"I'll look at it. Should I call David back in?"

She nodded.

David was dumbstruck. "I'm sorry about your decision. Are you sure?"

Cat shrugged. "No, but I'm not comfortable with your suggested revisions. And as you're not comfortable with the manuscript, we're at an impasse. It's probably better to part company now, isn't it?"

"Will you sell the novel elsewhere?" Cat looked up at the aggression in his tone.

A smile lifted Creighton's thin lips. "We're considering our options, David. Right, Catherine, shall we continue our discussion with a gin and tonic in front of us?"

An hour later, Creighton had told her to sit tight, given her a cheery wave and left her in the echoing cavern of Kings Cross station. The train she'd booked was cancelled. The next was in half an hour, but she felt restless and in need of another drink. She watched people move backwards and forwards on the concourse, peering up at the announcement board or down at their phones. Her mind was curiously blank.

For the first time in five years, she wasn't at all sure what would happen next. Usually, at this stage of a book, she'd be asked to rubber-stamp the cover design and blurb. Now she wasn't even sure if the book would be published.

She checked her bank account on her phone. Hmm. She had probably another three months of living carefully before she really hit the skids. Then... God, then what? Her savings were gone, thanks to the garden wall. Leaving Stephen and moving to Cleveland House had taken a sizeable chunk of her money. Although her first book had been a best-seller, the royalties from that had kept her afloat through the books that hadn't sold so well. And then, of course, there were the funds that Stephen had spent.

She wrinkled her nose as she saw a pink-haired young woman peck an older woman, probably her mother, on the cheek. Mum patted Pink Hair on the shoulder, smiled, and waved her through the barriers. It looked affectionate, uncomplicated.

Cat would almost rather starve on the streets than approach her parents for money. They'd sigh and go on about her brother, Saint Anthony, and his sensible job. *He'd* never come to them for money... Cat had never been sure why the fifty grand 'loan' for the deposit on Anthony's first house didn't count as help, but after a while she'd stopped asking. Anthony was different because he had a wife and family. Cat was just 'dabbling in writing' while they waited for her to come to her senses.

Cat squared her shoulders. It would work out. She'd write some short stories and publish them herself on the major ebook platforms. She could offer her services as a ghostwriter. Hell, Creighton might even find her another publisher. She was down, but she wasn't out.

She took out her phone and found Lauren's number. "Hi, it's me. Our celebration was premature – the publisher's pulled out. Fancy a drink? I'm at Kings Cross."

Lauren said nothing for a moment. "I'll be there in twenty minutes. Don't move!" she said, and hung up.

Chapter 26

E mily sighed as she turned away from the fernery. Soon the missing ferns would arrive and she could complete it as she had planned. She pulled the brim of her hat over her face. Molly had already scolded her for the freckles that were appearing as spring turned to summer and the sun gained strength. Her maid had threatened more lemon juice for her face and tutted whenever she caught sight of Emily's hands.

"I'll get that beeswax mix, ma'am," she'd said, with a tinge of disapproval in her voice. Emily examined her fingernails and grimaced. It wouldn't do to have hands like a skivvy when James finally returned.

Whenever that might be. She spied a torn stem on a rosebush and, searching in her pockets, found her scissors to snip it away. Apart from the gentle twitter of the birds, the air was quiet. A strange contentment grew inside Emily as she strolled back to the house.

James' face had been expressionless when he left. A son for Freddie made their childlessness a threat to James' succession, and her heart ached for him. She willed herself to remain calm, but there had been little she could say. He left without a backward glance.

There was one blessing attached to James' sudden departure for London: his mother had followed him back to town the day after.

Emily closed the verandah door and glanced around the drawing room. Her easel sat empty, and she pushed away the temptation to begin another illustration.

She settled in the low armchair by the window, journal in hand. The sunshine made the ivory pages gleam bright, and she wondered how she could express herself in a manner befitting a lady.

A full minute later, she was still holding the dip pen poised. The sunlight gleaming off the engraved gold brought to her mind another morning soon after she and James were married.

"I have something for you," James had said. He passed the slender package to her. Smiling, she unwrapped the tissue paper.

"Oh! How lovely!" Emily held up the hexagonal-shaped pen to examine it. "It's so beautiful! Where did you get it?"

"From Birmingham – they make the best pens there," he responded, watching her weigh it in her hand. "I hope it is not too heavy?"

"No, no, it is perfect! I must write something..."

She rose and rummaged in the nearby desk for paper. He laughed as he watched her toss envelopes and blotters to one side. "I thought the pen would inspire you to greater thoughts in your journal," he said, amused.

"Indeed. Of course, I only write female drivel *now*, but this will improve my reflections, I am sure." Emily concentrated on her hand as she wrote her signature.

"Minx," chuckled James, and picked up his newspaper again.

Staring at the pen, finely engraved with leaves and acanthus motifs, she dipped it again in the black ink. She wrote slowly, then faster as words seemed to tumble out of her onto the page.

I hope soon for J to return. Our relationship, which had seemed so full of fire, is now flickering to embers through lack of fuel. And although it is gross and unfeminine to admit such thoughts, I feel desire gnawing constantly at me, as though I could not be whole without his embrace. At night I pace the floor yearning for the relief that congress with him brings. My passion churns through me and unreleased, I am sickened. I am ashamed to be so carnal when I should fulfil the role of angel, but— Oh! Fill me up! Help me make us a family!

She stared at the journal, her cheeks fiery as she read her words. She slammed the journal shut. It was an accurate reflection of the person she had always been: the person that James had fallen in love with. She would not change it.

WATSON APPEARED IN THE DRAWING ROOM, LOOKING FOR ALL THE world as if something unpleasant lurked under his nose. He coughed apologetically and the conversation between Emily, Charlotte, and Mrs and Miss Sherwood-Taylor faltered.

"The Animal has escaped into the garden," he said, as though announcing a death. "Molly is trying to recapture him. And your lady-ship's plants have arrived."

Emily jumped to her feet. "Lucky has escaped? Oh, this is too bad of him! Mrs Sherwood-Taylor, are you or your daughter frightened of dogs? He is still a puppy, but a little boisterous."

Mrs Sherwood-Taylor smiled. "No, ma'am. We are rather more robust than Mrs Phillips," she added smugly, and Emily saw a twinkle that surprised her.

"Then can I risk offending propriety and leave you here to hunt for him?"

"We shall come with you. The day is fine and I should like to see the fernery again," said Miss Sherwood-Taylor, standing up and brushing down her sage-green visiting gown. Emily thought the colour became her rosy complexion and said so. Miss Sherwood-Taylor dimpled at her, and for a moment Emily wondered how the reverend had sired so pretty and plump a daughter.

The ladies stepped into the garden, Emily leading them while she called for Lucky. Though the door to the glasshouse was now firmly closed, Emily did not want a repeat of the anxious time she had endured after the dog had eaten poison.

"He's over here, ma'am!" Molly said. "But he won't come to me."

"Lucky! Lucky, come here, you vile animal!" Emily cried. Lucky, trailing ivy and slightly grubby, trotted out of the shrubbery, panting. She snatched him up and examined his lead, chewed beyond repair. Molly made to take Lucky's collar, but Emily shook her head. "The weather is fine. If our guests do not object, let him stay with us."

"I could almost be glad that he escaped! Now we may walk around your garden and the fernery," said Mrs Sherwood-Taylor. Remembering the reverend's views on 'lady gardeners', Emily hid her surprise. The daughter looked on, much amused.

"Have you examined the new plants, ma'am?" Charlotte said innocently. Mrs Sherwood-Taylor added her voice to the pleas to see the new ferns.

In releasing the ferns from their boxes and placing them for planting, Emily found contentment and exercise. Perhaps it would enable her to sleep, rather than tossing and turning in unsatisfied restlessness.

EMILY RAISED HER HEAD FROM HER BOOK AS SHE HEARD THE front door open and close. The post came promptly at nine, twelve, three and six o'clock, which was fairly convenient for Cambridge, although of course in London there were at least ten deliveries through the day. Had James written? She had written four times, each time asking for news. Surely he would write today.

The knock at the door heralded Watson, who came bearing a missive from Aunt Sybil and a letter for James.

"Put it in his study, please," Emily said, making her voice light to hide her disappointment.

She opened the envelope bearing Aunt Sybil's angular writing – more angular than Emily recalled. "You are getting old, aunt," she sighed, then made herself comfortable to read the scolding that the letter no doubt contained.

Aunt Sybil did not mince her words:

I understand from Mrs Cleveland that you are doing what I expressly told you not to, and falling under the illusion that you can flout the behaviour expected from one in your situation. While I was fond of your mother, her wilfulness attracted the opprobrium of society and people have long memories. You were fortunate that James shared your love of learning and overlooked her follies. Pray, do not make him regret his indulgence! While Lady Chester, being a widow of independent income, may do as she pleases, you, Emily, must not transgress the boundaries of society. You have not fulfilled your role in presenting Sir James with an heir. Should you not do so, he may well regret his decision to marry you.

Mrs Cleveland has described to me your escapades concerning your fernery, and your insistence that women may be serious students of science – I am speechless at your folly! You will desist at once. Your fernery may be very fine, but let that be an end to it. Bend your energy to making James a good wife.

By the time she reached the end of the letter, Emily's jaw was clenched with irritation. Her mother-in-law had been busy.

James had loved her for her mind when they met and encouraged her learning to an extent which surprised and even shocked some of his friends. James and she did not care; they revelled in their reading and conversations.

Or at least, they had until she lost the baby. Then he had changed, although recently she had seen glimpses of the man she married.

Emily paced her sitting room before striding to her writing table. She drew a sheet of paper towards her, reached for her pen, and found, to her irritation, that her inkwell was dry. She reached for the bell, then changed her mind. She would borrow ink from James' study.

James' study smelled of books and brandy. Emily breathed in, closing her eyes while she imagined him at the mahogany desk. Opening her eyes, she moved towards the desk to find the inkwell. Her gaze fell on the letter that had arrived, and she froze. The handwriting was that of Dr Schenley, the slanting letters bold and sly.

Why had Dr Schenley written to James? She picked up the letter. Could she open it without being discovered? Then she dropped it on to the desk as if it had burned her. After deceiving James about the illustrations, would she now open her husband's private correspondence?

Emily pulled her shoulders back. Grabbing the inkwell, she scurried out, her mind ablaze with imaginings.

An hour later, Emily had recovered sufficiently to write a polite rebuff to Aunt Sybil, inviting her to see the fernery for herself if she should care to visit. "Watson, please see that this catches the afternoon post," she said, handing it to the butler as he arrived to announce lunch. "And could you also see to it that this inkwell is returned to Sir James' study and mine is refilled."

She made a poor meal. The stark black handwriting of Dr Schenley floated before her eyes, and thinking about what the letter might contain gave her a headache. Her aunt's words echoed in her head: *You have not fulfilled your duty in presenting Sir James with an heir. Should you not do so, he may well regret his decision to marry you.*

With a groan, she rested her forehead on her hand, her temples throbbing. So lost in misery was she that when Watson returned with his silver tray, she started.

"My apologies, ma'am. This arrived for you."

A letter from James. She snatched it off the tray.

"Shall I ask Mrs O'Donnell to prepare a tisane, ma'am?"

"Pardon?"

"For your headache."

"Oh! No, thank you. I shall call if I need you."

Emily buried herself in the letter. James was coming back in two days – but oh, he sounded so disheartened!

My proposal is completely defeated. I had no support – not even from the liberals I counted my friends. Women are likely to be held solely responsible for the contagion sweeping through our armies, and the penalties will be infamous.

Freddie is in transports over his son. I am not. I am longing to take comfort in your arms when I return on Friday.

She felt a frisson run through her. James loved her. He would not collude with Dr Schenley. He was merely bruised from a brush with men who did not share his compassion or his views.

With mixed emotions, she rose to tell the household that Sir James would be returning.

Chapter 27

Emily

Sunday 28th May 1862: Revealing the truth is much like ripping a dressing from a wound. It is painful, it stings and the skin is sore afterwards – but is there not a tinge of relief that the lie is now open to the air?

Cat had only just taken off her jacket from her trip to David Sanderson when her phone buzzed. It was Harry, sending a text.

—I have news – are you in?

Cat froze. News? Was it about the stalker? No, of course not – he couldn't talk to her about the case. Had he got his promotion?

—Come over, she replied.

Five minutes later, there was a knock at her door. Flinging it open, Cat found Harry wearing such a look of pride on his face that she knew at once.

"Oh my God, you passed your Board!" she breathed, and he nodded, grinning. She threw her arms around his neck and hugged him hard. "That's brilliant! You're a legend, Harry Moore!"

He chuckled and returned the hug, their bodies slotting together just like they used to. For a precious second, his limbs pressed against hers. Then, as if by mutual agreement, they moved apart.

"This calls for champagne, only I don't have any," said Cat. "Will a glass of wine do?"

"That'd be great."

Cat busied herself with glasses and uncorked her last bottle of wine. She bit her lip. If they downed this bottle, there was no more. And given today's news, she would need to cut back on alcohol. But she pressed her worries down and poured two glasses with a flourish. "Tell me everything!"

Harry bombarded her with acronyms and names of people she didn't know, but after a few attempts to get him to speak plain English, she gave up and listened to the joy and pride in his voice, making noises of appreciation.

After about half an hour, Harry stopped abruptly. "You didn't understand much of that, did you?"

Cat giggled. "I thought comprehension was optional, but it doesn't matter. It's wonderful news and I'm mega pleased. Especially after your experience in the Met."

Harry nodded and sat back, cradling the glass of wine in his long, tanned fingers. "Yeah, that's finally over."

"So what's next? When do you take up your position?"

A pause. "There isn't one for me in Cambridgeshire, I'll need to move forces."

Cat stared at him as the ground lurched beneath her. "Yes. Yes, you said. Will you mind commuting, or—" She swallowed. "Or will you move house?"

He gazed at her with silver-grey eyes. "I'm not sure. I don't want to rush into anything."

Cat's stomach flipped as a wild thought passed through her brain like quicksilver. She nodded and twirled the stem of her wineglass. "Sounds good," she said, for want of anything better.

Silence fell. "How's your day been?" Harry asked, at last.

Cat looked down. "Bit of a disaster, really. The publisher doesn't like the book, so my agent will be hawking the manuscript around other publishers."

"They didn't like it?"

"Nope." Panic swelled in her chest and she grabbed the wine bottle. "Top-up?"

"But you're a best-seller! What are they thinking?"

Harry's indignation soothed Cat's battered spirit, and she managed a smile. "This book is different: not my usual girl-about-town stuff. It's so different that they didn't like it."

"What's different about it?"

That was a good question. Cat spoke slowly, feeling her way. "After getting away from Stephen, I felt as if there was a side to me that I'd never known before. I valued different things. It's why the rewrites took me so long, because the first draft was a bit... Well, it was superficial. I was effectively writing a whole new book, and it's dark in comparison to my previous books."

"What's your novel about?"

Cat hesitated. Was Harry just being polite? No: they'd discussed her writing when they were together. "It's about a woman called Louise who has a dreadful relationship with her mother, full of bitterness that Louise doesn't understand. When her mother dies, Louise finds out that she left a legacy to someone called Iris. Louise has never heard of this person, but traces her and finds out that Iris is her half-sister. Iris is really hostile because *she* knew she had a half-sister, and she was really hurt that Louise and her mother never got in touch when she fell pregnant. Iris has been bringing up her little boy on her own and she's very hard up. Then the little boy falls ill and they both fight to get him the care and treatment he needs. It's a story of female friendship, I suppose."

"Did you base it on your relationship with Lauren?"

"Sort of. Lauren and I have been through some rough times together. When I was looking for an agent I barely got a response from anyone, and doing a job I hated was when she was starting out in events and trying to support her mum."

"Your publisher sounds like an idiot for turning it down."

She shrugged. "I had a good chat with Lauren at King's Cross after meeting the publisher. She's helped me work off the initial angst."

"Did you tell her about the photos?"

"No, the police told me not to mention it. Why?"

"No reason." Harry paused. "They're right: keep it to yourself. Have you received anything else?"

"No, thank God. But who's doing this, Harry? In my heart I know it's Stephen, but he seems to be in the clear."

"Not Geoff?"

"God, I don't know. I don't think I know anything any more."

"I know, I know. But at least that milk bottle made the police sit up and take notice."

"I hope so. It makes me wonder what they'll do next – well, I'd rather not think about what they might do next."

Harry gave her a hug, and Cat luxuriated in the softness of his cashmere sweater against her cheek. "Try not to worry," he murmured into her hair. "We'll catch them soon."

CAT RUBBED THE SLEEP OUT OF HER EYES AS SHE WAITED FOR THE kettle to boil. The sun glinted off the chrome handle of the corkscrew and she put it in the cutlery drawer. Outside, it looked as if it would be a lovely day. It would do her good to tidy up the garden. Maybe even mow the lawn, if Harry would lend her his mower.

Pouring hot water over her teabag, she mused over the evening. Fried-egg sandwiches were hardly haute cuisine, but last night they had been the food of the gods. Remembering the conversation with Harry made her smile; he was excellent company. She threw the teabag in the bin and stared out of the kitchen window. Her eyes caught the graceful arc of a fern leaf, but there was no sign of Batman the robin. She padded to the patio doors. Normally the bird was waiting impatiently outside her window. That was strange.

The ground was dry underfoot. She'd be okay in her slippers and thanks to the walls, no one could see her. Cat slid the doors open and stepped into the bright morning. A gentle breeze blew, and she inhaled it – then caught a strange scent. Frowning, she walked further into the garden, trying to place the smell. Her gaze fell on the lawn; some of the grass looked as if it was dying. She frowned. That was new.

As she followed the path to the fernery, her eyes widened.

Plants drooped, blackened and wizened. The wall, once providing nooks and crevices for small ferns, glistened in the rays of the early morning sun. She gasped and quickened her pace. Every piece of greenery was blasted, the leaves curled up on themselves and dying. Then she placed the smell.

Someone had soaked all her ferns in bleach.

CAT WAS PUTTING ON GLOVES, STILL IN HER WRAP AND PYJAMAS, when Harry came round. "What's happened?" he asked.

"Some bastard has poisoned my garden!"

"Is that bleach I can smell? Cat, don't touch anything! Have you phoned the police?"

She stared at him. "Not yet. I'm trying to save some of my plants!"

"No, leave everything as it is!" he snapped. With one hand on her arm, he took out his phone. "PC Davis please? It's DCI Moore. Phil, there's been another incident at Cat Kennedy's. Can you get here? Yes, I'll hang around, but I need to be in the office at eleven, so step on it, eh?"

He hung up and spoke more gently to Cat. "I'm sorry I shouted, but there might be a bleach bottle around with prints on it."

Cat's mouth dropped open and a strangled noise came out of her throat. Harry put his arm around her shoulders, urging her gently towards the patio. "I'd hate to see your slippers ruined," he added, nodding towards her furry monster feet.

She shook her head, the stench of bleach beginning to make her head swim and burn the back of her throat. Tears gathered in her eyes and she blinked rapidly.

"I'm so sorry," Harry said softly.

Cat shook her head in irritation. "I'm not upset – well, I am, but I'm more bloody *furious*! Sneaking about in the night, murdering innocent plants – it's a cowardly, despicable thing to do. I hate this. And I'm getting to the stage where I'm more angry than afraid!"

Harry looked alarmed. "Cat, don't get reckless. If it's Stephen, he's waiting for you to do something unwise."

"*Unwise?* Like fighting back with some of the moves you taught me, rather than scuttling away like a scared rabbit?" She huffed and swung away, but Harry caught her arm.

"Cat, I'm scared for you. Whoever's doing this is getting bolder and they obviously aren't too squeamish to get their hands dirty. Remember the mouse? I don't want them trying anything with you!"

"I've been controlled enough over the last five years to last a lifetime!" she spat, wrenching her arm free. "No bastard stalker is going to do it again!"

Cat turned away just as she heard the slam of a car door. The police had arrived. She let them in and ran upstairs to dress. As she looked out of her bedroom window, she gasped at the words she could now see spelt out in the shrivelled lawn.

YOU'RE NEXT KITTY CAT.

PC DAVIS WAS STARING AT ONE OF HER WITHERED FERNS AS CAT strode outside, now dressed in jeans and a T-shirt. Harry stood by, quiet and watchful. A forensics officer in blue gloves and goggles was taking photographs and putting soil samples into test tubes.

"Found anything?" she asked, after a few moments.

PC Davis flicked his gaze over her folded arms and rigid stance. "We're just about to search the glasshouses," he replied evenly.

"Watch out for the tin in there: It's arsenic," she said.

PC Davis nodded. "Ready, Tony?" he asked his colleague, who nodded.

"You'll need better gloves," Cat said. "There's broken glass everywhere. Let me lend you some." She ran into the house.

"Thank you," murmured the policeman as he pushed his large hands into her leather gardening gloves.

Cat grimaced. "Better than nothing, eh?" She watched Tony pick his way across the littered floor, followed by PC Davis.

Harry glanced at his watch.

"Won't you be late?" Cat said, and instantly regretted her snippy tone. Come on, Cat, pull it together. It's not Harry's fault that there's a madman writing on your lawn in bleach and killing your plants.

"I'll text. A few minutes won't matter." He moved away. When he returned, she mouthed an apology.

"It would be great if they found something, but I'm not sure they will," he said. "Your stalker has been clever so far. There were no prints on the milk bottle, and unless they've been very careless this time... Look, Cat, are you sure you haven't spoken to anyone about all this?"

"I mentioned one of the earlier attacks to Creighton, because it was interfering with my writing and I had to tell him why I was late with the manuscript. But that was about a month ago. Oh, and I told Lizzie about the first text message, but nothing since."

Harry nodded. He seemed to be only half listening.

Forty minutes later, the policemen tiptoed out of the glasshouse and Tony pulled off Cat's gloves. "Nothing," he said. "You ought to remove the arsenic. What's it doing in there, anyway?"

"The Victorians used it for killing rats and weeds years ago," Cat

215

said. "I keep meaning to get rid of it, but there's always something else to do. And I've no idea where to take it."

"I've got to go into the office, but don't touch it, Cat," Harry said. "I'll take it to the chemist at the weekend."

PC Davis took out his notebook. "I think we've done as much as we can here. You might consider CCTV at the entrances to your garden and your front door."

With what? thought Cat, thinking of her bank balance.

"Tony will run the tests and write his report," PC Davis added.

"And will he report that some maniac has killed my plants with bleach?" Cat failed to keep the sarcasm from her voice and Harry shot her a warning look.

"If we had any clues about who holds a grudge against you, maybe we could make more progress," PC Davis said, without expression.

"My controlling ex-boyfriend isn't enough to go on?" Cat shot back. "Or the Victoriana obsessive who's already tried to buy me out of this house? Perhaps he wants to *scare* me out now!"

"We'll call on Mr Johnson and ask further questions. However, I *will* refer this to my sergeant, and ask him how he wants to proceed with Stephen Fergusson," PC Davis continued calmly.

"CID?" asked Harry. PC Davis nodded and Harry seemed to relax a little.

"We might be able to do more if the case gets referred," Tony commented, packing his kit away with neat, precise movements. He grinned at her. "CID love to be the cavalry; they'll find whoever's doing this."

They left, and she was alone with a hose and the wasteland that was her garden.

Chapter 28

Emily saw James' carriage pull up from her bedroom window. The train from London had been late, if the clock on the mantelpiece was to be trusted. The set of his shoulders showed how despondent he was.

Emily ran out to greet him and James' face lit up as she rushed downstairs, a lock of hair escaping as she did so. She sighed as he wrapped her in his arms. After a moment, he held her away from him and looped the hair behind her ear.

"I missed you so much!" Emily breathed, and he nodded, pulling her into the drawing room away from the stares of Watson and the servants. Once the door was closed, he drew her to him and kissed her deeply. A shiver of sensation went down to her toes, and she felt her flesh tingle as he held her tight.

Too soon, he drew away. "You look tired, James," she murmured.

"It's been a torturous few weeks. I seem to have been in committee every hour of every day."

She led him to the sofa and rang for refreshments. "Let me get you something to eat and drink; then you can tell me."

Fifteen minutes later, James sat back and sighed.

"I'm always amazed at the restorative properties of a cup of tea," she observed, handing him another scone.

He chuckled and she watched in satisfaction as he began to relax. He ate the scone, then threw down his napkin and pulled her into the crook of his arm.

Emily stroked the front of his waistcoat and listened to him breathing in the quiet room. "What happened?" she asked.

After a pause, he began to speak, his voice low. "I advanced my constitutional argument that a law applying solely to one half of the population was not to be countenanced, but so many members were unconvinced that I found myself alone. It did not help that they portrayed the women involved as harpies, purveyors of debauchery and desecraters of moral standards, infecting the troops and endangering the nation's safety."

"But even if the compulsion was only on the female side, surely their impact is only indirect?"

"There is that, but it wasn't the main thrust of my contribution. Sadly, what I said did not hold sway with my colleagues." James sighed. "The committee also held the discussions at very odd hours of the night. The lack of a transparent debate is something that has weighed heavily on my mind."

He fell silent, and Emily searched her brain for something to console him. Then he spoke again. "I am sure my father would have known how to present the argument. He was a decisive leader of men, but I found myself wavering on so many things that I could not emulate him. I feel oddly at sea, as though all the things I knew as indisputable facts have suddenly become unstable."

Emily's breath caught in her throat. Part of her was thrilled that James could not emulate what she knew of his father, while the other part ached for his defeat. She sat upright and clasped his face between her hands.

"My darling, how you have wrestled with your conscience! I am proud of you for doing your utmost to protect those whom everyone else in society has shunned, while balancing that with the needs of the country. What might have been repugnant to many, you tackled with enormous bravery. No, James, don't huff at me! The underbelly of our society is no place for the fainthearted – you lend your voice to those who would otherwise have none! I know you are worthy of every man's admiration."

His eyes searched her face as though uncertain. Emily returned his gaze and slowly, he pulled her closer and kissed her. It was a kiss that sent Emily's head spinning: gentle, tender and full of promise. When he drew away, her lips parted. "Are you tired, James?" she whispered.

His eyes widened. "I might be. Are you suggesting the kind of afternoon nap that we used to have, my love?"

"I am: I feel it would be restorative. Shall we go up for a few hours?" Emily smiled.

James' eyes glittered. "Would you lead the way?"

She grasped his hand and took him upstairs.

EMILY'S EYES FLUTTERED OPEN. JAMES' GAZE WAS FIXED ON HER face. "I'm sorry, I must have dozed off," she said, and made to sit up.

"No, stay where you are," James said softly. "There's no need to move, is there?"

She relaxed, relishing the smooth cotton pillow under her bare shoulders.

James smiled. "All right?" he asked.

She grinned. "Yes, I feel wonderful."

"Naughty puss!" He tweaked her nose and smiled, stretching his arms above his head. The sheets fell down to his waist, revealing his smooth shoulders and broad chest. Even in her sated state, Emily's stomach clenched again.

Good Lord, how shameless was she? She averted her gaze and drew a deep breath. James' brown eyes gleamed with understanding and he chuckled deep in his throat. He reached for her and with a small yelp she found herself straddling his lean thighs. "James!"

"Don't protest. You like it; I know you do."

She grinned, her face washed with colour.

He paused, pushing her heavy hair away from her face and tracing a line between her breasts, then sighed. "I should tell you about Freddie," he said, and she stayed silent. His lips tightened. "I paid a visit to Freddie and Cecily, and Ernest."

"Ernest is their baby son?"

He nodded. "Mother and son are hale and hearty, and Freddie looks like a dog with two tails." She caught the bitterness in his voice. "I offered my congratulations and stayed about an hour. At the end of my visit, Freddie himself saw me out. He assured me as delicately as he could that he had no expectations of the title, as we were likely to set up our own nursery imminently."

Emily blinked. "How kind of him," she murmured, not sure what to say.

James grinned at her. "Indeed, my love, I did not know whether to take offence or shake his hand and thank him, the impertinent cub! But he turned beetroot red as he spoke to me, so I am inclined to give him the benefit of the doubt and consider him sincere."

She sat back and pulled the coverlet over her shoulders. James winked. "Perhaps we need to prove him right."

Emily was unable to prevent a rush of anxiety that chilled her veins.

James put his head on one side, recognising her unease. "Emily, what's wrong?"

"I hesitate to make our lovemaking into something mechanical," she said slowly.

His eyes glinted under sleepy lids and he shifted his hips slightly, making her gasp as his erection pressed into her. "You have always been so sublimely responsive," he said thoughtfully. "I remember to this day how glad I was to feel your passion when we first married." His hand moved down and stroked between her damp curls. She moaned. "Is that mechanical?"

He cupped her breast, running a thumb over her nipple, which sprang into life at his touch. "You have taught me as much as I have taught you about intimacy, and I adore that we share a joint delight." He sat up suddenly and kissed her throat and a purr escaped her.

Emily placed her hands on his shoulders and pressed him back into the pillow. "You've made your point," she panted. "But I shall need reassurance every time, James."

He groaned as she shifted above him, curling his fingers around her hips as she sank down onto him. "I'll bear it in mind," he gasped as she began to move.

"So you can understand his despondency," Emily concluded, when telling Charlotte about events the following day.

Charlotte tapped a finger against her chin, nodding. "Yes – even though he conducted himself with honour, sometimes that is of less consequence than the victory."

Emily refilled her cup. "James felt his father might have been more successful in his endeavours—Charlotte! Are you all right?"

Charlotte had choked on her tea, and was wiping her chin with her lace handkerchief. She dabbed at the droplets on her skirt and waved Emily away. "I shall be well presently," she muttered, standing up briefly to brush herself down. "I beg your pardon, but did you ever meet Henry Cleveland?" she asked when she had taken her seat again.

"No: he had just died when I met James in Hatchard's."

Charlotte paused, her face uncertain. Emily patted her hand. "Please don't hesitate to speak your mind. I doubt James' father would have taken James' position."

Charlotte leaned back against the sofa, blowing her cheeks out.

They both laughed. "I am so relieved that we can speak plainly to one another!" said Charlotte.

"James holds his father in high esteem, though they apparently held opposing beliefs," Emily murmured. "He reveres his memory, and that of his elder brother, Charlie."

"Charlie is dead?"

"He died in the Battle of Inkerman."

Charlotte sucked in a breath and shook her head, her eyes wide with sympathy. "A terrible business. I read such nightmarish reports of the fog that blinded our troops. Though the Russians suffered the worst casualties, it was such a waste of allied lives! Indeed, a waste of *all* lives!"

Emily clasped her hands together, marshalling words that she had thought many times, but never had the courage to say. "James' father and brother haunt our lives," she began. "They provide the yardstick by which James measures his life. And I fear James will always find his life wanting, unless he goes into battle."

"And become another pointless casualty, slaughtered to serve the cause of men who simply wish to preserve their positions?" Charlotte huffed. "Friends of mine at Westminster say that fifty thousand men died to make Palmerston Prime Minister."

"Charlotte!"

"I know, my dear," Charlotte said, her mouth lifting in a wry smile. "You did not know that you harboured a rebel, I take it? In my view, which is unfashionable at best and treasonous at worst, war is a sport for aristocrats, played at as great a distance as can be managed."

Emily stared at Charlotte, who continued, "I am not sure what would be worth dying for, but Henry Cleveland viewed men's lives as dispensable where protecting trade was concerned. Including, it seems, the life of his eldest son."

Emily remained silent, remembering a bitter conversation with James about his brother some years earlier.

"We aligned our interests with the Ottomans to prevent Russian expansion and protect our precious trade routes, but Charlie knew nothing of this. He thought he was fighting for his country, when in fact he was fighting for a basket of oranges."

Emily stared unseeing into her cup, the thoughts in her head falling into place. "Apparently James' father was inconsolable when he learnt of Charlie's death," she murmured. "He suffered such a shock that he was never the same afterwards. He died only a year later; Mrs Cleveland says he died of a broken heart."

"Perhaps he had not accounted for the pain of losing his son," Charlotte replied calmly.

Emily shifted in her seat. Half of her was astonished to be having this conversation at all. She understood – had been *made* to understand – that had it not been for James' determination, his mother would not have so much as looked down her nose at Emily. It was out of the question that she might criticise the Cleveland family.

"Given his progressive stance on this parliamentary affair, I wonder why he is adamant that you should not publish your illustrations," said Charlotte. "Many gentlewomen do, and botany, as the reverend insists, is a very feminine pastime."

"It would lower me even further in his mother's eyes," Emily said immediately. A love match might be tolerated, but having failed to produce an heir, Emily had sunk in Mrs Cleveland's estimation. She had already struck a blow at the Cleveland lineage, and James' mother would brook no further assault on it. To publish an illustration would simply be vulgar.

"You must tell him soon," Charlotte warned.

SHE WAS DREADFULLY LATE. WITH A LITTLE HELP FROM MOLLY, Emily scrambled into another dress created by her maid and the clever fingers of the local dressmaker. While still grey, the silk had blue tones in it, and dark-blue cord adorned the bodice and skirt. In the mirror, she caught Molly's satisfied nod as she fastened the back.

Emily smiled, pleased with her reflection. Her eyes gleamed in the pale light from the window and her skin glowed.

"There you are, milady. As good as I can manage in ten minutes." Molly stepped away.

"You're a marvel," Emily replied, and hurried downstairs.

"You look splendid, my dear," James observed as she entered the drawing room. "Is that a new dress?"

Charlotte swivelled to look at her. "My, that looks as if Mr Worth himself might have designed it!"

Emily smiled. "I fear Mr Worth is considerably above me! No, this was made by a local dressmaker, guided by my maid Molly."

"Who is this Worth?" James enquired, and Charlotte launched into a description of the designer, his clientele, and the expense of his gowns. "Why should you not have a dress by the man himself, Emily? Why are you making do with copies?" Shocked, she registered his annoyance. While her own family could never have afforded a dress by the Paris-based designer, Sir James Cleveland certainly could.

She was searching for words when Watson announced Reverend Sherwood-Taylor and his wife. Emily jumped to her feet to welcome them, but a glance at James' face informed her that the conversation about the dress was by no means finished.

The reverend made his bow and Charlotte engaged Mrs Sherwood-Taylor in conversation. The reverend spoke of a recent storm and the damage it had wrought on the church roof. Emily declared that she had feared for her newly planted fernery. James responded civilly and before the reverend had even asked for one, offered a donation.

"How magnanimous of you!" The reverend beamed and rubbed his hands together. He continued to mutter the word 'magnanimous' as he reached for his tea, then looked up. "But I forget myself!" He turned to Emily. "Lady Emily, I have a journal for you! I felt sure you would welcome a publication so focused on your particular passion. Margaret, do you have it?"

Emily watched Mrs Sherwood-Taylor reach for her reticule and extract a magazine. A cold lump grew in her stomach as the reverend handed over the latest edition of *Phytologist*. Her gaze fell on Charlotte, whose own eyes had widened at the potential disaster: Emily's illustration would be in this edition.

Emily snatched up the journal. "How kind!" She clutched the journal and, after flicking blindly through a few pages, put it firmly down the arm of the sofa. James, she saw, was glancing at his pocket watch.

"There are some truly excellent illustrations," trilled Mrs Sherwood-Taylor. "I declare, you might almost feel the fronds of the ferns!"

James looked up and his eyebrows drew together.

"Printing techniques have developed considerably over the past few years," Charlotte said hurriedly.

Emily picked up her cup with a hand that trembled, abandoning the conversation to her guests. She longed to seize the journal and leave the room, but that was impossible. The visit dragged on. The journal on the sofa seemed to glow, attracting the attention of all.

Charlotte stood up to take her leave, giving Reverend and Mrs Sherwood-Taylor a hint that they too should depart, particularly as the reverend had achieved his aim of a generous donation for the church roof. James nodded to their guests and while Emily escorted them to the hall. She took leave of her guests, then hastened to the drawing room as soon as the front door was closing.

James looked up as she ran in, his eyes like stone. She stopped dead, a buzz starting in her ears as she registered the hurt and anger that marred his handsome face.

Between finger and thumb, he slowly raised the journal, open at a page with an illustration of a maidenhair fern. "I wondered where your painting had gone, Emily. Now, that has become very clear."

Chapter 29

Emily

Sunday 20 May 1862: The servants creep around as though there has been a death. J and I have barely spoken for three days and my muscles ache with tension. J is pale and unhappy, and looks at me strangely. Indeed, I am beginning to feel as if my recovery never happened and I am back in London again, dreading every day. While the discord between us looms large in my head, I feel another disaster approaches, though I know not from which direction.

At least ironing would be a change from pulling out dead plants, Cat reflected. She'd saved a couple of ferns, but there were immense holes in the fernery where once there had been healthy greenery. The bleach smell was fainter, but still lingered; it explained why Batman hadn't come to her windowsill.

Cat forced herself to concentrate as she shook the creases out of a T-shirt. Was it wearable? She held it at arm's-length and scrunched up her nose. No: she'd look like she'd fallen out of bed. Sighing, she threw it on the back of a chair and unearthed the iron from a cupboard.

Her phone rang and she recognised the number of PC Davis. "Cat?

I wanted to tell you that we've spoken to Geoff Johnson. He's been visiting London and he couldn't have damaged your garden. He has a very solid alibi."

"What about Stephen?"

"We haven't been able to speak to Stephen yet as he's away from home. We'll let you know when we do, but I don't want you to build up your hopes. We've no prints and nothing on street CCTV to prove that he was anywhere near your property."

When the call had ended, Cat stared out of the window. When was this going to stop? She'd install a security camera as soon as she could afford it. She'd buy one now, but her credit cards were maxed out. Maybe this was the one time she should ask her parents for money...

She blew out her cheeks. Yes, this was an emergency. She needed to call her mother and ask for a loan.

Cat dialled her mother's number and it went to voicemail. "Hi Mum. Er, can you give me a call? I need to talk to you about something. Love to Dad."

She was fighting with the legs of the ironing board – hell, she didn't use it that often – when her phone rang again and she swore. It was probably her mother, ringing when Cat was struggling with household equipment. Finally she moved to the dining table, where the phone buzzed against the smooth wood. The display showed Unknown Number and she went cold. For a few seconds, she watched it ring and ring.

Her nerves were stretched tight when she snatched up the phone. She accepted the call, put the phone to her ear, and said nothing. Come on, you weirdo, talk to me.

"Playing hard to get, kitty-cat?" the metallic voice said, sounding amused. "I'll still come for you, whether or not you talk to me."

"Oh, bugger off," Cat said in disgust, and disconnected. She grinned at the rush of power that coursed through her. "Arsehole," She went to make her T-shirt presentable.

LATER THAT AFTERNOON, SPURRED ON TO IRON ALL THE CLOTHES in the ironing basket, Cat was on her last T-shirt when she heard a knock at the front door. She glanced at the app on her phone to see who was outside. Lauren, with a scowl on her face.

She ran to throw open the door. "Um... hello?" Cat said.

Lauren threw her hands up. "Sorry to arrive unannounced, but your bloody phone's turned off! I wanted to show some sister solidarity after those pillocks turned down your book." She pulled Cat into a hug.

"Don't be daft, it's lovely to see you! Are you okay? You look pale," Cat said as she headed to the kitchen.

"Man trouble," Lauren said, bitterly. "And before you ask, you don't want to know."

"I wish you could find a decent bloke. There must be some decent guys in North London."

"You'd think so, but sadly I only find the bastards."

Cat frowned as she caught the tension in Lauren's voice. She finished making tea and placed the mug in front of Lauren, noting the lines of strain under her eyes. "Are you sure you don't want to talk about it?"

Lauren hesitated and Cat thought she saw the sheen of tears in her friend's eyes. But Lauren shook her head firmly. "No sweetie, it's too dull for words. Thanks for asking."

"Are you staying?"

"I was hoping you'd let me hang out and lick my wounds, unless you're busy?" Lauren glanced at the laundry. "Why the domesticity? You hate ironing!"

"I know, but I figure that if I have to talk pretty to potential new publishers, I'd better look as if I can string a sentence together."

Lauren took a swig from the mug, closed her eyes and sank back against the sofa cushions. "God, I needed this. So you haven't reignited your passion with Harry?"

"I've barely seen him since he got his new job."

He'd been in contact by text, but Cat didn't mention this. The texts had been tentative, careful from Harry's side.

"I'm pleased he didn't interrupt the edits!" Lauren laughed. "He's very distracting."

"Wrong, all wrong... God, now who is it?"

"Busy, busy," grinned Lauren and continued to sip her tea.

Cat ran to answer the door. "Oh hi, Harry." He was gazing at Lauren's car.

He turned and smiled at her and she felt as if the sun had come out. "I saw you had guests, but I wanted to ask if you fancied sharing a take-away tonight?"

"Sure. Lauren's here, but she can join us, can't she?"

His silver-grey eyes rested on her for a few seconds and he smiled. "Yeah, of course. Are you okay? Any unpleasant phone calls?"

She stared at him, then stepped onto the front step, pulling the door to behind her. "This lunchtime. How did you know?"

"That's interesting. Have you mentioned it to anyone? No? Good, keep it quiet." He raised his voice. "Right, shall we get this evening organised?" He strode past her. "Hello, Lauren, fancy sharing an Indian takeaway tonight? Take pity on a lonely copper looking to celebrate his promotion."

"Promotion? Are you allowed to talk to plebs like us now?"

"Normally you need to make an appointment, but it's your lucky day! And because I'm crashing your evening, it's my treat."

Lauren laughed. "If you're buying, it's a date!"

"Great, I'll drop the menus round." He turned to Cat. "Text me your order." He left, whistling, and Cat was thoughtful as she returned to the drawing room.

"What happened to your lawn?" Lauren said, peering out of the patio doors in the twilight. Her voice sounded strange to Cat. She glanced at Harry, who was placing foil trays carefully on the dining table.

"Cat's had a few problems with local kids," Harry said calmly.

Lauren, very pale, turned to face Cat. "What problems? Why haven't you told me?"

Cat grinned apologetically. "It's relatively recent. And what with the book and everything, it's kind of low down the pecking order."

"*Low down the pecking order?* What the hell has been going on?"

"They dripped something corrosive on the lawn," Harry said, opening a carton of something with bright yellow sauce. "The lawn will recover eventually. That reminds me, Cat, I've got some lawn seed back at mine. You can reseed it when you've cut out the damage."

"You're incredibly chilled about this, Cat." Lauren said, looking hard at Cat.

Cat rubbed her nose, avoiding Lauren's gaze. What on earth will she say when I tell her about the ferns? "It's disturbing, but I have new locks on the garden gates."

"I've got that contact for CCTV, don't let me forget to give it to you," Harry added.

Cat blinked. They hadn't spoken about CCTV.

"Shall we eat?" he said casually.

Lauren folded her arms. "I can't believe your *ex* knows more about what's going on than I do!"

"He lives next door, Lauren! How could he not know? And you've been so busy with the new job..."

"Have you told the police?" Lauren asked. Again, Cat caught an urgency in her voice that seemed out of place.

"Of course she has. It's criminal damage," Harry said, reaching for a spoon. "Aren't you going to eat? I bought the dish you wanted—"

"How the hell can you talk about food when Cat's home is being threatened? When *Cat* is being threatened?"

Harry shot her a level look. "*Is* Cat being threatened?"

Lauren threw up her hands. "Isn't she? Pouring bleach on some-one's lawn is hardly friendly, is it? I can't believe you're so freakin' calm about what's happened!"

Cat stared at Lauren, feeling the floor fall away from her. Nausea swirled in her stomach. "We never mentioned bleach," she said, at last. "But that's what it was."

Lauren froze, staring at her.

"Interesting," Harry said softly, taking his phone out of his pocket and dialling a number. "Phil? Yeah, think we got him – or rather, her. Sure, come now." He ended the call.

Lauren stumbled to the sofa and reached for her bag. "I'm leaving," she said, her voice shaking.

Harry stepped quickly in front of her. Lauren turned to look at Cat. "Surely you don't believe this crap. I'm your best friend!"

Cat opened her mouth, but no sound came out. The world seemed blank, drained of colour. *Lauren* had done this? Her best friend?

When Lauren moved, Cat barely saw it: it was so fast. Harry fell to the floor, blood on his forehead, and lay still.

"Harry!" she cried and moved towards him, but Lauren whirled to face her, eyes wide and staring, with something in her hand.

Cat dived towards the verandah windows, wrenching them open and tumbling into the garden.

ONCE OUTSIDE, CAT PULLED IN GREAT LUNGFULS OF AIR AND screamed as loud as she could. Her head was dizzy with the implica-tions. Her *best* friend, her friend from school, had scared her, threat-ened her, damaged her garden...

And what about Harry? Oh God, was he dead? Blackness swamped her for a moment. Then Lauren came through the patio doors and Cat darted towards the fernery. Lauren followed, and for a few minutes they played an increasingly desperate game of cat and mouse in the walled garden.

Panting, she finally ended up by the greenhouses. Lauren, her expression set, walked slowly towards her.

Oh, shit. Breathe. Don't panic.

"I can't believe you've done this!" she cried. Lauren set her jaw and continued to move forward.

Cat planted her legs firmly, trying to remember what Harry had taught her. When Lauren rushed at her, Cat ducked so that Lauren's wild swing missed her. She grabbed Lauren's wrist and twisted it underneath her arm. Lauren gave a cry of pain as Cat forced her arm up her back and stumbled against the greenhouse door. The pane shattered and Lauren crashed against the rickety shelves. Cat watched in horror as the tin on the top shelf wobbled and fell, showering Lauren with grey-white dust. Lauren began to cough.

"Oh no!" Cat looked around wildly. Her discarded gardening gloves were on the wall of the fernery. She rushed to grab them, pulling them on as she ran back.

"Lauren, it's arsenic! Keep your mouth shut!" she shouted as she ran into the greenhouse and dragged Lauren away from the deadly clouds of powder and on to the lawn, Cat rolled Lauren over so that she was face down. With a terrified glance at her, she ran inside the house.

Chapter 30

When she saw James' face, as he held out the journal that contained her illustration, Emily stopped dead, her heart in her mouth.

Oh God, what can I say? I could deny it... No: that would be pointless and would only inflame James further. She put back her shoulders. Cringing might appease James, but she would feel horrible. So she took a deep breath and walked steadily into the room. "May I see?"

He handed over the journal and she examined her illustration. It was beautiful, eclipsing the others she found when she leafed through the pages. Her face warmed, and she knew she had turned pink.

"What do you have to say for yourself?" James snapped.

My illustration is superb. Are you not proud of me? "I am sorry if it displeases you."

"Displeased? Emily, I don't know what disappoints me more – that you submitted without my permission or that you deceived me!"

"The submission was anonymous," Emily protested. "I only agreed that they could use it on that condition."

"Emily, you are so naive! The publisher must know who you are to agree to your conditions."

She was silent. James' eyes narrowed. "Unless you submitted through someone else. In that case, a potential gossip-monger appears as a friend."

Emily shook her head, unwilling to drag Charlotte into the matter. Emily was not worried about Charlotte revealing who had submitted the illustration. Charlotte would never gossip about her.

James studied Emily. "It was Charlotte Chester, wasn't it? Good God, a woman who already sets gossips' tongues wagging! I should never have let you form such a close acquaintance."

"Charlotte, as you yourself said, is a woman of character," Emily responded tartly. "And I do not know why you are at odds with her, because she holds views very similar to yours! She is a true, loyal friend, and would no sooner betray me than you would!"

At that, the colour rose in James' face. His mouth moved, but no sound emerged. Eventually, he managed to speak. "What else have you neglected to tell me? I sincerely hope, given that you have deliberately disobeyed me, there is no more."

"I submitted the illustration before you hinted that my work wasn't good enough," Emily said, her tone even. "But after that conversation I was so angry that when the journal wrote to Charlotte that they would welcome more of my paintings, I sent a second one."

His eyes widened in disbelief. "As they want more of my work and are happy to pay me for it—"

"*What?*" James roared.

Emily flinched but pressed on. "Given that they were happy to pay me and wanted more of my illustrations, I calculated that my terms of anonymity were more likely to be kept." She folded her arms over her thumping heart.

"How much did they pay you?"

She told him. He bit back a curse and paced the room. He looked hurt and bewildered, and part of her could not fault him for that. She had lied to her own husband!

"I begin to wonder what is wrong with your wits, Emily," he said, and she started at his choice of words. "I own half of Cheshire. My

234

family tree stretches back to William the Conqueror. Yet you copy the designs of a dressmaker when I could easily buy an entire wardrobe for you. And then you deceive me, and sell your paintings—"

"Is a little economy such a dreadful thing?" Emily protested, stung. "I am in Cambridge, not Paris. It was easier to have something made here than set sail for France! And I did not ask for payment for the illustration – the journal offered it!"

"But why did you take it?"

"Because I *earned* it!" she cried. "You *give* me everything! It was exhilarating to receive twenty pounds, knowing that I had created something worth the money!"

Neither spoke, yet the audible breathing which signalled their anger and frustration filled Emily's ears.

"I never thought you would throw the generosity of your allowance in my face. This must cease," he said flatly. "And my mother must never hear of this."

Emily bristled. "So I must stop doing something I love, something valued by others, something that no one even knows is connected to this family, because you fear what your *mother* would think? James, we are trying for a child. I did not know I already had one!"

He gaped at her as she left him.

EMILY BLOTTED THE JOURNAL, SWALLOWING HARD. SHE WATCHED the raindrops trickle steadily down the windowpane. The sky was leaden grey, mirroring the atmosphere in Cleveland House.

Lucky, sensitive to her dismal mood, licked her hand. She smiled, stroking his head. "Do you need to go out, Lucky? I'm sorry the weather is so abominable."

"Should I take him into the garden, ma'am?" Molly put aside her mending and rose to her feet.

Emily shook her head. "No, I shall take him out. It will help my head."

"Is it still aching? Shall I fetch a tisane?"

"The headache is gone, but my head feels stuffy. I shall take my umbrella and get some fresh air."

After locking away the journal, Emily slipped her arms into the coat that Molly held for her and attached the leash to Lucky's collar. Would James be downstairs? The house had been silent since breakfast.

With Lucky trotting beside her, Emily walked downstairs. From the hall, she could see that James' study door was ajar. She paused. This situation could not continue: it was making her nauseous.

She knocked softly and stepped into the room, but it was empty. She sighed.

Lucky, who was never allowed in James' study, took the opportunity to sniff around. To Emily's dismay, he jerked his leash away and scurried under the desk.

"Lucky, you little horror! Come back at once!" Emily reached under the desk, banging her head as she grabbed Lucky's leash. "Ow!" She straightened up slowly, holding on to the dog, and rubbed the crown of her head.

As her vision settled she saw a letter unfolded on the desk, with a blank sheet of paper beside it; it looked as if James was about to write a reply. Her breath caught in her throat. "Dr Schenley!" she whispered, cold seeping through her veins.

As though hypnotised, she sat down in the massive leather chair and picked up the pages covered with Dr Schenley's cramped black handwriting. The world receded as she read the letter, dated two days earlier.

Sir—

I apologise for such a long delay in responding. I have been at a medical conference in Paris and I travelled to Germany to see colleagues afterwards.

Saddened as I am to receive your communication, I am not surprised by Lady Cleveland's demeanour, which I would initially diagnose as hysteria. It is clear to me now that her discontinuation of the laudanum when I last saw her was a portent of this wider malady. What you describe to me is a classic symptom of disorders in the womb and reproductive organs, as the article I sent you some months ago indicated. I have since spoken to the venerated Dr Acton, and he agrees with me that women are more susceptible to the loss of a child than men. Your wife's behaviour is the outward demonstration of disruption to the unassailable bond between the psyche and the body. As the Lancet states: 'madness... is a sufficiently common result of disturbed ovarian function.' Your news of this latest development is a natural consequence of the progression of the disease.

I am happy to accept your commission and will visit you when I have the business in hand.

I remain your obedient servant,
  Dr Robert Schenley

Emily gasped and grabbed the edge of the desk to steady herself. Pain at James' betrayal and fear of Dr Schenley's 'commission' made her faint. Lucky whined. She grabbed his leash and walked blindly out of the room to the garden. Unheeding of the rain, she headed towards the fernery.

The dull light showed the ferns to advantage: raindrops sparkled from their feathery fronds and lacy leaves. The path winding through the rockery seemed to offer protection from the weather and from life, and gradually Emily's pulse returned to normal. The fernery seemed to call to her, soothing her anxiety. Ferns had survived for millennia. They would have known some trials, yet here they still flourished.

As the minutes passed, determination grew in her. She would fight this injustice. She was not insane because she wanted to grow ferns and publish illustrations!

In her heart she knew that James loved her – but he was being led astray by Dr Schenley and the ghostly voice of his father, whose views about women had been forged in another age. Surely, though, times were changing?

"Lady Cleveland?" Watson called from the house.

The fernery concealed her, and for a wild moment she considered remaining silent. But Lucky barked and betrayed her, and with a sigh, she walked to the end of the fernery path.

Watson strode across the lawn, holding an umbrella. "Begging your pardon, ma'am, but you'll catch your death of cold in this rain!" He thrust it over her, and she smiled her thanks.

"I must be quite mad, mustn't I?" Emily said lightly, and let out a peal of laughter when he frowned.

She composed herself as she entered the house. Quips like that could get her locked up.

EMILY HEADED TO HER SITTING ROOM. WATSON ASKED IF HE should send Molly to her but she shook her head. "The fire will soon dry me, but please bring some tea." When he left, she shut the door and put a hand to her forehead, her thoughts racing.

You must be calm and think rationally, she told herself, and took a seat in her favourite armchair by the fire. To her dismay, though, rather than rational thoughts and clever stratagems, she could focus on nothing but Dr Schenley's black handwriting. When Watson returned with the tea, she was still staring into the fire.

Roused at last, she wrote a note to Charlotte. James had forbidden visits from Lady Chester but had said nothing about correspondence. In her heart she knew this was sophistry: James would still be angry. However, James' fury did not outweigh her fear of being trapped by Dr Schenley. Emily sealed the envelope, reflecting that practising deceit led to more.

A knock at the door revealed Molly with one of Emily's Indian shawls. She bobbed a curtsy and settled the rich fabric around Emily's shoulders. "Beggin' your pardon, ma'am, but Watson mentioned that you'd been caught in the rain. I thought you might welcome the shawl."

Emily managed a smile and thanked her.

"Don't want you ill again, ma'am."

Emily gave her the envelope. "Ensure that this makes the post, please, and speak to no one about it. Do you understand? No one." Molly nodded, eyes wide. "And tell Watson to bring any reply to me, and me alone."

Molly slipped out and Emily breathed deeply, her fingers clutching the silky, warm, peacock-coloured threads of the shawl. She had asked Charlotte not to reply directly, but to send back a book with an innocuous note to signal that she would help. She picked up her embroidery and mindlessly plied her needle.

Two hours later, Watson appeared with a small parcel. It was a copy of *Jane Eyre*. Emily's mouth twisted at the placing of the bookmark: the revelation of Bertha Mason, Mr Rochester's insane wife. Charlotte's note read:

> *Ma'am – I return the book you were kind enough to lend me. I trust you are well. Yrs affectionately, Charlotte Chester.*

Tucking the book into the shelf by her bed, determination swelled in Emily's breast. She would prevail.

Chapter 31

Emily

Tuesday 31st May 1862: Cleveland House and the fernery are a balm to my spirits: by some strange power they bring me solace and comfort. I would not willingly leave this place, particularly as summer comes. I pray I do not have to!

T he call handler's voice was calm, which steadied Cat's shattered nerves. "So – a head injury and arsenic poisoning? He's unconscious, you say? Is the patient breathing?"

"I don't know!" She ran over to Harry and saw that his head was still bleeding. That was a good sign, wasn't it? She felt for a pulse, trying to slow down her panicked breathing. Be calm, Cat. She finally felt a beat under her fingers. "Y-yes, he's breathing."

"Okay, that's good. Do you know the recovery position?"

"Yes, I learned it at school."

"Excellent. Turn him over, make sure the airway isn't restricted, and put a blanket over him."

Cat pulled the rug from the sofa and tucked it around Harry's shoulders. She drew a shaky breath and stroked his white cheek with her hand.

"Right, now the arsenic victim. Where is she?"

"In the garden. I turned her face down, so she'd swallow less of the powder."

"Good. Are you contaminated too?"

Cat looked down at her dusty jeans and top. "Yes. Should I change my clothes?"

"Probably, but most importantly, wash your arms and hands really well – then you won't transfer poison to any new clothes or anyone else. Hang in there: the ambulance will be with you shortly."

"Should I try to wash the dust off Lauren, too? The person in the garden?"

"That would be helpful, but then she'll be outside and wet. Use a flannel or a wet towel to wipe the poison from her nose and mouth, but wear gloves if you have them." There was a pause. "The ambulance is three minutes away. I'll stay on the line. You get washed up."

"Right. Thanks."

Cat ripped off her clothes in the bathroom, kicking them into a corner, and stuck her head under the shower. Then she scrubbed her hands and arms and padded through the bedroom to find jeans and a fresh sweater. She grabbed a fresh towel for Lauren, soaked it in water and ran downstairs.

Hunting under the sink, she drew out an unused pair of rubber gloves and ran into the garden, her eyes lingering on Harry as she passed him.

"Okay, I'm in the garden," she told the call handler.

"Gloves?"

"Yes, I'm wearing them."

"Excellent. If it's powder, don't get too close," warned the voice.

Lauren was still on the ground, coughing. She was also crying. Cat put the phone down, knelt beside her and touched her shoulder. "Lauren, let me wipe some of the powder off. The ambulance is on its way."

Lauren looked up, her eyes panicked, and Cat wiped her face with the wet towel, trying to get the poison away from Lauren's mouth and nostrils.

"Was it you? All the letters and calls?" Cat asked quietly. "Did you steal my key and creep around outside, taking photos like some pervert?"

Lauren was silent.

"I know it was you, Lauren." Lauren said nothing. "What is wrong with you? What have I done? Haven't we been friends for years?" Cat cried.

"Stephen said you were using me, just like you used him."

"What? I used *Stephen?*"

"Yeah. You lived off him when your third book tanked." Lauren sneered. "And then you dumped him when you'd squeezed him dry."

Cat gaped at her. "Is that what the little shit told you?"

Lauren glared at her. "I've always been around to help, haven't I? He said you were using me, and you'd forget me when you had the next bestseller. He told me you destroyed him!"

"*I* destroyed *him?*" Cat could barely keep her voice from shaking with anger. "That bastard practically kept me under house arrest! He emptied our joint account and took most of my royalties! When I left him, I had one bloody suitcase from the flat we shared! Creighton had to get someone to break down the door so that I could leave, because the little shit *locked me in*! I told you endless times how controlling he was, but you never listened, did you?"

"What? No, that can't be right. Stephen would never do that."

"No? That time you called to take me out on your birthday, when he told you I wasn't well? I was fine, but I was hiding in the bedroom because he told me I was a disgrace, and that I shouldn't be allowed out looking like I did!"

"I—"

"Then there was the time he told Creighton that he wasn't the right agent for me and I needed someone in tune with modern tastes. *I* didn't say it, Stephen did! Or the time he went through my wardrobe and threw away half my clothes because he thought they made me look like a tramp. Or the endless bloody rules – when to turn the heating on or off, when I could have a shower, what hairdresser I could go to... You don't know the half of it. I'll ask Creighton to tell you the story of my escape, if you like," Cat said bitterly.

"You're just making this up!" Lauren cried. "You're right – it *was* me! I didn't sent the first message – Stephen sent that – but all the others," she said. "Every time you changed your phone you sent me the new number. I got the mouse from a pet shop. I took the gate key when I put away your shopping that time. And I ruined your garden. Stephen asked me to..."

Cat gasped, pierced by the confession. "I can't believe he took you in!" A light went on in Cat's brain. "Oh, God. You're in love with Stephen. That's why you've done all this vile stuff!"

A moment passed and then Lauren's face crumpled.

"Let me guess – he slept with you," Cat said bitterly, but not expecting Lauren to nod. She gaped and for the first time, tears appeared in Lauren's eyes.

"He – he never even looked at me while you were around! I tried to tell myself that if you made him happy, that was enough for me – but it wasn't! When you dumped him, I thought we would be together at last ... and he had sex with me."

Cat's mouth fell open. Lauren continued, her voice rising. "The next morning, he bloody *cried* and said it was a mistake! He said he could never love anyone but you, because you'd stolen his soul!"

Cat folded her arms, feeling nauseous. "Oh yes, that sounds like Stephen. Do something awful, then blame it on someone else. And this is why you sent me those vile texts? Did he *ask* you to?"

Lauren nodded and Cat's ears buzzed with fury. "What else did he make you do?" she demanded. "Because he will have made you do a lot, knowing Stephen!"

Lauren closed her eyes and turned her head away. "He convinced me to pull out of going to South Africa so I could keep sending the texts... When I told him we were going too far, he said he'd my boss about my dyslexia..." Lauren coughed again.

Where was this bloody ambulance? Cat heard a distant siren and pushed her rage aside. "That's the ambulance, Lauren. I'll be right back."

She ran inside as the crew knocked on the door, and wrenched it open. "Thank God! In here!"

One paramedic knelt to examine Harry and Cat waved the other towards Lauren. She'd barely drawn breath when her phone rang. Startled, she answered it automatically.

"Beanie, I've been trying to get through for ages!" said her mother.

Cat shook her head in disbelief. "Sorry, Mum, I'm busy."

"But you rang me! And I wanted to speak to you about Anthony's birthday. It's in two weeks!"

Cat rolled her eyes. "Mum, I'm *very* busy. I'll talk to you later."

"But—"

Cat disconnected the call. Of all the bloody times...

A groan made her spin around. Harry was conscious. The paramedic was speaking softly to him. Slowly, Harry raised himself on his elbows. Cat wrapped her arms around herself; her heart was banging against her ribs. The paramedic shone a light into Harry's eyes, then moved their finger from right to left while Harry's eyes followed it. "A couple of sutures and you'll be good as new," he said cheerfully after looking at Harry's head.

Harry gazed at Cat, who gave him a watery smile. "I'd hug you, but I may still have arsenic on me, so best not," she said. He nodded, then inhaled sharply as the paramedic dabbed his wound.

"Will he be all right?" she asked.

"He'll have a headache, but there's no concussion, so yes. We'll take him in overnight."

"No," Harry said at once. "I'm not going to hospital."

"We'll see," said the paramedic. He glanced at Cat. "Could you go and check how my colleague's getting on?"

Reluctantly, Cat left Harry and went into the garden.

THE PARAMEDIC WAS WEARING WHITE PROTECTIVE CLOTHING AND had donned plastic goggles. She was taking Lauren's blood pressure. She looked up at Cat. "Stay back, please. Have you changed your clothes?"

"Yes, and I had a quick shower." The paramedic nodded and the BP monitor made a noise. She frowned. Cat kept her distance, but Lauren looked terrified.

"Can you tell me what happened?" the paramedic asked.

"Lauren fell against the shelf in the greenhouse and the tin fell on her."

"What was the poison doing there?"

Cat took a deep breath. "I believe it's been there for years. The Victorians used to use it for killing weeds."

"That so? Well, at least you were smart enough to wipe her down – that will have helped. What were you doing in the garden? No, you stay quiet," she said sternly to Lauren.

Cat gritted her teeth. "We were having a row about an old boyfriend."

"The bloke with the head injury?"

"No, another one."

"Ah. So where does the bloke with the head injury fit in? How did he get hurt?"

"I didn't see," Cat said, thankful that she was telling the truth. "One minute we were sharing a takeaway, the next Harry was lying unconscious."

"Hmm." The paramedic addressed Lauren. "We'll get you to hospital. You're going to feel very unwell in the next half hour. If we're going to stop the effects of the poison, we'll need to get a move on." She spoke into her radio.

Lauren's eyelids drooped.

"Lauren! Stay awake!" Cat barked.

The other paramedic arrived, also in a protective suit, carrying a stretcher. Gently, they picked Lauren up and carried her to the ambulance. The tears made streaks in the powder that still clung to Lauren's face.

Cat reached out and gripped Lauren's hand. "Just get well. I know what Stephen is like and you're just another of his victims. We can sort all this out afterwards," she murmured.

Lauren, her eyes closed, nodded, and the paramedics lifted her into the ambulance.

Then the police arrived, sirens screaming and lights flashing. Cat scowled at PC Davis as he and two other officers piled out of the car. "You took your bloody time!"

"Looks like you've been having fun," he commented, slamming the car door. "Where's DCI Moore?"

"In the house, having his head bandaged."

"What? Show me."

Cat led them into the drawing room. "You ought to come to hospital and get a scan," the second paramedic was saying to Harry, with a frown. "There may be a fracture."

Fat chance, thought Cat.

"I'm fine: you've checked me over. I just need painkillers and a decent kip. Phil, tell this lovely man I'm fine."

"I think you should take him into hospital," PC Davis said. "He's clearly delusional."

Harry swore, and the paramedic shook his head. "Suit yourself. Call 999 or get yourself to hospital if you feel dizzy or sick."

"I have a hard head," Harry replied. Tutting, the paramedic left.

"Want to tell me about it, sir?" PC Davis said, casting an eye over the food congealing in foil boxes on the table.

Harry told the story of how Lauren had given herself away. "And then she hit me with the pepper grinder—"

Cat goggled. "The pepper grinder? *My* pepper grinder?"

Harry nodded, then winced and rubbed the back of his neck. "Yeah, it's over there." He pointed to the pepper grinder which had rolled by the leg of the table. It was a lucky blow, but I was out like a light. What happened to you, Cat? You're wet."

"We ran into the garden and Lauren came at me, so I did one of the self-defence moves Harry showed me. She went flying, crashed into the greenhouse and knocked the arsenic all over herself. The paramedic told me to wash it off me and her, hence my wet hair. Stephen fed her a load of lies..." Cat paused, wondering how much to say.

"And?" prompted PC Davis.

"Lauren took matters into her own hands, but she was being manipulated by my disgusting ex," Cat said.

"Did she admit to the criminal damage and the harassment?" demanded PC Davis.

Cat nodded, reluctantly.

PC Davis scratched his chin. "We did a check on the phone number the perpetrator used to call you," he said. "The phone was only used to call your mobile. There was another call this afternoon – thanks for the tip-off, sir." He glanced at Harry, who nodded in acknowledgement. "We did a quick trawl of our CCTV feeds and found someone answering Lauren's description topping up the data at a garage a couple of miles down the road."

Cat ached all over and her head throbbed, but in addition, she was full of vicious rage. Even now, Stephen was interfering with her life and screwing up her friendships. Harry reached over and clasped her hand, but pulled it back when PC Davis's eyebrows rose.

Cat's hands were shaking and she clasped them together. "What will happen now?" she said. "When can I see Lauren?"

PC Davis closed his notebook. "After we've spoken to her."

"Will you charge her?"

"It depends on what she says, and if she's prepared to talk about the pressure Fergusson put her under." PC Davis stood up and nodded to the other officers.

"Will you please let me know when I can go to the hospital?" Cat asked urgently. "She's covered in arsenic. She could be really ill!"

"I'll call you after we've talked to the doctors and the paramedics.

Please don't leave Cambridge."

Dazed, Cat walked them to the door. When she came back into the drawing room she looked at Harry, his hair midnight dark against his pale face. As he stood up, he swayed, and Cat flew to catch his arm.

"You're fine, eh?" She heaved a sigh, suddenly exhausted as the last of her adrenalin trickled away. "Look, you'd better stay with me in case anything happens in the night. Don't get any ideas, this is just medicinal."

He looked at her, his silver eyes glinting in the light. "It will be. I'm in no fit state for anything else."

ABOUT THREE IN THE MORNING, CAT WOKE WITH A START, AN alien, yet achingly familiar sensation disturbing her. Harry was on his stomach, sound asleep and his arm had sought her across the double bed. His large hand curled around the curve of her waist and he tugged her toward him. For a moment, she resisted but then softened: it would wake him if she pulled away. So she shuffled backwards into his lean body and as his warmth seeped into her skin, she drifted back into slumber.

THE SMELL OF COFFEE DRAGGED CAT FROM SLEEP. SHE OPENED her eyes and memories of the previous night came flooding back. Harry was beside her bed, holding a mug.

She propped herself up on her elbows, her ancient pyjama top straining, and peered up at him. His bandage had slipped off during the night and an enormous bruise, purple and black, had bloomed on his temple.

"Morning." Harry placed the mug on her bedside table and sat on the window seat.

"How's the head?"

"Sore."

She nodded and sipped the coffee. She needed the loo, but she didn't want to get out of bed while Harry was watching.

"Thanks for this," she added, raising the mug. "What time is it?"

"Just gone nine. I need to go to work. I just wanted to check you were okay before I left."

"I'm fine," she said. "But I'm not sure what happens next with Lauren and Stephen."

"They'll talk to Lauren when she's sufficiently recovered: don't contact her in the meantime. They'll arrest Fergusson on suspicion of involvement of harassment. PC Davis will be in touch to ask you further questions when he's spoken with the CPS – the Crown Prosecution Service."

"Will they go to gaol?"

Harry shrugged and rose to his feet. "It depends if the CPS thinks it has enough evidence to prosecute. But, yes, if they take it to court, Lauren could go to gaol. If her lawyers can show she was being coerced by Fergusson, she might get a lighter sentence. At the very least, she's caused criminal damage."

"And Stephen?"

"Fergusson may face a charge but that's not certain. We'll try..."

Cat looked into the mug, her anger simmering. God, would he get away with his behaviour yet again? While Lauren, deluded, deceived Lauren, took all the blame?

"Listen, there's a long way to go yet," said Harry. "Try not to worry."

She nodded and managed a smile, remembering the warmth of an outstretched arm from last night.

"Thanks for staying with me last night," Harry said.

"I couldn't have you flake out on me – especially as it was my pepper grinder."

He grinned. "I'll see you later, Cat."

Chapter 32

E mily pressed her fingers to her forehead, weary with thinking about Dr Schenley's commission and James' involvement. The house was silent and sad. Even though summer was coming, James' attitude chilled her to the bone. He seemed a statue: distant, cold. Emily had considered her predicament from every angle, when an idea pierced the gloom of her thoughts. If she was with child, surely James would not send her to an asylum.

She rose and paced the drawing room. She must become intimate with James again. She did not know how long it would take the doctor to organise whatever he was commissioning, but she needed to effect a reconciliation as soon as possible. She was mid-stride when the door opened and James appeared.

For a second, there was complete silence. Then Emily recovered herself. "Would you like some tea?"

James looked as uncomfortable as she felt. His skin was pale, making his dark beard stand out even more starkly. There were dark rings under his eyes and his brown gaze was dull. She wanted to go to him, to soothe his pain and hers, but remained where she was. For a moment he did not respond, then, gathering himself, nodded and sat down opposite her.

She rang for Watson. "Thank you," he said, his voice husky.

"You're welcome. Ah, Watson, please bring tea, as Sir James has joined me."

Watson backed out of the room.

Silence fell again, and the ticking of the clock seemed unnaturally loud. Steeling herself, Emily folded her hands in her lap and waited. At last, Watson returned. Proud that her grip did not tremble, Emily poured James and then herself a cup of tea. She passed his cup without a word. She took a sip, then said in a low voice, "I hate it when we are at odds."

James sighed, but before he could speak Emily continued. "I have disobeyed your wishes and for that, I am deeply at fault. I had not recognised how my foolishness might impact the family's reputation. I am very sorry." She wanted to say more, but no words would come.

James looked at her. "I appreciate how unused you are to the burden of responsibility that comes with belonging to a family as ancient as mine," he said, each word dropping like a lead weight. "While I hold considerably more progressive views than my father did, I must show the respect due to my family." He paused. "It is more than that, though. You deceived me, and that grieves me sorely."

Emily wiped a tear from her cheek. "I know: I have been stupid. What can I do? You must know that I love you, and I want to make you proud of me."

"Emily, you have always made me proud. The difference you have made to the garden and this house has astonished me. But lying to me! I thought our marriage was strong enough for you to trust me."

Emily was silent. How could she say that since their baby had died, he had been too distant for her to share her thoughts honestly? That his immediate response to her illustration and the fernery had squashed any inclination to tell him what she wanted? She could see how hurt he was, and tried to soothe his pain. "I have done wrong and I shall do better – I promise. Can you forgive me?"

James sighed, but she glimpsed relief in his eyes. "We shall see." After a moment, he left the room.

Emily stared uneasily at the door. At least they were speaking to one another again. She would need to rely on her womanly wiles for the rest.

EMILY YAWNED AND STRETCHED OUT AN ARM, HOPING TO FIND James. The sheets were cool: he had obviously risen earlier. She closed her eyes, reliving the night and blushing at the memory of her wanton behaviour.

She had chosen a gown with a lower-cut décolletage than she would usually wear for a family dinner at home. They both made an effort to converse and she made her responses warm and low-voiced. Peeking at him from under her lashes after the first course, she found his eyes fixed on her and a slight flush on his cheeks. She had known then that they would lie together. He opened the door to her bedroom and she nodded at Molly, who disappeared like mist. Wordlessly, she drew him to the bed and kissed him hard; he'd taken her that first time without even removing his jacket.

She turned over and bunched up the feather pillow under her head. No one had ever spoken to her about the intimate side of marriage before she wed, she mused. It had all come as a rather wonderful surprise, although she knew others had found it a shock.

To the amazement, bemusement and then the increasing delight of James, she'd relished his lovemaking. As they grew better acquainted, Emily paid especial attention to the things James liked. Cupping him in her hands, sucking his nipples, and arching her back while he was inside her drove him to distraction. She'd also noted what *she* liked, and particularly what would bring her to orgasm quickly if they had little time. One summer, when James was away for six weeks touring his estates, Emily even learned how to pleasure herself. She knew it was sinful and resisted as long as she could, but she knew how to find relief, and did so when the yearning grew too strong.

During her illness after the baby died, James had avoided her bed. Now, though, wounded as they were, he could not resist her. Nor she him, she sighed, her lips parted as she recalled his thrusts the previous night. If vigour influenced her chances of getting with child, she would be enceinte now!

She shifted in the bed, growing hot with need, and felt the aches caused by the passion of the previous night. She sat up and reached for the bellpull with a soft groan. Lord, she needed a bath. And to open some windows: the whole room smelled of their lovemaking.

EMILY PAUSED AT THE TOP OF THE STAIRS AS SHE HEARD WATSON show someone into the drawing room. She frowned. It was very early for a call – not yet eleven – and from the faint voices she could hear, they had two visitors.

Watson closed the doors to the drawing room as she reached the bottom stair. "Who has called, Watson?"

"Dr Schenley and Dr Edward Robinson, ma'am. They have requested an audience with Sir James."

Emily's blood froze in her veins. As if in a dream, she stepped towards the drawing-room door and Watson opened it for her. She took a deep breath and swept into the room.

Dr Schenley looked astounded, but the other man rose to his feet. He was portly, with thin grey hair combed across a balding pate, and he smelled of menthol. She nodded at him. "Dr Edward Robinson, at your service," he said in a light voice.

"I am Lady Cleveland," Emily said, as pleasantly as her cold lips would allow.

The two men exchanged glances and Dr Schenley smiled. "Ma'am, how nice it is to see you."

Emily regarded him without expression. "I'm sure it is, Dr Schenley."

After an awkward pause, Dr Robinson began to ask Emily questions. How was she feeling? Was she sleeping well? Had her nightmares returned?

Emily stared at him, then turned to Dr Schenley. "Have you discussed my health with this man without my permission?"

"A matter of professional interest," he said smoothly. She clenched her hands until her nails dug into her palms.

"Dr Schenley!" James exclaimed from the door. "I was not expecting you. Oh, Lord – I take it you did not receive my letter."

The doctor smiled. "No, I am afraid not. May I introduce my colleague, Dr Edward Robinson? Your correspondence may have arrived after I left; I came as soon as I could. It was a matter of some urgency, was it not?"

The men shook hands and James glanced at Emily, standing rigid by the fireplace. "Emily, I beg your pardon, but might I have a few moments alone with these gentlemen?"

Emily fought with herself to control her fear and hold on to her anger. "Am I the topic of conversation, James?" She saw guilt cross his face. "I see," she said, and sat down on the sofa. "Then no, I shall not leave."

James blinked, and his jaw set firm. "Dr Schenley talked to me of a rest cure that he assures me would be of benefit to your suffering. He knows of such a place of rehabilitation and suggested that I might place you there for a month."

"And Dr Robinson is here to provide the second signature to commit me as insane, I suppose."

"No! No, I never said that you were insane!" James cried.

"I fear we need to consider what has happened, Lady Cleveland," Dr Schenley said, moving in front of her and shaking his blonde head. "You left off the laudanum I prescribed. Following this, you committed several acts of unfeminine behaviour. You adopted a scruffy mongrel, ripped up the garden and began to keep unsuitable company."

"Unsuitable company?" Emily frowned, then her eyes widened. "Do you dare to describe Lady Chester as unsuitable company, Dr Schenley? I shall make sure she hears how you judge her!"

He smiled. "Sir James told me that you were rude to his mother *and* Lady Botham. And when I made further enquiries, Mrs Cleveland told me that Mrs Jenson had thought you agitated."

"I see." Emily silently cursed her mother-in-law.

"And then you became obsessed with the garden and the ferns," James muttered. "Indeed, you were so determined to be involved that you pushed everyone aside to undertake manual work."

Emily turned to him, astonished. "James, do you hear yourself? There are women who hunt ferns and put themselves in danger to collect them, travelling the country in pursuit! My intention to *plant* them can hardly be viewed as the beginning of insanity, surely?"

James shook his head. "You must understand how it looks to the casual observer. You had such radical ideas of selling your illustrations... It was then that I wrote to Dr Schenley. He was away in Paris and did not reply until I was in London, doing committee work and paying my respects to Freddie. In truth, by this time, I had begun to think that you were indeed happier and more settled." His eyes clouded, and Emily surmised that he was thinking about the threat to the succession. "I replied to him when I returned."

Emily kept her face impassive; her husband's account tallied with the letter she had read in his study. "But Dr Schenley appears not to have received your letter," she pointed out. "What did your letter say, James?"

"That I felt a rest cure was unnecessary, since you were as well as I'd ever seen you."

"So Dr Schenley's visit is unnecessary," said Emily, hope dawning.

"Not at all!" exclaimed Dr Robinson. "There is much to investigate in these symptoms, with causes beyond the female mind."

Emily threw him a look of pure dislike. "I can assure you that I do not lack mental capacity, doctor."

"And then you told me that you had sent not one but *two* illustrations to the journal," said James.

"I have already apologised for that."

"Yes, you have. And while I was angry – very angry – I reflected on your words and thought that you made a good case."

"I did?"

He grimaced. "I can still remember your face when you suggested that there was already a child in the house."

"Good God!" breathed Dr Schenley, exchanging glances with Dr Robinson.

Emily flushed. "I was upset, and with good cause, but that was a disgraceful thing to say to my husband," she said quietly. There was a moment's silence, and she turned to Dr Schenley, "So, what did you hope to achieve today?"

He smiled again and Emily narrowed her eyes. "Sadly, Lady Cleveland, I did not receive any communication from Sir James. Therefore I have commissioned your stay at Green Birch—"

"Green Birch?" Emily cried, remembering the newspaper article she had read. She turned to James. "You were going to send me to Green Birch?"

James frowned at Dr Schenley. "He assured me that it was the most appropriate and comfortable place."

Emily leapt to her feet and seized his hands. "James, promise me you will never send me to that place! I have read about it – the women imprisoned there live in squalor and filth!"

"Madam!" Dr Schenley protested.

James looked alarmed. "No, no, of course not! Emily, calm yourself!"

"Sir James, these are the symptoms to which I referred!" Dr Schenley said. "Hysteria, becoming argumentative, unfeminine behaviour... Combined with Lady Cleveland's unusual enthusiasm for intimacy, her symptoms are absolutely consistent!"

Emily's mouth dropped open and she turned to James. "You told *him* of our lovemaking? James, how could you?"

James flushed. "He said that women of your class did not succumb to the baser urges as men do."

Emily placed her hands on her hips. "So you are *complaining* about my enthusiasm?"

"No, no!" James said hastily, flushing to the roots of his hair.

"Although I did recommend that Sir James should refrain from coitus," Dr Schenley remarked.

Emily threw up her hands. "Why? Sexual congress is natural! Or do you want to make us all mad, so that you can lock us away in your terrible institution?"

James opened his mouth, then frowned. "*His* institution? *Is* it his?"

"Oh, yes, husband! The longer I am incarcerated, the more money he earns!"

James turned to Dr Schenley, who for the first time looked uncertain. "Is it truly your institution?"

Emily moved towards the door.

"No, we must examine the patient!" Dr Robinson darted in front of Emily and put his hand on the door, then took her arm to lead her back to the sofa. He pulled gently, then with more vigour as she resisted.

"Unhand me, sir!" she hissed.

James stepped forward. "Enough, Dr Robinson," he said, his voice brooking no argument.

Dr Robinson let go and, mustering all her dignity, Emily walked steadily out of the room. Once outside, she ran upstairs. Her heart felt as though it was breaking. How could James even consider sending her away? How could he betray her in this way?

And while James seemed supportive at the moment, Dr Schenley was jealous of his reputation and the arguments would not cease now she had left the room. She needed to get away in case the doctors managed to persuade James that she ought to be committed.

Molly was in Emily's bedroom, tidying. Lucky was snoozing in his basket, but leapt up when he saw her, ears flapping and tongue hanging out.

Emily closed the door and leaned against it, panting a little. "Ma'am?" Molly asked doubtfully.

"Pack a bag, please: I am going away. Dr Schenley is downstairs!"

Molly stared at her, then snapped into action. "Shall I ask for the carriage first, milady? Lay out the gowns you want; I can always follow with more later."

"Excellent thinking, Molly. I hope you will be able to join me in a while." Molly nodded, then ran out of the room.

Emily opened her armoire, yanked out three dresses, and flung them on the bed. She gathered her hairbrush and her journal and picked out some jewellery before closing the lid on her jewellery case. It seemed like stealing to take the family jewels which James had given her. She would leave it all here and take nothing but her clothes.

Molly returned and grabbed Emily's coat, holding it out for Emily to slip her arms in. Emily jammed a hat chosen at random onto her head. Molly tutted, and urged her into the chair. "Best not to look as if you were running, ma'am," she murmured, and placed the hat more gently on Emily's dark curls, securing it with a hatpin. Shaking with nerves and fear, Emily nodded at her maid in the mirror.

In less than a minute Molly stood back, satisfied, and pressed Lucky's lead, gloves and a reticule into Emily's hands. "Thank you – you're a good girl," Emily whispered. "I shall send for you when I can."

She walked carefully downstairs with Lucky, excited at an additional walk, at her heels. She heard raised voices from the drawing room. "Sir James, I must insist! We are of the professional opinion that your wife may be unhinged! Her behaviour, her history—"

She closed her ears to James' response, fixing her gaze on the front door. When she reached it, she even managed to smile at Watson, who opened it and handed her into the carriage.

"Shall I tell his lordship when you will return?" Watson asked.

Emily hesitated, settling Lucky on the floor of the carriage before responding. "Just tell him not to worry," she said at last.

Watson's brown eyes were sad, and she tried to smile at him. "Thank you, Watson. Lady Chester's mansion, please," she said to the driver.

He snapped the whip and the horses trotted down the drive. In less than fifteen minutes, Emily had left her husband.

Chapter 33

Emily

Sunday 20th August 1862: I attended church today and was struck by the reading from Proverbs, which I have taken to heart. Love prospers when a fault is forgiven, but dwelling on it separates close friends.

"You greedy little thing!" Cat told Batman, who fluffed his feathers and flew off, a piece of crust in his beak. Cat grinned and walked to the dining table with her tea.

On the table lay a thin, cheap envelope. Cat sat down to read it, knowing it was from Lauren's mother.

Lauren had stayed in hospital for nearly three weeks as they treated her for arsenic poisoning, and there had been damage to Lauren's liver which might have long-term consequences. But even when she left hospital, the fallout for Lauren had been huge. Though the judge had given her a suspended sentence, she'd been fined for the damage to the garden and her company had sacked her. She was now a steward in what even Cat recognised as a dodgy firm which provided security for small festivals. The pay was pathetic, the hours long.

It had been the most difficult thing she had ever done to face Stephen in court; she felt her pulse tick up at the memory even now, two months on. She had felt his fury against her and against Lauren, who had looked small and scared, flanked by police officers. It was almost as though he blamed them for putting him there. It had also been frustrating to watch as Stephen, with the help of an expensive lawyer escaped with a fine. Even though there was now a restraining order against him, the one silver lining from the whole sorry mess, she could see the smirk on his face as he stepped out of the court room.

"Bloody Stephen," Cat muttered, pushing her chair away and pacing around the dining table in frustration. She knew how plausible he was. It was hardly surprising that Lauren, with her insecurities, had been so thoroughly taken in.

While Lauren wasn't allowed to contact Cat, Cat had asked if Lauren's mum might correspond on her behalf. The letter was brief, as Lauren's mum was dyslexic too. Cat could only imagine the time and effort that had gone into it.

She's starting to settle a bit in the new job. The money is rubbish, but she never complains. Me and her sister keep an eye on her and her probation officer is pleased, though Lauren can't wait until suspension of the sentence is done. Maybe then she could call you for a chat? she wrote. *She's so ashamed of what she done. She won't blame you if you don't want to speak, but it would cheer her up no end.*

Cat propped her chin on her hand, gazing out of the window at the late-summer sun. She remembered Lauren's face as she realised her obsession with Stephen had been based on his lies, all fuelled by his mammoth ego. Lauren had shouldered all the blame, as Stephen knew she would. The evil, evil bastard...

Yes, she would take Lauren's call – perhaps even meet up for coffee, if Lauren's mum came too. She hunted for a pen and paper to reply. Goddamn it, don't I own writing paper? Ten minutes later, defeated, she pulled the laptop towards her and dashed off a chatty, light note. Not gushy – anything gushy would make Lauren uncomfortable. She sent the note to the printer and looked for an envelope.

"Crikey, how did the bloody Victorians do it, sending mail five times a day? Mind you, they all had servants," Cat muttered. She'd need to walk down to the village for a stamp. She might do that after lunch.

But until lunch, what? She could play around with ideas for the next book, but apart from that the day looked like most others lately. Empty and lonely. She'd even rung her mother the other day to break the monotony. She'd heard nothing from Harry for a little while as he battled with his new job in Essex police. He'd been texting her during the trial, offering support virtually, if he couldn't be there in person. She'd seen him a couple of times, but only briefly. He was staying in Essex with an old friend, a female superintendent. She'd been careful not to think too closely about that.

Heat crept up her face. She could feel his arms wrapped around her as he slept. At least she'd kept him safe for the night, she told herself.

Her mobile rang, shattering the silence of the morning. "Good morning, Catherine!" Creighton boomed.

Cat grinned. "Hi, Creighton! How are you?"

"All's well here. I wondered if you were at home today?"

Cat's stomach flipped. Oh my God, what was wrong? She couldn't remember the last time Creighton had ventured outside of the M25.

"Um, yes. Is everything okay?"

"Of course, Catherine! I have news!" Creighton chuckled. "You think I'm resigning as your agent, don't you?"

"Well, I – um..."

"Catherine, have faith! Have you any food in the house?"

Cat's mind rooted through the kitchen cupboards and the fridge. No, she hadn't. She'd set herself a weekly budget for food and she'd already eaten through it. And today was Wednesday. Unless she turned up like a waif on Lizzie's doorstep – again – it was cornflakes, porridge or toast for the rest of the week. "I haven't been to the supermarket, I'm afraid," she said. She was flat broke, but Creighton didn't need to know that.

"Righty-ho, don't fret! Shall I arrive about twelve thirty?"

"I – yes, that's fine."

"See you then! Cheerio!"

Cat stared at the phone, unable to line up her thoughts. After a couple of minutes, she leapt up, grabbed her keys, and headed out to post the letter.

IN THE END, CAT DECIDED TO BUY A BAGUETTE, A SMALL PIECE OF meltingly lovely Camembert cheese and some pate from the wonderful French bakery in the village. She had to have something in the house when Creighton came, after all. She smiled at the girl as she paid for her purchases, then jumped as a snide voice said in her ear, "How is your case coming along?"

Cat turned to see Geoff Johnson, wearing an iridescent T-shirt from a seventies rock group. She took a step away and her eyes narrowed. The man was a gossip. She wouldn't put it past him to talk to the newspapers.

"All sorted, thank you for asking. And thank you for being so patient during the investigation," she said sweetly.

His mouth dropped open, then a crafty look spread over his face. "So has the perpetrator scared you out of the house? If you feel uncomfortable in that big house, all alone, my offer still stands. Although I'd need to take the damage you've done to my reputation into account," he said, watching her.

"The episode has made me more attached to the house, actually," Cat replied, and as she said it, she realised it was true. Despite the costs, she wanted nothing more than to stay at Cleveland House – as Gam had known she would.

Geoff opened his mouth to speak and Cat cut in. "I'm expecting someone for lunch – must dash."

"What happened with the court case?" he called after her.

"No time! Thanks again!"

SHE HAD ONLY JUST FINISHED DUSTING WHEN THERE WAS A KNOCK at the door. She shoved the cloth and polish into a drawer and ran to answer it, smoothing down her cotton top.

Creighton was standing there with an enormous picnic basket and a bouquet of cream roses. Cat was speechless for a moment, then remembered her manners. "I'm sorry, come in! That's quite the bunch of flowers!"

"Do you own a vase?" Creighton said, looking into the house with undisguised curiosity.

Cat kissed his cheek and took the basket from him. "Of course! Good grief, what have you got in here? Come through."

She put the basket on the kitchen counter and found a vase. As she was filling it with water, she was aware of Creighton walking around the hall, looking up the stairs and into the drawing room, making admiring noises.

"To what do I owe this honour?" Cat asked, placing the roses in the centre of the dining table.

Creighton's elegant eyebrows arched. "Dear girl, do I need an appointment? I wanted to see this splendid house in the flesh, and I wanted to discuss something with you." He pulled out a chair and sat down.

Oh God, he hasn't sold the book. Cat sat down opposite him and began to tap on her hands.

"I have interest from Templeton's," Creighton said.

Cat stopped tapping, one finger frozen in mid-air. "Templeton Publishing?" she whispered. "*The* Templeton Publishing?"

Creighton nodded, a smile on his thin lips. "It's for two books, with a possible extension for another two, so you need to think about the outlines before we do anything else. They might be persuaded to offer an advance, but if they do, you *will* need to deliver what they ask for."

"Oh, Creighton! They *really* liked the book, then? That's great! I've been offering editing to other writers and doing the odd bit of teaching..."

"Pooh!" he chided gently. "You really must believe in your talent, Catherine. I knew they'd love the book. It was just a matter of getting to Joe."

"You took the book to *Joe Templeton*?"

"Darling, I've been in the business a long time." Creighton wagged a finger. "I'd be a poor agent if I couldn't reach the managing director. He's suggested you work with Elise Swift, one of their young editors. A bit of a rising star, I understand. But before we get into the details, I need a look at this wonderful house."

Cat grinned, her heart so full of joy and light that it was like being drunk. She might not have much in the house, but it was beautiful. She led Creighton upstairs while he exclaimed over the stained glass and the cherry wood bannister. A tour of the guest bedrooms followed, all bare apart from the odd rug.

"This is your bedroom?" Creighton said as she pushed open the last door. His gaze swept the room, then came to rest on her. "Ah yes, the chair I bought from you. When do you plan to replace it? The room looks somewhat ... spartan."

Cat laughed, embarrassed. "Oh, new furniture can wait. If we get an advance, I might make you an offer to buy it back!"

Creighton looked away. "Perhaps we can negotiate. I haven't found a place for it yet." He tried to look innocent, and failed completely.

Cat hugged him. "Shall we eat?"

"Lead on, dear girl."

Four hours later, Cat waved him away. As the taillights of his Jaguar disappeared through the gates, she heard the booming bass line of a rock song float on the still summer air.

Harry was back.

CAT SLAMMED THE DOOR OF LIZZIE'S ANCIENT CAR AND BEAMED at the new ferns lined up like glossy green soldiers on the drive. It had taken some time, but she'd gradually replaced the soil and compost in the fernery, hunted for fern sales and now she was ready to replant.

Lizzie chuckled as she locked the driver's door and came to stand with Cat. "You look like a kid at Christmas."

Cat grinned at her. "I can't believe how impatient I am to get started!"

"Isn't Harry helping this time?"

Cat shook her head. "I haven't seen him for a while, what with the new job." He hadn't called. Not that I need him to, she told herself, ignoring her smarting pride.

"Shame. So—" Lizzie hoisted a fern into her arms. "Shall we get on?"

The conversation stayed general for the next two hours as Lizzie and Cat tenderly settled the ferns into their new home. The late August sun was scorching and Cat's tongue was sticking to the top of her mouth. She called a halt. "I have sparkling water in the fridge. Fancy a glass with some elderflower cordial?"

"That sounds wonderful," Lizzie said, sitting back on her heels after planting a maidenhair fern.

When Cat returned with a tray, Lizzie had put out two folding chairs under the tree which shaded the fernery, and was fanning herself with her hat.

"I'm working you too hard!" Cat said, handing her a glass tinkling with ice. "You can supervise for the rest of the afternoon."

Lizzie laughed and drank deep. "I'm fine for a bit longer, never fear."

Cat shaded her eyes and looked across the garden, washed out by the strong sunshine.

"How's Lauren?" Lizzie asked quietly.

Cat shrugged. "She's doing okay: her mum and sister are taking good care of her. She's got a job of sorts and her mum wrote to say she's seeing a therapist."

"Will you see her again?"

Cat hesitated. "I'd like to. We were best friends for years."

Lizzie pursed her lips. "You need to take care. The woman threatened you! She hit Harry and ruined your fernery!"

"I know, but she's not a character from *Killing Eve*! She was taken in by that bastard Stephen. Having been in the same position, I'm sympathetic." Cat leaned over and clasped Lizzie's hand. "I'll be very careful. I won't see her on my own; I thought we could meet with her mum."

"And what about that vile man, Stephen Fergusson?"

"I'm furious that he got nothing more than a fine and a restraining order. If I ever see him again, he'll be the one in danger!"

"It's been an eventful few months, hasn't it?" Lizzie said, after a pause.

Cat snorted with laughter. "It has! But what with Stephen, losing Gam, changing direction in my writing in such a big way I had to find a new publisher and this, it's been an eventful six years. I reckon I can cope with anything now."

Lizzie squinted at her. "Hmm. You're not invincible, Cat."

"No, but I'm much stronger than I was. With your help, I've rebuilt the fernery. I rewrote my book, and it will be published. My parents don't understand what they call 'my writing phase', but I've realised that they're never going to understand – and that's okay. I have an amazing agent who believes in me and my writing, and now *I* do too. Before, I thought I'd just got lucky. Now I see that I've got talent, and while I won't earn a fortune, I'll manage."

Lizzie smiled. "I helped May build the fernery that was there when you arrived. She loved it too."

Cat grinned and raised her tumbler. "To Gam!"

"To Gam!" They chinked glasses.

Silence fell, and when Lizzie spoke again, Cat had to lean forward to hear her soft words.

"Gam's greatest wish was that you would live your life the way you wanted to. She couldn't, but she was desperate that you would. She knew you wanted to be an author. That was why she left you Cleveland House – so that if you needed to, you could sell it and keep writing, rather than be trapped in some dreadful job that would suck the life out of you."

Cat frowned. "What do you mean – she couldn't live as she wanted?"

Lizzie turned her head away, her cheeks suddenly hectic with colour. Cat blinked, and it was as if the world came into focus. Constant companions, always laughing together. Lizzie's regular-as-clockwork visits to the care home, even when Gam grew so ill that she barely recognised anyone. Lizzie had been with Gam when she died. And Cat remembered her white, stricken face at Gam's funeral, and how she had shared with Cat the endless, slow trail back into the light.

"Lizzie, were you lovers?" Cat asked gently.

Lizzie nodded wordlessly, tears running down her lined face.

Cat dropped to her knees and put her arms around Lizzie's shuddering, thin body. She held her until the tears stopped, then got to her feet, wiping her face on her sleeve. "You should have told me. I'm glad you had each other: you made her very happy," she croaked at last. Lizzie nodded and scrabbled for a handkerchief to mop her eyes.

Eventually, Lizzie sniffed, tucked her hanky in her pocket, and patted Cat on the shoulder. "I wanted to tell you for such a long time, but May was so very private that it didn't seem right. She dreaded the Civil Service finding out, although I know things are different now. I'll tell you more over dinner sometime." She took a deep breath, then sighed it out. "But now we need to finish the fernery."

Cat stood up and grinned. "It sounds quite a story. Watch out – you never know what I might use in a book!"

"I'd sue," Lizzie replied crisply.

Chapter 34

Lady Chester put the book she wasn't reading on her lap and looked across her luxurious sitting room. Emily was sitting in the alcove where the light was best, concentrating on the fern she was painting. Nonetheless, she knew she was being observed. When she was satisfied, she sat back and dipped the sable brush in the water. "Charlotte, you have something on your mind," she said, wiping the brush and moving to the soft leather Chesterfield.

Emily's instinct to trust Lady Chester had proved absolutely right. Charlotte had held Emily while she wept, cheered her when she was disconsolate and chivvied her when she felt sorry for herself. She had forced Emily to take the air and pick up her paintbrush again, and tempted her with morsels of dainty food. She had, in short, been a true friend.

Charlotte smiled. "I know James has written again," she replied, placing the book on a Chinoiserie side table with something like relief. "What did he say?"

The first letter from James had arrived with Molly nearly eleven weeks previously. It had apologised, then demanded she cease her fool-

269

ishness and return. Emily had read it, lost her temper, and passed it to Charlotte. Charlotte cast an eye over its contents and threw it in the fire.

Emily had flitted around Charlotte's rooms like a ghost for the first fortnight, starting every time anyone knocked at the imposing front door. But gradually, with much reassurance from Charlotte, she began to relax. It was then that she wrote her reply to James, putting down what she wanted on paper for the first time in her life.

There had been an agonising wait for James to respond. When his letter finally arrived she tore it open with trembling fingers, half-dreading what she would find.

I loved you at first sight for your spontaneity and your free spirit, he wrote. *I fear that in our time together I have diminished the very things which I cherish in you,* he had written. Emily's hands shook so badly that she dropped the pages. She scrabbled for pen and paper, but after starting several times, she tossed the ruined pages away and headed into the garden.

Lady Chester's garden, tamed into parterres and elaborate borders, was not to Emily's taste, but the fresh air cleared her head. Half an hour later, she picked up her pen. *I would like to correspond with you. Our letters should be honest about what we feel and want from our life together. This may be more difficult for you than before – I believe your grief for the baby and your anxiety for an heir has warped our original relationship – but I should like to try.*

After a painful two-day wait, James wrote again. His letter was rather formal but agreed to her suggestion. After this, barely a day elapsed without a letter, and sometimes two. Charlotte was highly amused by the constant arrival of the postman.

Emily pulled the latest letter from her pocket, smoothing it on her lap.

Charlotte raised an eyebrow. "Have you slept on it?"

Emily laughed softly. "I am foolish, I know. But we are corresponding honestly now, as we did when we first married."

"May I know what he says?"

Emily unfolded James' letter. There was one sentence that she particularly wanted Charlotte to hear. "Listen to this! *'I enclose several letters from what I imagine are fern societies: they announce their enthusiasms on the envelopes in crests and monikers. I expect they are clamouring to see your fernery. Although Seth does his best, he does not have your skill.'* Charlotte, does that not sound as though he is proud of me? That he recognises my talents?"

"Indeed, my dear. But have you forgiven him yet? Perhaps it is time to meet him."

Emily looked up from the letter. "You may be right. We seem to understand one another much better than we did, and I desperately want a reconciliation. I miss him."

Charlotte nodded. "Have you heard from your aunt?"

Aunt Sybil, naturally, had objected to Emily's sojourn with Lady Chester. Her last letter had declared that she would wash her hands of her niece if Emily did not end her foolishness and return, as a good wife should, to her husband. In Emily's reply, she had politely asked whether Aunt Sybil could protect her from the machinations of doctors who had vested interests in having her committed. If so, she would promptly return to James.

"No," Emily said sadly. "In time she may reply, I hope." She was silent for a moment, then shook herself. "Mr Irvine has solicited an article about the construction of the fernery at Cleveland House, and asked for an illustration of the plans."

Charlotte frowned. "Will that not prove awkward if you are not living at Cleveland House?"

Emily tossed her head with a mischievous smile. "Oh, I intend to return to my fernery! It is simply a matter of timing. And I shall have some control over the publication of the article, shall I not?"

Charlotte stared at her, then threw her head back and laughed. "Oh, Emily! Yes, my dear – you may control many things."

Emily peeked through the heavy curtains as James dismounted from his horse. Her heart stuttered. He looked pale, and his cheekbones seemed sharper. He glanced up as though he felt her gaze and she jerked away from the window.

A few seconds later, the ring of the doorbell echoed up the sweeping stairs. Emily moved to the dressing-table mirror. The dark blue-grey velvet bodice flattered her porcelain skin, and biting her lips from nerves had made them rosy. Her jawline was more defined, but she put that down to exercise in the garden rather than fasting.

Emily drew a deep breath and smoothed her skirt with palms that were suddenly damp. You are all you need to succeed, she repeated to herself, and bent to catch her reflection in the mirror.

"You look divine, my dear. Please don't fuss," Charlotte said gently. "He is in the yellow drawing room."

Emily nodded, and Lucky licked her hand.

"You should take Lucky with you," Charlotte added.

Emily considered, then clipped on Lucky's leash and patted his wiry, straw-coloured head. Perhaps he would be her talisman.

Despite her intense desire for this meeting, her heart thudded against her ribs as she followed Charlotte down the impressive staircase. At last she stood before the door of the yellow drawing room. Lucky whined, his tail wagging furiously.

Charlotte touched her arm. "You need only to ring for a footman to come at once. Do not let him bully you." She looked into Emily's eyes. "Do you know what will make you happy?"

Emily nodded.

"Then ask for it."

LUCKY SHOT FORWARD SO SUDDENLY THAT THE LEASH SLIPPED from Emily's grasp. James, standing rigid by the fireplace, doubled over as the small dog leapt at him. Startled but laughing, he caught Lucky and hugged him. "Someone is pleased to see me," he said wryly, raising his dark eyes to her face.

Despite her vow to remain collected, Emily felt a blush rise to her cheeks. "Please be seated. Lucky, get down!" She clicked her fingers and Lucky, not at all abashed, trotted over, tail wagging. She sat down on the brocade sofa and he sank at her feet, putting his head on his paws.

James flicked out the tails of his coat and sat on the sofa opposite. Although she had long considered how to begin the conversation, now that James was present all her careful sentences fled from her brain.

James cleared his throat. "You look well," he said, his dark glance sweeping over her.

"Thank you, I am quite well. Lady Chester has been all that is generous." A pause. "How are you?"

"Well enough."

Another pause. "May I—"

"Are you—"

They both spoke at once. James shook his head with a slight smile. "After you."

Emily took a deep breath. "I am pleased to see you. May I ask what has caused you to seek an audience with me?"

"Our correspondence is no longer sufficient. We have much to discuss." His eyes seemed glued to her.

Emily was profoundly grateful for the arrival of tea, as it distracted her from James' presence. She had to manage this conversation correctly, or she would be lost. After a few moments, the footman closed the doors and Emily fussed with crockery. "I have found your letters enlightening," she said as she passed him his cup. "It has been an honest exchange between us, and I am grateful for it."

James rubbed his chin and looked away, reddening.

"What happened after I came to Charlotte?" Emily asked. "In all

273

our letters we have not discussed this, other than that you have declared that Dr Schenley is no longer welcome at the house, or as an acquaintance."

"When I discovered that you were not in the house, I threw them both out. I could not waste precious time talking to them. I rode over that very day."

"Here?" Emily asked, her eyes widening. Charlotte had never mentioned that to her. Had she really denied Sir James, a Member of Parliament, access to her house?

"Aye. I was told that Lady Chester was not at home. I could do nothing but return to Cleveland House, and return I did, in no small temper."

Emily thought of the first letter demanding her return, and light dawned.

"I feared you might never return," James murmured, looking at the rug.

Emily moved to sit beside him. When his eyes lifted to hers, she clasped his hands. "What has happened to us, James? When we first married, I thought ours was a marriage of equals – indeed, you told me it was so! When I—" She stopped, her breath catching in her throat. "When I lost the baby, everything changed. I felt we had drifted apart, and I did not know how to bring us back together." Her voice clogged with tears.

James pressed her hand. "I did not know how to return to you! I felt my grief, and yours, very keenly, but I considered my tears unmanly and indicative of weakness."

"They were simply natural," Emily said gently. He nodded, and there was silence for a moment.

"Your distress ignited mine. I felt it was more use to stay apart than let our united grief overwhelm us."

Emily sighed. "Knowing that you shared my feelings would have helped me. It would have helped us both!"

"Instead of being the first barrier between us," James replied. They sipped their tea, reflecting, and silence fell.

"How shall we proceed?" James asked, turning to her.

Emily considered. "I yearn to be a proper wife to you, but I also need to be useful," she said slowly. "I need more stimulation than making calls and hosting dinners. I wanted so much to campaign by your side! I created the fernery partly to show that I can do more than direct servants and make calls. Charlotte feels that I have talent, and so does the editor of the *Phytologist*. I want to study botany and ferns, to exercise my mind and keep it whole and healthy! You have heard others praise my efforts. With study, I can improve further and make you proud of me."

James pressed her fingers. "I am already proud of you. But deeper study will take a great deal of time and energy. I do not want you to make yourself ill again."

"I wasn't ill – I was grieving!" She drew a deep breath. "I shall not over-exert myself," she said, with more confidence than she felt. "I intend to read, attend lectures, and continue to paint, and the editor of the journal has asked me to submit an article about the fernery at Cleveland House. I shall only do so with your permission, of course, since it is your house."

"How good of you to remember," James murmured. Emily looked at him anxiously, but his eyes were twinkling.

"I would like to learn more about your campaigning, and Lady Chester will happily educate me," she added.

James was quiet. Her heart sank, but she waited. She would not compromise.

"You know how your mother suffered from society's view of her," he said. "Anything out of the ordinary is never ... straightforward."

Emily cleared her throat. "I know. I shall do it alone, but I would welcome your support."

"Is our marriage dependent on my support?" His voice was serious.

She wrinkled her nose. "I love you. But I would prefer you to love all of me, not only the elements that society considers acceptable."

He said nothing, and she was about to lose her nerve when he stood up. Eyes wide, she too rose.

He cupped her face in his hands. "I loved all of you – bold, impossible, unconventional – when we married. It will be a joy to become reacquainted with the parts of you I have forgotten." He kissed her gently. "I shall support your endeavours wholeheartedly. We will face society together. I miss you. Will you come home?"

She gazed up at him and nodded, her heart swelling. Lucky, waking up at that moment, thumped his tail in approval.

Chapter 35

Emily leaned out of the carriage window but could only glimpse the approaching station through the steam and smoke. Then she saw Watson on the platform with Lucky, trying to ignore onlookers' sniggers at the scruffiest of dogs. Lucky was unsure about the giant puffing machine sliding into the station and whined in protest. The butler bent to ruffle his ears, and Emily deduced that Lucky had wriggled his small body into Watson's heart.

The train stopped with a jolt. A porter appeared immediately and opened the door, handing her down to the platform.

"Welcome back to Cambridge, ma'am," Watson said, as Lucky barked a greeting and strained at his leash to reach her.

"Thank you, Watson. I'm pleased to be home. You may let him go."

Lucky hurtled towards her and, disregarding her travelling dress, she bent to pat him and have her face licked. "Yes, I'm pleased to see *you,* too!" she chuckled. She picked up the dog with a whoosh of breath. "Mrs O'Donnell has been overfeeding you," she said, with mock severity. "If you do not take care, Lucky, we will need to put you on a reducing diet!"

Watson led the way to the waiting carriage. "I trust ma'am has had a useful trip to London?"

"Yes, I have learned so much! It was invigorating."

"Indeed, ma'am looks very well, if I may comment."

She beamed. "I feel well, thank you."

The carriage moved off, and she raised her face to the late-September sun.

James' study door opened as she stepped into the hall and he strode to embrace her. "My dear, I'm glad to see you!" Lucky bounced around their legs as he kissed her; Watson discreetly turned away and asked the footman to take her valise upstairs.

Finally released, Emily twinkled at James and resettled her hat. She took off her gloves and unbuttoned her coat, shrugging it into Watson's waiting hands. "It's lovely to be home! And the lecture was so *interesting*..." She linked her arm through his and tried to explain a full day's lecture in the time it took them to reach the sitting room. "I may have not been quite clear, but it was so fascinating. I met many interesting scholars, as well as amateur enthusiasts like me."

He gazed at her, his eyes flicking over her face and figure. "Do I have a smut on my face?" she asked. "The train is fast, but so very dirty!"

James chuckled softly and a warm glow spread through her body as he took her hand and stroked her fingers. "I was just admiring your beauty, my love. You are in looks."

She leaned forward and caressed his cheek, running her fingers against his beard. She kissed his lips slowly and gently and heard his breath catch as she nibbled at his mouth. He shifted towards her. Feeling mischievous, she jumped to her feet. "I must change – I cannot sit here in all my dirt!"

James blinked and hurriedly composed himself.

"I shall ask Molly to take Lucky for a long walk. Perhaps you could come up for us to continue our conversation in, say, an hour?" She saw the flame flash in his dark eyes.

"You are incorrigible," he murmured, but his face was lit with joy. She grinned at him over her shoulder as she swept to the door.

JAMES SIGHED AND STRETCHED HIS ARMS ABOVE HIS HEAD. His eyes gleamed as he surveyed her tumbled curls on the pillow. Emily shifted sinuously on the smooth sheet, deliciously replete and tingling all over. Her gaze slid over James' broad shoulders and his muscled chest, sprinkled with dark hair. She noticed the graze on his shoulder where she had dug her nails into his flesh and stifled a giggle.

"What?" James asked. He craned his neck to see the damage. "You little vixen!"

She kissed him and he hugged her close. "How was London?" he asked.

"Noisy, rather dirty. I saw Lady Botham briefly." Not briefly enough, she added, to herself. "It's astonishing to think that one man has devised a system for categorising all living things – a true phenomenon! It excites me that I am learning the foundations of true botanical knowledge."

"Indeed?"

As encouragement it was mild enough, but Emily turned eagerly to him, propping her head on her hand as she explained that the Linnaean system gave all organisms a two-part name: one to help botanists and doctors identify its genus, and the other its species. To his credit, it was a good five minutes before James looked dazed with all the Latin.

"Though he is rightly lauded for his work, some detractors consider that his pursuit of the taxonomic system was spurred by his lack of prowess in illustration," she added, with some acidity.

279

James laughed. "Which is essential for any good botanist," he commented, and kissed her nose.

"Indeed," she said, with a smug grin. "What a timely reminder – I must respond to Mr Irvine, who wants more illustrations." She threw back the covers and slipped on a dressing gown. "What news is there of your parliamentary business?"

James lay back and watched her tug a brush through her hair. "I am rather dreading returning to the House," he said. "Shaftesbury is seeking my support for the Ragged School Union, and I am undecided."

"Why so?"

"Because of his views on the Lunacy Commission. He is adamant that those laws are sufficient and opposes the suggestion to make the certification of insanity more difficult."

Emily paused in her brushing, and her lips tightened. Then she gave the tangle in her hair a sharp pull. "These are schools for impoverished children, are they not?" she asked calmly.

James sighed and stared at the ceiling. "It is wholly to advance his evangelical beliefs, which I do not share. I wanted your views, given our most recent experience. I would hate this to be a barrier between us."

She put down her brush and turned to study him. "Do the children benefit?"

"Giving them hours away from drunken, brutal parents? Oh yes, they benefit. And for all my concern about his focus on religious education, the moral guidance the schools provide may keep the little ones out of the gutter. I hear rumours of a ragged school for wild girls, too."

"Education for women? Whatever for?" Emily scoffed, and squealed as he threw a pillow at her. She fell onto the bed, her fingers seeking to tickle him, and in seconds, he was shouting and wriggling away. Breathless, Emily sank onto her heels as he tumbled out of bed to escape her. "It will come, mark my words!"

His dark head, hair tousled and face alight with laughter, appeared over the side of the bed. Grabbing his clothes, he ran.

Two hours later, Emily was wincing as Molly tightened her corset. "Ma'am, I dare not pull it much tighter..."

"Can you fasten the gown?"

"I think so – but pardon me for saying that I don't think you'll fit into it next week."

Emily laughed softly. "I agree. Thank you, Molly."

She glanced at Lucky, sound asleep in his orange crate. She had bought him a brand-new basket, but after a few restless nights, Molly put the crate back. He had slept in there ever since.

As Molly slid a pearl comb into her hair, Emily wondered how she would fare that evening. Not the dinner – Mrs O'Donnell's delicious cooking was enough to satisfy the most exacting guests. But afterwards... that would be the challenge.

She walked carefully downstairs and into the drawing room, where James was watching the sun begin its slow descent behind the garden wall. It had been a long summer. Now, in September, the sun seemed to have found fresh energy and the air was mild.

He swung round as she entered the room. For a moment he said nothing, and she stood there, a little nervous under his regard.

"Exquisite, my dear," he murmured, and crossed the room to plant a tender kiss on her cheeks. "You look radiant. I am so happy to see you in this colour."

She smoothed the jade silk, her fingers lingering on the silver knots of embroidery at her hips fashioned into fern-like shapes. "I have been in mourning for a long time. Perhaps too long."

He nodded and was about to say something when Watson announced their guests. Lady Chester and the Reverend Sherwood-Taylor, his wife and daughter had arrived.

"It's such a beautiful evening," Charlotte declared. "May we stroll for a few minutes in the garden?"

Watson and a footman threw open the doors and the party trailed after Emily, happy to listen as she described the new beds laid only at the end of August.

Charlotte linked arms with Emily and drew her into the fernery. "You look so well!" She leaned back to take a better look. "You have put on flesh, which is always a good sign. Your face appears fuller." She pursed her lips, considering.

Emily laughed, but would not be drawn. She pressed Charlotte's hand. "You know I cannot thank you enough—"

"Then do not to make the effort," her friend responded crisply. "We are friends, and this is what friends do for one another. Mrs Sherwood-Taylor, let me compliment you on your delightful gown!"

At the end of the evening, Charlotte kissed her cheek. "You can always return, should the need arise," she murmured, and Emily felt her cheeks flush.

"What was that?" James asked when all their guests had left.

Although she did not want it, Emily picked up the teapot. She sipped, and managed not to grimace at the iron taste of stewed tea.

James gently took her cup and saucer away. "You have been distracted all night. What is amiss?"

Emily tried to gather her thoughts. "James, you love me, do you not?"

"Can you doubt it?"

"I have been happier this past month than I ever have in my life. I never want this time to end. I have found such joy with you and in my botanical work. My studies show me how much I love to learn, and I wish to continue."

James looked wary. "You speak as if this was all ending. What would interfere with it?"

Emily took a deep breath. "A baby."

James trembled slightly as he placed his tumbler of whiskey on the table. "Are you certain?" His voice was husky, low.

"Yes. It's been three months."

He sank to his knees beside the sofa and grabbed her hands, smothering them with kisses. "Oh, Emily!" He threw back his head and laughed. "Emily, how wonderful you are! How precious, how fragile—"

She pulled her hands away and jumped to her feet. "No, James! I built that fernery with my bare hands; fragile is the last word you should use to describe me. I will not be made an invalid for a completely natural process!"

"But—"

"Nor will I give up my work! I am strong enough to do both."

Her words met a deafening silence, and her heart thumped against her ribs. Then she too fell to her knees. "James, I implore you, let me continue my illustrations and my writing! I am only half a person without them."

James gazed at her, then slowly raised his hand and pushed a stray curl from her forehead. "I am only half a person without *you*, Emily. I cannot lose you!" he said hoarsely. "You must rest, and not exert your-self. Last time—"

"Last time I had a man in charge of what should be women's work," Emily replied. "I promise you faithfully that I shall not over-exert myself. I promise in the name of God that I shall do all in my power to protect our child. I shall rest, drink potions, and do everything else my midwife tells me to – but don't forbid me to paint, write or garden. It would suffocate me!"

He rose and helped her back on to the sofa. For a moment there was silence, then she slipped her hand into his. He squeezed her fingers, and tears of relief started in her eyes.

James placed a warm arm around her shoulders, drew her to him and kissed her forehead. "It will be as you wish. Here is our agreement: you will keep your mind and spirit busy, but take enormous care with your body and our baby. Do you agree?"

"I agree," said Emily, smiling through her tears.

SETH LOOKED PUZZLED BUT HELD HIS TONGUE, FOR WHICH EMILY was grateful. It was indeed a strange thing to do. Rationally, she could not explain it – but this was what she needed to do with her journal, now complete. She wrapped the book in oilskin and closed the tin box, her gloves making her fingers clumsy. The lock was modest but would ensure the journal was protected. It would be her last journal. From now on she would speak her mind, not write down its thoughts.

A kick made her gasp. She smiled and rubbed her swollen belly.

Emily glanced around the fernery, still asleep in the December cold, and smiled. Tomorrow was New Year's Day. The year ahead held much promise, as did the life she carried.

As Seth levered one of the stones from the wall, Emily recalled the bizarre dream that had disturbed her slumber in the early hours. A very tall, slender woman with grey-green eyes and long dark hair strode through the fernery wearing pantaloons and a loose shirt. While the woman's attire had shocked her – the pantaloons showed every line of the woman's legs – Emily was certain that she would like her, much as she liked Charlotte. An instinct told her that this woman would read her journal and value it, although Emily had no clue how it would fall into her hands. Now that she had made her decision to write no more journals, Emily needed to put this last one in the place where she had seen the woman in her dream.

Seth gave a grunt as the stone fell to the ground, his breath like smoke in the cold air. "There you go, my lady," he wheezed.

Emily bent as best she could to peer into the wall. "Yes, that will serve perfectly," she said, smiling. She handed the box to Seth and he slid it into the gap between the stones. Then he tapped the stone he had removed sharply with his trowel and it broke in half. Another tap, and he was left with a piece of stone an inch thick to fill the remaining hole.

Emily beamed at him. "Excellent! Please fix that in position. I do not wish the journal to be revealed, so make sure the stone is properly secured."

He nodded. "If I might make so bold, ma'am, t'aint right that you should be out here freezing! I'll see this properly done, have no doubt, but shouldn't you go in?"

Emily laughed. "I shall check your handiwork in the spring! Thank you, Seth."

She carefully made her way back across the lawn, which sparkled with frost. As she reached the verandah door she turned to look, but the fernery and her journal were out of sight.

Chapter 36

Emily

Friday 8th September 1862: I feel as light as air! Mr Irvine has today written to ask my permission to reprint my latest article, as it is in such demand! J is like a dog with two tails, sharing in my delight. This will pale, though, before the news I intend to give him this evening.

Tears pricked Cat's eyes as she closed the journal and stroked the battered leather cover. Despite reading the diary several times, its story still caught at her heart. She leaned back against the sofa and stared into space. Emotion welled in her chest as she reflected once more on the unknown woman who had thrown her heart and soul into the fernery, and through it had gathered strength to battle so many other things.

At least Emily had recovered sufficiently to have the family she yearned for. Cat's investigation through the ancestry sites had revealed that Emily had given birth to no less than six children: the first a boy called David, followed by twin girls, then another boy, another girl, and a final son. Their lives, and their own families and stories, spread like a series of veins through history. Emily had lived until the age of ninety-three, and died just a year after her husband James.

Without much hope, she checked whether a magazine called *Phytologist* still existed. She found, to her astonishment, that despite several changes of ownership and a change of name to *New Phytologist*, it was still in print. However, the editor could find no mention of Emily Cleveland as an illustrator.

Someone on one of the ancestry sites had sent her a grainy photograph. It showed a couple, upright and proud, surrounded by their children. The man was dark, though a silver streak was visible at the front of his hair, with a close-trimmed beard. The woman sitting very close to him was small and slender, with a child on her knee. Her face was delicate, but Cat saw a firm mouth and intelligent expression. Yes, this was the Emily whose diary she had read, and she looked very similar to the woman who had appeared in her dream. Which was impossible. Cat chided herself for an overactive imagination.

None of the information Cat had uncovered, though, explained how Emily's diary had come to be buried in the fernery. However, Cat felt sure that even if she dug up the whole fernery she would find no further trace of the writer. The last entry in the journal had made that clear:

Since J and I have reconciled, I have little need of a journal. It takes me away from speaking to him and other interesting people, to talk to myself instead.

Cat grinned. She wished she could have known Emily – she felt sure they would have been friends. She touched the journal again; the leather seemed warm. She would keep it for her children, if she ever had any.

And what strange parallels in their stories! Emily had built the fernery; Cat rebuilt it. Emily had an enemy in Dr S, whoever he was, while Cat's enemy had been Stephen, the arse. Both Emily and Cat had grown in confidence: Emily through designing and building the fernery, and Cat through her writing and rebuilding Emily's work. Creighton had been Cat's guardian angel, and Lady C had been there for Emily. Emily had learned to be independent and demand control of her life. Cat had learned ... what?

Cat decided that was too difficult to work out and struggled to her feet. The sun streaming through the drawing-room windows was still warm, but the days were growing shorter. She was walking to the kettle when she changed her mind and reached for a bottle of wine. She deserved a drink, if only to celebrate Emily's success.

She was pulling the cork when her phone pinged. It was Harry.

—Heard about the sentences. Hope you're okay. Fancy catching up?

On impulse, she phoned him. "I've just opened a bottle of red. Shall I get a glass out for you?"

"Give me five minutes," he said. She grinned, and ran upstairs to drag a brush through her hair.

By the time he knocked on the door, she was as jumpy as a cat. He looked thinner, but energy radiated from him. His grey eyes flashed, and his smile was a little uncertain.

"Hi," she said, and wondered if she was grinning like an idiot.

"Hi." He walked into the drawing-room. I hope this isn't going to be awkward, she thought, and pasted a bright smile on her face.

"Shall we head outside with a glass?"

"Great idea," Harry said and stretched his neck as though trying to relieve some tension.

They walked towards the fernery. "You managed to replace everything?" he said, looking around. She nodded. "Impressive."

"Lizzie helped."

"I'm sorry I wasn't around to help."

"I didn't want to wait. It was something I needed to do."

"Have you heard from Lauren?"

"From her mum," Cat corrected. She told him about her decision to see Lauren after her suspended sentence was completed, and he nodded thoughtfully.

"It's big of you," he said.

"There's a long way to go to repair the relationship, but I think we've got a strong enough history. I know from bitter experience how bloody persuasive Stephen can be. I can hardly blame her for falling for his bullshit in exactly the same way I did!"

"Still big of you."

They sat on the garden chairs, glass in hand, watching the sun's rays slice through the trees. Finally, Harry turned to her. "I missed you," he said in a low, gravelly voice.

Cat coughed, not expecting him to be so direct, and was about to say something flippant when she looked at his expression – grave, expectant, worried.

"I missed you too." She said the words before she could change her mind.

He relaxed, and the smile he gave her warmed her to her toes. Hurriedly, she asked him about his job.

"Good, it's good. The new team doesn't contain anyone with my mix of experience, and working in London has given me some tricks they haven't seen. So at the moment, anyway, I'm flavour of the month." He sipped his wine.

Cat found herself looking at his lips and forced her gaze away. "How are your digs?" she asked casually.

"Fine, Jo's spare room is perfectly comfortable but that probably won't last much longer – her wife is pregnant."

Cat's lips parted. "Oh! I thought..." she trailed off.

"What did you think?"

"Nothing! Nothing... so you're not selling the house?"

Harry shot her an amused glance. "Nope. Is that important?"

Cat gathered her scrambled thoughts and came up with something inane. "Well, I just wanted to know if I might have new neighbours. Quieter ones, hopefully."

He chuckled. "Recognise the music?" he asked.

"How could I not? That album was pretty much the soundtrack to our relationship!"

"Yeah. That's been on my mind a lot lately," he said softly.

Cat sloshed more wine into her glass, just to have something to do with her hands.

Harry stretched out his long legs. "How's the writing? Have you found someone to publish your book?"

"Yep. It's a four-book deal, and they've given me an advance, so I won't starve for the next few months."

"That's great news!" He looked truly delighted.

Cat smiled. "I'm not getting carried away. If this book doesn't sell... I'm trying to stay calm and not spend all the money I've got." And pay off my credit card bill, she added in her head.

"When will it be published?"

"Spring. So I'm still that has-been author whose books got worse until I redeem myself with this one. I hope."

Harry's brows drew together. "You're too hard on yourself. I read all your books while I was on shift—"

Cat gasped. "You've read my books? Oh my God! Did you force yourself?"

"No, I did not," Harry said, with dignity. "I thought the first one was brilliant and I enjoyed the next one as well. I thought you lost your way a bit in the last one, but if you were with Stephen that's hardly surprising."

She shook her head in wonder. "I can't believe you read them."

"It was a labour of love," he said quietly, and she stopped laughing. Harry put his wine on the table and turned to her. "Cat, I'm no literary critic, but even a dull plod like me can spot talent. You've got it in spades."

Cat opened her mouth, then shut it. She clasped her hands and tried again, her voice strangled. "I know I'm talented, but I'm never going to be the next JK Rowling or Stephen King. I won't earn shed-loads of money or write one of those bestsellers you see on the shelves at airports."

His gaze was steady. "Are you happy?"

His question surprised her. "Yes. Yes, I am."

"That's what matters. I never cared about the money, you know, when we were together. You could be unpublished, and I wouldn't give a damn. I wanted you to be happy. Rich would be good, too, but happy trumps everything."

Cat hung her head, suddenly realising what she had in common with Emily. How had she missed it? She'd learned how to be happy, to forgive, and make the most of her talent. Just as Emily had done. Just as Gam had wanted. Her eyes filled with tears, and she looked up. "Oh, Harry, I've missed you!"

He muttered something unintelligible and reached for her. His fingers threaded through her hair to hold her close for a kiss. It was like coming home, and the spark that had always been there flared into life. Cat grabbed his shirt and pulled him to her and clumsily, they rose to their feet. She sighed, finally able to wrap her arms around him. His lean form moulded to her and their hips locked.

A few minutes later, Harry raised his head. "Cat ... do you think we should take it slowly? I don't want to break up with you again." He paused, choosing his words. "This time, Cat, it – it really needs to work. I need you to be sure."

Cat was stunned into silence. Then a rush of shame followed by iron-hard certainty flooded her head. She grasped his hand. "Yes, I am. Sure, I mean. We screwed up badly last time. We won't do it again."

His silver eyes searched her face. At last he found something that reassured him and wrapped her in his arms. "We should take it steady. I've changed, and I imagine you have, too."

She drew back and put her head on one side, considering him. "I could take your reluctance as a challenge and float around in all kinds of see-through garments if you like?"

He laughed. "Do you *possess* any see-through garments?"

She mentally flicked through her wardrobe: only sensible cotton came to mind. Damn. He knew her too well, even now. "I can go shopping," she said. He groaned and laughed at the same time. "Or you could just agree that we'll go to bed at some point and save me the money."

"You're a nightmare."

"I still have stockings somewhere," she said, thoughtfully.

He flushed pink. "I-I—"

Cat kissed him hard, running her hands down his shoulders to his belt. She felt him catch his breath as her hands paused at the buckle. She rested her forehead on his chin. "If you insist, you can take me to dinner and drop me at my front door. Then we can both have sleepless nights while we think of what we might have been doing."

"Cat, you're impossible!" Harry's expression was a mix of offence and yearning.

Cat stepped away with a sly grin. "Coming in? I promise not to pounce."

She held her hand out and he grasped it. They went indoors.

Afterword

If you liked The Fern Keepers, *please leave me a review.* It's an enormous help to indie authors like me with no advertising budget! And if you'd like to know when I'm releasing the next book in the series, sign up to my mailing list on my website - https://www. sarasartagne.com/keep-in-touch.

About the Author

Having wanted to be a journalist when she was a teenager, Sara actually ended up on the dark side, in PR. From there, it was a short skip to writing for pleasure, and from there to drafting her first book, a romance series where gardens feature in a BIG way. This allows her to indulge her passion for gardening, inherited from her grandmother.

There are three books in this series, *The Garden Plot*, *Love in a Mist*, and *The Glasshouse Effect*. What started as a trilogy appears to be morphing into a quartet, so watch out for the final story.

Sara recently moved from London to York and is loving the open skies and the green fields. And a HUGE garden! Going from an underground tube or bus every three minutes, bus timetables in a small Yorkshire town have been a bit of a shock...

A new collection, The Duality Series, are stand-alone books which features two stories, somehow connected. *The Visitor*, her first book in this series was released in March 2021 and Sara received a **Prestige Chill With A Book Award** for the novel in June 2021.

She loves hearing from readers who have thoughts about her books and characters - and even about gardening! - so please visit http://www.

sarasartagne.com (good for news and freebies!) or make contact on Twitter - @SSartagnewriter.

The Visitor
Love. Witchcraft. Unfinished business.

Two outsiders connected by love. Four hundred years apart.

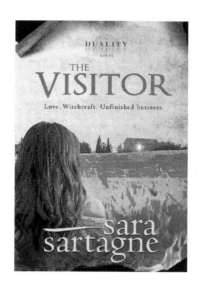

2019. Trainee teacher Stacie Hayward is spending the summer with her brilliant, academic family. And with her ghosts. It's a strange gift that she's had since childhood – and learned to keep quiet about.

When Stacie's parents invite American professor Nate to stay, Stacie's ghosts suddenly vanish. Then Stacie is visited by the ghost of a young woman who calls her cousin and who offers to protect her. But protect her from what?

1619. Sarah Bartlett, a young healer, is suspected of witchcraft. The only person to defend her is John Dillington, the new parson. But is he in love – or bewitched? And can he save her from the flames?

Alone and bewildered, Stacie uncovers more of her past and realises that choices made long ago are rippling through time to threaten her. History may be repeating itself – but this time, it's Stacie who's in danger.

The Visitor is the first in a new series of Duality Novels that always feature two storylines, somehow connected.

If you like contemporary romance interwoven with historical suspense and adventure, explore Sara Sartagne's new novel here.

A Bouquet of White Roses
English Garden Romance novella

Local businessman Sam Winterson thinks that Dawn Andrews is the most beautiful women he's ever seen and he's instantly drawn to her. There's just one problem. She's the florist for his *wedding*.

Dawn Andrews is no marriage-breaker. Trying to deny the fizz of feelings that happen when they meet is the best option, given the handsome young landscape gardener is literally engaged elsewhere. But when Sam rescues her from an assault outside a nightclub, despite her best intentions, Dawn's feelings begin to change.

It's a complete mess. With the wedding only five months away, can they ignore the mutual attraction, turn their backs on each other and carry on as if they'd never met?

A Bouquet of White Roses is a prequel novella to *The Garden Plot*, Book One in Sara Sartagne's **English Garden Romance** Series.

You can get it for FREE if you visit my website and sign up to my mailing list! Link here.

The Garden Plot
English Garden Romance 1

Sometimes love needs a plan...

Desperate to keep her company afloat, designer Sam Winterson doesn't need a relationship, she needs business! All that stands between her and the commission that might save her company is a mystery business-man. But when a proposed housing development threatens the tranquillity and beauty of her village, Sam's determined to stop it.

Reclusive widower Jonas Keane is not interested in the kind of woman who puts her career before her home and family. Been there, done that. Ordered to stay home to recuperate from illness is as frustrating as hell — but it allows him to oversee the renovation of his own garden while staying a silent partner in a housing development. What he doesn't expect is to run headlong into a budding romance with a blonde, pixie-faced gardener intent on upending his plans.

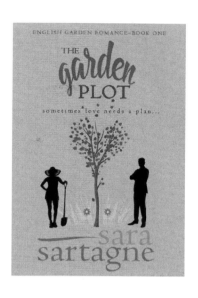

But Magda, Jonas' daughter is tired of her work-obsessed dad and his picture-perfect girlfriends. She has a plot of her own. When she plants the seeds of romance, can love blossom between a ruthless businessman and an outspoken gardener with a green conscience?

Fans of Jill Mansell and Katie Fforde will enjoy Sara Sartagne's debut novel, a sweet romance with a hint of spice and a HEA! Available on Amazon!

Love in A Mist
English Garden Romance 2

An aristocratic Englishwoman. A fiery Irishman. Two secrets they'd rather not share.

Ella Sanderson manages the farms and estate at Ashton Manor. She's an old-fashioned girl who knows what she likes. And she doesn't like the ultra-modern garden designed for the ancient house by horticulture's bad boy, Connor McPherson.

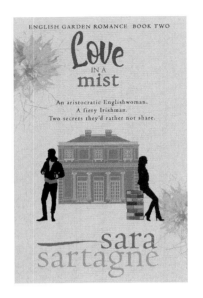

An aristocratic Englishwoman.
A fiery Irishman.
Two secrets they'd rather not share.

Connor is just the type of man she's learned to mistrust. Bright blue eyes and Irish charm may have captivated her employer Lady Susan—but not her! With all her protective instincts on high alert, Ella can't disobey Lady Susan's wishes for the garden, but she can just... not help.

Connor McPherson didn't want the commission, but as the garden will host his best friend's wedding, he couldn't refuse it. If the wettest English weather on record hasn't completely blown his chances of getting the build completed for the big day, he's also battling the snooty estate manager who couldn't be less enthusiastic.

The stage is set for fireworks between the hot-tempered Irishman and the cool, contained estate manager. But when mounting problems force them to work together, Connor realises that beneath her buttoned-up exterior, Ella has a passion equal to his own and a secret she's hidden for years.

As Ella fights to get the garden she hates built in time for the wedding she'd rather not attend and safeguard the manor from unwelcome publicity, she's increasingly drawn to the tempestuous designer. Who, she discovers, has his own secrets to protect...

Meet old friends from **The Garden Plot** *in the next in the series of* the **English Garden Romance** *series. Available from* Amazon!

The Glasshouse Effect
English Garden Romance 3

Her dream job. Her too dreamy colleague...

Magda Keane has been waiting for this job her whole life – creating her design for the exotic gardens in the huge Arcadia glasshouse. This assignment could grow her developing reputation – even get her a partnership.

There are just two problems...

The first is enigmatic Vincenzo Mazzi, the Italian engineer in charge of the solar panels powering the glasshouse. She's never forgotten how she threw herself at him, nor the humiliation of his polite rejection. The second is the unexplained failure of Vincenzo's system, which could blight her prospects quicker than an early frost.

For Vincenzo, having Magda on site, in the flesh, is enough to give him sleepless nights. He's been so intent on building his business, he's kept his passion under lock and key.

Even worse, strange problems with his tried and tested system are giving him an almighty headache. That, and working with Magda, threaten both his hard-earned reputation and his self-imposed restraint.

Will this shared pressure drive them further apart? Or draw them together to finally face the attraction that never went away?

*The latest book in the **English Garden Romance** series. Available from* Amazon!

Printed in Great Britain
by Amazon

17428210R00176